**Praise for *USA TODAY* bestselling author
Margaret Daley and her novels**

"This terrific family story does a fantastic job of
dealing with serious issues."
—*RT Book Reviews* on *Once Upon a Family*

"*Heart of the Family*…is a wonderful story on many
levels and will have readers shedding tears of
happiness."
—*RT Book Reviews*

"A gripping story about second chances and living
in the present."
—*RT Book Reviews* on *A Love Rekindled*

"Emotionally charged and emphasizes…the power
of forgiveness."
—*RT Book Reviews* on *A Daughter for Christmas*

USA TODAY Bestselling Author

MARGARET DALEY

Guarding the Witness
&
Bodyguard Reunion

HARLEQUIN® LOVE INSPIRED®CLASSICS

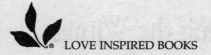

LOVE INSPIRED BOOKS

Recycling programs
for this product may
not exist in your area.

ISBN-13: 978-1-335-21891-9

Guarding the Witness & Bodyguard Reunion

Copyright © 2018 by Harlequin Books S.A.

The publisher acknowledges the copyright holder of the individual works as follows:

Guarding the Witness
Copyright © 2013 by Margaret Daley

Bodyguard Reunion
Copyright © 2014 by Margaret Daley

www.Harlequin.com

Printed in U.S.A.

CONTENTS

Margaret Daley, an award-winning author of ninety books (five million sold worldwide), has been married for over forty years and is a firm believer in romance and love. When she isn't traveling, she's writing love stories, often with a suspense thread, and corralling her three cats, who think they rule her household. To find out more about Margaret, visit her website at margaretdaley.com.

Books by Margaret Daley

Love Inspired Suspense

Lone Star Justice

High-Risk Reunion
Lone Star Christmas Rescue
Texas Ranger Showdown

Alaskan Search and Rescue

The Yuletide Rescue
To Save Her Child
The Protector's Mission
Standoff at Christmas

Guardians, Inc.

Christmas Bodyguard
Protecting Her Own
Hidden in the Everglades
Christmas Stalking
Guarding the Witness
Bodyguard Reunion

Visit the Author Profile page at Harlequin.com for more titles.

GUARDING THE WITNESS

Trust in the Lord with all thine heart; and lean not unto thine own understanding. In all thy ways acknowledge him, and he shall direct thy paths.
—*Proverbs 3:5–6*

To all my readers—I appreciate you all
for reading my books. Thank you.

PROLOGUE

Bodyguard Arianna Jackson flexed her fingers over her holstered Glock at her side, ready to draw at a second's notice if she sensed her client, Esther Perkins, was in danger. She cased the garage as she and Esther moved toward the door to the utility room of her client's house.

"Every time we come back from my lawyer's office, all I want to do is sleep for the next week," Esther said with a deep sigh. "At least we didn't stay long this time. I'm glad to be home early. If my husband had bothered to show up, I'd still be there."

Esther's lawyer had refused to conduct the meeting without Thomas Perkins present to finalize the details of the divorce. Therefore the meeting was cut short, actually never started. That was fine with Arianna. Whenever they left the house, the chances went up that her client would be hurt by her husband, whom Esther had found out was part of a huge crime syndicate in Alaska. "Hang back until I check each room."

"As soon as this divorce is over with, I'm getting as far away from my soon-to-be ex as I can." The forty-five-year-old hugged her arms to her chest and stopped right behind Arianna. "I won't live in this kind of fear. He's a violent, horrible man."

Arianna unlocked the door into the house and eased it open, listening for any abnormal sounds. Silence greeted her, and the urge to relax her vigilance tempted her for only a second. She'd learned the hard way never to do that while working as a bodyguard. She had her old injury to her shoulder—a bullet that went all the way through—to remind her.

When she was satisfied it was safe for Esther to enter, she motioned to the woman then trekked toward the kitchen, making a visual sweep of the room before moving into it.

A sound, like a muffled thud, penetrated the quiet. Arianna immediately pulled her gun from its holster and chambered a round, then swung around and put her finger to her mouth to indicate no talking. Waving her hand toward the pantry, she herded her client toward it. At the door she whispered into Esther's ear, "Stay in here. I'm locking the door. Stay back away from it. I'm checking the sound out. You know the drill."

With a shaky hand, Esther dug into her purse for her cell to call 911 if she thought it was needed.

And because her client didn't always do what she was supposed to unless Arianna spelled it out—and because there was a way to unlock the pantry from the inside—she added, "Don't leave the pantry until I tell you to."

Her blue eyes huge, Esther nodded, all color draining from her face.

With her client secured—at least as much as she could be with a possible intruder in the house—Arianna crept forward. She scanned each room as she made her way through the lower level. Another dull thump echoed through the air. She knew that sound— a silencer. Coming from the library. A muted scream followed almost immediately. Every sense heightened to a razor-sharp alertness.

The couple who lived here with Esther was gone for a few days to a funeral. No one should have been in the place. Increasing her pace, she covered the length of the hallway in a few seconds and flattened herself against the wall to one side of the door that was ajar.

Peering through the slice of space into the library, she spied a large man about six and a half feet tall standing over Thomas Perkins, who was bound to a chair with his hands tied behind his back and a gag in his mouth. He bled from the shoulder and thigh—a lot. Esther's husband tried to scooch back from the towering man, moaning through the cloth stuffed in his mouth, his eyes dilated with fear.

The assailant leaned down and removed the gag. "No whining. Just tell me where the ledger is or the next shot will be in your heart."

"There isn't one," Thomas Perkins said between coughs, still trying to move away from the man.

"Yeah, right. I know you have one in case you needed to use it against me. Your mistake was talking about it to the wrong person."

She wasn't paid to protect her client's soon-to-be ex-husband, but she couldn't stand by and watch an assailant murder him. Fortifying herself with a steadying breath, Arianna nudged the door open, pointed the gun at the attacker's heart and said, "Drop the weapon or I'll shoot."

The large man's hand inched upward.

"I don't play around. I'll only have to shoot you once to kill you instantly."

The man's fiery gaze bored through Arianna. "You've just made the biggest mistake of your life."

ONE

Two months later, a helicopter banked to the left and descended toward the clearing where Deputy U.S. Marshal Brody Callahan's new assignment, Arianna Jackson, was being guarded by three marshals. His team would relieve them, so he used his vantage point above the forest to check out the area. Knowing the terrain that surrounded the safe house had saved his life several times. The cabin backed up against a medium-size mountain range on the north and west while the other two sides were made up of a wall of spruces, pines, hemlocks and other varieties of trees that stretched out for miles. A rugged land—manageable only as long as the weather cooperated. It was the end of July, but it had been known to snow at that time in Alaska near the Artic Circle. He had to be prepared for all contingencies.

As they dropped toward the clearing, Deputy U.S. Marshal Ted Banks came out of the cabin, staying back by the door, his hand hovering near his gun in his holster. Alert. Ted was a good marshal Brody had worked with before.

The helicopter's landing skids connected with the

ground, jolting Brody slightly. Over the whirring noise of the rotors, he yelled to the pilot, "This shouldn't take long."

With duffel bags in hand, Brody jumped to the rocky earth closest to the cabin while his two partners exited from the other side. Brody ran toward Ted, who held out his hand and said in a booming voice, "Glad to see you."

"Ready to see your wife, are you?"

"Yep. I hope you've honed your Scrabble skills. This one is ruthless when it comes to the game. I'm going to brush up on my vocabulary with a dictionary before I play her again."

"I've read her file." Arianna Jackson was the star witness for the trial of Joseph Rainwater, the head of a large crime syndicate in Alaska, because she'd witnessed Rainwater killing Thomas Perkins. The man had bled out before the EMTs arrived.

"Doesn't do her justice. I don't have anything to add to my earlier phone report this morning. C'mon. I'll introduce you two." Ted peered over Brody's shoulder at his partners, Kevin Laird and Mark Baylor, approaching them while carrying a bag and three boxes of provisions. Ted nodded to them before turning to open the door.

As Brody entered, he panned the rustic interior with a high ceiling, noting where the few windows were located, the large fireplace against the back wall, the hallway that led to the two bedrooms and the kitchen area off the living room. Three duffel bags sat by the door. Then his gaze connected with the witness he was to protect.

Arianna Jackson.

Tall, with white-blond hair and cool gray eyes, she

resembled a Nordic princess. Still, he could tell she was very capable of taking care of herself from the way she carried herself, right down to the sharp perusal she gave him. From what he'd read, Ms. Jackson had been a good bodyguard caught in a bad situation. Her life would never be the same after this.

She tossed the dish towel she held onto the kitchen counter, never taking her gaze off him. She assessed and catalogued him, not one emotion on her face to indicate what she had decided about him. That piqued his interest.

"These three are our replacements—Brody Callahan, Kevin Laird and Mark Baylor. This is Arianna Jackson," Ted said. Then he headed toward the door, the tension from his body fading with each step. "It's been quiet this past week except for a pesky mama bear and her cubs." He shoved into Brody's hand a sheet of paper with instructions on how to avoid a bear encounter.

"Good. Have you seen anyone in the area?"

"Nope, just the wildlife. We are, even for Alaska, out in the boonies," Ted said, giving him a salute. "Hope the next time I see you is in Anchorage. Goodbye, Arianna."

Brody looked from Ted, almost fleeing, to Carla Matthews not far behind him, to Dan Mitchell, the third Deputy U.S. Marshal on team number one, who would be on vacation on a beach in Hawaii. Brody clenched his jaw, curling his fingers around the handle of his bag so tightly his skin stretched taut over his knuckles. Carla shot him a piercing glance before disappearing outside. Slowly, Brody released his grip on his duffel bag, and it dropped to the floor with a thud.

Good thing Ted and Dan worked with Carla. He had

once and wouldn't again. He'd learned the hard way to never get involved with a colleague. In fact, she'd been one of the reasons he'd transferred to Alaska from Los Angeles. It had been a hard shock to find out she'd been recruited to be on the detail protecting Arianna Jackson. At least she would return to L.A. when this trial was over.

Brody swung his attention to his witness, who watched team one leave. These assignments were never easy on anyone involved. The pressure was intense. Never able to let down your guard. And with Ms. Jackson the stakes were even higher because Joseph Rainwater was determined his crime syndicate would find her and take her out, along with anyone else in their way. And the man had the resources and money to carry out that threat.

Her gaze linked with his. "The bedroom on the right is where you all can bunk," Ms. Jackson said in a no-nonsense voice as she rotated back to finish drying the few dishes in the drain board.

Patience, Lord. I'm pretty sure I'm going to need every ounce of it this next week. He was guarding a woman who was used to guarding others. He doubted she would like to follow orders when she was used to giving them.

Brody nodded to Kevin and Mark to go ahead and take their duffel bags into the room assigned to them by their witness. Then Brody covered the distance between him and Ms. Jackson. "We need to talk."

She turned her head and tilted it. One eyebrow rose. "We do? Am I going to get the lecture about not going outside, to follow all your ord—directions?"

"No, because you guard people for a living and you

know what to do. But I do have some news I thought you deserved to know."

Her body stiffening, she faced him fully, her shoulders thrust back as though she were at attention. "What?"

"Esther Perkins is missing."

Arianna clenched her hands. "No one would tell me anything about Esther other than she was being taken care of. She didn't witness the murder. She couldn't testify about it. What happened?"

"Rainwater thought she might know something concerning the ledger and went after her. Or rather he sent a couple of his men since Rainwater is sitting in jail. We moved her out of state while she tried to help us find that ledger even from long distance."

"So the police never could locate it?"

"No. They figure it has to be important since Rainwater personally killed a man over it. Usually others do his dirty work. The ledger probably details his contacts and operation. Thomas Perkins was in a position to know that information."

"So how did Esther go missing? Maybe she just left the program." She knew that was wishful thinking. When she'd stressed the importance of staying put, the woman always did. She'd been scared of her husband and now knowing who he'd worked for she was even more afraid.

"No, the Deputy U.S. Marshal running the case said it didn't look like she had. It had been obvious there had been a fight. There was blood found on the carpet. It was her type."

Her fingernails dug into her palms. Anger tangled with sadness and won. "She didn't have a detail on her?"

"She was relocated with a new identity thousands of miles away."

"Then maybe you have a leak somewhere." She pivoted back to the sink, her stomach roiling with rage that a good woman was probably dead. This all wouldn't have happened if they had stayed at Esther lawyer's office for another hour or so. Why, God? It had tested her faith; and now with the Rainwater situation her doubts concerning the Lord had multiplied. As had her doubts about herself.

For the past four years she'd worked for Guardians, Inc., a group of female bodyguards run by Kyra Hunt. In that time, she had seen some vile people who would hurt others without hesitation. She'd thought she had been tough enough for the job, especially with all she'd seen in the military in the Middle East during several tours. Now she was wondering if this was a good time to change jobs.

The continual silence from Brody after her accusation made her slant a look over her shoulder. A frown slashed across his face, the first sign of emotion from him.

His gaze roped hers. "It's more likely Esther contacted someone when she shouldn't. Let slip where she was. We've never lost a witness *if* they followed the rules."

"Take it from me—this isn't easy to do. Walk away from everyone you know and start a new life. I can't even call my mother or anyone else from my past." Arianna had always called her mom at least once a week, even when she was on a job, to make sure everything was going all right, wishfully hoping one of those times her father would talk with her. He never had, which broke her heart each time. Not being able to at least talk with her mom, except that one time right after the incident in the Perkinses' library, added family heartache on top of everything else.

"All I can tell you is that the U.S. Marshals Service is doing everything they can to locate Mrs. Perkins."

Left unsaid was "dead or alive." She closed her eyes, weariness attacking her from all sides. Since coming to the cabin, she hadn't slept more than a few hours here and there. The marshals had moved her from Anchorage because they'd worried the safe house had been compromised. If that place had been, why not this one?

That question plagued her every waking moment. It was hard to rest when she didn't know the people involved in her protection. When she did lie down, she'd managed to catch some sleep because she had her gun with her. She'd brought extra money, a switchblade and her gun without the marshals' knowledge. In case something went down, she wanted to be prepared. That was the only way she would agree to all of this. She would see to her own protection. She didn't trust anyone but herself to keep her alive.

Not even God anymore. That thought crept into her mind and prodded her memories. She wouldn't think about the reason she'd left the army, much to her brothers' and father's dismay. But how could she trust again when one of her team had sold her out? In the end it wasn't the Lord who had saved her. She'd saved herself.

That was when she'd vowed to protect others. She never wanted another to live in fear the way she had—

scared she would go to prison for a crime she hadn't committed.

She turned toward the marshal, appreciating what her clients must have felt when she'd guarded them and told them what to do. "Promise me you'll let me know if you all find Esther. She was my client. I feel responsible for her."

"You did everything you could. If you hadn't been there, she would have been dead next to her husband."

"And now she may be dead, her body somewhere no one has found yet. May never find."

"Yes," Deputy U.S. Marshal Brody Callahan said over the sound of the helicopter taking off.

The blunt reality of what might have happened to Esther, and still could happen, hung in the air between Arianna and the marshal. She went back to drying the lunch dishes. Anything to keep herself occupied. If this inactivity didn't end soon, she might go running through the woods screaming.

Mark Baylor, the oldest of the three marshals, with a touch of gray at his temples, strode to the door. "I'm gonna take a stroll around the perimeter."

Usually one marshal stayed outside while two were inside—often one of them taking his turn sleeping. That was the way it had been set up with Ted and his team.

"Do you need any help?" The deep, husky voice of Brody Callahan, the marshal who seemed to be in charge, broke into her thoughts.

"With cleaning up?" she asked, surprised by the question.

"Yes."

She glanced back at him. Six inches taller than her five-feet-eleven frame, Brody carried himself with confidence, which in its own way did ease her anxiety about her situation. His figure, with not an ounce of fat on him and a broad, muscular chest, spoke of a man that kept himself in shape. "I've got it under control." *About the only thing in my life that is.*

"We equally share the duties while we're here."

"That's good to know. I don't cook."

"You don't?"

She finished drying the last plate. "Never had a reason to learn. I went from living at home with my family to the army. Then when I started working for Guardians, Inc., I found myself on assignment most of the time with wealthy clients who had cooks." She shrugged. "The short amount of time I was in Dallas I ate out or ate frozen dinners."

"That's okay. I love to cook," Kevin Laird, the youngest of the marshals, announced as he came into the living room.

Brody chuckled. "That's why I like to team up with Kevin when I can. He can make the most boring food taste decent."

"Good. I'm not averse to edible food." Arianna moved out of the kitchen area, trying to decide what she should do next. *Let's see…maybe a crossword puzzle. Or better yet, solitaire.* She still had at least fifty varieties to work her way through. The thought of more days like the past week heightened her boredom level to critical.

She began to pace from one of the few windows, drapes pulled, to the hearth. It was empty and cold. They couldn't have a fire even at night when it did get chilly since it indicated someone was at the place. She counted her steps, mentally mapping out an escape route if she needed it. Her thoughts were interrupted when Kevin spoke up from the kitchen.

"This is a park ranger's cabin. Where's the guy that usually stays here?"

"On an extended vacation." Brody prowled the living room in a different direction from her.

"Does he know we're using it?" Arianna asked as she peeked out the window. The previous set of marshals had told her about the cabin, but only now had she started to wonder what the tenant had been told.

"No, the cabin belongs to the park service. No one knows you're here or that the U.S. Marshals Service is using it to protect a witness. A bogus agency has rented it while the park ranger is gone. They think we're here on vacation." Brody parted the drapes and looked out the only other window in the room.

"When's he due back?" Arianna spied a bull moose in the thick of the trees. Seeing the beautiful animals was the one thrill she got being where she was. She loved animals, but because of her job, she hadn't been able to have any—not even a goldfish.

"Not for two more weeks. Do you see it?" Brody's gaze captured hers, nodding in the direction of the moose.

"He's beautiful. I wish I could go outside and take a picture. I took the Perkins assignment because it was in Alaska. After I finished guarding her, I was going to take a long overdue vacation and do some touring of the countryside up here. The most exciting thing that's happened to me this week was the helicopter ride to this cabin. Breathtaking scenery."

"Don't even think about going outside to snap a picture."

She held up her hands, palms outward. "I thought you said I knew the drill and didn't need to hear your spiel."

"I've changed my mind. You sound like a bored witness. That kind can do things to get themselves killed."

"I am bored. I don't even have the luxury of a television set. Most of the time I don't watch it, but I'm desperate. How in the world do you do this job after job?"

"I'm on an assignment to keep you safe. I can't let down my guard ever or allow for any distractions. You should know what that means."

His intense, dark brown eyes drilling into her exemplified strong will and fierce determination—traits she shared. He was a person she should be able to identify with if she stopped feeling sorry for herself—something she rarely did. But she hated change, and the changing of the guard not half an hour ago bothered her more than she'd realized. She now had to get to know her three new guards, and she still couldn't shake the thought that her safe house in Anchorage might have been compromised. She'd feel better if two of the female bodyguards from Guardians, Inc. were here with her instead. She knew where they were coming from.

"How about chess?" Kevin asked from the kitchen area, gesturing to the chess set perched on a shelf, while Brody crossed to the door.

"I don't play it. Where are you going?" she asked Brody as he opened the door.

"Outside. I'm relieving Mark."

"But he just left."

"Yeah, I know."

"Can I come with you?" the imp in her asked.

He frowned and left, the door slamming shut.

"Ms. Jackson, I can teach you to play chess. It'll take your mind off what's going on." Kevin moved into the main part of the room.

"Nothing is going on. That's the problem." She strode toward the table and took a chair. "Sure. I might as well learn." She checked her watch. Noon. It was going to be another long day.

Finishing his last trip around the perimeter of the cabin, Brody took a deep breath of the fresh air, laced with the scent of earth and trees, then mounted the steps to the porch. When he reached the door to the ranger's cabin, he panned the small clearing. Nearing midnight, it was still light outside. The temperature began to drop as the sun finally started its descent. When moving to Alaska, the only thing he really had to adjust to was the long daylight hours in summer and equally long nighttime ones in winter. At least in Anchorage where he was living it was farther south and the days and nights didn't get as skewed as they did up here nearer the Arctic Circle.

Inside the cabin, he left the shotgun by the door for Kevin, who was relieving him on patrol. He turned to find Arianna sitting on the couch, staring at him. Her gray eyes with a hint of blue reminded him of the lake he'd flown over this morning.

"Did you see the mama bear that's been hanging around the cabin lately?" she asked and went back to playing solitaire.

"No. Where's Kevin?"

"Right here. Sorry. I figured I needed a jacket since the sun was going down." Kevin picked up the shotgun and exited the cabin.

"So it's just you and me since Mark is taking his turn sleeping."

For a second he thought he saw a teasing gleam in her eyes before she averted her gaze to study the spread of cards on the coffee table in front of her. He sat in a chair across from her. "Have you won any games?"

"Two probably out of fifty." She raised her head. "Wanna play Scrabble?"

"I've been warned about you and Scrabble."

"I took you for a man who likes a good challenge." A full-fledged smile encompassed her whole face.

"And baiting me guarantees you'll have an opponent."

"Yep, kinda hard playing Scrabble with yourself. No challenge really."

"You're on. Where's the game?"

Arianna gestured toward the bookcase behind him. "I think I'll leave the ranger who lives here a thank-you note. I don't know what I would have done without some of his games. I brought a deck of cards and some books, but I went through the books in the first four days and I'm sick of playing solitaire. Do you have any idea when I'll get to testify and can move back to civilization?"

"No. Rainwater's attorney gets big bucks to delay the trial as long as he can."

"Because he's got people out there looking for me."

"Yes, you know the score. If you testify, he'll most likely go down for murder. Without finding the ledger Rainwater killed Perkins over, you're the main witness in his trial. Without you, he'd probably get acquitted, if they even went ahead with the trial."

"Something very incriminating must be in the ledger Rainwater was looking for."

"Perkins kept the books for Rainwater. The public set has been sanitized not to include anything incriminating. We think Perkins kept a second ledger with all the dirt on the man. As you know, risky for Perkins to do, but it could be invaluable to us. Rainwater has gone to great lengths to find it."

"We can't afford for people like him to win. I'm even more determined to testify."

"And he's as determined to stop you." Brody rose and retrieved the box with the Scrabble game in it, then laid the board and tiles out on the coffee table. When he sat again, he pulled his chair closer. "Ready to get trounced?"

"Is that any way to speak to a poor defenseless witness?" Arianna said as she laid down seven tiles for a score of seventy-six points.

He looked down at his letters and could only come up with a twelve-point word. Now he was beginning to understand what Ted meant. Forty minutes later it was confirmed. She was *very good* at Scrabble.

"What do you do? Study the dictionary like Ted threatened?"

"No. Don't have to. I have a photographic memory, and I enjoy reading a lot. Once I see something, I remember it."

"So that's how you could give such a detailed description of what went down the day Thomas Perkins was murdered."

"The gift has helped me in my job. When I go on a new assignment, I case the house or wherever I'm staying with the client so I can pull up the layout in a hurry in my mind. It has helped me on more than one occasion, especially in the dark." She gathered up the tiles and began putting them into the box.

"I do something similar although I don't have a photographic memory."

One corner of her mouth lifted. "I consider it one of the weapons in my arsenal."

He laughed, folding the game board and laying it on top of the tiles. "That's an interesting way to put it."

Arianna yawned. "I'd better call it a night and try to sleep."

"Are you having problems sleeping?"

"Yes. Wouldn't you if you were in my position, with all that's been going on?"

"We're guarding you. You don't have to be alert and on the job."

"Actually the quiet is too quiet. I'm glad to hear an occasional animal call in the night."

"I grew up in New York City. The first few years after I left I had the hardest time with the silence at nighttime. Until I was assigned to L.A., I was located in smaller cities. Now when I get it, I love it. My house is outside Anchorage where it's—"

A blast from a shotgun exploded in the air.

As Arianna dove over the back of the sofa with a wall of the cabin behind her, Brody moved toward the door. Another gunshot sound reverberated through the quiet.

Mark rushed down the hallway, weapon drawn. "What's going on?"

"Stay with Ms. Jackson. I'll go check."

Suddenly there was a rattling on the window on the left side of the room as if someone or something was tearing at the screen. Brody moved toward it. A roar split the air as he opened the blinds to find a grizzly bear attacking the window. The screen hung in metal shreds from its frame. The huge animal batted it away, only a pane of glass now between him and the bear.

"Stay put, Arianna." Brody signaled for Mark to keep an eye on the window where the bear was.

Where is Kevin? His heart pounding, Brody charged toward the exit, knowing his Glock might not be enough to stop a bear coming at him or Kevin. In the gray light of an Alaskan night this far north, he saw his partner backing around the corner of the cabin while squeezing off another shot into the air.

"I'm behind you, Kevin," Brody said as he approached him.

The tense set to his partner's body relaxed. "She's leaving. Finally. When I was making my rounds, two cubs came out of the woods close to where I was. Mama bear followed not five seconds later. I tried not to show any fear and backed away. She came toward me—not charging, but making sure she was between her cubs and me. When I fired my first warning shot in the air, both of the cubs ran into the woods. She didn't."

Kevin kept his gaze fixed on the departing bear while Brody watched the front of the cabin. When the threat disappeared into the woods, they both headed for the porch.

"Good thing she doesn't know how to open doors or windows. It took three shots to scare her off," Kevin said, then positioned himself by the steps.

"She's establishing her territory. Next time stay closer to the cabin and don't play around with a grizzly sow and her cubs. They are very protective of their babies."

"Believe me I'll stay glued to this place. I don't want to tangle with one of them."

"I'll be turning in soon. Mark will be on duty in the cabin. I'll relieve you in five hours." When Brody reentered the cabin, Arianna stood behind the couch. "What part of get down do you not understand?"

"The last order you gave me was stay put." She pointed to the floor. "I stayed put. Besides, Mark was here."

Brody shook his head. "I guess I'll have to spell it out for you next time."

"There's gonna be a next time with that bear?"

"If she's hungry enough or we threaten her cubs. Obviously she didn't like Kevin near her cubs or shooting his gun—even in the air."

"Oh, good. If she comes back to us, I'll get to take a photo."

"Photo? Of a bear charging you?"

"No. Don't you remember you've ordered me to stay in the cabin? I'll be watching from the window. No charging bear will be coming at me. Now that's not to say she won't come after you or your partners…"

He chuckled. "I'll make sure I'm not your model for that picture."

Mark laughed, too. "I'm going back to bed for the little time I have left. I'll leave you two to hash things out."

As Mark left, Arianna said, "When I finished a job in Africa, I went on a photo safari. One of the rare vacations I gave myself. After this job I was going to take a second vacation and see some of the wildlife. I don't think that's going to work out unless I can get the wildlife to come to me."

"Give me the camera. I'll take a picture for you."

"Not the same thing. Besides, the bear is long gone by now. At least I hope so." Another yawn escaped Arianna. "That's my cue to say good-night."

"Good night. Mark will be back in here—" he checked his watch "—in an hour."

"Sleep tight then."

"Don't you mean sleep light? After all, I am guarding you."

"Every bodyguard has to grab some good sleep if he or she is going to do a good job. And believe me, I want you to do a good job protecting me."

He studied her body language as she said those words. "I think you believe what you said, but you also believe you can take care of yourself."

She smirked. "I'm gonna have to work on fooling you better."

"No one, not even myself, is invincible. We all need help from time to time."

"And who do you turn to?"

"God and my partner on the job. In that order."

Her eyes widened for a second before she rotated toward the hallway and headed toward her bedroom.

Brody watched her leave, flashes of his own experience questioning God's intention going through his mind. He'd been the lead marshal on an assignment in Los Angeles. The witness he'd been guarding ended up being gunned down on the way to the courthouse because the cell phone in his pocket was used to track his movements.

Brody shook the memory from his mind. That was the past. He couldn't change it, but he could learn from it. Now Brody needed to be the sharpest marshal he could be. He wasn't going to lose another witness on his team.

When Mark relieved him later, Brody strode toward his bedroom. His glance strayed toward Arianna's closed door. She was an interesting woman whose life would never be the same. How would *he* deal with giving up all he knew and starting over?

Her earlier adrenaline rush finally subsiding, Arianna removed her Glock from under the mattress and put it on the bedside table within easy reach. That was the only way she would be able to get any kind of sleep. When she lay down and closed her eyes, the image of Brody Callahan, laughing at some of the words she came up with, popped onto the screen of her mind. Though she'd won the Scrabble match, he hadn't gone down without a fight, challenging a few of the words she'd used that he didn't know. But mostly she remembered his good nature at losing to her.

Sleep faded the picture of her and Brody facing each other over the Scrabble board and whisked her into a dream world that evolved into a nightmare she hadn't had in a year—one where she was shoved into a prison cell. As she swept around to rush out, the bars slammed shut, the sound clanging through her mind.

The noise jerked her awake. Her eyelids flew open. Silence greeted her and calmed her racing heart.

Until she heard a muffled thud—as though a silencer had been fired.

TWO

The distinctive sound of a gun with a silencer discharging nearby yanked Brody from sleep. As he rolled out of bed, he grabbed his Glock from his bedside table. Kevin and Mark didn't have silencers on their weapons, which meant someone had made it inside. Had there been more than one shot? Since he hadn't heard his partners' guns going off, he had to assume something happened to them. What had he slept through?

Hurrying toward his door, he shoved deep down the thought of the worst occurring. He couldn't afford to be sidetracked. He had to be as detached and professional as possible. There would be time later for emotion.

He eased open the door a crack and listened. Silence ruled. For a second he wondered if he'd dreamed hearing the sound. Hoped he had. Then a whisper of a noise alerted him to Arianna easing her door open slightly. His gaze seized hers, and he knew she'd heard the same thing. It wasn't a dream.

The cabin had been compromised. Fortifying himself with a deep breath, he swung the door open wide and stepped out into the hallway with his Glock pointed toward the living room. To his side he noticed Arianna stepping into the corridor. He shook his head. She ignored him and continued out into the hall with a gun in her hand.

He shouldn't be surprised she'd brought her own gun to the cabin. He would have in her place. But still he frowned and tried to convey silently that she get back into her room.

A low moan coming from the living room refocused his full attention on the threat in the cabin. Short of handcuffing her to her bed, she would be backing him up. Waving her behind him, he crept down the hallway. At least this way he could shield her.

Toward the entrance into the living room, he slowed and flattened himself against the wall then inched forward. Much to his dismay Arianna copied him but on the other side of the corridor. She brought her Glock up, both hands clasping it. She ignored the displeasure he knew showed on his face, her gaze trained on the living area.

At the moment, survival was the most important objective. He gave up trying to have Arianna hang back. He knew from all the reports she was very capable of handling herself so he indicated she cover the left side of the room while he took the right. They entered in unison.

One large man was dragging Mark's body out of sight while Brody glimpsed another intruder by the front door.

"Drop your weapons," Brody said, preparing for them not to obey.

The guy moving Mark ducked down behind the kitchen counter while the one at the door raised his gun and fired. Arianna squeezed off a round at the shooter then stepped back behind the wall into the hallway for cover. While that intruder went down with a wound to the chest, Brody dived behind the couch and crawled forward to get a better angle on the attacker in the kitchen. He popped up at the same time Brody aimed his Glock and took the man out. The thud resounded through the cabin when he crashed to the floor.

Brody rose, swinging around in a full circle to make sure there were no more assailants in the cabin. Arianna had disappeared down the hallway, and the sound he heard now of doors opening and closing as she checked each room raised his admiration for the lady's skills.

When Arianna came back, he said, "I'm checking outside. There may be more. I need to see where Kevin is. You'll have to see if Mark is alive. From his injury, I don't think he is." But he prayed his partner was. And Kevin.

"Be careful. Sending two men to kill four doesn't make sense."

"I know. That's what concerns me." As he approached the intruder by the door, he leaned over and felt for a pulse. "This one is dead."

Arianna arrived in the kitchen. "So is this guy."

He opened the door. "What about Mark?"

Ducking down behind the counter, Arianna answered in a heavy voice, "Dead."

That was what he'd thought. With a head wound Mark hadn't had a chance to get a shot off. And to get into the cabin they had to go through Kevin. A young marshal with only a year's experience. Again he reminded himself to tamp down his emotions. Later he could mourn the dead. His only goal was to protect Arianna.

"Lock this after I leave." Dread at what he would find blanketed him as he slipped through the front door out onto the porch. Already the night sky started growing light as sunrise neared at four-thirty.

No one was on the porch. Alert, every muscle taut with tension, Brody descended the steps and slinked toward the left side of the cabin. When he rounded the corner, a man plowed into him, sending him flying back. Brody managed to keep a grip on his gun even while his arms flung out. The impact with the ground caused the air to swoosh from him. The bulky assailant crushed him into the dirt, sitting on him, knees pinning down his arms and fists pounding into Brody's upper body and face. Stars swam before Brody's eyes. From deep inside him he drew on his reserve, fueled by a spurt of adrenaline. He was the only thing standing between Arianna and death.

Between punches Brody sucked in a shallow breath, laced with the scent of sweat, then poured what strength he had into freeing one of his pinned arms. When he did, Brody cuffed the brute on the side of the head with his Glock. The man's drive slowed. Brody struck him again with the butt of the weapon.

His assailant growled and swiveled his upper body, grasping the hand that held the weapon. His attacker wrestled Brody for the gun, trying to twist his arm— possibly to break it. The Glock hovered between them. Brody focused all his will on an effort to regain control of the weapon. His chest burned with the lack of oxygen. The gun wavered inches from Brody, the barrel slowly turning toward him. A dark haze edged into his mind. Brody sent up a silent plea to God, and with a last burst of strength, he halted the Glock's momentum, then he began turning the end toward his assailant's torso.

Brody pulled his finger around the trigger with the man's hand still covering his. Brody stared into his attacker's dark eyes as the bullet exploded from the weapon, striking his assailant's chest. He jerked then slumped over, pinning Brody to the ground.

His ears ringing, the scent of gunpowder filling his nostrils, he shoved the man off him and scrambled away, never taking his eyes off his attacker. In the dim light of predawn he felt for a pulse. Gone. He checked the man's pockets for ID. There was none, but he found a switchblade with blood on it. Brody searched the area.

What happened here? Where is Kevin?

Tension stretched every nerve to beyond its limit. Rising, Brody kept scanning the terrain as he circled the cabin, using the shadows to cover his presence as much as possible. By the time he reached the porch again, he was even more confused by what had happened. Kevin was nowhere he could see, and he hadn't encountered anyone or anything else suspicious.

When he knocked on the door, he said, "It's Brody." He noticed the drapes over the window move, then a few seconds later the click on the lock sounded in the quiet. Too quiet. No birds tweeted. No howls of the wolves he'd heard earlier. The hairs on his nape stood up.

How did the assailants arrive? Not by helicopter. He would have heard that. By four-wheel drive? By foot?

The door swung open. Arianna took one look at him and dragged him inside. "I hope the other guy looks worse."

"He's dead. I can't find Kevin. At least he's not near the cabin or in the open area."

"I almost came out when I heard the gunshot to check on you."

"What stopped you?"

"Whether you believe it or not, I can follow orders. I figured if someone killed you, my best chance was in here, and if you got the jump on one of them, you'd be back. I was going to give you another five minutes before reassessing what I needed to do. In the meantime, I checked the pockets of these two. No identification on them. All they brought with them was their Wilson Combat revolvers and this." She held her palm flat with a piece of paper on it. "A detailed map to this cabin."

"Great. They didn't just stumble upon us."

"You thought they did?"

"No, but I could dream they had and no one else knew about the cabin yet. At least until I could get you safely away from here."

Arianna's mouth pinched into a frown as she stared at the nearest dead assailant. "As you know, we have to assume the worse. Did the guy outside have anything on him?"

"He had a switchblade with blood on it and no ID."

Her gaze returned to his face. "No gun?"

"In a holster at the small of his back under his jacket. Not the best place to draw quickly. I surprised him coming around the corner. We're getting out of here."

"You're not calling this in?"

"No. Something isn't right. How did these guys find us? Where's Kevin?"

"Do you think he's dead, too, or that he let someone know I was here?"

"Don't know, and since I don't, I can't trust anyone until I know more. My job is to keep you alive to testify. I intend to do my job. Even more now. Rainwater has made this personal." Brody strode into the kitchen and washed the blood off his hands and face. "Get one of the marshals' duffel bags. Stuff what you think we can use in it. We don't have transport out of here, so we'll have to go on foot and find a place to camp. Bring food that is easy to carry. We won't use a fire to cook."

"Yeah, too risky."

He gestured at his bloody clothes. "I'm changing and gathering what I can from the bedrooms. I imagine the ranger has a lot of what we may need for camping."

Arianna snapped her fingers. "Be right back." She rushed down the hallway and returned a half minute later with her camera.

"I don't think this is a good time to take pictures of the wilderness."

She smiled. "Not the wilderness but these two animals. When we get back to Anchorage, I want to make sure we find out who they are and who they work for."

"That's easy. Rainwater."

"But who they are might help us get Rainwater for a murder of a federal agent."

He covered the distance to the hall. "Are you sure you weren't a cop before this?"

"No, but when you protect others you learn things. Change and take care of those cuts or I will. There's a first aid kit in the bathroom."

"Don't have the time. I'll do it later. I want to leave in ten minutes. We don't know who else is out there and how long it will take them to realize these guys didn't succeed. When they figure that out, they'll come looking for us."

The thought there could be more than three sent to

kill them spurred him to move as fast as his throbbing body allowed. Now that the adrenaline had faded, the pain came to the foreground. But he wouldn't allow it to interfere with what had to be done.

After snapping pictures of both of the intruders, Arianna found a backpack in the storage closet off the kitchen and decided to use that instead of one of the marshals' duffel bags. Easier to carry and since it was large it would hold about the same amount of items. As she stuffed what food she could into the bag, she glimpsed Mark on the floor nearby and steeled her resolve to bring to justice the person responsible for his death.

As a soldier she'd seen death, sometimes on a large scale. As a bodyguard she hadn't been exposed to it much in the past four years. She'd worked hard to keep it that way by protecting her clients the best she could. But now there were three dead bodies in the cabin and at least one outside, possibly Kevin's, too. She'd wanted to help and protect people without the death. But it had found her that evening when she'd witnessed Thomas Perkins's murder and wouldn't let go.

After scouring the kitchen and living room for anything they could use, she hurried to her bedroom and grabbed what she might need from her own possessions. The last things she put into her backpack were the camera and flashlight. Although the night was only about four hours long, they might need the light, especially if they had to find shelter in a cave.

"Ready?" A rifle with a scope clutched in one hand and his duffel bag in the other, Brody stood in the entrance to her bedroom, dressed in clean jeans and

T-shirt with hiking boots, a light parka and his Glock strapped in his holster at his waist. His face still looked as though the man had used him as a punching bag. When they were safely away from the cabin, she intended to treat those cuts.

She slung the pack onto her back. "Yes. Do we have all the ammunition?"

"Yes, what there is. I wish we had more rounds for the rifle, but for the handguns we should be fine. I found a map and a compass in the ranger's bedroom closet." He swung around and started for the front door.

Arianna followed. "I hate leaving Mark like this."

Brody stepped out onto the porch. "I can't call this in. I don't want anyone to know the assassins didn't succeed in killing us all. I don't know how they found us. I can't trust anyone."

"And we can't even take the satellite phone with us," she murmured, thinking about the GPS in cell phones. Great way to track someone.

"Not if we don't want more assassins finding us. We're on our own and I don't intend to make it easy for anyone to track us." Brody used the pair of binoculars hanging around his neck to scan the terrain stretching out before them.

"What happens when we reach Anchorage?"

"I'm not sure. I'll have to stash you someplace safe until you can testify because I intend to get you to that trial. Rainwater isn't going to win this one. One of my men, possibly two, are dead because of that man." He checked the compass then descended the steps. "Let's go."

"If they come after us, they'll know we're heading for Anchorage. There aren't too many ways in."

"I know. That's why we aren't going straight there. We're heading east toward Fairbanks, not southwest. They'll be watching all the direct routes to Anchorage."

"But we have to still get to Anchorage."

"Once I find some transportation, I'll figure out a way. I can't see us walking the whole way to Anchorage anyway. Time is against us. If they can't kill us, they'll still succeed in freeing Rainwater if you don't show up to testify."

"That isn't going to happen." She'd already waited so long for the chance to testify, spending almost two months in Kentucky until the U.S. Marshals Service had moved her back to Alaska. Two months separated from her family and friends. Her employer at Guardians, Inc. only knew that she had gone into the Witness Protection Program, and after that, she had to cut all ties. "I didn't go through the last two months for nothing." She ground her teeth, wishing she could grind her fists into the face of the person responsible for giving the cabin's location away.

"Even if you didn't get to testify, I doubt Rainwater would want you alive."

Arianna slanted a look at the harsh planes of Brody's face. Determination molded his features and steeled the hard look in his brown eyes. "That's my thinking, too. If I have to give up my life, I want it to be for something."

After Arianna took a picture of the third assailant, she and Brody headed toward the trees. The sun hung low on the horizon as it started its ascent. A dense stand of spruce, willow and birch up ahead offered them shelter from being in the open. Brody increased his pace the lighter the day became. When the thick wooded area swallowed them into a sea of green, he slowed his gait.

"If you need to rest, let me know. I tend to push."

"That's fine by me. But I do think we need to stop and take care of your cuts. Did the guy have a ring on?"

"You know at the time I didn't think about that. I was just trying to stop him."

"The cut over your eye is oozing blood. So is the one on your right cheek. Doesn't the scent of blood attract predators?"

"I guess it could. I didn't think about that, either. Too busy trying to figure out the best way to proceed. We'll stop for a brief rest after we've gone a little deeper into this forest."

"Maybe the U.S. Marshals Service will discover we're missing before the bad guys realize their assassin team didn't succeed."

A frown descended on Brody's beat-up face. "But who do we trust? I still can't figure out how they knew where we were. Few did. And the map that guy had was very precise."

"And another burning question is Kevin's whereabouts." Arianna pictured the young marshal with the ready smile. Did he betray them? What happened to him? Money lured a lot of people to do evil things. "I don't want them to find him dead, but what if he gave the cabin's location away? That was the first time he was on duty outside, and the assassins just happened to get inside the cabin without anyone knowing. They surprised Mark or we would have heard a commotion."

"That's what I'm wrestling with. I don't want to think it's one of us, but I have to consider that. Or—" Brody paused for a long moment "—it was someone from the first team at the cabin, especially because of the detailed map. Until we were flown in, I couldn't have drawn the kind of map they had. If it was Kevin, how could he have gotten the map to them ahead of time?"

"It has to have been an inside job, especially in light of the safe house being compromised in Anchorage. I don't believe in coincidences. Two places compromised in a case? Doesn't happen without inside information."

"And Rainwater has deep pockets. He's a crook but money can be influential."

As they went through a thicker area of trees, branches slapped against Arianna's arms while she threaded her way through the woods right behind Brody. "In a perfect world, money and power wouldn't count."

"It does in this world, and Rainwater has a lot of both. But somewhere along the line, we're going to have to trust someone, especially if we want to figure out who's behind this."

"I have to. My life will depend on that. I can't go into the Witness Protection Program with the thought that some marshal might have betrayed me and could do it again. Rainwater, even if he gets off, won't stop until I'm dead."

"Agreed." He halted and faced her, intensity vibrating off him. "We have to discover who is behind this and get you to Anchorage to testify."

Blood trickled down his cheek. The urge to touch him and wipe it away assailed her. "This looks safe enough to stop for a few minutes. I need to take care of your cuts. You're still bleeding."

"A limb hit me in the face. Probably opened a few cuts that had clotted." Brody glanced around. "How about over there?"

"Fine." Arianna trekked to a less dense patch under a group of mountain alders. Dropping her pack on the ground, she relished the weight being off her shoulders for a few minutes. "Sit while I clean your cuts and bandage a couple of them." She retrieved the first aid kit and opened it.

"Did I tell you I'm not a good patient?"

"No, but too bad. I can't afford for you to get an infection."

"I doubt—" At that moment, she wiped the deepest cut on his cheek with a pad doused in alcohol, and he yanked back. "It's obvious you're no Florence Nightingale."

She grinned, winking at him. "Never claimed to be. I'm sure we shouldn't stay here long so speed is important." She moved on to the next wound.

"Yeah, the farther away we are from the cabin the safer we'll be."

He stayed perfectly still, his gaze fixed on her. She tried to ignore it, but it was hard. Her stomach clenched into a tight ball. His eyes seemed to penetrate deep into her—as though trying to discover her innermost secrets. She had no intention of sharing those with him or anyone.

"Close your eyes. I want to take care of the one near your left one. I wouldn't want to get alcohol in your eye."

His gaze narrowed for a few seconds before he shut it completely. She dabbed the pad on the cut, relieved for the short break from his intense look. Slowly the knots unraveled in her gut. With his eyes closed, she got a chance to scrutinize him without him seeing. His features weren't handsome, but there was a strength and ruggedness to them that gave a person the impression he knew how to take care of himself. That appealed to her. Probably too much.

Caring about a person who was protecting you wasn't

wise. Just as caring about a person you were protecting wasn't wise. Her hand quivered as she pressed a small bandage over the cut near his eye, then proceeded to put two more on the other ones that kept bleeding.

"What made you go into the private sector as a bodyguard?"

His question surprised her, and yet it shouldn't have. He no doubt was assessing her and deciding if he could trust her to protect his back. Whether he liked it or not, they were in this as a team. "Instead of law enforcement?"

"Yes."

"Money and the freedom my job allows me. When I left the service, I knew I wanted to use my skills to protect people. In my different tours in the army, I saw a lot of defenseless people who were victims of their circumstances. Guardians, Inc. is a business but Kyra Hunt, my boss, also helps people who can't usually afford to have a paid bodyguard."

"When I knew I would be protecting you, I did some checking into Guardians, Inc. It's a top-notch company with a good reputation."

"Kyra only employs the best."

"And she hired you?"

She laughed. "I'll try not to be offended by that remark."

"Don't be. I've read about your assignments. You're very good at your job."

Ignoring his remark, she taped the last bandage into place. "I'm finished. You're not as good as new, but it will have to do." She put the packaging from the items she'd used back into the first aid kit, not wanting to leave any evidence they had been there behind for someone to find.

His eyes remained closed.

"You didn't fall asleep on me, did you?"

"No, I was running through my mind what went down at the cabin, trying to figure out what happened, how they might have known where we were. How did they get there? Who would have talked with them?"

"Any clues?"

His eyelids slowly rose, and his look snared hers. "No, and now we don't have the time to dally and try to figure it out. Let's go." He pushed to his feet.

Arianna stood, stretching to ease the tightness in her shoulders and back. "I'm ready." She reached for her pack when a roar echoed through the stand of trees. A familiar roar.

She shot up and whirled around. Through the woods a large grizzly bear standing on its hind legs stared right at them.

THREE

Forty yards separated Arianna from the grizzly, still perched on its hind legs. Watching. "Is this the same one that was at the cabin?"

"Don't know. I don't see any cubs around."

"Oh, good. *Another* bear. What do we do? Run? Climb the tree behind us?"

Brody turned his head slightly but still kept tabs on the brown bear by slanting a glance toward it. "Don't look directly at it."

"But—"

Before she could finish her sentence Brody straightened as tall as he could, raised his arms and waved them. "Bears are curious. I'm challenging it. Follow suit." Then in a shout he said, "Leave us alone," over and over.

Arianna mimicked what Brody was doing, hoping he knew what he was doing. She was all for spinning around and running as fast as her legs could carry her.

The grizzly dropped to all four legs. It charged them but stopped about twenty-five yards away.

"This isn't working." Arianna's heartbeat sped, her

mouth dry. She might not have to worry about Rainwater's men.

"Back away slowly, still waving your arms and shouting."

"Isn't this calling attention to us?"

"Yep, but a gunshot would make more noise. Carry farther."

One step back. Then another. Arianna looked sideways at the bear. It stood on its hind legs again, pointing its nose up in the air as though the grizzly was sniffing it. She kept moving, going between two trees.

"Are you sure we shouldn't climb a tree?"

"Grizzly bears can climb a tree."

"What else can they do?" Arianna asked, watching the animal lower itself onto all fours again.

"Swim and run fast."

The bear roared.

Arianna gasped while Brody brought the rifle up.

The grizzly gave one last vocal protest then loped off toward the east, disappearing in the thickness of a stand of pines.

Brody rotated around. "Let's get out of here before it changes its mind and returns for us."

"Now you're talking." But as she hurried away, she glanced back every few steps to make sure the bear wasn't behind them. The pounding of her pulse echoed through her mind.

"We need to keep moving. It's been several hours since we were attacked. If I was running that mission, I'd be wondering why my men hadn't come back and go investigate."

"The Marshals Service will investigate when you don't call in this morning."

"Yes, so the best thing for us is to put as much distance between us and the cabin. We don't want anyone to know where we are, not even the marshals. When we get to Fairbanks, we can check the news to see what, if anything, is being said."

Arianna slowed her pace and twisted around once more to make sure the bear wasn't following them. She'd heard stories about a bear tracking a person, appearing every once in a while then attacking. She didn't want to be one of those stories. All she saw was a thick, green forest around her—a perfect place for someone—or some animal—to hide and wait for the right time to strike.

After a couple of hours of walking as fast as they could through dense woods and rugged terrain, Brody spied a place that probably had been used as a campsite in the past. Thankfully it showed no signs of recent use. "Let's stop and eat something." He pointed at a crop of rocks. "I'm going up there to scout out our surroundings." He took out his compass. "And make sure we're going in the right direction."

"Did I tell you I don't cook?" Arianna said with a laugh. "So all you'll get is something easy. Like peanut butter sandwiches without the jelly, and I'm afraid the bread has been squashed."

After finding his first foothold, Brody peered at Arianna already digging into her backpack. "Right now anything sounds good. I'm starving."

"So am I."

Her gaze linked with his, and he glimpsed the toll the past hours had taken on Arianna. There were many people he'd guarded in the Witness Protection Program, but some were criminals. The ones like Arianna always got to him. The ones who weren't trying to cut a deal or avoid the consequences of their actions, but were simply testifying because it was the right thing to do, no matter what the cost. He couldn't imagine giving up his life and having to start a new one. But she would have to once the trial was over.

He climbed the outcropping of rocks until he reached a perch where he could lie down and scope out the area without being seen. He was most concerned with the terrain between them and the cabin.

The wind whipped against his face, carrying the scent of burning wood. A campfire nearby? Frowning, he focused the binoculars in the direction they'd come. A roiling mushroom of dark smoke billowed into the sky.

Was the cabin burning? The forest around it?

He trained his binoculars on the area, trying to see anything that would give him an idea of what they were up against. He couldn't tell. After checking all the surroundings, he scrambled down the rocks and hurried to Arianna.

"We need to keep moving."

She handed him a sandwich. "Take a few minutes to eat." Studying his face, she pushed to her feet. "What's wrong?"

"There's a fire behind us and the wind is blowing this way. I'm guessing it's four miles back, but it has been dry in this part of Alaska, so there's a lot of dry timber between us and the forest fire." He took a bite of the sandwich, hefted his duffel bag and then slung his rifle over his shoulder. "Let's go. We'll eat and walk."

"You think Rainwater's men started a fire at the cabin? Why would they do that?"

"Maybe to cover up any evidence. To cause confusion. They had to know the U.S. Marshals Service would know when something happened at the cabin."

"The fire means a lot of firefighters will be in this area."

"Making it harder for us. Rainwater's men can infiltrate the firefighters, using that as a cover for being here."

Arianna nodded as she finished the last of her sandwich. "Which way?"

"There's a river up ahead of us." He checked the compass then pointed northeast. "We'll have to cross it. It should be low because of no rainfall in the past month, but we'll still have to swim."

Arianna slowed her gait. "Is there a way around the river?"

"It stands between us and Fairbanks. Why?"

"I can't swim well. Just enough to get by."

"You can't?" He'd never considered that. "Why not?"

"I almost drowned as a child. I was caught in a flood. Rushing water scares me. Is this river like that?"

"Yes. At least when it's low you can see the rocks." He wished there was another way to get across other than swimming. Arianna had already gone through enough.

She stopped and swept around toward him. The pallor on her face highlighted her fear. "I can do a lot of things. Climb up tall structures. Parachute out of a plane. Snakes, rats, spiders don't bother me, but rushing water does. I'm only okay in a pool—still water."

He hated to see the fear in her eyes, but there was nothing he could say to make it better. "We don't have the time to find a way around the river. We have to cross it and there isn't a bridge for miles. Besides, those will be watched."

Closing her eyes, she drew in a deep breath. "Okay."

She rotated back around and started forward, her strides long. But Brody had glimpsed how scared she was and wasn't sure how they would get across the river that was a favorite of those who liked to ride the rapids.

Brody came down from climbing a tree to check the progress of the fire. His grim expression spoke of their dire situation even before he said, "It's moving fast. Faster than us. Animals are fleeing the area—an elk herd is off to the right of us. But what is even more alarming is that I saw three dogs with several handlers—all armed. No uniforms on so we need to assume unfriendly."

Dogs. Tracking dogs were hard to evade. Determined and relentless described the ones she'd worked with in the past in the service. "We're boxed in then with the river on one side and the fire and dogs on the other."

"Yes, and they are about two miles ahead of the fire so let's getting moving."

Arianna thrust a bottle of water into his hand. "Drink, and eat this protein bar. We're gonna need to keep our energy up."

After taking a swig of water, he started out at a fast clip, making his own path through the forest. "We've got to eat on the run. No other way."

As she set into a jog, Arianna wolfed down her food. Her muscles burned from exhaustion and only her strong determination kept her putting one foot in front of the other. She refused to dwell on what she would face at the river. The scent of the fire intensified even as they moved away from it. When she inhaled deep breaths as she ran, she couldn't fill her lungs with enough oxygen. Pain in her side stabbed her, her breathing grew more labored with each stride she took.

She periodically looked over her shoulder, checking the area behind her. At any second she had to be prepared to encounter people. Whether friend or foe didn't matter because they couldn't take a chance on being seen.

Brody came to an abrupt halt, his arm going up to indicate he heard something ahead of them. Arianna nearly collided with him but managed to stop in time.

He pointed to the left then whispered into her ear, "Someone's coming."

Arianna glimpsed something orange where he'd indicated. She scanned the forest, saw a place they could hide and tugged on Brody. She just hoped it wasn't a tracker with a dog or their hiding would be in vain.

As quiet as possible, she crept through the underbrush with Brody at her side. Lying down on the forest floor beneath some dense foliage, she pulled her gun, praying she didn't have to use it. Brody brought the rifle around and aimed it in the direction where he saw the orange.

Two men dressed as hunters, rifles in their hands, trekked *toward* the fire. While in Kentucky, Arianna had familiarized herself with every person known to be associated with Joseph Rainwater. She had planned on going back to Alaska as prepared as she could be. The larger of the two that passed within ten yards of their location was Boris Mankiller, an appropriate name for him because he was believed to be one of Rainwater's most valuable guns for hire.

Mankiller and his comrade halted about twenty feet away. Mankiller made a slow circle, his rifle raised as though he sensed them nearby. Her heartbeat hammered so fast and loud she wondered if he heard it.

Brody signaled he had his rifle pointed at Mankiller. She lifted her Glock and targeted the man's comrade, her breath bottled in her lungs.

One minute passed. Mankiller pointed at the sky in the direction of the fire. Arianna glimpsed the growing smoke, obscuring the sun and leaving a dimness in the forest as if it were dusk instead of the middle of the day.

The two parted—one went to the left while the other moved to the right and slightly toward the fire, fanning out. She saw through the foliage another pair of guys a hundred yards away. She leaned toward Brody and whispered, "They're trying to close in on us."

"They may be part of an inner ring around the cabin. We need to watch for any people forming an outer circle. Let's go. It's even more important to get to the river."

When he said the word *river*, a ripple of fear snaked down her spine but her fear of the water was far outweighed by fear of the men after her. In this small part of the forest she knew that Rainwater had four men looking for them. Multiply that over the large area of this wilderness and he must have hired a small army to look for her and anyone left to protect her.

Sneaking out from under the brush, she ran while crouched right behind Brody, swinging her attention back every once in a while to make sure no one had spotted them. Her back hurt from being hunched over and her thighs screamed in protest at the punishing pace Brody set but she didn't dare voice a complaint.

Forty-five minutes later, Arianna stared down at the raging river, its water churning like a boiling pot of liquid. She froze at the sight.

Brody came up beside her. "You okay?"

She opened her mouth to answer him, but no words formed in her mind, her full attention glued to river. Reminders of when she had been young and swept away from her parents in something similar inundated her. Her younger sister had died in the flood. Arianna had tried to save her, but her grip on Lily had slipped away. The last thing she remembered was her sister's scream reverberating through her head against the backdrop of the gushing sound of the water—a raging turmoil.

Brody grasped her arm and swung her around. He waited until her gaze latched on to his before saying, "All you have to do is get yourself across the river. I'll take care of everything else. Okay?"

She nodded, her mouth so dry she should be happy to immerse herself in water. She wasn't. Fear held her immobile, unable to take a step toward the bank.

She hadn't known how hard controlling her fear had been until her army unit had been forced to cross a swollen river. Watching one of her comrades swept away by the power of the water brought her childhood trauma to the forefront after years buried deep in her subconscious.

"We don't have much time to get across the river and hide before the dogs track us to here."

Her attention drifted away from the water to focus on Brody. "What do you need me to do?"

"We need to wade in the water along the edge as far

upstream as we can go, then go straight across. They'll assume the current will take us downstream."

"Or they might assume the opposite. Either way we'll be taking a chance. Actually with all the men I have a feeling are out here, they probably can cover both areas."

"Don't forget they can't be openly looking for you. By now the U.S. Marshals Service is all over here, too."

"If only we knew who to trust."

"Can't take the chance. You don't know how much that pains me to say."

She stared into his brown eyes, full of sadness. "I was betrayed by a team member, so yes, I do know how you feel."

"When we have time, you'll have to tell me about that." He took her hand and started down the incline to the river.

Scaring off a bear was nothing to Arianna, but this was a big deal. She stepped into the water until it was swirling about her ankles. Still grasping her hand, Brody led her a few more feet out to where the river came up to her knees, then he trudged upstream. The feel of his fingers around her fortified her with the knowledge she wasn't alone to face her worst fear.

After about a hundred feet up the river, Brody rounded a corner and came face-to-face with the water racing over a mound of rocks. Blocked from going any farther in the shallow part of the river, he stopped and took her backpack. He opened it and gave it to Arianna to hold.

"You can't swim holding the rifle and a duffel bag," she said.

After removing some rope from his duffel bag, he

piled it into the backpack then began adding other items. "I know. I'm putting what I think we need the most in the backpack. The rest I'll sink in the middle of these rocks. It'll be hard to find."

He left food or items that would be ruined from being dunked in the river in the duffel bag, then scrambled up the rocks. When he slipped and fell back into the river, Arianna rushed to help him. Suddenly she realized she stood in thigh-deep water with a strong current tugging at her. Panic seized her. She shoved it down. She had no time to be afraid. The alternative was to stay on this side of the river and try to evade tracking dogs and men with rifles.

She waded to Brody and helped him up, taking the backpack from his hand. "I'll toss you it when you get up on top of the rocks."

This time he succeeded without the burden of carrying the pack. She threw it to him. He caught it and disappeared from view. Arianna hastened back closer to shore and waited. Two minutes passed and worry nipped at her composure. She thought about shouting his name over the rushing sound of the water, but that might only lead the dogs and men to their location.

Opening and closing her hands, she gritted her teeth. She'd never been good at waiting. *Lord, I know I haven't been talking with You lately, but please help Brody and me get to Anchorage safely. Rainwater needs to go to prison for what he did. I need You.*

The last sentence had been the hardest to say because she'd come to depend on herself so much in the past four years. *I don't know if I can make it across this river without Your help.*

As she stared at the rushing river, the earlier tension

eased. Suddenly Brody popped up over the rocks then lowered himself down into the water.

He sloshed to her and took the rope and backpack. He slung the backpack over his shoulders, then lifted the rope. "I'm tying this around your chest. This'll be your line to use. As long as you're attached, I should be able to help you. Don't go in until I reach the other side."

He moved farther out into the rapids, water hitting the rocks and spraying up into the air. With long, even strokes, he headed for the opposite bank at an angle. He didn't stop until he was over on the other shore. Waving to her, he held up the rope and signaled for her to start.

Sucking in a steadying breath that did nothing to fill her lungs, she waded as far as she could, fighting to keep herself upright with the strong current. Even though Brody had swam at an angle upstream, he'd ended up about ten feet downstream. Was that far enough away from where they first went into the river? But even more important, could she keep herself from being swept up in the current?

Two seconds later she plunged into the river, using all the strength she had to dog-paddle toward the other side. Water splashed over her head, and she went under, swallowing some of the river water. Panic threatened to take over. Again she fought to squash it as she struggled to the surface. Her head came up out of the water, and she gasped for air at the same time the current slammed her against some rocks. Black swirled before her eyes.

FOUR

Brody saw Arianna go under halfway across the river, and his first impulse was to drop the rope and go into the water after her. Instead, he searched for something to tie the rope to then he'd go after her, using it to guide him to her. He used a tree nearby, keeping his eye on the area where she went under.

As he hurried into the river, she surfaced feet from some large boulders. Before he could do anything, she crashed into the rocks like a wet rag doll. Next the river swept her limp body, bobbing up and down, into the fast current, heading away from him.

The rope grew taut, the thin tree he'd tied it to bowing but holding strong for the time being. Gripping the line, he held on to it and swam the fastest he could with one arm. The rush of the river tossed him about and drenched him as he tried to get to Arianna.

Then the churning water swamped him, pushing him under, and he lost sight of Arianna.

Pain jerked Arianna from the black void. For a second she didn't know where she was until the same feeling of drowning from when she was child overwhelmed all her senses. Her chest felt as though it were about to explode. She needed to breathe. She couldn't. Water encased her like a tomb. She couldn't see through the murkiness as she tossed and twisted in the river.

I can't panic.

Lord, help.

A memory punched through the panic. Brody had tied a rope around her. A lifeline. She fumbled for it, her fingers grazing the rope about her torso. When she grasped the length connected to Brody, she willed what strength she had left into her arms and pulled. One hand over the other. Again. And again.

Light filtered through the dim water. The surface. Air. She moved quicker while her lungs burned in excruciating pain.

I won't—let—Rain—

She broke free of her watery tomb. Oxygen-rich air flooded her starved lungs. Her thinking sharpened. That was when she realized her grip on the rope started slipping. She clutched it and began dragging herself toward shore. Her gaze latched on to Brody only a few yards from her in the river. Although still tossed about, she fixed her full attention on him as he came closer.

When she reached him, he enclosed an arm around her, a smile on his face—the most beautiful thing she'd seen in a long time.

He treaded water. "Okay?"

She nodded.

"Hold on to the rope. I'll be next to you."

Those words made her feel totally taken care of and protected. Something she did for people, not the other way around. The calmness that descended surprised her because they still had half the river to cross. Was this what she instilled in her clients—this sense of security? Then she remembered in her time of need calling out to the Lord. That was when she was able to calm herself and get to the surface.

When she pushed to her feet a couple of yards from the bank, her shaky legs barely held her upright. Brody slung his arm around her and helped her to shore. She collapsed on the ground, still inhaling gulps of air as though she couldn't get enough of it, like a person left in a desert without water.

Hovering over her, he offered her his hand. "I wish I could give you a minute to rest, but we can't stay here. No doubt the men and dogs will end up at this river soon. We've got to keep moving."

"I know." She fit her hand in his, and he tugged her to her feet. "And you don't have to worry about me. I know what has to be done."

He grinned, untying the rope from the tree and reeling the long length in. "I'd like all my witnesses to cooperate like this. Maybe I can hire you to teach them."

"Sure, but I think that would be breaking a number of WitSec rules," she said, using the shortened nickname for Witness Security.

"Yeah, I guess I'll still have to keep trying to train my witnesses myself." Brody picked up the backpack and slung it over his shoulders, then reached for the rifle.

"Let me carry something."

"Let me play the male here and take both."

"Can't give up that gun? Now that doesn't surprise me. But I can take the backpack at least part of the way."

Brody gave it to her, then climbed up the bank of the river.

Arianna tried clambering up the incline behind him

and nearly slid back down. She gripped a small tree growing out of the mini cliff and kept herself stationary. The swim had taken more out of her than she realized. "Okay. You can have the backpack for now."

Standing above her on the rise, he bent over and grasped one arm then hoisted her up. "When we get away from the river, we'll stop and eat something while I take care of your injuries."

Finally, at the top of a small ridge, Arianna glanced down at herself. Cuts and marks that would probably become bruises later covered her arms. She hoped the jeans protected her legs or she'd look like she'd been through a meat grinder. She touched her face and winced. When she peered at her hand, blood was smeared on her fingertips.

As they progressed across a clearing toward the forest at the bottom of a mountain range, her body protested each step she took. Everything had happened so fast in the river, but she must have been knocked against the rocks pretty hard to feel this bad.

An hour later at the bottom of a mountain beneath a line of trees, Arianna sat at the base of an aspen and leaned back against its whitish trunk. "This isn't gonna be easy to go over."

"No, but this range goes for miles. Walking around isn't an option with the clock on the trial ticking down."

"Not a complaint. An observation. With the right equipment I love to climb mountains."

"Sorry, all we have is rope, and I'm not sure how good that will be for us." Brody took out the first aid kit. "Let's get you patched up. Your cuts aren't bleeding anymore, but I'd feel better if they are cleaned. I remember a wise woman telling me that cuts can get infected."

With Brody only a half a foot from her, she wished she had a mirror in all the items she'd thought to bring. His nearness did strange things to her inside. As he looked into her face, the chocolate brown of his eyes mesmerized her, holding her tethered to him without the use of any ropes. His touch as he tended to her injuries was gentle, in direct contradiction of his muscular, male physique. Through the sting of alcohol, she concentrated on him.

"I don't know much about you personally, and since I didn't have the advantage of reading up on you before you came to the cabin, maybe you could tell me a little about yourself."

His hand stilled; his gaze locked with hers. "What do you want to know?"

"Are you married?" came out before Arianna had time to censor her question. Although she really wanted to know, she could have phrased it a little less obviously. "I mean you aren't wearing a wedding ring, but some men don't. Is there a wife waiting for you to come home? Children? I mean not that it's important..." She clenched her teeth together to keep from making it worse by explaining why she'd asked. That was when she realized how dangerous his touch, his nearness was. She forced herself to look at a point behind him.

"I have no one to worry that I won't be home. This job requires a lot of time away from my home, not to mention putting my life on the line to protect a witness. I won't subject a wife to that kind of uncertainty."

"That was the way I felt about my job, first in the army and then with Guardians, Inc. I was usually gone from my home three weeks out of four, sometimes more. Not easy to have a relationship that way."

"Sounds like our lives are similar."

"Not exactly, at least now. My bodyguarding days were over when I became the star witness against Joseph Rainwater."

"I'm sorry about that." He took out a pair of scissors. "I want to cut the sleeves off your shirt. They're shredded anyway."

She glanced at the ruined shirt and nodded. "When I get a chance, I'll be chucking it. Not a souvenir I want to keep of this trip."

His laughter filled the air. "True."

Arianna looked away from him again before she forgot how serious their situation was.

"It's my turn to ask you a question. Why did you leave the army? From what I read about your service record, you were very good at your job."

"Being in the army had been in my blood since I was a child. My father served in the army as do two of my brothers. A third brother is a Navy SEAL, and my family hasn't let him forget it. I'd planned to stay in."

"What changed your mind?" Brody cleaned each scrape and cut on her right arm, his fingers whispering across her skin.

Goose bumps rose on her flesh. She knew he saw them and wished she could control her reaction to his touch and proximity. "The army didn't appeal to me anymore." She couldn't share what had happened to her. It was too personal. The team member's betrayal still cut deep.

"How did your family feel about your decision?"

"Hey, I believe—" she twisted toward him "—it's my turn to ask a question."

"I can't get anything by you," he said with a contrite look.

She chuckled. "I may be exhausted, but I'm still sharp up here," she said and tapped her temple. "What made you become a U.S. marshal?"

"Probably the same reason you became a bodyguard. To protect those needing to be protected. I had a friend in school who was bullied by a group of boys. I found myself standing up to them and liking the feeling of protecting Aaron. I hated seeing what those kids were doing to him. He didn't want to go to school. He stayed in his house. It changed him."

"But you often guard criminals that have agreed to testify for a lesser sentence or protection in the program. They're not exactly innocent."

"Yes, but their testimony gets some criminals convicted that are often untouchable without their testimony. Besides, if those criminals weren't protected, they would be killed for daring to testify against the people running things. Everyone should be able to do what is right, to start over in life." He put the antiseptic swabs he didn't use back into the first aid kit. The ones he'd used, he stuck in the backpack pocket where trash went. Nothing was left behind to be found by the people after them.

"I've discovered everything isn't black-and-white," Arianna said. "There's a whole lot of gray in life."

"That's a good way to put it." After withdrawing another protein bar, he gave it to her. "This isn't much, but we really shouldn't take any more time to rest. Let's get over this mountain first."

As Arianna looked up the slope, thousands of feet high, the scent from the blaze on the other side of the river invaded her surroundings. Through the break in the tree canopy, she caught glimpses of the haze caused by the fire. "Yeah, we need to get over by nightfall."

"What nightfall?"

"I know it's not much, but it does get dark for a few hours. I've had to come down a mountain in the night. Not fun."

"Maybe there's somewhere we can rest up there. Find a place where we can see if anyone is coming up this side."

Arianna moved until she found a large hole in the canopy and shielded her eyes from the sunlight. "There doesn't look like there's one, but maybe there's a cave tucked in up there for us."

Several thousand feet higher than the surrounding forest, Brody situated himself between two boulders, lying flat on the ground and looking upon the terrain below. Using the binoculars, he scoped out the area between the mountain and the river.

Activity across the river near where they had come out of the woods caught his full attention. They were too far away to see if it was Mankiller, but there were three men and two dogs. Not good. And where was the other dog he'd seen earlier?

Still, they might be able to rest and sleep for a couple of hours. He hoped the men chasing them were smart enough not to try to climb the mountain in the dark. Arianna and he had had a hard time doing it in daylight.

Arianna crawled up next to him. "Anything?"

He passed her the binoculars. "What do you think we should do? Stay and rest a little or keep going?" She was in good condition. From Ted's daily reports he knew she worked out each morning, keeping in shape.

Even after that battering she took in the rapids, she still wouldn't stop.

She turned toward him, one eyebrow raised. "You're asking my opinion?"

"Yes. You're part of this two-person team. If you can't make it, then there's no reason for us to try to hurry down the other side."

"Even if I was dead on my feet, there's no way I would pass up a challenge like that. I can make it down the mountain. We have enough rope to do the Dulfersitz rappel method. It was what climbers used in the 1800s before all the safety equipment we use today was created. It works, especially in this situation. Rappelling is a faster way down the other side of the mountain. It's dangerous, but the alternative is even more dangerous."

"Yeah, Rainwater's men are catching up with us."

"We'll have to leave the rope dangling from the mountain because we'll have to tie it to an anchor up here."

He peered at the three men and dogs across the river. "We have no choice. I've never rappelled, but I've done some rock climbing on indoor walls."

"You're in good hands. I've done it a lot."

She'd trusted him that he would get her across the river. He would trust her this once to get him down the mountain rappelling, but beyond that he couldn't totally put his trust in anyone. He crawled back away from the edge and stood when the rocks behind him gave him cover from the men after them. "I'm game. If you can swim across a raging river, I can go down the mountain the fast way."

"Not the fastest. That way would kill you." She grabbed the rope and searched her surroundings. She made her way to a rock jutting up and tested it to see if it was firmly in place. "I'll anchor the rope to this." After tying the rope to the boulder, she knotted the ends of the rope. "I wouldn't want you to rappel off the end of it."

"Thanks. I wouldn't want to, either. You think it will reach all the way?"

"Let's see." She went to the edge and dropped it over. "It's about a hundred feet to the ledge. The rope almost reaches it. We'll have to drop the last yard, but it looks pretty flat and there's enough room. The rest of the way looks easier—probably like what you did at the indoor rock wall?"

"I know I don't take the rope and hand over hand creep down it."

"No. I'll show you how you need to do it, then I want you to try. You'll go first." Arianna put the rope between her legs then brought it around her front, across her torso and over her left shoulder. She held the rope anchored to the boulder in her left hand and the other end of it in her right one, behind her and near her waist. "This will help you control your descent. Do you think you can do it?"

"There's only one way to find out." When she stepped away and gave him the rope, he took it and mimicked her earlier position.

"Good. Now when you lower yourself over the ledge, you're going to walk yourself down the side of the mountain. Slow and steady. When you get down there, I will lower the backpack and rifle to you, then follow after that. Okay?"

"I don't like leaving you up here by yourself."

"No choice. Besides, I can—"

"Take care of yourself. I know. I've seen you in action. Even in the river you didn't give up."

"Giving up isn't an option. I told you I'm not gonna let Rainwater win. I saw what he did to Esther's husband and most likely he's responsible for doing something to Esther." Her voice roughened as she finished her sentence.

His respect for her went up another notch. She continually amazed him. In all the witnesses he'd protected, he'd never encountered someone quite like her. "Let's do this."

He walked backward to the edge of the cliff, paused and looked at her, her long white-blond hair pulled up in a ponytail. The wind played with it, causing strands to dance about her shoulders. Her eyes appeared silver in the light.

Easing himself over the ledge, he let the rope slide slowly in his grasp. His heart rate spiked as he began walking down the almost ninety-degree rock facade. He peered up at Arianna watching him, worry apparent in those silver-gray eyes.

He forced a smile of reassurance to his lips although that was the last thing he felt. "I'm fine."

"You're doing great. Are you sure you haven't done this before?"

"Yep. I think I'd remember it," he said, his hands burning from the scrape of twine across his palms. No wonder climbers used gloves. Too bad they didn't have any.

An eternity later he came to the end of the rope, and finally looked down at where he was. Three feet to the wide ledge. With a deep breath, he pushed out of the makeshift harness slightly and dropped. When his feet landed on the stone surface, he bent down, absorbing the impact from the ground with his legs.

Immediately he straightened and shouted, "Piece of cake. I've got a new hobby when we get out of this. Send the backpack and rifle down."

"Coming." Arianna raised the rope, tied the objects on it then lowered them to him.

Not long after that, she started rappelling down the side of the mountain. What took him ten minutes she did in seven. He wished when this was over that they could rappel together with the proper equipment, especially gloves. But after she testified, she would leave Alaska for a new home, in an undisclosed place. With her location compromised, she wouldn't return to where she had been before coming to Alaska to testify. Whoever was behind the cabin attack might have discovered her previous residence.

When she planted her feet on the ledge, he finally breathed normally. Although she knew what she was doing rappelling, their equipment wasn't something most climbers would use and the sport was dangerous, even in desirable conditions. These were less than advantageous. Desperate was a better description.

He inched toward the edge to stare down at the rest of their descent to the base of the mountain. "Once we are about halfway, we should be able to walk. It might be a steep one, but we won't have to climb down."

The stone shelf ran about fifty feet across. Arianna moved down its length and stopped not far from one end. "Let's go down here. It isn't the easiest way, but it slopes into a different area from where you're standing so if they find the rope and bring dogs in from below this will give us more time."

He approached her and peered around her. The angle was seventy or eighty degrees, which wasn't much better than what they had done, but a lot of rocks jutted out to use as steps. "Agreed."

"We'll go together. There's room for us both to descend near each other. I'm carrying the backpack. You can sling the rifle over your shoulder."

"You can tell you like to be in charge."

"In this case it's only because I've done this probably a lot more than you. Balance is important and the backpack might throw you off. Doing this in an indoor place is different from outside with the elements."

"I bow to your superior experience." He bent forward at the waist and swept his arm out.

She chuckled. "It's nice we have different skill sets or no telling what kind of trouble we would be in by now."

He turned in a full circle. "It'll be dark in an hour and a half."

Arianna took the backpack and shrugged into it. "The bottom part of the mountain will be a cinch after this."

Twenty minutes later Brody hung in the middle of the rock wall, Arianna about a yard from him, below him slightly. The skill she exhibited marveled him. Too bad this wasn't the time or place to admire them. He couldn't lose his focus on protecting her. Admiring her would have to wait. She'd slowed her descent because of him.

His left hand grasped onto a hold, and then he found a rock outcropping for his right one. Next, he lowered himself until he found a foothold that would take his weight and brought his left foot to it. When he shifted to place his right foot on a one-inch ledge, he began looking for his next move.

"Doing okay?" Arianna called up to him.

"Yes." He leaned toward the left, reaching for an indentation in the rock facade.

His right foot slipped off the foothold, plunging into the air.

FIVE

Arianna looked up to check on Brody's progress, and was just in time to see the ledge where his right foot gave way. For a second his leg hung in midair. He floundered, teetering for a second, before he finally lost his balance and plummeted.

When his body hit against a small stone ledge, the rifle shimmied down his flapping arms and dropped to the ground below. He clasped the rock shelf, breaking his downward fall.

Arianna swallowed a scream and moved as fast as she could to get to him. He hung under the protrusion, trying to secure his hold. In the midst of rushing, she lost her grip but hadn't moved her feet yet. She searched for another hold and dug in, determined to get to him before he lost his grasp. His legs flailed as he searched for a place to put his feet.

She was capable, but she didn't want to do this alone. She needed help. *Please, God, keep him safe.*

She probably wouldn't have made it across the river without him. She wasn't going to let him die. Feeling utterly helpless at the moment, she mumbled over and over a prayer of protection for Brody.

When she was a couple of feet from him, she saw his arms begin to slip from around the stone outcropping. She lunged toward it with her right foot as his grasp first on the left then the right came loose. Recklessly she leaped totally onto the small ledge and went down to grip him. Her fingers grabbed air.

All she could do was watch Brody crash downward the remaining few yards. As he lay collapsed, completely still at the bottom, Arianna hurried her descent.

Please, please let him be alive.

A constriction about her chest squeezed tighter the closer she came to him. She jumped down the last feet and shrugged off the backpack as she knelt next to him. With a quivering hand, she felt for his pulse at his neck. It beat beneath her fingertips, and relief shivered down her.

A second later, the sweetest thing she'd heard was his groan. Then he moved.

"Take it easy. Where do you hurt?"

Carefully he rolled over and looked up into her face. "Everywhere."

"That doesn't surprise me. You had quite a fall. That's why you don't climb without ropes and safety gear."

One corner of his mouth quirked up. "Thanks for telling me now. You could work on your timing."

"I do believe you're gonna be all right if your comebacks are any indication."

"What about my head? It's throbbing."

She probed his scalp, producing an "ouch" from him. "You might have a concussion. You've got a nasty gash to go with all the new scrapes you acquired on your plunge downward. Don't you remember I said it might be the fastest way down but not the safest?"

"I'll keep that in mind next time. Wait, there isn't going to be a next time. I don't think rock climbing and me go together," he said as he struggled to his elbows, flinching as he planted them on the ground to prop himself up. "At least the ground isn't tilting too much."

"Tilting? It's flat right here."

"Oh, then things may be worse than I thought." As he pushed himself to a sitting position, he closed his eyes.

"Is your world spinning?"

"In slo-mo, but yes, it's spinning."

"Then we aren't going anywhere for the time being."

"We can't stay here. We need to get the rest of the way down the mountain."

Arianna peered up at the dimming sky—some of the darkness from the sun going down, some from the smoke of the fire. "Not in the dark. It's bad enough navigating over rough terrain when you are in top physical condition, but when you're suffering probably from a concussion, no." She emphasized that last word.

"Did anyone ever tell you that you're bossy?"

"A few clients have, but they usually came to appreciate it in the end."

Putting his palms on the rocky earth beside him, he shoved himself up and immediately crumpled back onto the ground. "Okay, we'll stay here and have something to eat, rest a little bit but not long. I'm leaving in an hour and you're coming with me."

"I could argue with you."

"You could, but I'm an injured man. Surely you wouldn't add any more distress to me than a fall from twenty feet up a side of a rocky mountain."

"Oh, please, don't pull the woe-is-me card."

He eased back onto the ground and closed his eyes. "I'll just rest for a few minutes."

The comment was said casually but with a thread of pain that heightened her worry. "You going to sleep?"

"No, just trying to alleviate some of the tap dancers in my head. They're having a jolly ole time at my expense."

Arianna brought the backpack around and rummaged inside until she found the first aid kit at the bottom. When she opened it, she saw that some of the contents were ruined from the swim in the river, but the pain relievers in the packets weren't. She shook out two tablets and opened a new bottle of water. "Here, take these. They might help."

Lifting his head, he grimaced. He took the pills and swallowed a mouthful of liquid. "I've got a feeling this is like throwing a pail of water on a raging fire." He settled back on the ground. "Do I look as bad as I feel?"

Her gaze trekked down his length. His torn shirt matched hers after her encounter with the rapids and his scrapes against the rocks left welts and abrasions all over him. "I never thought you were the kind of guy who worried about his good looks."

He opened one eye. "I have good looks?"

"I'm not answering that question. It might swell your head even more."

He smiled. "You're not half-bad, either."

"I'm warning you now. I'm cleaning as many of your scrapes as I can with the limited first aid kit we have. I think we have almost exhausted its contents. We seem to be accident-prone."

"And the river...didn't help...either. I'm glad you..." His voice faded the more he spoke until no words came out.

She felt his pulse again. Strong. That reassured her. About all she could do was pour antiseptic on the worst of the wounds. There was no gauze left that wasn't wet with river water. They needed to find somewhere she could really tend to his new injuries. When they reached civilization she was going to insist on trying to find some kind of help.

As she finished what she could do with the antiseptic, she sat back and retrieved another protein bar, their mainstay. Before this was over, she would never want another, but at least it gave her some energy. She counted how many they had left. Three. A lot of the food never crossed the river with them.

After two hours of standing guard and fending off the mosquitoes, she woke Brody and said, "We better get going."

"How long did you let me sleep?"

"Do you feel better?"

"Yes. How long, Arianna?"

"I gave you enough time to get some rest."

"How about you?"

"Someone had to stand guard, but it's time to go now."

"Time? It's way past the time." He shoved himself up, darkness shrouding him in shadows.

Arianna helped him to rise to his feet. When he put weight on his right leg, he sank down. Quickly she wrapped her arm around him and held him up against her. "What's wrong?" The night made it difficult to see details, only an outline of Brody.

"My ankle. I did something to it."

"Lean on me. Do you think it's broken?"

"No." He shifted and must have put his foot down because he jerked back. "Maybe. But this will not hinder us. We keep moving if I have to hobble the whole way. No matter what, you'll get to Anchorage to testify."

"We'll hobble toward Fairbanks on one condition."

He snorted, but gestured for her to continue.

"You'll let me help you and the first time you can get medical attention you will."

"Yes, ma'am."

"And no lip or you'll hobble all the way to Fairbanks without my help." She thrust the protein bar she'd saved for him into his hand. "You're gonna need all the energy you can get."

"Where's the rifle? I can carry that."

"In several pieces. So it's in the backpack. Can't leave it." Slowly Arianna started down the slope, letting what moonlight there was illuminate their path. "Here's some water to wash the bar down."

He took it. "Did you get any rest?"

"And leave us unguarded? No way. Remember I'm a top-notch bodyguard and don't forget it."

"But I'm supposed to be guarding you."

"So I'm the client?"

"Yeah, so to speak."

"I thought we were a team."

He stopped and twisted toward her, sticking the water bottle in his jean pocket and then settling his hands on her shoulders. "We are and for just a few minutes I could forget about the pain shooting up my leg and the throbbing in my head to enjoy some fun bantering. Thank you, Arianna."

She didn't need to see his face clearly. She felt his

gaze on her as though he could pierce through all her barriers and touch her heart, one she had kept protected for four years. She'd been dating the man who'd framed her for giving out intel to the enemy. She'd been used. She wouldn't forget that feeling.

"C'mon. Quit this dillydallying."

He laughed. "Dillydallying?"

"A word my grandmother loved to use with us kids. Quit dillydallying. Move it. She would have made a great drill sergeant." She resumed their hike down the bottom half of the mountain.

"It sounds like you have fond memories of your grandmother. Is she still alive?"

"Yes, as far as I know." Another family member she couldn't see. Sadness enveloped her. A lump rose in her throat, and she swallowed several times, but she couldn't rid herself of the fact she wouldn't be surrounded by her family at the holidays as oftentimes in the past. "She was my role model."

"I'm sorry about what you're going through."

His gentle tone soothed her. In the last few months she'd tried not to think about having to give up all she'd known—people, career—to start new. She'd focused on bringing Rainwater to face justice. But soon she would have to deal with it. For now, though, she would concentrate on getting herself and Brody to Anchorage alive.

In the distance a wolf bayed, reminding her that all they had now to protect themselves were two Glocks. They wouldn't stop a charging bear.

Midmorning of day two, with the backpack on, Brody leaned over and picked up a piece of wood that would be perfect as a walking stick. "Honest. My ankle is probably only twisted. The ACE bandage gives me some support, and the pain is bearable. I promise," he added when he saw Arianna's skeptical look.

"I see you wince when you put too much weight on that foot."

"That's your imagination."

"Hardly." She scanned the field before them. "I'll feel better when we get across it. I hate being out in the open."

He lifted the binoculars and swept the area before them, noting the dry meadow, the vegetation shorter than usual. He spied some elk at the edge. "Me, too. But it's not far and I don't see anything suspicious."

"That kinda worries me. Nothing since we crossed the mountain. I smell smoke so the fire is probably still burning."

"Forest fires can be hard to contain. When I lived in California, we had one that nearly reached my housing subdivision. I only lived in an apartment, but I certainly didn't want to lose all my possessions. We had to evacuate, and all I could take with me was what I could get in my car."

"What was the first thing you decided to take with you?"

"My laptop with all my pictures on it." He let the binoculars drop to his chest and looked at her, thinking of all she'd had to give up. Much more than he would have if the fire hadn't been contained.

"Of family?"

"Yes. I had everything digitalized."

"You don't have a backup service?"

"Yes. But when I get lonely, I like to look at them." Which had been often of late. He loved Alaska but he felt cut off, especially in the winter months, from his friends and family in the lower states.

"Are your parents alive?"

"My mother's in Florida. She remarried after my dad died. I don't have any siblings, but I have aunts, uncles and cousins. We usually have a big gathering once a year. I try not to miss it." Brody strode next to Arianna, realizing she was keeping her pace slow because of him. He sped up his step. They still had a way to go to get to Fairbanks—not to mention Anchorage.

She matched his faster gait, sliding a glance at him. "I'm fine. Don't worry about me."

"Who said I was worried?"

"Your expression. It takes more than a fall from a mountain to get me down." He cocked his head and listened, bringing his finger up to his mouth to indicate quiet. The sounds of a helicopter filled the air.

Arianna rotated in a circle, looking up at the sky.

He grabbed her hand and half ran, half limped toward a cluster of trees in the middle of the field that would offer shelter from prying eyes. The whirring noise grew louder. They needed to be under the trees before the helicopter came into view. If someone was looking for them, they would be scanning the terrain.

Three yards away.

Arianna glanced back. "The helicopter's coming from over the mountain."

Brody moved to the side and dropped down, dragging her with him. "This brush should hide us until we get to the trees. We'll have to crawl under it."

With Arianna beside him, he crept on his belly toward the trees, pulling the backpack along the ground in order to fit under the brush.

"This reminds me of my service in the army. I did this many times."

"I can't say I've had the pleasure."

A few feet to the green canopy. He peered back and realized the chopper would fly right over the pasture.

Even under the trees, he continued to crawl until they were safe in the center of them. Slowly he rose and faced the helicopter as it swooped across the field. He could see its flight path without viewing the chopper because the wind from its rotors stirred up the dust and flattened what vegetation there was. The herd of elk panicked at the noise and ran toward them. They pounded through the stand of spruce, firs and pines.

Pressing up against a large trunk on the backside of a black spruce, he glanced over at Arianna who had done the same thing. His gaze riveted to hers as the helicopter flew overhead and the elk passed by. In the middle of the tense situation a connection sprang up between them. They were in this together. She wasn't a U.S. marshal, and yet he knew she had his back. That feeling heightened his respect for her and the regret about the ordeal she had to go through just for being in the wrong place at the wrong time.

Why, God? This wasn't the first time he'd asked the Lord that question. From all he'd read about Arianna and seen over the past few days, she did a good job helping guard people who needed it. Now she would never be able to go back to that job. How would he feel if he couldn't do what he did?

"Did you see any writing on the helicopter?" Arianna asked, pushing away from the tree she'd hugged. "It was too dense over here."

He had glimpsed only one word through a slit in

the green canopy. "In gold lettering I saw the letters CAR. I'm not familiar with a helicopter service with that name, but then I don't know all of them. It wasn't military or government."

"Which means we have to assume it was part of Rainwater's search for us."

"Yep. Let's get into the forest. We'll be safer there."

"I hope you don't regret saying that." She picked up the backpack from the ground. "My turn to carry it." She started out, throwing a grin over her shoulder.

He limped after her, chuckling to himself at her attitude. *Take charge. I can do anything you can. So refreshing.* His usual witnesses weren't anything like Arianna. As he watched her a few feet ahead of him, he liked what he saw. And in that moment he realized he'd better watch where his thoughts were taking him.

Arianna Jackson was off-limits to him. She would testify and then disappear, and he wasn't interested in a relationship without long-term commitment. His relationship with Carla had taught him at least that much.

At the edge of the forest she turned and watched him, her eyes intense, her confidence conveyed in the way she carried herself. Planting one hand on her waist, she grinned. "Marshal Callahan, I do declare you're a slowpoke."

"Is that another phrase your grandma likes to say?"

"Yes, she's a Southern matriarch. She rules her husband and household with a sugarcoated firmness I've never been able to match."

He stepped into the dimness of the forest. "Have you ever been married?"

"Your dossier on me didn't tell you that?"

"All I know is that you're currently single."

"Nope. Although I had two serious boyfriends in my life, neither one led me to the altar."

"What happened?"

Striding next to him because the forest floor didn't have a lot of underbrush, she tilted her head toward him. "I had three older brothers who were standing between any guy and me. They made it tough on any boy in high school or college who was interested. Only one guy was stubborn enough to date me seriously and even he got run off eventually. I had to join the army to get away from their hovering."

"Ah, so your other boyfriend was while you were in the army?"

She nodded.

"Was he in the army, too?"

A frown crunched her forehead. "Yes, though his loyalties lay elsewhere. Thankfully for my sake his dubious character was uncovered before it was too late."

"For the altar?"

"No, for me to be sent to prison."

"Do you want to talk about it?"

"No, it's the past. I want to forget it." The steel thread woven through her words and the pursed lips underscored how hard that was for her.

"But you haven't."

"No, still trying. We haven't talked much about this, but it seems one of your fellow marshals betrayed the location. How does that make you feel?"

"Angry. Determined to find out who did this and make him pay."

"I still feel angry, too, even though I know who was responsible and saw him face justice. I know I should forgive and move on, but I can't. I figure you know what I experienced."

"Yeah, knowing what we're supposed to do and doing it can be two very different things."

"I can't do what God wants me to do. After what happened, I left the army. It wasn't the same for me. My dad thought I should have stuck it out and stayed. Dirk was responsible for sullying my reputation, and although he was caught and stood trial in the end, some still thought I was in it with him. I tried staying but realized all chances of promotion were gone. I disappointed my father and our relationship changed. When we saw each other at family gatherings after that, it was like we were two polite strangers."

"What were you charged with?"

"Selling intel to the enemy." Her frown deepened. "I would never betray my country."

"I'm sorry that happened to you." The sound of a stream nearby echoed through the trees. "I hear water." Brody looked ahead through the binoculars. He pointed to the left. "It's over there. It would be a good way to throw the dogs off if they come this way."

"Stream or river?"

"The wading kind of water. C'mon I'll show you."

As Arianna trudged toward it, she said, "Since I spilled my guts to you—and, by the way, I don't make it a habit to do that—I get to ask you a few questions."

"Okay," he replied warily, noting a gleam in Arianna's gaze.

"I noticed a certain amount of tension between Carla Matthews and you when you came to the cabin. Why?"

"You are good. I thought I covered that pretty well."

"Not well enough. You both tensed up, exchanged looks that could freeze a person."

"I guess I need to work on that."

"I doubt the others noticed. I'm very good at reading the subtle messages. Her eyes narrowed slightly, and she drew herself up straighter. A tic twitched in your jaw, and you made it a point not to look at her."

"Definitely I'm going to have to work on my unreadable expression."

"So why was there tension between you two?"

"I was hoping you would forget the question." He stopped at the edge of a stream, the water flowing gently over round rocks in the bed.

"Nope. Do you really think you can wade through this stream? Look at the rocks."

"I don't have a choice. If they bring the dogs into this forest, they'll pick up our scent. We need to do what we can to confuse the trackers."

"And we probably won't hear them coming." After taking off her tennis shoes and socks, she stepped into the cold water. "Use the stick but also hold on to me."

"What if you go down?"

"Then let go and let me go down. You don't need to twist your other ankle. I'll go first and you follow where I go."

He put his hand on her shoulder and trailed behind her into the water. "We need to walk as much in the center as possible where it's deeper."

"Deeper. Not my favorite word when connected to water."

He squeezed her shoulder. "I'm right here. Nothing is going to happen to you."

"I know. This is nothing compared to a raging river.

Have you been coming up with an answer to my earlier question?"

"You're relentless."

"No more than you."

"I'm not going to get any peace until I answer you, am I?"

She laughed. "Don't make it sound like some kind of torture. I've told you things I don't normally share with people I've only known for a few days."

"But what a couple of days they have been. It's not torture so much as me being unaccustomed to sharing at all."

"I bet you were fun on the playground as a kid."

"I'm talking about sharing feelings, not toys. I have a hunch you don't share much, either."

"Who am I gonna tell my secrets? My clients? I'm on the road all the time. Not conducive to long-term friendships and I don't share with casual acquaintances."

"How about me?"

She looked back at him, took a step forward then another and nearly went down. Letting go of his stick, he caught her. Her cheeks flamed.

"I'm sorry I distracted you."

Facing him, she narrowed her eyes. "No, you aren't. You're using delaying tactics. Back to the original question."

He sighed. She was right—no point in stalling anymore. Besides, after what she'd shared with him, she deserved his honesty. "Carla and I dated for a while. She was way too intense for me. I realized our relationship, if you could call it that, wasn't leading anywhere and broke it off. She didn't appreciate it. Since we worked together, I couldn't say she was stalking me technically, but there were times when it felt like it. Weird things started happening to me. Calls in the middle of the night. A flat tire when I'd go to work in the morning."

"Flat tires aren't that unusual. I've had my share."

"Three times over five weeks?"

"No. It sounds like someone wasn't happy with you. Is that why you left Los Angeles for Alaska?"

"Not entirely. I lost a witness."

"Like disappeared?"

"No, like was killed."

"Not that this witness is worried, but what happened to the other one?"

He wasn't going to lie to Arianna, but he did not share that dark time with anyone. "Nothing to concern you. The situations are totally different."

As they rounded a bend in the stream, Arianna halted, then moved back. "I see the top of a car on the left side up ahead."

He stepped around her, brought the binoculars up and surveyed the situation. "There's a tent. I don't see anyone, though. It may be campers."

"Or?"

"Or someone looking for us."

SIX

"Make a wide berth around them?" Arianna asked, searching the terrain for any sign of the people connected to the car.

"Let's check them out more closely. They could be our way out of here. The best way to evade dogs is a car. Can't track us when the scent vanishes."

Arianna eyed the steep incline on the left side of the creek. "How's your foot?"

"Numb from the cold water, but I think that's helped it. Like a pack of ice."

She nodded toward their route out of the stream. "I'll go first, and if you need help up the slope, I can give you a hand."

Picking her way through the rocky bottom, she made it to the side, Brody right behind her. "This should be easy after the mountain."

She grabbed hold of the trunk of a small tree and used it to hoist herself up and over to the forest floor above the creek. Favoring his good leg, Brody followed suit, rolled over and sat up to put his socks and boots on over his soaking wet ACE bandage. Arianna was on her feet and peering around the bend in the stream toward the car and campsite.

"What do you think?" Brody asked, close to her ear.

She swallowed her gasp at his sudden quiet appearance next to her. "Still don't see anyone. Maybe they're hunting or fishing. We'll need to go closer."

Using the foliage and tree trunks to hide them, Brody and she sneaked closer. She focused her attention on the campsite while he scoured the area for any sign of the car's owner.

Fifteen yards away from their objective a rustling sound to the right near the camp stilled Arianna's movements. A man and woman around the age of fifty came into the small clearing where the tent was pitched. He carried a rifle and they both had binoculars around their necks.

Arianna ducked back deeper into the underbrush. "What do you think? After us or two campers on holiday?"

He fixed his gaze on the couple. "I see a camera in the woman's hand. At first glance they seem all right."

"But…"

"Appearances can be deceiving. You and I have both encountered that in our lives."

Immediately Arianna thought of Dirk and then the latest person—the marshal who had betrayed her location. "Let's move closer and listen to what they're talking about. I'm not quite ready to just walk into their camp without more info."

"I like how you think—cautiously."

"There's time for action and time for waiting and seeing what happens."

"Not for long. We can't stay anyplace long."

"Why not?" asked a low-pitched female voice behind them.

Arianna peered over her shoulder. A young woman, no more than twenty, stood with her shotgun aimed at them. Arianna thought of going for her weapon at her side.

"I wouldn't if I were you," the girl said. "Both of you turn around slowly and start doing some explaining."

When Brody was fully around and facing the stranger, he nodded toward the gun. "Why don't you point that thing somewhere else?"

"I will when you explain what you meant by not staying long in a place."

"There's a forest fire not far from here. We've been running from it since yesterday. We had to leave our camping equipment and about everything we had and make a run for it. The last we saw the fire, the wind was blowing it this way. I'm surprised to find anyone here," Brody said, using his soft, nonthreatening voice.

The young woman relaxed slightly. "I smelled smoke. That's why I went up the tree to see if I could find out where it was coming from."

"Oh, then you saw the fire." Arianna watched the girl's body language intently. The more she looked at her the more she thought she was probably a teenager.

"Yep, but the wind has changed directions. It's blowing more directly north now. I think we'll be safe." The girl gestured with her shotgun. "If you're out here, those side arms ain't nearly as effective as a rifle or shotgun, especially for bears. We camp here every year and a couple of times bears have been a problem."

"Jane, who are you talking to?" a male voice asked.

"That's my grandpa," Jane said to them, then shouted,

"A couple running from the fire I seen." Again she made a motion with her gun. "C'mon. I'll introduce you to my grandparents. They don't live too far from here."

Arianna looked at Brody, who nodded. "We'd love to meet them."

With her arms out to indicate she wasn't reaching for her Glock, Arianna slowly rose. Brody did the same.

"Go ahead," Jane said, pointing toward the campsite, her shotgun still aimed at them.

When Arianna passed close to Brody, she whispered, "I'm not liking the gun pointed at us."

"Me, either." He slid a look back as he limped toward the campsite.

"What's wrong, mister?" Jane asked while trailing behind them.

"I fell and twisted my ankle."

"Running from the fire?"

"Yes."

As they entered the campsite, the man stood near the fire pit with his rifle up and fixed on Brody. It had been strained before with the teenager, but now the tension shot up like the fire devouring the forest across the river.

As Brody bridged the distance to the older man, he said, "That's as far as you come. Who are you?"

"I'm B.J. and this is my wife, Anna. I understand from your granddaughter you live around here."

He scowled. "What of it?"

Jane had been downright friendly compared to her grandfather. Arianna glanced at the woman not far from the man. Her hard expression, gaze glued to Arianna, did nothing to alleviate the stress.

"Nothing. Just trying to carry on a conversation. That coffee on the fire smells wonderful."

"Jane, git the rope. I think these two are who those officers were looking for."

"We're not running from the law but the fire." Arianna clenched her hands at her side, more worried about the two officers than this couple and their granddaughter.

Brody sidled closer to Arianna. "What makes you think that, sir?"

"You fit the description of the fugitives. You're wanted for starting that fire. If the wind had shifted, my home would be in the middle of it."

"What law enforcement officers?"

"State troopers. They came through this morning early."

Jane appeared at her grandfather's side, holding a length of rope.

Arianna exchanged a look with Brody. Were those Rainwater's men dressed as state troopers or did someone truly think she and Brody were behind the fire? But that didn't make sense. Wouldn't the U.S. Marshals Service step in and inform them about what was going on?

"Both of you take out your guns slow and easy then toss them over here," Grandpa said, lifting his rifle higher and aiming at Brody while Jane pointed hers at Arianna. "No shenanigans. First B.J. then Anna." He slurred their fake names as though he didn't believe a word they had said.

All the while Brody followed the older man's directions, Arianna assessed the situation, trying to find a way to get the upper hand. None presented itself without one or both of them being shot before she could use her Glock.

"Jane and Maude, tie them up. Remember I have the

rifle trained on you two. I kilt a charging bear by hitting it between the eyes. Girls, use that tree over there."

"What are you gonna do with us?" Arianna knew no good would come from being turned over to those "state troopers."

"Send Maude and my granddaughter to tell those state troopers about you."

"Where are they?" Brody asked as Grandma Maude jerked him toward the tree.

"Out on the highway not too far from here. They told us they have some kind of command post. If I seen anything I was to let them know."

"They just came up to you and asked you to help them?" Arianna uncurled her hands, trying to relax herself in order to move at a second's notice. The first opportunity…

"No, I saw them in their uniforms. I asked them. They were mighty surprised to see me and Maude bird watching."

"Are you sure they were real state troopers?" Arianna asked as Jane gestured for her to move to where Brody was now tied against the trunk.

"They were. I seen state troopers before, and they looked just like them. Maude, make sure he's tied tight. Don't want them getting away. Jane, the same with her."

Jane yanked the rope until it cut into Arianna's wrists. When Maude walked back toward her husband, Arianna whispered, "Jane, we aren't criminals. We were running from the fire and trying to get to the highway. Please help us."

"I can't. I was up in the tree. I saw those two men. Grandpa doesn't lie."

"What's taking ya so long, girl? You and your grandma need to go git help."

Jane peered around the tree trunk. "Just making sure she ain't going nowhere."

"Jane, if you bring those men back here, they'll kill us and maybe you all, too."

Jane's eyes widened. "Why? We ain't done nothing wrong."

"Neither have we."

Jane bolted to her feet. "They ain't going nowhere, Grandpa."

"Good. Check their pockets. Make sure they don't have anything they can use to get free."

Jane patted her down and found the money and the switchblade Arianna had, then turned her attention to Brody. She removed his wallet but didn't look at it. Jane hurried to her grandparents. "They don't have nothing now."

"Good. I think I'm going with you two. We'll tell them where these two are and then go home. It's getting late anyway and we'll let the state troopers take care of these criminals. Let's pack up."

Arianna craned her neck around to see the family packing up and tearing down their tent probably in record time. "What are we gonna do? She took my knife."

"I'm working on it."

"The ropes?"

"Yep."

"I can't budge mine. Jane followed her grandpa's instructions to a tee. In fact, my hands are starting to feel numb."

"Grandma doesn't have as much strength as Jane. I might be able to work these loose."

The sound of the car starting filled the clearing. Out of the corner of her eye she glimpsed the green vehicle drive away. "At least we know which way the highway is."

"That's the highway where the *state troopers* have set up a command post."

"Then it's probably not the way to get to Fairbanks."

"It's the only way out of here going that way. On the bright side, they left us our backpack."

"The guns, too?"

Brody chuckled. "If only that were the case. No, they took them."

"So even if we can get away, we have no weapons or money." Arianna twisted her hands over and over to try to make the rope give some. It was cooperating—barely. "How are you coming with getting free?"

"It may be a while. Grandma was stronger than I thought."

"How long do you figure we have?"

"It's hard to tell. I doubt this is far from the highway, but I don't know where this command post is."

"Could it be the real state troopers?"

"Notice Grandpa didn't mention if the troopers gave our names, just our description, so I guess it could be. The U.S. Marshals Service would be careful about what they reveal. The site was compromised. That will make them cautious about who to trust, especially in this high profile of a case. Rainwater has a lot of influence. We probably don't know how deep and wide it goes."

"That's not reassuring."

"It wasn't meant to be."

Arianna worked hard to loosen the ropes around her hands. If she got them off, then she could get out from under the one around their chests and untie the twine around her feet. As she moved, the rough bark dug into her back. A small price to pay if they could release themselves.

A noise penetrated her desperation to undo the ropes. A car. "That was fast. The command post must have been close. Or maybe it's someone else, and we can convince them we've been robbed, which is the truth. I had four hundred dollars." She yanked herself around as far as she could to see the vehicle when it appeared. The rope cut into her chest, making breathing difficult.

"What were you going to do with four hundred dollars? This trip to Alaska was all paid for by the U.S. Marshals Service. You certainly weren't going shopping or sightseeing."

"I've been on better paid vacations than this one. It was a comfort for me just in case something like this happened. If I needed to run, at least I had some money to help me disappear."

"I suggest we start praying this is the real state troopers and no one on Rainwater's payroll."

As the sound grew closer, Arianna did pray. At the moment she couldn't get herself out of the mess she was in without the Lord's intervention. Tied to the tree as they were, they were a great target for any of Rainwater's men who wanted to practice their shooting.

Friend or foe? Please, Lord, let it be a friend coming.

The front of the vehicle came into view—green-colored. Grandpa, Maude and Jane had returned. Were they alone? Her heartbeat slowed to a throb as she waited to see who was in the car other than their three captors. Although they had tied them up, the family was a better option than fake highway patrol officers.

But even when the vehicle came fully around the bend, the dark windows made it impossible to see inside. Arianna slumped back against the rough bark, dragging smoke-scented air into her lungs.

"If it's just them returning, we need to get them to untie us," Brody said from the other side of the tree.

"Jane might listen. As I talked to her, she paused when she was tying me up. I don't think she liked the idea of doing it."

"But she follows her grandpa's orders."

She heard the car come to a stop. How in the world did she ever think that she could do this alone? While in some tough situations in the army, she hadn't thought she could get by without God's protection. Even while she was awaiting trial in a prison cell, she'd turned to Him. She'd allowed her bitterness toward Dirk rule her life. To make her doubt the Lord.

A door opened—the noise carrying in the quiet clearing. Arianna tensed. "What's going on?"

"It's only the family returning," Brody murmured, surprise in his voice.

"That's a good sign. Maybe they couldn't find the command post because there wasn't one."

"They weren't gone long enough to have gone far. Grandpa is heading this way."

"With his rifle?" Arianna whispered.

"Yes, but pointed down. I don't think he goes anywhere without it."

The crunch of the other man's footsteps resonated through the forest. Coming nearer. Was this good or bad? The thump of her heartbeat hammered against her skull. The past few days' tension gripped her.

"Why didn't you tell me you were a U.S. Marshal?" Grandpa asked, tightness in the question.

"You finally looked at my wallet?"

"Yep. When Jane showed me, I turned around." The older man came around so Arianna could see him, too. "Are you one, too? Where is your ID? Jane didn't find any on you."

"Most of my belongings burned in the fire, but I'm not a marshal."

"Who are you?"

"I told you. She's Anna. We were camping like you when the fire hit. We aren't the people the state troopers are looking for. In fact, there has been a bulletin I've seen about someone pretending to be a state trooper then robbing people. Did the ones you talked to show you an ID and badge?"

Grandpa scratched his balding head. "Well, now that I think about it, no they didn't. I just assumed since they were dressed in uniform. You think they weren't state troopers?"

"Maybe. What kind of description did they give for the couple they were looking for?"

"A man and woman about thirty or so. The woman is a blonde while the man had dark brown hair."

"That could fit a lot of people. But it isn't us."

"I don't know. You should have said something to me."

Arianna saw the doubt flitter across Grandpa's face. He took a step back, raising his gun. "We might as well tell him the whole truth. I'm a U.S. marshal, too. That was why I was armed. All I can say is that my partner and I are on a case we can't talk about." She hated to lie, but she had no choice when their lives were on the line.

"Why didn't you tell me before I left you tied up?"

"If you found there was a command post and the state troopers were real, we figured we would explain to them when they came," Brody said in an even, patient voice.

"If I hadn't found them, what if I had just kept driving and went home?"

"We knew you weren't that kind of man. We could see you were only trying to do the right thing." Arianna bent toward Grandpa, the rope about her chest only allowing her to go a few inches. "We need to keep our presence hush-hush. Can you do that?" She spoke in low tones as if she were imparting top secret intel to the man.

Sweat popping out on his forehead, Grandpa put the rifle on the ground, knelt next to Arianna and began untying her. "I won't say a word, not even to Maude and Jane." He glanced at his family leaning against the car, Jane's arms crossed over her chest, chewing on her bottom lip. "You're B.J. and Anna on vacation. That's all they need to know."

"I appreciate that."

As Grandpa turned to free Brody, Arianna loosened the rope about her feet, then rubbed her chafed skin, especially around her wrists, and rose. For a few seconds she debated whether to go for the rifle or not. It was close by the man's feet, but that move might produce results that would make this situation worse. She would stick with her story and hope they got out of this alive and not turned in to the "authorities." The two state troopers who'd stopped by earlier in the day were still out there. Looking for them.

Brody stood and offered his hand to Grandpa.

"Thanks for coming back. We need citizens who try to do the right thing."

Grandpa beamed, straightening his shoulders even more. After he picked up his rifle, he started for his car. "We'll give you a ride wherever you need to go," he said then paused, rotated toward them and continued in a low voice, "Unless you need to stay because of your job."

Brody sent Arianna a conspiratorial look followed by a wink, which Grandpa didn't see. "The fire has changed everything. We need to get back to the headquarters where the operation is running. A ride to Fairbanks would be great. From there we can get where we need to go, but if anyone asks, I hope you can keep it quiet."

"I understand. Not a word from me, especially since you're being so nice after I had you tied up. One of my favorite shows to watch is about the U.S. Marshals Service. I certainly know what you two do to keep this country safe. Keep up the good work." He turned to his family and announced, "We're taking them part of the way to their destination."

Jane glanced up through her long bangs. "You ain't mad at me—us?"

"No, you all thought you had two criminals, and you did something about that." Arianna forced a big smile to her lips, not letting down her guard one bit, especially since they still had to drive by the "command post."

But twenty minutes later, Grandpa threw a look over his shoulder at Brody and said, "The command post should have been back there. You were right. Those two were phony state troopers. I should call—"

"That's okay. I'll inform the right authorities when

we get to our destination. Just remember in the future to always ask for a badge and ID and look at it closely."

"I'll remember that." Grandpa touched his temple. "It don't take but once for me to learn a lesson. Remember what B.J. said, Jane."

"Yes, Grandpa." Jane dug into her pocket and withdrew the switchblade, running her fingers up and down the knife casing. "This is yours. I forgot to give it back with the money."

Arianna curled her hand around Jane's outreached one. "You keep it. I imagine you can find a use for it living in the woods."

Jane's expression brightened, a grin spreading across her face. "When I go hunting, it'll help me skin the critters. We use almost every part of the animals I bring home."

"Yep, keeps us fed well," Maude finally spoke after being quiet since they got into the car.

"Our favorite is rabbit stew," Grandpa added.

Hunting had never appealed to Arianna, even more so with her job. She'd seen what her clients had gone through being hunted by someone who intended to kill them. Having traveled all over the world, she knew many people still hunted for their food. But she'd never been able to go hunting with her dad or brothers in the mountains of North Carolina.

Brody slid his hand over hers on the seat between them in the back of the car. She spied the raw skin on his wrist from the rope. Its sight only reinforced the ordeal they had been through so far. Exhaustion embedded itself in the marrow of her bones.

Brody leaned toward her ear and said, "Rest. It's your turn. I'll stay alert."

Arianna laid her head back against the cushion. With Brody next to her, watching over her, she would be fine. That and the fact she felt the Lord was watching over her, too. Sleep whisked her away almost instantly.

Arianna snuggled up against Brody as they entered the outskirts of Fairbanks. She'd fallen asleep right away, and other than rolling her head and resting it against his shoulder, she'd hardly moved. Even when he'd slung his arm around her and pressed her against him, allowing his body to pillow her in her sleep, she'd stayed deep in a dream world.

"Where to, B.J.?" Fred—Grandpa had given Brody his name partway through the trip—asked from the driver's seat.

"Could you take us to the train station on Johansen Expressway?"

"Yep. I know where it is. My cousin came in on the train a few months back to visit us."

Arianna stirred within the crook of his arm. Her eyes blinked open. A few seconds passed before she reacted to being cradled along his side. She didn't move away, but instead smiled at him. "I was tired. How long was I asleep?"

"An hour and a half," Fred answered from the front. "B.J. told us how long you two had been evading the fire. Heard on the radio they're sending in firefighters from all over to help contain it. Thank the Lord, the winds are still blowing it away from our cabin."

Arianna sat up straight. "That's good. Hopefully the wind will die down, and they'll be able to put the fire out. That area is beautiful."

"Yep, it sure is. Maude and me have lived there for

twenty years. It's about all that Jane knows. She came to live with us when she was a baby."

As Fred expounded on what he'd taught his grand-daughter, Brody kept his gaze fixed on the area they were passing through. He didn't know Fairbanks that well, but he knew its basic layout.

Ten minutes later when Fred pulled up near the Fair-banks train depot, the clock on the tower indicated it was almost three. Brody glimpsed a black SUV parked near the depot with two men in it. He had a bad feeling about them. "Stop here. We'll walk the rest of the way."

"Sure, but we can pull right up to the door if you want. Or we can take you to the airport or bus station."

"No, this is fine." Brody opened the door, grabbed the backpack at his feet and climbed out of the car. He leaned back in to help Arianna out.

"Sure, I understand." Fred winked. "We three will forget we even saw you two. Mum's the word."

"Thank you. We appreciate your help." Arianna slid across the seat and stood next to Brody. "I'll be praying your cabin remains untouched."

"You do that, Anna," Fred said as she shut the door.

Brody waited until the green car disappeared from view before grasping Arianna's hand and starting in the opposite direction from the train station.

"This isn't exactly in the middle of downtown."

"No, but the town isn't far. We'll find a restaurant to eat at where we won't look too much out of place. Our appearances leave something to be desired."

"I should be offended," Arianna said with a laugh, "but I can still smell the smoke on these clothes. I hope we can find some place to change and take a shower. Do you think we can take a chance on a hotel room?"

"No, but I have an idea. Someone we can trust to help. Charlie Owens. He's a retired FBI agent. I'm sure he still has contacts. He's been in Alaska a long time and only recently retired."

"Why him?" Arianna asked as they crossed a street, getting closer to the downtown area.

"I saved his life last year. We were working the same case. We've kept in touch since he left the FBI, but it's not common knowledge—nor is the fact that I pushed him out of the way of a bullet. No one needed to know Charlie was caught unaware. He was leaving the FBI in a few weeks, and I wanted nothing to take away from that, so I left it out of the report. He used to live in Anchorage but moved up here."

"I'm not sure about that. It might be safer to find some hotel and pay cash for a room."

"I'm pretty sure the train station was being watched as all the other ways out of Fairbanks. I wouldn't be surprised if the surrounding towns have people in them looking for us. You're very important to Rainwater. We don't know which hotel clerks have been paid off to alert someone if two people fitting our description come in to rent a room."

"Then we'll find some place in a park to sleep."

"I'm sure all areas are being checked. That's what I would do if I was looking for a fugitive."

"Okay, you've convinced me. If you trust Charlie Owens, then fine. Just don't plan on me trusting him. With all you've said, should we even risk going somewhere to eat?"

"Good point. I think that was my hunger speaking back there." Brody looked up and down the street, saw a store that might have a pay phone and continued. "Let me call him. See if he's home. If not, maybe we could disguise ourselves and still go to a restaurant and eat. I think it would be better than wandering around Fairbanks until I can get hold of Charlie."

"I can put my hair up, wear sunglasses and put a hoodie on. That ought to change my appearance enough."

"C'mon. Let's go in here. You shop for the sunglasses while I call Charlie." He walked down the aisle toward the pay phone in back. "Stay in my sight."

Brody made the call after getting his friend's number from information. He let it ring until it went to Charlie's answering machine. Deciding not to leave a message, he hung up.

Arianna popped up next to him with a pair of big sunglasses on. "How do I look?"

"That's good. Your eyes are very distinctive—and beautiful."

Two rosy patches graced her cheeks.

"You definitely have to do something about your hair. That's a dead giveaway even from a distance."

"I'm not cutting it. I'll wear a wig before I do that. I kept it short in the army. This is four years of my hair growing out."

"And I like it. Let's see if there's a hat or wig in this store."

"I saw a display of throwaway phones. We could purchase one of them. They aren't easily traceable, and then we don't have to find a pay phone. They aren't as common as they used to be."

"Good point. Let's grab what we need and clean up the best we can in the store's restrooms. I'll keep calling Charlie every half an hour until we get him."

Thirty minutes later, Brody walked out of the store with his arm around her as if they were in a relationship. The people looking for them might not think of them as a couple. They kept to the back streets, assessing the area where they were going before making a move. When Brody found North Diner, it was nearly deserted because it was in between lunch and dinner. He took a booth at the back with a good view of the entrance that was close to the restroom and a back way out of the restaurant.

Arianna opened her menu. "I'm starved. I could eat one of everything on this menu. I don't think I want to see a protein bar anytime soon."

After they placed their orders with the young waitress, Brody pulled out the throwaway cell phone and made another call to Charlie. His friend answered on the third ring, much to Brody's relief. He'd begun to think Charlie was out of town.

Brody checked the restaurant for anyone nearby who could overhear the conversation and then said low into the cell, "I need your help."

"I told you anytime you did to call. Does this have anything to do with what is happening northwest of Fairbanks? I've heard some chatter about recovering five bodies—murder victims. The fire destroyed most of the evidence. The authorities are looking for any other people who were caught in the forest fire."

"Do they know how the blaze started?"

"A dropped cigarette and a dry forest. But that's speculation. There was one body burned worse than the others. So are you involved?"

"I need to lie low. I don't want anyone to know I'm here. Not even the U.S. Marshals Service. Can you help?"

Charlie emitted a soft whistle. "This sounds serious."

"Lives are at stake."

"Where are you? I'll come pick you up."

Brody gave him the address of North Diner. "There's an alley out back of the restaurant. I'll be waiting there. How long will you be?"

"Twenty minutes."

"What kind of car do you drive?"

"A white Jeep. It's seen better days."

"Thanks, Charlie. See you in twenty." When Brody hung up, he continued. "I'm going to let the waitress know we want everything to go."

Brody strode to the counter and found his waitress. "We need to leave. We'll take the food to go and I'll pay for it now."

After the transaction was completed, Brody walked by the picture window, searching the street out front. A black SUV with dark windows drove slowly by. He ducked back, the hairs on his nape tingling. At the side of the window, he peered out to see where the SUV was going. It stopped and a woman climbed out of the passenger seat. He stared at Carla Matthews across the road as she went into a small hotel.

Was Carla here as a U.S. Marshal or one of Rainwater's lackeys?

SEVEN

Brody hurried to the counter. "Is the food ready?"

"In just a minute," the waitress said and went back into the kitchen.

Arianna rose with the backpack in hand. Looking at her disguise, he couldn't tell clearly she was Arianna Jackson, the witness the U.S. Marshals Service and Rainwater's men were searching for. He waved for her to head back toward the restrooms, making a motion to turn away from them. As she did, the waitress brought out a sack with the food in it. He left and limped after Arianna toward the back while the waitress returned to the kitchen.

Outside in the alley, Brody paced. "Charlie should be here soon. Stand by the door so anyone driving by won't see you."

"How about you?"

He stepped into the entrance of a shop on the other side of the alley. "There was a black SUV that dropped Carla off at the end of the block. They're canvassing the street. If they are, then Rainwater's men are here, too."

"Do you think Carla is the mole?"

"Maybe. And since I don't know, we can't approach her."

"Do you think someone let them know we're in Fairbanks?"

"Maybe. Fred Franklin might have decided to call the U.S. Marshals Service after all. If he did, then whoever gave up your location probably knows by now that the Franklins dropped us at the Fairbanks train station." Brody peeked around the brick wall down the alley on both side. He spied a black SUV pass on the street on his left side and darted back against the store's door.

"What's wrong?"

"Another SUV. Maybe another marshal is being dropped off on the next street. Either way, this is not good."

"Fairbanks is the closest major town from where we were. That may be why they're searching even though it's away from Anchorage. Fairbanks has better transportation to get us to Anchorage. They'll know we can't walk there and get there in time for the trial."

Brody plowed his fingers through his hair. "Yeah, I know, but I hate not knowing who to trust." In the past he'd trusted the members of his team. How would he be able to after this?

The sound of a car turning into the alley announced they weren't alone. Under his light jacket, Brody put his hand on his gun and inched forward to take a peek at what kind of vehicle was coming toward them. His rigid body relaxed when he saw a white Jeep.

"It's Charlie, but don't come out until I tell you to. If there's a problem, duck back into the diner. Hide in the restroom." Brody stepped out of the doorway to the store and stood several yards down the alley for Charlie to stop. He didn't want his friend to see Arianna until he'd talked with Charlie.

Brody slipped into the front passenger's seat and angled his body toward the former FBI agent. "Retirement has been kind to you."

"Do we have time for this chitchat? What's up? Why are you running from your own people? I saw a marshal I know get out of an SUV two blocks over."

"Who?"

"Ted Banks. He's hard to miss."

"I'll tell you everything when we get out of here and to your house."

Charlie put his hand on the stick shift to put the vehicle into drive.

"Wait. There's another passenger."

"The witness in Rainwater's trial?"

Brody nodded, got out of the car and said, "It's okay. Hurry."

Arianna darted out of the diner's doorway and jogged toward the Jeep, looking behind her then in front of her. She slid into the backseat as Brody took the one next to her.

"Charlie, this is Arianna, the witness I need to get to Anchorage ASAP to testify at Rainwater's trial."

"Nice to meet you," Charlie said to Arianna, watching her through the rearview mirror. "We'll talk when I get you to a friend's house—I'm watching it for him while he's salmon fishing. I suggest both of you get down until we arrive there."

Arianna scrunched down on the floor, facing Brody. He took her hand and held it. "Charlie saw Ted Banks a few blocks over so it's not just Carla here. Five bodies were found around the cabin—one burned worse than the others. He thinks that one was near the point of origin."

"Just passed another car that looks suspicious," Charlie said from the font seat. He made a turn then continued. "The firefighters have ruled out a lightning strike and they can't find any evidence of an accelerant being used, especially where they think the fire started. The guy I talked with speculated it was a cigarette."

Arianna frowned. "An accident?"

"We thought it might have been set deliberately, but are you saying that might not be the case?" Brody asked Charlie.

"With a cigarette it could still be deliberate. That way the fire would take a while to catch. It would give the person who set it time to get out of the area."

Arianna caught Brody's gaze. "It makes more sense if it was an accident. Burning the cabin doesn't accomplish anything other than calling attention to the place."

"Possibly. Or maybe there was something they wanted to cover up."

"Five bodies were found. That must mean they found Kevin."

"Unless there was someone we didn't know about."

"Were all the bodies found at the cabin?" Arianna asked Charlie as he pulled up to a stoplight.

The former FBI agent shifted as though he were staring out the side window. "The firefighter didn't say. I could find out."

"Only if it doesn't seem suspicious. I wouldn't want anyone paying you a visit." Brody moved to ease the pressure on his sore ankle.

"Believe me, I don't, either. We're almost at my

friend's house. Well, more like a cabin. I hope you don't mind staying in a rustic place."

Arianna laughed. "You should have seen where we've been. Anywhere with a roof over our heads and running water that isn't a stream is a big step up."

"There's a roof, running water, and even an indoor bathroom."

"Oh, that sounds luxurious. Is there a bed with a soft mattress?"

"Yeah, plus a couch."

The smile that graced Arianna's face lit her features with radiance. Her look appealed to Brody—way too much if he stopped to think about it. She was strictly a professional concern. Once she left Alaska after testifying, he could get back to his life—that was, if they made it to Anchorage alive.

She reached out to him and grazed her fingertips down his jaw. "We're gonna make it. We've got your friend's help. Rainwater isn't going to win."

The light touch of her hand on his face doubled his pulse rate. His throat thickened with emotions he never allowed on a job. He cared. She was cheering him up. Usually he was trying to do that with his witnesses, especially when the reality of their situation really sank in. All the waiting for the trial gave the witnesses time to think. To realize their lives would be radically different because they were doing the right thing.

"We're here. He doesn't have any neighbors close by, but I'm still going to park around back in his garage. That's what he calls it, at least. I call it a lean-to about to collapse."

Brody rose in the seat. "And you're parking your Jeep in there?"

"Out of sight is better than announcing to everyone where I am—just in case they run down people you know in the area to see if you've gotten in touch with them."

"Won't anyone think it's strange you're gone from your home?" Arianna climbed from the Jeep after Charlie parked it in a shed that really did look like it would blow down in a strong wind.

"Not my friends. They know I often just pick up and go somewhere. That's what retirement is all about."

"Then I hope they ask your friends."

"Either way, we can't stay for long. Tomorrow we'll have to figure out a way to Anchorage," Brody said as he limped toward Charlie's friend's place.

"I might have a way to get you there. I have a friend who has a ranch. She raises cattle and horses. She's been wanting me to help her take some horses down south. I'd told her I could do it at the end of the week. I'll call her and see about tomorrow." Charlie unlocked the door of the cabin. "This is the only way in and out, except the windows."

Stepping inside, Brody assessed the space, noting where the windows were and how easy they would be to access. "We have dinner in these bags. I think Arianna ordered half the menu, so there'll be plenty for all of us. I hope you're hungry."

Charlie's laughter filled the large living room that flowed into the kitchen. "Are you kidding? You've seen me eat out. I've been known to finish a twenty-five ounce steak and want more."

Arianna dropped the backpack by the brown couch then took the two sacks from Brody. "I'll go get this reheated. Dinner won't be long."

"Good. I'll call Willow and see about the horses for tomorrow." Charlie started to pick up the phone on an end table.

"Wait. Use my cell. It's not traceable."

Charlie hiked an eyebrow. "You really are worried someone will find you."

"This is important. Three of Rainwater's men found us at the safe cabin. If she doesn't testify, he'll be acquitted. She's most of the state's case against him."

"Yeah, I've been reading about the case. A nasty man. He may live in Anchorage, but he has his hand in a lot of things all over the state."

While Arianna strode to the kitchen and took the food out of the sacks, Charlie made the call to Willow. Most of the conversation took place on the other end. A faint flush brushed Charlie's cheeks. He turned away from Brody to finish what he was saying to the woman. Interesting. Charlie had never been married before, but from what he'd seen, his friend was attracted to Willow.

Charlie hung up and handed the cell back to Brody. "We're good for tomorrow. I'll go to the ranch and pick up the horses at seven, then come back here to get you two. At first Willow wanted to come with me. I discouraged her and reminded her about the fire west of here. She needs to be on her ranch if there's a problem and they can't contain it."

"She lives that close?"

"No, but I had to think of something to keep her home. Willow is the most delicate woman I know. Fragile actually. She's been sick until recently. Cancer. She's finally getting her life back."

"You care about her?"

Charlie's mouth twisted into a look that wasn't a

frown but not a smile, either. "Yeah, I guess I do. She's planning a special dinner when I get back. I told her I might be in Anchorage for a few days after I deliver the horses. I figure you're going to need all the help you can get."

"It won't be easy getting to Anchorage. I don't know who to trust, even in my own office."

Charlie stared at Arianna. "We'll get her to the courthouse."

Brody hoped so. He wasn't going to lose a witness, especially not Arianna. In spite of his best intentions, there was something about her that he liked—a lot.

Refreshed after a meal and a shower, Arianna stood in front of the mirror in the bathroom, examining the cuts on her face. She looked like she'd gone through a battle. In one way she had. She was fighting for her life—and Brody's.

But there was hope. Charlie had a way to Anchorage that might not alert the wrong people. She had no choice. If she didn't testify against Rainwater, she would never have a chance of surviving. She closed her eyes and tried to imagine a life in the Witness Protection Program. A new name. A new job. A new home. Since she left her childhood house, she'd never really had a place she could call home. Now she would. But what did she want to do with that life?

When she opened her eyes and stared again at herself in the mirror, no answers came to mind. That scared her more than anything. The unknown.

Then she remembered something her grandmother had told her when she was a child. When she was scared, fix her thoughts on the Lord. He was always there for her, rooting for her, supporting her so she really never was alone.

She'd forgotten that these past four years while trying to control her life, needing no one. Now she needed others to keep her alive, but mostly she needed the Lord to give her the hope it would be all right.

A knock at the door pulled her from her thoughts. "Yes?"

"Are you okay?" Brody's voice held the concern she'd come to cherish.

"Yes."

"Charlie has some information on what's going down at the cabin."

"Coming." Arianna ran a brush through her hair, putting it up into a ponytail.

When she entered the living room, Brody and Charlie stopped talking and looked at her. Brody's warm perusal caused flutters in her stomach. She sat near him on the couch while Charlie settled across from them in a chair.

"What have you discovered?" Arianna couldn't stop thinking about how Brody had been there for her every step of the way. Yes, it was his job, but she might not be alive today if he didn't do his job so well.

"A sixth man was found dead near the cabin. I have a friend who worked the fire. He said the sixth person was not far from the body at the edge of the tree line."

"The other four bodies were in or right outside the cabin?"

"Yes, the only way they'll be able to ID any of the bodies is with dental records, according to my friend."

"So they aren't sure who is dead, except they know they're all male," Brody said, tapping his hand against the arm of the couch. He looked at Arianna. "The U.S.

Marshals Service doesn't know if you're dead somewhere else or if you fled by yourself. Right now they think I could be any one of the six men."

"But Rainwater's men know I wasn't killed, that I fled."

Brody kneaded his nape. "Probably, but we aren't sure what they know. If they saw the cabin before it burned, yes they know. By the two fake state troopers who talked with the Franklins, we have to assume they know that you and a marshal are gone. That might give us an edge. They aren't sure who you're with."

"We know people are looking for us. That much is a definite."

"Yes, there's a widespread manhunt out for Arianna Jackson, possibly with a male accompanying her." Charlie pushed to his feet and walked into the kitchen. "Anyone want some coffee?"

"No, I won't get any sleep tonight." Arianna shifted toward Brody. "I'll take the first watch. You need to get some rest."

"You mean my two hours late last night wasn't enough?" he said in dead seriousness.

She smiled. "I know you're a marshal with superpowers, but going without sleep isn't one of them. Tomorrow will be a big day for us. We'll either make it to Anchorage or…" She couldn't quite say the alternative. Their lives were on the line but so was Charlie's now.

"I know, and my body is totally agreeing with you. Sleep is a priority."

"Yeah, that's why I'm going to stand guard tonight. I got eight hours last night," Charlie said as he folded his large bulk into the chair and took a sip of his coffee.

"Tell you what, friend. Arianna will take the first two

hours and I'll take the last two. You can stand guard for the four hours between."

"Done. Now let's talk about why you're keeping this from your own people. Who do you think is the mole?"

Brody's forehead creased, his jaw tensed. "It could be any one of the marshals on the first team or my team. It could be someone higher up."

"Are you sure it was a marshal?"

"Not one hundred percent, but how else can I explain the breach in our location? Our attackers had a map—they knew exactly where we were. It could have been Kevin because he would have had to radio in for Mark to open the door. Mark wouldn't have opened it without that. But then it could have been Mark, and after they took out Kevin, he let them into the cabin."

Arianna saw the anger and sadness warring for dominance on Brody's expression. "So you think it's most likely the inside man was one of the two marshals on your team?" she asked.

"It could still be someone from the first team. The word phrase we use if we're being forced to call in is the same for the operation. Those three marshals knew that phrase so one of them could have told Rainwater's men."

"What was the phrase?" Arianna knew the emotions Brody was struggling with. She'd dealt with the same ones with Dirk—was still dealing with them.

"All clear. No bear sightings." Brody's scowl deepened. "Kevin and Mark are dead. If one of them was the mole, Rainwater was definitely leaving no one around to testify against him."

"Not a bad strategy for the man who is in jail because Thomas Perkins was selling him out." All because of money and greed. Arianna squeezed her hands into tight fists, her fingernails digging into her palms.

"I'll do some checking and see what I can come up with. Find out if anyone has received some money lately," Charlie said.

"Follow the money trail?" Arianna rose, needing to work out her restless energy or she wouldn't sleep when her time came.

"Charlie here worked for the FBI because of his great computer skills. He discovered information most people couldn't."

The retired FBI agent chuckled. "Yeah, one of the rare times I was in the field, I had to be rescued by this guy." He tipped his head toward Brody. "In my years of experience I've uncovered a lot of wrongdoing by following the money."

"Are you a hacker?"

Charlie burst out laughing. "I hate that word. I'm more of a persuader who entices a computer to give up its secrets. I hate secrets, and I'll work until I can undercover them."

"Don't you have to have a computer to do that?" Arianna scanned the room and didn't see one.

"Yep, and that's why I want you to wake me up fifteen minutes earlier," Charlie peered at Brody, "so I can go get my computer. I live south, about a five-minute walk. That's how I got to know the guy who lives here. We'd keep running into each other while jogging. Willow is his sister." He downed the last of his coffee. "Brody, I found a cot in the storeroom and set it up for you. I'll take the bed since Arianna will wake me up before she needs it. Get a good night's sleep." Charlie strode toward the bedroom.

"Are you sure you want to take the first watch? You're the witness. You shouldn't take any watch."

"My life is at stake here, and I need you two rested. I'm perfectly capable of taking care of myself and even guarding you two." She balled a hand and set it on her hip. "Now go and get some sleep."

Brody rose in one fluid motion, a huge smile on his face, and closed the distance between them, stepping into her personal space. "You're quite good at taking charge."

"That's why I get paid big bucks to make decisions and assess situations."

"I had a recruiter for a big security firm who wanted me to come work for them. The pay was twice what I made, but I decided to stay with the U.S. Marshals Service. I had come off some big cases that had gone well. I almost called the man up after my time in L.A. when that witness was killed. But I didn't want to leave the service on a black note."

"If anyone else had told me they lost a witness, I'd be worried but not with you. I've seen you on the job. So quit beating yourself up over it. Things happen that we can't control. We think we have a situation handled and then everything blows up in our face."

The smile that curved his mouth also reached deep in his brown eyes. He inched closer and with another man she would have moved back. She didn't feel the need to with Brody. She cared about him and didn't want to see him wrestling with a problem that was taken out of his hands.

His eyes softened. He cupped her face. "Most women I've dated don't understand my job. You do."

"Not even Carla?" she asked, half in jest, half in seriousness.

"You would think, but she didn't. For her, doing her job was a means to a promotion. She made it very clear she wanted to move up in the ranks. Her witnesses were just cases to her, ones she barely tolerated. When she found out I had turned down a job that would have led to a promotion but taken me out of the field, she couldn't understand. But then I couldn't understand her attitude."

"I thought she was just mad because she was stuck in a cabin in the boonies because of me."

"She's definitely a big city gal." His hand slid around to her nape. "But I don't want to waste my time talking about her."

"No, you need to sleep because tomorrow..." Her words faded into the sudden electrifying silence, his mouth inches from her.

He didn't come any closer, but he was still close enough that she could smell the coffee he'd drunk earlier, the fresh clean scent from the soap in the shower. He would never make the final move so she wrapped her arms around him and settled her lips over his. For only a second there was a hesitation in Brody, then he took over the kiss, deepening it. He brought her up against him, so near she wondered if he could feel the pounding of her heartbeat against her rib cage.

The kiss she'd started ended all too soon when he leaned back slightly, his arms still locked around her. "We shouldn't do this. Not a good idea."

"I know. Emotions should never interfere with the case."

He nodded, laying his forehead against hers. "But

it felt right. I've never had someone who got me like you do."

Her throat jammed. She felt the same way, but there was no future for them, and she didn't do casual, no matter how much he tempted her. It was going to be hard enough for her to patch her life BACK together without a broken heart. She pulled away totally.

"Go to bed. Please." There was no strength behind her words, but she needed time to compose herself, shore up her determination not to lose her heart to him. There was no way she would ask him to give up his job for her—give up everything he knew for her. She *had* to and she knew how hard that was. But if he couldn't join her, then that meant a relationship between them wouldn't stand a chance.

"Good night." He crossed to the kitchen and disappeared inside, heading for the storeroom and his cot.

Arianna sank onto the couch, her hands shaking. That trembling sensation spread throughout her body. If only they had met under different circumstances. When she scrubbed her fingertips down her face, the action reminded her of her sore and bruised skin. She pushed away all thoughts of Brody and of what was to come. After she checked her gun in her holster at her waist, she prowled the room, occasionally peeking outside from the various windows in the cabin. Nothing out of the ordinary.

For the next hour she saw the same thing when she checked out the windows. Darkness began to settle over the landscape the closer midnight came. She played back through the bits of conversation she'd had with the members of the first team for any clue that one of them was the informer.

She remembered Ted talking about his twin boys starting college in a month. Not one child but two. That was a tidy expense nowadays. Did he need extra money for his children's tuition? Then there was Dan. He liked expensive vacations. He went on and on about how he and his wife loved to travel and the places they went. How did he pay for them? She had less of a sense of Carla's tastes or expenses—almost as though she didn't have a personal life. She did notice the woman's possessions were expensive—from her shoes to her purse to her clothing. The men wouldn't have realized the money it took to buy what Carla had, but she did. She'd worked for some wealthy clients who shopped and bought the same brands that Carla had with her.

Arianna looked at her watch—ten minutes before she was to wake up Charlie—then started her last walk around the inside of the cabin. When she pushed two slats in the blinds facing the front of the place, her gaze latched on to the smoke and flames she saw in the sky.

Arianna stared for a few seconds then whirled about and raced for the storeroom to wake up Brody. There was a fire not far from the cabin to the south. Wasn't that where Charlie's house was?

EIGHT

The moment the door to the storeroom opened and light from the living room flooded inside, Brody bolted up in the cot. "Why are you waking me up? If it's time for my shift, you should be asleep." He swung his legs over the side.

"There's a fire to the south. I'm gonna wake up Charlie. It could be his place. Even if it isn't, his house could be in danger." Arianna swung around and hurried to the bedroom. She had to shake him awake.

His eyes opened, and he frowned. "It's time already?"

"There's a fire toward where you live. You need to check it out. Are there a lot of trees around your place?"

"Yes. It's mostly woods." Charlie stuck his feet into his boots then scrambled to his feet and headed for the front door to the cabin. "Stay inside. I'm going to jog a ways and see what I can discover."

Brody stood by the window from which she'd seen the fire. "Be careful. Someone might have found out you're helping us. How easy is it for someone to figure out about this place?"

"It would take some work. I didn't get to know Paul

until after I retired. The same for Willow, Paul's sister."
Charlie opened the door then paused. "If I can get to
my house and it isn't burning, I'll bring back my computer. Forget sleep. I want to know who is behind this."

Brody shook his head. "I don't know about staying."

"Let me see what's going on before we decide."

Brody went back to the window to follow his friend's
progress across the yard in the dim light of dusk.

Arianna took up guard at another window. "I agree
with you. We need to leave. I discovered in my research
on Rainwater that his men like using fire. It can cover
up so much. I think some of Rainwater's men are getting close."

"It doesn't surprise me he has a few pyromaniacs
on his payroll."

"He has a variety of different skilled murderers. I
hope it wasn't Charlie's house."

Brody nodded his agreement. "I shouldn't have
brought him in on this." A minute later Brody said,
"He's coming back and he doesn't have his computer."

Arianna went into the bedroom. "I'm gathering our
stuff. We need to get out of here."

"Agreed." Brody opened the door before Charlie
knocked. "Your place is burning?"

"Yes, the fire department is there, but I didn't let
anyone know I was there. Two men stood out in the
crowd gathering. They aren't my neighbors. Also as I
was leaving, I saw Ted pull up."

"That was fast, even if he heard it over the radio."
Brody strode to the fireplace and took the rifle down
from over the mantel. "I'll make sure I get this back to
Paul. We need all the firepower we can get."

"We'll go to Willow's ranch. I'm leaving my Jeep

and taking Paul's old pickup truck. I think it'll get us there. Paul's been talking about selling it for scrap so there are no guarantees."

"It'll be better than your car. If they know you're helping me, then they'll be looking for your Jeep." Brody took the backpack from Arianna and slipped it over his shoulders.

Charlie went into the kitchen and came back out with a set of keys and a revolver. "I'll give this back to Paul, too. I feel naked without a weapon."

"I didn't see a truck in the shed." Arianna left the cabin sandwiched between Brody and Charlie.

"It's behind it, rusting in the elements. I think Paul would love to see it just rust to nothing."

When Arianna spotted the vehicle she could see that calling it a pickup was stretching it. "Will it work?"

"Only one way to tell." With a missing driver's door, all Charlie had to do was hop up onto the seat, stick the key in the ignition and turn it.

A cranking noise echoed through the stillness.

Arianna scanned her surroundings, imagining the loud sound alerting all Rainwater's men that they were escaping.

Charlie tried again and the engine finally turned over. "Get in. The tires are almost bare, but hopefully they'll last long enough to go ten miles to the ranch."

Brody and Arianna hurried around to the passenger side and actually had to open a door. But when she went to climb into the cab, she had to sit on the floor.

Brody crowded in after her and shut the door. "Let's go. It's probably better we're on the floor anyway."

"All I want is for this to get us to the ranch, then it can die." Charlie pulled around the front of the shed and headed toward the road. "For this time of night, there's more traffic than usual, but then a fire does attract spectators."

"So long as they keep their focus on the fire, we can slip away." Arianna sat cross-legged facing Brody, whose back was to the dashboard, the lights on it minimal.

In the shadows she could feel Brody's gaze on her while hers fixed on him. She told herself it was because there was nowhere else to look, but that wasn't it really. There was a connection between them she couldn't deny. She needed to get through the next few days alive, testify and then leave Alaska. In her new life, she could put all of this, including Brody, behind her. She needed to quit thinking about what she wasn't going to have. Any kind of relationship beyond this was impossible.

When Charlie hit a rough patch in the road, she bounced up and forward—into Brody. He clasped her to steady her, but instead of pushing her back where she sat, he held her still for a few extra seconds, his face near hers, his breath washing over her cheek. She remembered their lives were only crossing for a short time and finally managed to pull away, planting herself as far from Brody as she could. Which wasn't nearly far enough.

"Are we almost there?" she asked Charlie, a frantic edge to her question.

"A couple more miles. Sorry about the rough ride. The shock absorbers are one of many things not working on this pickup," Charlie said.

"We'll survive," Brody said as though talking through clenched teeth. He probably was—the bouncing couldn't be doing his ankle any favors.

When Arianna studied his outline in the darkened cab, the rigid lines of his body conveyed tension.

Arianna held on to what she could when the truck went over another bumpy spot in the highway. Charlie made a sharp right turn onto a dirt road. Her grip strengthened around the bottom part of the driver's seat.

"I'm parking a ways from the house. No use for me to go nearer until closer to seven in the morning. When I leave with the trailer, I'll return to pick you two up. I don't want Willow to know anyone else is going with me. The less she's involved the better for everyone."

Brody knelt, looking around as the pickup went off the road onto an even rougher path. "Does she have hired hands who would be out at this time at night?"

"Two hands, but I doubt they'd be around. One is her uncle and the other a friend of her deceased husband. They help her out. This is an area she doesn't use on the ranch. No cows or horses."

When Charlie stopped—or rather, when the truck spurted to a halt—Arianna opened the door, needing to get out, to breathe fresh air. Being confined so close to Brody, their legs touching, was not good for her concentration. She would check out the terrain since they would be here for six or seven hours.

For a moment she relished the cool night air, a light breeze blowing with no hint of smoke in it. An owl hooted nearby as if sending up an alarm someone was intruding. Otherwise silence reigned—except for the footsteps coming toward her.

She knew it was Brody before he stopped next to her and did his own reconnaissance of the woods cocooning them. "It's your turn to get some sleep. The bed of the truck isn't too bad. You can use the back-pack as a pillow."

"What are you and Charlie gonna do?"

"Take turns keeping watch. Don't worry, we'll try to get some sleep, too."

"Where?" She didn't know if she could sleep if he lay down in the back of the pickup, too.

Brody sweep his arm across his front. "The ground. I can sleep anywhere. Sometimes that's part of the job."

"Sleep sounds wonderful. I'm not sure I can after fleeing Paul's cabin. I should be used to not trusting anyone or anyplace, but I sure wanted to stay at his house for the night."

"Yeah, a comfortable bed is so much better than the ground or the back of a twenty-year-old pickup." Brody slipped off the backpack. "Use this if you can."

Her hand grasped the same strap he did, glancing across his knuckles. The touch only reminded her of the growing physical attraction she had for him. "Let's hope we can rest for the next six hours and not have to escape. I don't know if that truck can go another foot."

Brody chuckled. "It did sound like it died for good. Let's hope we don't have to find out. Surely our transportation in the morning will be better."

Sitting on an aluminum floor in a horse trailer was a step up from sitting on the floor in Paul's pickup, but Arianna hated not being able to see outside without standing up.

"The scenery is beautiful along this highway. You'll get glimpses of it through the windows." Brody took a place next to her at the front of the two-horse trailer. "It looks like we'll have hours to kill."

"Please, not that word." Arianna retied her hair into a ponytail, strands of it whipping about her in the cool breeze coming in from the partially open windows. "I'm glad we'll have pretty good cell reception along most of the trip. I want to be forewarned if there's a roadblock."

"The good thing about going this way instead of the Parks Highway is that there's less traffic."

"Yeah, but longer timewise. At least this mode of transportation isn't obvious."

"And there's an area you can hide in the storage part for the tack."

Arianna peered up at a mare looking at her with her big brown eyes. "When I was a girl, I rode all the time. I wanted to raise horses. I wish I could have talked with Willow instead of having to sneak into the trailer." Brody started to say something, but she held up her hand. "I know, the less people know what we are doing the better."

"Why did you like to ride horses?"

"Are you kidding? Most little girls at some time in their lives think about having their own horse. At least my friends and I did. But mostly I did because my dad loved to ride and it was a way for me to connect with him. We used to ride when he was home several times a week until I left for college. Now it doesn't make any difference."

"Was he gone a lot?"

Thinking about her father and the angry words they'd exchanged over her leaving the army closed her throat. When Brody looked at her, waiting for an answer, she swallowed several times and said, "He was always gone on some kind of mission. He was up for general and didn't get it the last time I saw him at Christmas. I've always wondered if what happened to me was the reason why. He certainly had done everything he could to get it."

"Have you talked with your dad about what happened? Explained your reasons?"

"I tried when I first came home. He didn't want to hear it." The kindness in Brody's eyes urged her to tell him everything. "What if I—died and my father and I never make things right? He would blame himself. Not right away but in the end."

"I can carry a message to him if you want."

A lump the size of Alaska lodged in her throat. She couldn't get a word out. All she could do was nod, tears shimmering in her eyes. She didn't cry. What good would it do her to bemoan her predicament? It wouldn't change anything. *Trust the Lord.* She needed to keep that in the foreground. But no matter what she told herself, a tear slipped down her face.

He caressed his thumb across the top of her cheek. "Don't think about it now. Let's get through the trial. I'll help you any way I can. It won't be easy, but you're tough or you wouldn't do what you've been doing. You survived someone trying to frame you. You've protected many others who needed your services and you didn't lose anyone." His voice caught on the last part of that sentence.

"Tell me what happened when you lost your witness."

"I was waiting at the courthouse, coordinating the security there when the car transporting the witness was ambushed. A marshal and the witness were killed and two marshals were wounded. It was a fast and brutal attack. Later we discovered the cell phone on the witness that led the assailants to his location."

She took his hand and held it. "I'm so sorry. At least I knew better than to bring along a cell phone."

"But not your gun or knife."

"That's different, and I needed them so it was a good thing that I had them."

Brody's eyes clouded. "Yeah, you did need them. You shouldn't have."

"In a perfect world. This isn't a perfect world." She squeezed his hand gently. "And you remember that. You told the man what he had to do, and he didn't follow directions. Remember, we can't control everything. I'm really discovering that lately."

"Yes, but the consequences affected so many. The families of the marshal killed and the families of the criminal's next victims. Without the witness's testimony, he was acquitted and within a year killed two more. One was a mother with two young children. I'll never forget seeing those kids at her funeral. They haunt my dreams."

"You didn't kill their mother. You can't think like that." Hearing the anguish in his voice made her want to forget what was happening and just comfort him.

"I have a hard time forgiving myself."

"And I have a hard time forgiving Dirk for what he did. What a pair we are. It's not easy to move on with that kind of baggage." She grasped his upper arm, trying to impart her support.

"I try not to think about it. I guess seeing Carla again brought it all back."

"You need to deal with it, not avoid it. Was the guy convicted when he killed those two other people?"

"Yes, I'm happy to say he'll be in prison for the rest of his life, but—"

She put her fingers over his mouth. "No buts. They aren't allowed. These past two months have given me a lot of time to think about my past. I've let Dirk's betrayal rule my life for the past four years. It possibly colored how I dealt with my dad's disapproval. I got defensive. Now I can't do anything about it. It was bad enough what Dirk did to me, but it's worse that I'm still letting him affect me. When this is all over, I intend to put the man in the past where he belongs. If that means I forgive him, then I'll find a way. I'll have enough to deal with trying to piece together some kind of life." *Without anyone I know. I'll be totally alone.*

"That part of being a U.S. marshal never appealed to me. My life may be a mess, but I can't imagine giving up everything and starting new."

His words only confirmed what she'd thought, and that no matter how much she was starting to care about him it would go nowhere. Arianna pushed to her feet, holding on to the side to keep herself balanced while the trailer was speeding down the highway. Pretending an interest in the mare nearest her, she stroked the horse's nose—anything to keep from looking at him. She was afraid she would start crying if she thought about how she was feeling and what her future would be.

"I'm sorry. I shouldn't have said that. You don't need to hear that now."

A band about her chest constricted her. She needed to say something to him, but she couldn't. Why did she meet a man she was attracted to when there was nothing that she could do about it? It wasn't fair, but then having to go into the Witness Protection Program was unfair.

Life isn't always fair. Do the best you can with what you're given.

Her grandma's advice slinked into her mind and began to ease some of the tightness in her chest. She inhaled a deep, soothing breath and said, "Yes, I do. You're right."

"I—" The throwaway cell rang, and Brody answered it. "I think that's a good idea. I'm starved." When he hung up, he rose and came toward Arianna. "Charlie is pulling into a place he knows up the road to get something for us to eat. They have restrooms on the outside of the building, so he'll park near them. That way we can sneak and use them without anyone spotting us."

"Good. I could use walking around a little. I was getting stiff sitting." She'd started to feel confined, something she felt when she thought about her future. She still didn't know what she was going to do.

As the trailer slowed down and Charlie pulled off the highway, Arianna patted the mare's neck, wishing she could get on her and ride away.

The driver's door slammed shut then Charlie slapped the side of the van. "We're here, and it's all clear. I'll be inside getting us something to eat. When we leave, I'll top off the tank. Don't know when we can stop next."

Brody peered out at the gas station/convenience store. "Let's go. I see another car pulling in for gas."

Exiting the side door of the trailer, she hurried toward the restroom. The length of the horse trailer and large pickup blocked her from anyone seeing her from the store or in front of it pumping gas. Brody was right behind her, moving quickly.

A few minutes later as she washed her hands and wiped a wet towel over her face, the sound of a knock made her stiffen. She swung around, staring at the door. Under her light jacket she had her gun. Her pulse rate jumped as she put her hand on her Glock and moved forward. "It's being used."

"Oh, sorry. I'll pay for the gas then come back."

Arianna went to the door and listened for the crunch of the pebbles layering the ground outside that indicated the woman walked away. When she heard it, she relaxed her tense shoulders. Waiting ten more seconds, she eased the door open and peeked out. Clear.

She rushed toward the horse van at the same time a man came around the end of the trailer. She halted as though caught doing something wrong. Making sure her gun wasn't visible, she pulled her jacket around, crossing her arms at her waist.

"Beautiful day," she murmured and continued her trek toward the pickup as though she was getting into the cab.

When the man entered the restroom, she rushed to the side door of the trailer and inched it open slowly, hoping the hinges didn't squeak too loud. The noise of the men's restroom door being unlocked spurred her to move faster. She clambered into the horse trailer, shutting herself inside and ducking down at the back. She prayed the man didn't check out the horses by looking into any of the windows. But the sound of his footsteps faded around the back of the trailer. She slumped against the side.

Where's Brody? If the restroom was free for the stranger, then he should have been in here. The urge to search for him tested her. She shouldn't. Not yet. But she didn't want anything to happen to him because of her. That she couldn't deal with—not with all the deaths so far associated with Rainwater murdering Thomas Perkins.

The side door open. Arianna drew her gun and brought it up as Brody said, "It's me."

She sighed and laid her hand holding the gun in her lap. A tiny voice in her head told her to wait to put it back in her holster. What if someone was with him, forcing him to reveal her?

But when he appeared in the entrance, he was alone. His gaze lit upon her Glock. "Were there any problems?" He shut the door.

"Where were you?"

"I went to the restroom."

"After that. A man came around to go in there and it was free. I thought you would be in the trailer. You weren't." Her voice rose with frustration and strain. *I want my life back.*

"Did he say anything to you or indicate he knew you?" Brody sat next to her, his left side touching her right one.

"No. His body language seemed okay, too. Nothing to alarm me. So where were you?"

"I saw a black SUV similar to the one that dropped Carla off yesterday. It stopped at the pump and the driver got some gas. He wasn't familiar, but I couldn't see if there was anyone else inside the car. I sneaked around the other side to get a better look. Once the SUV left, I hightailed it back here."

"So nothing suspicious?" Arianna whispered, aware their normal voices could carry beyond the back of the trailer.

"I didn't say that." Brody leaned close to her and lowered his voice even more. "I got the gut feeling there was someone else in the car. He kept looking at the passenger side when he was checking out the area around him. There was nothing casual about him. Vigilant. On edge."

"When he looked over here, did he react differently?"

"I couldn't tell. He was turned from me."

"I hope—" The sound of someone outside the horse trailer made her swallow the rest of her words.

"It's me," Charlie said before opening the side door. "Got you each a turkey and Swiss sandwich, a bag of chips and because I'm so nice a chocolate chip cookie." He glanced from side to side then continued. "There's talk of a roadblock on Glenn Allen Highway so we're going to Valdez and taking the ferry to Anchorage. We'll get into Anchorage after dark. That might not be so bad."

A few minutes later, Charlie had them back on the highway heading south.

Being so close to Brody wasn't safe for her peace of mind. She wanted to know everything about him and that was dangerous. The more she discovered the more she liked him. "I'm getting sore sitting on this hard surface. I wonder if I can do some yoga stretches, maybe work some of the stiffness out of my body." She scooted a few feet from him.

"Are you one of those people who can't rest even when you get the chance?"

"That about sums me up. I need to be kept busy but occasionally I do stop to play Scrabble or read a good book." She snapped her fingers. "I don't seem to have one with me."

"I should have had Charlie stop at the library on the way out of Fairbanks. Oh, yeah. He couldn't since we left before any library would be open."

"It wouldn't be a bad idea for you to do some of these

exercises with me. Nothing where we stand up and balance ourselves. I don't think going sixty miles an hour is conducive to that."

He twisted around and sank down, laying his head on the backpack. "Wake me if we're in trouble."

"I doubt seriously you'll be able to sleep through it. The sound of my gun going off in here will probably start a two horse stampede."

"So long as they go out the door and not back here." Brody closed his eyes.

Arianna sat cross-legged with her spine straight and the back of her hands lying on her knees. Washing her mind of all concerns, she let a calmness flow through her. From there she moved into a core pose, then a back bend followed by an inversion, throwing her legs over her head. The stretches felt great, removing her from all that had happened to her.

The cell rang. Brody popped up, digging for it in his pocket. "Yes?"

He listened, a frown curving deep lines into his face. When he hung up he said, "That black SUV is stalled up ahead. A woman, not Carla according to Charlie's description, is waving us down. He's going to blow by them."

The speed of the horse trailer picked up. Charlie swerved into the other lane and increased their pace even more. Brody knelt on the side they would pass the SUV and peeked out the window. He dropped down and went for his gun. "Two more men are getting out, both with big guns."

NINE

"Get back against the wall." Brody cocooned Arianna's body between him and the aluminum wall.

"Don't. Flatten yourself next to me." She tried to push him away.

"No." He poured all the authority he could into that one word. She was not going to die here on the road.

Shots blasted the air. Suddenly the trailer swerved toward the side of the highway where the SUV probably was. The speed of the trailer decreased. He dragged Arianna to the floor and covered her again.

"What's—"

The loud sounds of the crash reverberated through the trailer. The hard impact of it crashing into the SUV jolted him, and although he knew what Charlie had decided to do, he wasn't able to keep himself from being thrown off Arianna, sliding toward the back door. All around him, he could hear the hooves of the panicked horses as they stamped the floor and tried to stay on their feet.

When he looked back toward Arianna to make sure she was okay, her body rammed against his at the same time the mare brought a hoof down toward her head.

Arianna saw the hoof coming toward her and flinched away from it so that it only clipped her left shoulder. Pain bolted through her.

She looked toward Brody. The other mare crashed to the floor, not able to remain standing. Her eyes wide, the horse tried to get up, but the trailer was swinging around toward the truck. Coming to a stop, the trailer tilted at an angle as though hanging over a cliff. The area they'd been driving through was relatively flat. A ditch?

A woman's scream pierced the air. Shots sounded again, this time from a different gun.

Charlie's? Arianna got up on her knees and hands. "Okay?"

"Yes." Brody's gaze was riveted to the mare still on her feet, dancing about and tugging on her tethers. He rose, searching for his gun that had been knocked from his hand. "Calm her if you can."

As he struggled up the inclined floor toward the front of the trailer, Arianna gripped one of the mare's ropes and yanked her as far away as she could from the horse still lying on its side, her legs flailing. The downed animal's body banged against the side of the trailer, her head whipped back and forth against her restraints. The panicked horses' guttural cries ripped at Arianna's heart.

She looked out the window near her. They were tee-tering over a drop-off along the side of the road. The mare she held would counter the other's weight and help keep them from sliding down into the ditch. She stretched to see the bottom of the gully. She could see it, maybe eight feet down. She pulled even more to coax the mare the few remaining feet to the tack area at the front.

She would secure the mare to a bar, then follow Brody outside. She wouldn't stay in the trailer while there were at least three assailants. She hated leaving the frightened horses in the trailer but the only way out for them was through the back doors, which opened into the ditch.

Another round of gunfire pushed her faster. Charlie could really be hurt. The front of the truck he was driving took most of the impact with the SUV. As Arianna made her way to the small side door, the mare yanked on the rope. Her last glance back at the horse showed an animal with wide eyes, trying desperately to get loose. The one in the back of the trailer struggled to her feet, the rope tied to her halter still connected to the trailer.

Lord, watch over them. Us.

Arianna eased the side door open, her gun drawn, a bullet in the chamber.

On the ground lay one assailant, not moving, a bullet hole in his chest.

She checked his pulse then sneaked forward toward the cab of the truck. Where was Brody?

A noise on the other side drew her full attention. Glancing over the hitch that connected the horse trailer to the truck, she spied Brody struggling with another man. To the side of her, she heard a door creaking open. She turned toward that nearer and more immediate threat as Charlie tumbled out of the cab, blood running down his face.

Brody's attacker broke free of him and tried to run toward the SUV. Brody leaped forward and drove the man to the ground inches from the drop-off. The guy heaved up and rolled over, sending Brody and him into the gully. Rocks and vegetation stabbed him on his trek down. He landed in a couple of inches of runoff with his assailant on top of him, the air swooshing from his lungs, his face pressed into the water.

He had to take care of his assailant and protect Arianna.

With his face still in the few inches of water, Brody struggled to turn his head so he could breathe. His thoughts clouded from lack of oxygen. He felt his attacker's hot breath on his neck. Through the haze in his mind an idea came to him. With all his energy he used his head as a sledgehammer striking the man on him in the face. Momentarily his assailant let up, drawing back slightly. A howl of rage pierced the air.

Adrenaline zipped through Brody. Putting all his energy into hoisting himself up and throwing off his opponent, he thought of Arianna alone in an unfamiliar place with no way to get to Anchorage. He would not let that happen, which meant he couldn't die here today. He tossed the man off him and turned around, scrambling to his feet at the same time his attacker did. The man drew a knife, flicking it open. The eyes of the man were full of determination to kill him. Brody moved in a slow circle, scouring the area for any kind of weapon. There was none.

As Charlie sank to his knees, Arianna rushed to him. "Are you hit?"

He shook his head, drops of blood spattering onto the side of the road. "The windshield is shattered from the bullets. Probably a few fragments cut my face. It happened so fast. I'm fine." He started to stand but collapsed back down.

Arianna examined him. "I think you were grazed by a bullet."

"Could be. I aimed the truck at the SUV and the gunmen. I ducked as they sprayed the pickup."

"Stay put." She went to the opened door of the truck and searched for Charlie's gun. When she found it, she took it to him and put it in his hand. "I'm checking the area. Brody was wrestling one on the other side. One is on the ground. Where's the woman?"

"Don't know. I tried to return fire, but I must have lost consciousness briefly."

Arianna slowly rotated in a circle to check around her. Other than the dead body a few yards away, she didn't see anyone else on this side. With her gun in hand, she crept forward to round the front of the SUV. The truck had smashed into its side, T-boning it. That was when she saw another man pinned between the pickup and the SUV. His assault rifle was still clutched in his hand but there was no life in his shocked eyes. Arianna felt for a pulse just in case but found none. So at least three men and a woman.

Rainwater has to be stopped. Death follows him around.

Anger surged to the foreground, firming her resolve to make it alive to the trial to testify. No man should be above the law.

When she rounded the SUV, a woman flew at her, tackling Arianna to the hard ground.

Poised on the balls of his feet, Brody was ready to dodge the medium-built man. Every nerve alert, he tingled with anticipation of the attack to come. He smelled of mud, brackish water and sweat. The sun beat down on Brody, but a chill gripped him.

His gaze glued on his attacker, he waited for the move. Speed would be paramount. The man charged him, the knife pointed at Brody's heart. With his booted feet, he lashed out at the assailant's legs at the same time he grabbed for the guy's wrist. The assailant twisted his arm away. Brody pounded his right fist into the man's jaw while kicking him again.

The attacker fell to his knees, the knife dropping from his hand. Brody moved in and hit him in the face several times until the man crashed forward into the water. Gasping for air, Brody snatched up the knife, then rolled the assailant over. The man was out cold.

Brody removed the guy's belt and secured his hands behind him. He had to make sure there weren't any others on Rainwater's payroll around. He clambered up the incline to clear the scene and to find his gun and something better to tie up his assailant.

As her attacker went for Arianna's neck, choking her, she looked into the woman's crazed eyes.

"You killed him," the lady shouted over and over.

Gripping her wrists to pry her hands from around her neck, Arianna twisted and bucked, trying to knock the woman off her. Her oxygen-starved lungs screamed for air. A haze descended over her mind.

Suddenly her assailant was lifted from Arianna, and she gulped in precious breaths until the feeling of light-headedness faded.

Brody held the kicking and screeching woman against him. "Okay?"

Arianna nodded, grabbed her gun from the ground a couple of feet away and rose, her legs shaky for a few seconds. "I'll take care of her. Secure the crime scene. Charlie is—"

"Right here. I've called a highway patrol officer I'm good friends with. We can trust him. Someone will have to clean up this mess. A trucker is coming. We're going to have to do some fast-talking if we intend to get away before this place is mobbed. I figure we'll need to use your badge."

Brody looked toward the road. "Take care of the guy in the ditch. I'll take care of the people who want to help until your friend gets here. Arianna, get some rope from the trailer to tie up both of our attackers. Make sure the horses are still okay."

Images of this incident on Richardson Highway being splashed all over the news spurred her to move as fast as her sore body allowed. They had to contain this until they could get away or Rainwater's men would know exactly where she was.

"The trooper I left at the wreck owes me. He'll process the scene as slowly as he can, especially when it comes to notifying people about what happened on Richardson Highway. The two dead men will be picked up and the other two will end up going to headquarters since their injuries are minor. Johnson will tell the commander to check with the U.S. Marshals Service, but he'll delay that as long as possible."

"Thanks, Gus," Charlie said in the front seat of the state trooper's car, speeding back toward Fairbanks. "We need to be as far away from this as possible before Rainwater's men discover the way we're heading to get to Anchorage. They'll have those routes locked up tighter than an oil drum."

Gus chuckled. "Won't they be surprised when you aren't going that way."

Brody glanced toward Arianna sitting across from him in the rear seat in the vehicle. Her head rested on the back cushion, her eyes closed. "Who's this pilot that can fly us to Seward?"

"A childhood friend. He had a run-in with Rainwater's smuggling operations once when he was flying up north to St. Lawrence Island. He barely made it out alive. Believe me there was no love lost between them, but I didn't tell him who you are. Just to keep this quiet. There'll be a car waiting for you at the airstrip in Seward. Another trooper who I know isn't on anyone's payroll other than the state's arranged it. He doesn't know why I asked."

Brody had known from the beginning when they were running away from the cabin that he'd have to trust a few people to help him and Arianna get to the courthouse in Anchorage. But the more people they brought into the circle the more the chances increased that Rainwater's men could discover their whereabouts. That was not an option. At least he was the only one who knew where they would stay in Anchorage—if they could get there.

"While you were securing the two prisoners in the back of the trooper's car, I placed a call to Willow. She's heading toward the wreck site to pick up her horses. I was so glad I could reassure her that neither one was injured badly—just shook up and with a few minor cuts. I'm really going to have to make this up to her."

"Was she mad at you?" Brody asked, remembering

leading the horses out of the trailer right before the second state trooper showed up. One limped from a cut on her leg, but otherwise the mare appeared all right and calm once out of the trailer. He sure hoped there were no lasting effects to the animals.

Angling toward Brody, Charlie grinned. "No. She was more concerned about my injuries. I'm definitely going to have to take the woman out to dinner when this all settles down."

"She's a keeper, my friend." Brody looked toward Arianna again, relieved she wasn't injured. Her soft gaze trained on him lured him toward her. "Okay?"

Her eyes gleamed. "I'm relishing the calm while I have it. We both know how quickly that can change. One minute we're just riding along and the next we're ramming a car."

"Don't worry about that," Gus interjected. "We're almost to my friend's place. You'll be safe."

Her eyebrows rose, and she mouthed the word *safe*, as though in her world that wasn't possible.

Which Brody could see. They both were used to guarding people in trouble. What would it be like to not do something like that? To wake up each morning not worried about a security plan or if he had all the options covered?

Arianna fully faced him on the seat and said in a soft voice, "We left a mess back there."

"Once you've testified I can straighten everything out."

"I hope I can tomorrow. The prosecutor has only one witness left, according to Gus. That'll be cutting it close."

"But better in the long run. I'll only have to keep you

hidden in Anchorage overnight. Less time for Rainwater's men to find us."

"Once I've given my testimony the easy part is over with."

"This is easy? What kind of life do you normally lead?" he said with a laugh, trying to coax a smile from her. He knew exactly what she was referring to and to him the aftermath of the trial would be the hardest part of all of this—reinventing yourself.

"One I'm not sure how to let go. When you're used to a certain kind of challenge and excitement, how do you live without it?"

"Get excited about something else? Don't let the circumstances you can't control pull you down?"

She did smile then. "Both good suggestions."

He bent closer to her and whispered, "Don't forget tonight to write that letter to your parents. I'll see they get it."

"But I can't get a response from them. What if I refuse being in WitSec?"

"You put yourself and anyone around you in danger. They would use your family to get to you. They know that when a person goes into the program, all contact is lost so there is no reason to use your family like that. It has to be that way for yours and others' safety."

She sighed and closed her eyes for a few seconds. When she reconnected with him visually, there was a sheen to the gray depths, like light shining on silver. "I know. I would never put someone I love in danger."

A tall, redheaded man stood by a twin-engine plane at the end of a flat, grassy field. Gus slowed his car to a stop next to his childhood friend. "Hal thought this would be a better place to take off from than an airport—even a private one. He uses this field sometimes. It's not far from his property."

Arianna started to open her door, but Brody caught her hand on the seat between them and held it for a second. "Ready?"

"Yes," she murmured, then slipped from his grasp and pushed the door open.

No matter how tough Arianna was, this past forty-eight hours had taken its toll on her. She tried to put up a brave front, but occasionally when she didn't think he was looking, he saw the sadness in her eyes. It ate at him. This wasn't fair. She was doing the right thing by testifying against Rainwater, and yet she would pay the price as much as the crime boss. She was losing her family, her career, everything she knew and was special to her. Anger knotted his stomach. He shoved open his door and climbed from the car.

The next twenty hours would be the hardest of the trip. He figured that Rainwater had a chokehold around all the ways into Anchorage with spies everywhere.

Within ten minutes Gus's friend took off with Brody in the backseat next to Arianna. She stared out the window, silent since getting out of the car. While Charlie carried on a conversation with Hal, Brody studied Arianna's stiff posture, the tensing of her jaw as if she gritted her teeth. He wanted to comfort her with more than words. He wanted to hold her tight against him. He wanted to kiss her again.

The revelation made him frown. He cared for her and that wasn't smart at all. Although Carla had been a marshal, not a witness, he'd mixed his professional life with his personal one and that had ended badly. It was especially unwise to become involved with a witness. After his work was done, she would be whisked away. He would never see her again.

He swung his attention to the side window next to him and stared at the ground below. Mountainous terrain spread in all directions. Patches of snow on the peaks. Blue lakes. Green forests. Beautiful.

"Nearer to Seward, I'm flying under the radar. I'm going out over the water and coming in from that direction," Hal announced, pointing due south. "It'll take us a little longer, but I think that will be the best approach to the airstrip. If anything happens and we go down in the water, there are life preservers under your seats."

Arianna looked at Brody. "I always laugh when the flight attendants on the airlines go through the procedure for water landings when we're only going over land. I know it's some regulation that they must follow no matter what. But in this case, we may need to know the information."

"Don't worry about it. We won't go down. But if we do, the life preserver will hold you up until—"

As she held up her hand to stop him talking, a smile danced in her eyes. "I'm not concerned. It isn't rushing water. When this is over with and I get wherever I'm to live, I'm going to take swimming lessons. Dog-paddling isn't dignified. I should be able to do better than that. It's about time I conquer a childhood fear."

"Is that a challenge for me to conquer mine?"

"Not with me. Only with yourself. I'll never know if you conquered it or not," she said in a detached voice, then returned her attention to looking out the window.

His throat closed. He clenched his jaws so tight that dull pain streaked down his neck. He wanted something different for Arianna, for both of them, but her fate was sealed when she'd witnessed Thomas Perkins's murder. He was thankful she believed in the Lord. He would be with her and give her the added strength she would need to start over.

"Do you know of a helicopter company with the letters CAR?" Brody asked the pilot, wanting to concentrate on the present—not the future.

"The only one I can think of is a small outfit called Carson Transportation. Why do you want to know about them?"

"We saw them flying over the fire area."

"They fly tourists and sometimes reporters to different places around here. They have a good reputation in Fairbanks."

Arianna looked at Brody. "So it might have been innocent."

"Maybe. Or maybe they didn't know who they were dealing with."

Nearing land, Hal turned toward the north. Brody spied the runway up ahead, not long enough for large airplanes. The next few hours would be dicey. *Lord, we need all Your help. People like Rainwater shouldn't get away with murder.*

Arianna clutched the edge of her seat as the plane touched down, only releasing her grip as Hal taxied toward the small terminal.

When Brody climbed from the plane, he offered Arianna his hand, not sure she would take it. But she did. The feel of it in his caused him to thank the Lord for getting them this far.

Charlie joined them. "Gus said a white Chevy would be parked in the lot near the main building."

* * *

At the car, Charlie searched under the back tire on the driver's side. Rising, he held up a set of keys. Both Brody and Arianna slipped into the backseat while Charlie settled behind the steering wheel and started the engine.

As Charlie pulled out onto Airport Road, Brody said, "We need to get a change of clothing. If those two back at the wreck have been interviewed, Rainwater's men may know what we're wearing and how we're disguised."

"Good point. I know just the place. I've been to Seward a couple of times so far this year. Besides, this is tourist season and everything is in full swing."

"I suggest we also find a place with makeup. I've been thinking we should age ourselves. It might help," Arianna said.

"Have you had any experience in doing that?" Brody asked as he kept his attention trained on what was going on around them. He felt Arianna's presence next to him deep down—an awareness that went beyond the visual. He could be in a totally dark room and know she was there. Maybe it was her scent, but something he couldn't explain linked him to her.

"Yes, two years in high school and one in college. I loved working behind the scenes in stage productions."

Surprised by this new bit of information, Brody briefly skimmed his gaze over her before returning to his vigil. "I never would have thought you'd do that."

Her chuckle peppered the air. "You probably envisioned me as a tomboy growing up."

"You do have three brothers, and you're the only girl in a family steeped in the military."

"My mother and grandma, true Southern belles, had a strong influence on me. I liked girly things."

"And yet you went into the army."

"Warrior by day and diva by night."

"That I'd like to see. Wait, I've seen the warrior part."

Arianna laughed again. "Then I'll give you an aging diva. That ought to throw people off."

Later when Brody escorted her to the Chevy, Arianna felt like a new person in a flowered dress with added padding in a couple of places to give the appearance of an extra thirty pounds. Heavy makeup had changed her with a few age spots on her face as well as wrinkles. Wearing a wig of gray hair, she'd aged herself by forty years. She curved her shoulders to give the effect she was humped over and used a cane. Her shuffling gait carried her slowly to the car. She waited until Brody opened the door.

Once everyone was back in the car—a Chevy with Aurora Tours painted in black on the sides—she admired the look that Brody had come up with. He wore a ball cap with blond hair sticking out, hiding his dark color beneath. He'd sculpted a big belly that flowed over his belt. Wearing a light jacket, black shorts with white socks almost up to his knees and sandals, he looked the image of a tourist who hadn't read about the cooler temperatures in Alaska even though it was the end of July.

"Now all I have to do is touch up your face a little." Arianna opened the bag with her jars, tubes and brushes. "This makes me feel like I'm back in high school, but I'm the drama teacher."

Charlie rotated around, wearing a gray wig, too, and a long moustache. His attire was similar to Brody's.

"Ready to go. There shouldn't be any roadblocks—at least from law enforcement. Good thing you thought to have Gus get the higher-ups to call off looking for Arianna with roadblocks."

"So if we see one, we'll know they're Rainwater's men. I doubt they would do that so close to Anchorage. Too easy for the real state troopers to come upon them." Brody closed his eyes as she put light color foundation around them.

"But they'll have lookouts watching all the ways into Anchorage." Arianna darkened the skin under his eyes to give him circles, then shaded his nose to make it more prominent.

"Yeah, we can't act suspicious, either," Charlie said from the front seat.

When she finished the makeup job on Brody, she inspected her work. "You look good for an old man."

He patted his fake large stomach. "One who is definitely out of shape. Won't be able to run a hundred-meter race in ten seconds."

She whistled. "That's great for an amateur."

Brody puffed out his chest, which looked funny with the belly. "I'll have you know I was on the track team in high school and college."

"So while I was a drama geek, you were a track star."

"I won't say the star, but I did pretty good." His gaze brushed over her. "And I can't imagine you being a geek anytime."

"Oh, but I was. We moved so much I never felt I fit in anywhere. I was quite shy in high school. Being in drama allowed me to make up characters and become them. I even toyed with being a drama teacher once. Briefly."

"What changed your mind?"

"A Jackson serves his, or in my case, her country. That is the tradition. Even my mother was a nurse in the army when she met my dad."

As Charlie left Seward, he increased his speed. Arianna relaxed to enjoy the scenery. This area had been on her list of places to explore after her job two months ago ended. Seward Highway was a scenic road meant to be taken slow with many stops to see what Alaska had to offer. But she hoped they didn't stop at all. She would breathe easier when she was in the safe house in Anchorage—at least until tomorrow when they would leave for the courthouse.

I'm in Your hands, Lord. I know You're with me.

Those thoughts gave her comfort. She'd done all she could—prepare and pray.

As Charlie drove through a pass, mountains surrounded them, hemming them in, while steel-blue lakes dotted the terrain. In the sky an eagle soared near the water's edge. Beautiful. Tranquil. She shoved down the yearning to spend time here. That could never be.

Charlie decreased his speed. Arianna looked out the windshield as the traffic got thicker and slower.

"I think there's a wreck up ahead," Charlie said in a tight voice. "I don't like it one bit."

In another half-mile, the stream of cars came to a standstill. Brody leaned forward. "It looks like a semi on its side. That's going to block traffic for a while."

"I feel like a duck sitting on a lake surrounded by hunters waiting for duck season to open," Charlie said.

Charlie's image said it all. "That is what we are," Arianna said, scanning the area and cars parked around them. People began getting out, talking to their neighbors stranded on the highway with them.

Charlie drummed his hand against the steering wheel as more people poured out of their vehicles. "It's going to look strange if you don't get out, stretch and view the magnificent scenery."

A frown carved more lines into Brody's face. "I know. Let's give it a little time. Maybe they'll move the truck soon."

Charlie craned his neck. "I think I see two down and this couldn't have happened more than fifteen or twenty minutes ago because we're close enough to see the wreck. This is tourist season so the traffic is thicker at this time."

"Great. I don't want us to stay out too long. If we do, we need to minimize our interaction with others."

Arianna peered at the groups of people forming, talking. A couple of people opened the trunks of their vehicles and dug into a cooler then began passing around drinks. "This may turn into one big party. I think we need to mingle with the crowd. Few are staying in their cars."

"You two mingle. I'll stand back and watch. That'll fit with my role as tour guide," Charlie said.

Arianna turned to Brody. "We'll be Ethel and Bob Manley in Alaska for the first time."

"You're enjoying this," Brody said, his frown deepening.

"No, but we can make the best of this situation. Our disguises are good. We just have to act the part of an older couple who have been married for forty years."

"Where are we from? You've got everything else figured out," he said with a smirk.

She playfully hit his arm. "Don't be a grouch." Snapping her fingers, she smiled. "Better yet, be an old grouch. A good role for you. I've dragged you to Alaska, and you didn't want to come. We live in Florida. You're rather be on a beach."

"Anything else?"

"No, just go with the flow. And keep things simple."

"Yes, Ethel."

Charlie left the car and opened the door for Arianna.

When Brody rounded the back of the car, she took his arm and strolled toward the side of the road, "Isn't this beautiful? A lot better than a hot sandy beach."

"No," he grumbled. "I'm too cold. They should plaster all over those tourist brochures how cold it is here."

"It's not cold, Bob. I told you shorts weren't needed. Besides, you have such bony knees."

Brody stopped and stared down at his legs. "I do not."

Arianna patted his arm. "Dear, let's not argue. It's a gorgeous day." Not far from another couple, probably in their forties, she gave them a smile. "Are you two from Alaska?"

"No, visiting like you. We couldn't help overhearing." The blond-haired woman stuck her hand out. "I'm Laura and this is my husband, Terry."

After they exchanged handshakes, Terry asked, "Did you take a cruise here? We just got off a ship. We'll be flying out of Anchorage in a few days after we see this place."

Brody rocked back and forth on his feet. "Nope. Get seasick. I put my foot down when Ethel wanted to take a cruise to Alaska. We settled on flying here. We're leaving Anchorage next week."

"What are y'all doing?" Laura asked, looking Arianna up and down as though checking her out. The couple seemed harmless, but she knew this could turn into a dangerous situation if they let their guard down. She'd seen it in the Middle East with suicide bombers.

"Seeing the countryside. A couple days ago we went to Denali National Park so today we went down to Seward. On our way back to Anchorage." She leaned more on her cane. "All this walking is taking a toll on my knees."

"What did you like the best about Denali? We're going there tomorrow." Laura stuck her hands in the deep pockets of her light jacket.

Exhausted, Arianna searched her mind for what she read about the park. Bits and pieces of information about Denali materialized, but her attention strayed when a large man approached through the crowd and paused nearby, close enough to hear what she said.

Brody tossed his head toward Charlie leaning against the car. "Our guide over there drove us to Savage River Trailhead. Got to see a great view of Mount McKinley. We took a bus tour from there because the rest of the roads aren't accessible for private cars. We saw moose, lots of birds, caribou, fox and wolves."

"Don't forget the grizzly we saw from the bus. Good thing we were inside and he was outside." Arianna fanned herself. "Wow, that got my heart pumping." She watched the muscular man in jeans, cowboy boots and plaid shirt move farther away and plant himself near another group of people talking. She released a breath slowly. "I'd just as soon see a grizzly in the zoo, not the wild. Huge. She had two cubs with her. I heard they are ferocious about protecting their young. Aren't they, Bob?" She elbowed him in the rib.

He'd been staring into the crowd with the man. "Uh-huh. Sorry, sweet pea. Looking around at this place. You reckon we're gonna be here long? I could use a nap."

Terry nodded. "I could, too. I'm on vacation. A nap is a requirement." He peered toward the wreck blocking the highway. "Looks like the state troopers are here and some kind of big tow truck to get the semis moved."

"Honeybun, I need to sit down. My knees are starting to hurt being on my feet for so long today. Nice to meet you two." Arianna gave each one a smile then hobbled toward the Chevy with Brody trailing her.

Even with her head down, she slanted a glance around. Another man halted next to the muscular one who had stopped near them and said something to him. Both men hurried away.

Charlie opened the back door for her, and she eased onto the seat like she was seventy years old, putting the cane in front of her and holding its knob at the end while Brody and Charlie pretended to be in a deep conversation about where to go when they got to Anchorage— loud enough that people could easily hear.

Another lone man strolled not far from them, checking something on his cell. A photo of one of them? Arianna grinned at him then purposely looked away as if she had not a care in the world. But she noticed that Brody kept track of him, a hard glint in his eyes.

When a cheer went up a few hundred feet nearer the wreck, Arianna struggled to stand slowly although she had so much energy from the adrenaline in her body she could dance a jig for the crowd's entertainment. The back end of one semi was being moved to the side of the road.

"About time," Charlie mumbled, his mouth pinched

in a frown. "I've seen at least three or four suspicious persons inspecting the people in and out of their cars."

Everyone watched the second semi being towed away and clapped. Arianna sat again, and this time closed the car door. Tension vibrated through her. She should be used to this kind of stress. It was her job. But she cared too much for Brody, even Charlie. She didn't want anything to happen to them because of her.

Charlie slid into the front seat while Brody climbed in next to her. Charlie started the car. Brody exhaled and lounged back.

A loud crack boomed.

TEN

Brody pushed Arianna down onto the backseat and covered her body with his. He pulled his gun from its holster at the same time she did.

"False alarm. I think it was a car backfiring. No one behind us is reacting," Charlie said and drove forward slowly as the traffic began to move.

Brody eased up and looked around. "You stay down just in case."

"We're all in danger. Not just me."

Brody focused on his mission to keep Arianna alive to give her testimony. He could not think of anything beyond that—certainly not how much he cared for her. "Don't worry about me or Charlie."

"But I do."

He glanced down at her, caught the worry in her eyes and wanted to dismiss it. He couldn't. Most likely his own expression mirrored hers. "I can take care of myself."

"I could say the same thing, but we both know this is bigger than the both of us. Rainwater is sparing no effort to get me."

"Then we'll have to rely on someone even bigger."

Her gaze locked with his. "The Lord?"

He nodded.

"I'm trying."

He tore his attention away from her before he neglected his duties. She was so close and yet forbidden to him like the apple in the Garden of Eden. As they passed the wreck site, four Alaska state troopers were at the scene, the back of one truck still lying on its side off the highway now. "This was no accident."

Charlie snorted. "Yeah, I was thinking the same thing. A planned roadblock. It allows his men to check the people traveling to Anchorage up close and personal. I wonder what stunts they staged on the other highway into Anchorage."

"At least there's more than one way into Anchorage." Brody did another scan of his surroundings, noting the thinning of the traffic now that they were past the wreck, and clasped Arianna's arm to help her up.

"We'd be disappointed if they hadn't tried something. We'd really be worried about what was going on." Arianna settled back, straightening her gray wig.

"Speak for yourself," Brody said with a grin. "I would have been perfectly happy if they hadn't tried anything. Ah, the wonderful feeling of serenity. I would have relished it."

"What's that? In our line of work, we live with the tension."

Brody's stomach churned with that tension she talked about. His vacation was coming up soon. He'd originally thought of taking it in Alaska, camping in the wilderness. Now he wanted to get as far away as he could from where he worked. Maybe Dan was right about a beach in Hawaii, listening to the waves crash against the shore. Calm. No conflict. No life-or-death stakes. A place where he might be able to put his priorities in order.

"What are you thinking? You're so quiet."

Arianna's question drew him back to the reality of their situation as they raced toward Anchorage. "My next vacation."

"Where?"

"A beach."

"I thought you liked Alaska and the wilderness."

"I've had my fill of this for the time being."

"No salmon fishing on a beach?"

"There are other kinds of fishing on a beach." He could almost feel the waves wash over his feet, his body start to relax totally. He released a slow breath. The only thing missing was Ari...

Charlie began slowing down again. Brody pushed all thoughts of beaches and vacations to the background and sat forward. "What's happening, Charlie?"

"Two state troopers on the side of the road with a parked car. Traffic is slow. Rubbernecking."

As they passed the three cars on the side of the road, Brody surveyed the situation. Two troopers had a man between them, talking to him. The man was shouting, his hands balled.

Arianna clasped Brody's arm. "That man looks like one of Rainwater's men I saw when I was researching his organization."

He remembered Arianna's photographic memory and asked, "Who?"

"Stefan Krasnov. It looks like he's being detained and he isn't too happy about it."

"I've heard that name." Brody studied the man in question, trying to recall where and what.

"He's been in Russia for the past two years. I guess he's back now."

"You really dug deep."

"I like to know everything about who wants me dead."

This was why he liked her. She was professional and good at her job—one similar to his. She understood his work. If only they had met differently...

He shoved that thought into a box, shut the lid and stored it deep in his heart. It wasn't to be.

"The sighting of Krasnov means there'll be other people waiting all along the road. We can't let down our guard even with only fifty miles to go."

Charlie's thoughts reflected Brody's. It wouldn't be over until the trial was over and Arianna was safely relocated.

The outskirts of Anchorage came into view. Arianna's heartbeat hammered a fast staccato through her body. She curled her hands in her lap. This was it. Tomorrow at this time it would be over and she would fly out of here shortly afterward.

But a lot could happen in twenty-four hours. She uncurled her fists and wiped her sweaty palms together.

Brody covered her hands. "Okay? We didn't have any problem the last fifty miles. That's a good thing."

"Did you notice that Seward Highway was littered with state troopers?"

"I'm hoping that was Gus's doing somehow. His way of protecting us the best way he could. No roadblocks but plenty of state troopers."

"I think it was Gus." Arianna saw another car had been pulled over closer to the city but didn't recognize the person being detained.

"Go north on the Old Seward Highway. You can get off up there." Brody indicated the turnoff. "We're going across the city. At least it's after the rush hour so we should be able to move quickly."

When Charlie drove onto the older road, he said, "I

don't know about you two, but I'm starved. I'd like to find a drive-through and pick up something for dinner. We can take the food to the safe house."

Arianna glanced at Brody. "I'm hungry, too. Will there be something to eat at the place?"

"Probably not much. It's Dan Mitchell's house. He's out of town in Hawaii."

"Why there and how are you going to get inside?" Arianna asked.

"Dan is possibly the guy who gave you away. He was on one of your protection teams. They won't look there because if it was him, they'd never suspect him of sheltering us. Plus I know he doesn't have close neighbors. He's got almost an acre of land right outside of town."

Both of her eyebrows hiked up. "Did the man give you a key to his place?"

"Isn't it obvious? I'm going to break in. If he's on the take, we'll find evidence inside. If he isn't, he won't mind in the end."

"That's stretching things a bit."

"I suppose we could go to my apartment, but I have a feeling Rainwater has someone watching that place and all of my friends'. Dan isn't a friend, just a colleague. I know quite a bit about his house only because he loves to talk a lot. I've never been there." When Charlie reached the intersection with Third Avenue, Brody said, "Turn right. He lives off Westover Avenue."

"It is convenient he was going to Hawaii and wouldn't be in Alaska when everything went down," Charlie said as he went into a drive-through of a fried chicken chain.

Hunger tightened Arianna's stomach. "I'll take a whole chicken."

"I'll second that order." Sitting up, Brody scanned

their surroundings the whole time Charlie ordered and didn't relax until they'd pulled out of the parking lot and continued the trek toward Dan's house.

Charlie parked around back at the place. "We'll move it when we get the garage open. I don't like leaving the car for everyone to see."

"He would have left his at the airport so there should be room."

Charlie stepped up to the back door before Brody and slipped out a lock pick to begin working on opening it. The dim light of dusk painted the landscape in shadows.

"We get more nighttime hours here in Anchorage. It's not even eleven yet, and the sun is going down. That might help us." Arianna scoured the wooded area around Dan's house, taking the left side while Brody watched the right—like a team, not a word spoken. They just did it naturally as though they shared each other's thoughts.

"I'm in. His security system was easy to circumvent if you know what you're doing. I do." Charlie swung the door wide and stepped inside first.

What was she going to do when she left tomorrow night or the next morning? She glanced at Brody's strong profile and knew she would miss that everyday for the rest of her life. She couldn't deny the feelings she had developed over the past few intense days. She tried to tell herself that with time, she would forget him. Certainly what they had been through wasn't a good foundation for a normal life. So maybe her love for Brody wasn't really real. It sure felt real, though.

"After you, Arianna," Brody whispered into her ear. She hadn't even heard or seen him move closer.

Charlie came back into the kitchen. "I've opened the garage. I'm moving the car in there."

"We'll check the house, then we can eat." Brody moved to the right while Arianna took the left side of the one story house.

As Arianna passed through each room, she checked any space someone could hide, and she also noted places to examine more thoroughly after they ate. Maybe they could help Brody figure out if Dan was the marshal who had sold her out. When she went into a game room, she came to a stop a foot inside the entrance. Trophies of the man's kills hung on the wall—stuffed and staring at her. She shivered and focused on searching the place rather than paying attention to the deer or bear over a shoulder watching her every move.

Brody appeared in the doorway. "Did you find anything?"

"Nope, but I see you have a laptop. I was beginning to think all Dan did in his spare time was kill animals and then mount them. Do you see the gun over the mantel? It could take care of a bear for sure."

"I can use it when we go to the courthouse tomorrow. If it stops a bear, it'll stop a man, even the huge one we saw called Mankiller."

She flicked her hand toward a table. "The ammo is in there and plenty of it. Did the laptop have anything on it?"

"I haven't looked through it yet. We'll eat then take a look at it."

"When are we going to leave for the courthouse tomorrow?"

"Probably as soon as we can. We don't know what roadblocks we'll face. I know when we show up the D.A. will have you testify right away. I want to keep a tight schedule. Only let the necessary people know at the last minute. I don't want to give them a chance to intercept us."

"Most likely there are some of Rainwater's men around the courthouse as we speak," Charlie said. "I'm sure they've been there from the very beginning."

"Yes, but if they knew when we were coming, there would be more."

"Come up with a plan yet?" Arianna strode toward the kitchen and the bucket of cold fried chicken.

"Working on it. I want to sketch the floor plan of the courthouse the best I can from memory."

Charlie placed the bucket of chicken in the center of the kitchen table. "I zapped the baked beans. The coleslaw is fine as is. To tell you the truth, I could eat the containers they come in. I'm that hungry."

Arianna laughed. "I'm with you. All this running from the bad guys has increased my appetite."

After they sat, Brody bowed his head. "Lord, I know You'll be with us tomorrow. Help us to deceive Rainwater's men and allow Arianna to testify against Rainwater, and return safely. Bless this food. Amen."

"After we eat, I'll get on the computer and see what I can find about the different marshals." Charlie took several pieces of chicken and passed the container to Arianna. "I love doing computer searches."

"I'll map out what I can of the courthouse. I wish I had your photographic memory, Arianna."

"I was there with Esther Perkins that first week I was protecting her. I didn't see all of it, but I may be able to help you."

"Great. Also, I have a friend in the L.A. U.S. Marshals' office who I worked with for several years. He may be able to help us delve into who might be the mole."

"Does he know Carla Matthews well?" Arianna tried to picture Brody and Carla together and the image wouldn't materialize. They were so different, but when work was most of a person's life, often people started relationships with coworkers. She had with Dirk and regretted it.

"He isn't a fan of hers."

Charlie reached into the bucket and drew out another piece of chicken. "You know this house is a nice one. Mitchell or his wife must have some money to afford this."

Arianna surveyed the kitchen, which looked like it had been recently remodeled with top-of-the-line marble countertops and ceramic tiles. All the stainless-steel appliances were new. "You're right. Does Dan's wife work?"

"No, she quit her job a while back. They're trying to have a family." Brody finished the last of his baked beans, doing his own assessment of his surroundings. "It seems I remember Dan talking about buying a cabin recently on a piece of land near a lake. He loves to hunt and fish."

"No, you're kidding," Arianna said with a smile. "I'd never get that from the trophies on the wall in his game room. His pool table was a beauty, too. His banking information might be somewhere in the house. I'll do a thorough search."

"You've worked with all these marshals. If you had to choose one right now, who do you think it is?" Charlie took a long sip of his coffee.

"I've known Carla the longest. She's a good marshal, very professional on the job. Off the job is totally different. It's like she's two separate people. That's sends up a red flag to me. I think Kevin is still too fresh and new to be corrupted. He's always thought he could change the world single-handedly."

Arianna rose and took her trash to throw away. "And he's a great cook. I think I'm still hungry and only thinking about food."

"Me, too," Brody said, crossing to the refrigerator

to look inside. "Ted Banks is good at following directions, but I don't think he's a leader. From what I heard around the office, he messed up on a detail when he was the lead. Our chief hasn't given him one since. I think he realizes where he is will be about it for him, so if he's got ambitions to make more money, Rainwater might have seemed like his only choice." He shut the fridge door.

"Don't forget Ted has two children starting college."

"From what I hear that'll set him back a pretty penny." Charlie cleaned up the table. "Any food in the refrigerator?"

"No, unless you like eating mustard and ketchup." Brody sighed and leaned against the counter. "Mark Baylor was close to retirement. He was talking about doing it at the first of the year. He was quiet, reserved. By the book. I really hadn't gotten to know him as well as Ted and Kevin."

"Anything that stood out to you, Arianna, while you were at the cabin that first week?" Charlie sat again and opened the laptop.

"I'm not sure my assessment of Ted is quite the same. I saw a marshal that did well running team one. Efficient. Insisted all the rules were followed. I was impressed with how sharp he was. I tried to sneak outside one morning just to stand on the porch in the crisp, fresh air. Ted was right on it."

Arianna waited to hear Brody's admonishment, and it came on cue. "What if the attackers had been outside then? They would have had a clear shot of you."

She lowered her head, her cheeks heated. "I know. It was stupid but I was so tired of the inside of that cabin. It was day six. I thought I could pull it off, have a few minutes outside by myself while the guard made his perimeter round and get back inside unnoticed. Ted opened that door so loud it startled me."

"How about your boss?" Charlie asked while opening, skimming and closing files on Dan's computer.

"I'd say no, but can't totally rule out anyone. He's up for a promotion and I can't see him throwing that away. But then money is a powerful persuader."

"I'll check on assets and anything that may seem out of the ordinary on the five marshals and your boss. Arianna, I'll leave Mitchell to last. See if you find anything in this house to help me."

"I'm calling my buddy in L.A. then Gus. I need to know what has been discovered. He was going to look into it. He may know something by now."

"Like the identity of the sixth victim. We left five behind—if you count Kevin, although we didn't find him." Arianna headed for the hallway. "I'll see if I can find you some paper to use to draw the floor plans of the courthouse."

Arianna started with the master bedroom, a large room with massive pieces of oak furniture. She found a printer with paper in it and took a couple of pieces to Brody who was deep in a conversation with the marshal in L.A. Then she headed back to the master bedroom to search it thoroughly.

In the back of the closet on the top shelf, she discovered a lockbox and carried it into the kitchen. "I need your picking tools."

Charlie gave them to her, and Arianna worked on opening the strongbox. She found the Mitchells' financial papers and other important documents in it. Brody was between calls, so she said, "Come over here. I've hit a gold mine." She passed half the stack to him. "Maybe we can find all the answers in here."

Charlie whistled. "You should see the place Dan Mitchell is staying at in Hawaii. A five-star hotel. He spent lots of money on this vacation."

"Over ten thousand to be exact." Brody waved the sheet of paper he held. "This is the bill and that's not including the food they'll eat."

"How can he afford that on his salary? Federal employees at his level don't make that kind of money." Charlie continued checking emails on the computer.

"You all do realize if Dan is the one none of this can be used against him." Arianna passed more financial papers to Brody and Charlie.

"At this moment I need to know who the mole is. That's more important. Someone can build a case against him later." Brody shuffled through the stack he had, stopped and tapped his finger on the top one. "I think I know how he got his money. Dan's great uncle died last year, and he received a hundred thousand from the estate."

"He never said anything to you all at the office?" Charlie asked, then closed down the email and began researching Kevin Laird.

"I remember he went to Oregon for a funeral last year," Brody said. "That's all. He got the money two months ago. It looks like that's when he planned the vacation and bought the cabin."

"And had the kitchen remodeled, a widescreen TV delivered and ordered a new vehicle that should be delivered next week. My, he's been busy going on a shopping spree." Arianna put back some of the financial sheets into the strongbox. "If I received a hundred K, I have to admit I would plan a dream vacation. But then I'd save the rest since being a bodyguard isn't a lifelong..." Clearing her throat, she took the rest of the papers from Brody and stacked them back the way she took them out.

Brody clasped her shoulder, massaging his fingertips into it. "I'm sorry. You'll do great whatever you decide to do."

She refused to lift her head or he'd see the tears in her eyes. Slamming the box closed, she locked it then started for the master bedroom to put it back where it belonged.

Brody caught up with her in the hallway. "Are you okay?"

When she kept her face turned away, he moved into her line of vision and cradled her face in his hands. She saw him through a sheen of tears. The look he gave her nearly did her in. All she wanted to do was go into his embrace and have a good cry. She hadn't since this all started. She needed to, but she wouldn't allow her emotions to rule right now. They would divert her from what she needed to do: find the mole.

But his tender touch on her face and his eyes soft with concern made her wish everything was different—that they had met under normal circumstances.

She inhaled a deep breath and covered his hands with hers. "Yes, just trying to assimilate the fact my life as a bodyguard is over, that I won't be able to use my skills to protect others. That's all I've known for so long. I'm not used to having to trust others with my safety."

"I know what you mean. Trusting comes hard in our line of work. But the more I've looked at your situation the more I realize I'm going to have to trust someone in the D.A.'s or the U.S. Marshals' office or both. Not everyone is on Rainwater's payroll. I just have to decide who isn't. A mistake could get you killed."

Or him. Her heartbeat thumped, its sound echoing through her mind like a death knell.

"I know you'll do the best job possible. There comes a time when I have to put myself in the Lord's hands. Let's do what we can and turn the rest over to Him."

He smiled, a gleam in his brown eyes that seemed to shine straight through her. "You're right."

Kiss me. She started to lean toward him, then she pulled back, finally putting some space between them. "I'd better get back to finishing my search, then I'll take a look at your floor plans of the courthouse. I still think we need to figure out the most likely places an attack could come from."

"I'll draw them as soon as I call Gus for an update."

Arianna strode toward the hallway to the bedrooms, then turned to peer back at Brody. He glanced over his shoulder and their gazes connected. Never in her life had she seen such an all-consuming look. She felt possessed and cherished in that moment. She grasped the corner edge of the wall, willing strength back into her legs, her knees.

There was no way she wouldn't end up hurt. She loved Brody Callahan and no amount of berating herself was going to change that fact. And when she had to leave him behind, the hurt would be far worse than when she discovered Dirk had betrayed her.

ELEVEN

"Still no ID on the sixth corpse at the cabin?" Brody asked Gus a few minutes later as he sat across from Charlie at the kitchen table.

"No, but they were able to ID Mark Baylor and one of the assailants—a Bo Wilson. He was the body outside the cabin along the side, behind some shrubs."

"He was my attacker when I was looking for Kevin. So they don't know who the two men inside were yet? Too bad the camera with photos of those men was ruined when we crossed the river. It might have made the job easier with pictures."

"No, and the two bodies in the cabin were badly burned to the point it will be harder to ID them. They're looking into Kevin's dental records. He rarely went to the dentist according to his mother. One of the bodies at the edge of the woods had a satellite phone, but they don't know who it is."

Brody drummed his fingers against the tabletop. Gus had proven himself to be trustworthy. He could be Brody's chance to get Arianna into the courthouse safely. "We're going to need your help tomorrow morning. I know you don't live that far from Anchorage. Can you come here?"

"I'm glad you asked. I want to see this through. Rainwater's men made a mess for us state troopers to manage today on the roads into Anchorage. He needs to find out the good guys will win every once in a while."

"I can't trust anyone in the Marshals' office, so it'll be just us," Brody said.

"I know a couple of the security officers at the courthouse. I have one we can trust. He's my cousin."

They just might have a chance. "I'll be calling the prosecutor first thing tomorrow morning to coordinate getting Arianna there."

"So where are you?"

It was the question Brody had been waiting for. Did he have a choice? Not really, but this felt right. He gave Gus Dan's address. "Come around back. Although he lives in a fairly isolated place you never know when someone Dan knows could come by and wonder why a state trooper's car is out front."

"Will do. Be there by six tomorrow morning. I'll be bringing my cousin, Pete Calloway."

After hanging up, Brody slid the white, blank sheets toward himself and began sketching what he remembered of the courthouse.

Charlie peered over the top of the computer. "You said something about talking to the prosecutor tomorrow. Is there a chance he's one of Rainwater's men?"

"If he is, he didn't give the location away because all the man knew was that Arianna was here in a safe house in Alaska. No, leaking the location boils down to the five marshals and my supervisor."

"I thought you didn't think it was your boss."

"I hope not, but I can't be one hundred percent sure."

"It isn't going to be easy tomorrow. There's only a day or two left for Arianna to testify. That narrows the timeline."

Brody tapped the pencil against the paper, staring at what little he'd drawn so far.

"Nervous?"

"I'd be stupid if I wasn't concerned. I'm having to depend on others for her safety."

"From what you've told me, you've always had to—except maybe in the woods when you were running from the assailants and dogs. But even then that couple and their granddaughter helped you two."

"You're right. Rainwater doesn't own everyone in Alaska."

Charlie laughed. "It just might seem like he does with everyone shooting at us. Tell you what, I'm going to wait hidden outside until after Gus comes. Most likely if he's going to betray us it'll be then. But honestly I don't think he will. If he was going to, the best time was when he was driving us away from the wreck."

"He's bringing his cousin who works security at the courthouse."

Charlie scowled. "I didn't know he had a cousin."

Brody's head pounded with tension. "Do you know any of Gus's family?"

"Nope. Never needed to. But I'll run a check and make sure he really has a cousin working at the courthouse."

"I'd feel better if you did. He's Pete Calloway."

"What's wrong?" Arianna asked from the doorway.

"Nothing really. Gus and his cousin who's part of the

security at the courthouse will be helping us tomorrow. They'll be here around six."

"Then why would you feel better if Charlie does something?"

Brody hadn't wanted her to worry. He'd do enough for the both of them. "Charlie's checking on Gus's cousin. We like to know what we can about a person we're working with."

"I agree. I always checked out the people I was working for and with as well as anyone associated with them. I don't like surprises." Arianna sat at the table. "I didn't find anything else here that would help us. What did Gus say about the crime scene at the cabin?"

"They identified Mark Baylor and the assailant I killed at the side of the cabin with dental records. Nothing yet on the other four."

"So we don't know if one of the bodies in the woods was Kevin?"

"No. It seems Kevin didn't go to the dentist much. It's taking a little longer to track his dental records down." Brody wanted to smooth the tired lines from her face. He remained seated at the table. Everything was too complicated as it was.

"I've been thinking while searching the house. What if Kevin isn't dead? We never saw his body. The additional bodies in the woods could be the people who started the fire, but instead of getting away, they got caught in it."

"So what are you saying?"

"That Kevin could have been the mole."

"What if he's one of the bodies?"

She shrugged. "It doesn't totally clear him if he is.

Rainwater has no problem double-crossing his associates."

"I've got something," Charlie said in an excited voice. He looked up from the laptop and smiled. "Mark Baylor. I got an email from a techie friend who was running a background check on the names I gave him before we left Fairbanks."

"You contacted someone about this without my knowledge?" Brody gritted his teeth, feeling as though he had no control over the case.

Charlie stared at him. "Yes, and I didn't tell you because I also had him look into you. I left no one out. I never did when I worked a case. I wanted to know what I was getting into."

Brody returned his look for a long moment. If he'd been in Charlie's place, what would he have done? Probably the same thing. That was why he liked and respected the man. He was thorough and relentless. He relaxed his stiff shoulders. "So tell me a little about this guy. Is he a hacker?"

"There is very little he can't get into with time. He doesn't live in Alaska. He used to work for the FBI and went freelance with his services."

"What did he find?" Brody rose and came around to look over Charlie's shoulder at the same time Arianna did.

"Mark was in debt up to his eyeballs. Serious debt. He was close to having his house taken by the bank. That's until last week when he paid off all the back payments."

"Did he pay off the house?"

"No, at least he was smart enough not to do that.

My friend is tracking the money trail and will let me know what he finds. I think it will lead to Rainwater."

"Why? Look at Dan. He inherited his money." Brody had to put aside the fact he liked Mark. He had to be impartial.

"Three reasons. Mark hasn't inherited any money, when he goes on vacation and sometimes long weekends, he flies to Las Vegas and you could say I have a gut feeling about this."

"Has he found anything else about the other marshals?"

"Carla has expensive taste in clothes."

"So if it's Mark, then they killed their informant. That'll send a great signal to future informants." Arianna covered her mouth to stifle a yawn.

Brody crossed to the coffeepot and poured a large cup. Lack of sleep was catching up with all of them. "Gus and his cousin will be here around six. We all need some sleep. One person can rest while the other two stay on guard and dig through info. Arianna, do you want to sleep now or later?"

"I'd rather stay up now."

"That's okay," Charlie said. "My eyes are tired from looking at the screen for the past couple of hours. I'll turn it over to you two. See what you can find about Gus's cousin. Try Facebook. You'll be surprised what you can discover on social media sites." Charlie slid the laptop toward Arianna while Brody retook his seat at the table.

When the former FBI agent left the kitchen, Brody took a long sip of his coffee and stared at Arianna over the rim of his mug. "Pete Calloway shouldn't be too hard to locate if he has an account on Facebook.

There probably aren't too many with his name living in Alaska."

"It may not be a public account."

"True, but we can start there and do a Google search."

"This world is getting so small. I never had the time to do any of this social media and now that I do, I can't. I don't think WitSec would be too happy if I had an account on any of the social media sites under my new name."

"Probably not a good thing. Even if Rainwater is put in prison, he'll be controlling his organization from there."

"Sad when we know who the criminals are and can't do anything."

"But you are." Brody snared her look, his gut twisting at the thought of all Arianna was giving up to make sure justice was done. She would be "punished" along with Rainwater.

"Brody—" she tore her gaze from his "—thanks for including me in the guard duty."

"I know you. You wouldn't have gone along with it if I didn't."

Her chuckle filled the air. "We've gotten a crash course in each other over the past few days."

He loved hearing that sound from her. "But I wouldn't recommend it for ordinary people."

"What happened at the cabin could have easily ended differently. You're good at your job. You're a light sleeper."

"I could say the same thing about you."

"Well, now that we've complimented each other, I'd better try to find Pete Calloway on the internet since he'll be here in five hours or so," she said. "You would think after all that Gus did for us earlier today that we could trust his judgment and cousin."

"This job has made me jaded. That's the part I hate about it. I want to believe in the good in people but..." Brody shoved back his chair, not able to put into words how the years in law enforcement had changed him. Sometimes he didn't like what he was becoming— totally cynical and distrustful. He realized it when he thought of Gus's cousin. He thought of it when he heard Charlie had his friend check him out. "I'm going to walk through the house, then step outside and walk around. Don't let me in unless I say it's getting cold."

"Sure."

Brody hurried from the kitchen, needing to put some space between him and Arianna. It was becoming harder for him to separate his professional and personal life with her. He wanted her to testify, but there was a part of him that didn't want her to for a while so he could spend more time with her. Not a good way for him to think.

Arianna looked at her watch. Four-thirty in the morning of the day she would testify. After that, her name and life would officially be changed. The thought scared her more than she wanted to admit. Her future was unknown. Not only where she lived but what she would do.

Then there was Brody. She wouldn't see him after this. She rubbed her hand over her heart, pain piercing through it. In such a short amount of time, she'd fallen in love with him. She'd tried not to. She knew no good would come of it in the long run. There was no future for them. No dates. No watching the sunset with not a care in the world for anything but each other.

Then she remembered that time fleeing the dogs and Rainwater's men when they were going over the mountain. They had paused and stared at the night sky as an aurora blazed an eerie green across it. A special moment she would never forget. When she'd looked into his eyes, she'd known then even if she wouldn't admit it to herself that she could and probably would love Brody Callahan. And she couldn't even really tell why other than she felt a connection to him she'd never had with another, not even Dirk.

Through a slit in the blinds, she peered out a window and saw the growing light in the sky as dawn neared. Gus and Pete would be here soon. According to what she discovered on the internet, Pete was exactly what Gus had said. The man had a wife and two children. He had been working security at the courthouse for ten years.

A little voice inside her said that didn't mean he couldn't be on Rainwater's payroll. But somewhere along the line she had to trust the Lord. He was with her; she couldn't do this by herself.

Arianna knocked on the bedroom door. "Brody, it's time to get up."

Before she had a chance to step away, he opened the door, their bodies inches apart. The hairs on her arms stood up, tingles zipping down her spine. The urge to embrace him and take that kiss she'd wanted all evening washed over her. She backed away.

"Did you sleep?" she asked to fill the silence.

"Yes. I set the alarm on my watch."

"Scared I'd leave you to sleep until Gus came?"

His eyes twinkled. "Yep."

"Only because you let me sleep half an hour longer than I should."

"You've got to be sharp today to testify. We don't want Rainwater's crafty lawyer getting the better of you."

"I'm not gonna let this all be for nothing. You may enjoy hiding out, but it's totally overrated as a form of entertainment."

Brody threw back his head and laughed. "I'm going to miss your wit."

She paused at the end of the hallway, turning toward him. "Only my wit?"

A look came into his eyes that stole her breath. It consumed her. It enticed her toward him. A step then another and she was past the bedroom door.

He took her face within his hands and combed his fingers into her hair, holding her still. "I've been telling myself I shouldn't kiss you. It's wrong. But you'll be gone by tomorrow, and I'll regret that I didn't."

He leaned down, brushing his lips across hers. Soft. Heart melting. As his hands slid down her neck and spine, he molded her against him, increasing his claim on her. She surrendered as she never had before to the sensations bombarding her from all sides. The warmth of his embrace. The scent she had come to identify with him—clean and slightly earthy. The intensity in his kiss.

She could forget everything but him. The danger he was in because of her. The hurt she would feel when they parted. The unfairness of it all that she'd finally met a man she could love with her whole heart.

When he pulled back a few inches, he framed her

face and rested his forehead against hers. His ragged breathing sounded in the quiet, mingling with her own.

"I wish we had met differently," he murmured and dragged himself away.

He stared off into space for a moment, and she could see his professional facade fall into place. "The second you step out of this house you will wear a bulletproof vest at all times." He strode toward the kitchen. "Any news while I slept?"

"Charlie couldn't find anything on Ted other than some loans for his twins for college tuition. He borrowed quite a bit but that isn't unusual with the high cost of college."

"So we really don't know for sure about anyone."

"No, although Mark is still looking the most suspicious. Charlie also looked into the helicopter pilot who brought you and your team to the cabin. A state trooper with a stellar record."

"What did he find out about Kevin?"

"The only thing is that his brother is stationed at the air force base here."

Brody halted and swept around, frowning.

"Did you know that?"

He shook his head. "I thought his family lived in Seattle."

"They do except his older brother and family."

"He never said a word in the nine months he's been here. That's odd. We were on a couple of details together. You get to know someone then. Long hours with not a lot to do."

"Yeah, I know." She felt she knew Brody though they'd met only a short time ago.

He let Arianna enter the kitchen first. "I haven't said

anything, but after we plan how we're going to get to the courthouse and inside, I'm paying the prosecutor on this case a visit away from the office. He needs to know you're here and will be at the courthouse."

Arianna stopped, blocking his entry. Her gaze automatically swept the room, taking in the exits and the empty seat where Charlie had been sitting before he went outside to wait for Gus and Pete. "Where are you gonna meet him?"

"His house. I know it's risky, but the leak of our location wasn't him because he didn't know where we were. I need to be there before the police escort him to the courthouse. Whatever we decide on how to get in, he'll make it easier for us. There'll only be three of us besides Pete on duty, to protect you and get you inside. Rainwater will have a lot more men than that. Nothing can go wrong."

A knock at the back door caused Arianna to gasp, so intent had she been on Brody and what he was going to do. She understood why he needed to do it, but she didn't like it. What if Rainwater's men were watching the prosecutor's house? What if Brody was caught and killed?

The very thought pained her more than she thought possible. It had always been easy for her to detach her emotions from what she was doing. That was how she survived in dangerous situations. This time she couldn't.

Brody pulled his gun out of the holster, peeked out to see who was there then opened the door. Gus and his cousin came inside.

Charlie followed the pair into the kitchen. "I didn't see anything unusual out there. It doesn't look like anyone followed you two."

"At this time of day few are up and about. That made it easy to spot anything unusual. We didn't see anything suspicious." Gus smiled at Arianna. "Good to see you're all right. I worried about you until I heard from Brody last night. This is my cousin. Pete, this is the little lady we're gonna make sure testifies today. I have some good news. Pete is the security officer on the back door into the courthouse today."

Brody crouched near a group of shrubs, close to the deck, in the backyard of Zach Jefferson's house. Fifteen minutes ago the lead prosecutor on the Rainwater case had opened the blackout drapes on a window upstairs—probably his bedroom. He was single, living alone. Brody would wait until the man came downstairs. He knew from past dealings with the prosecutor he was a heavy coffee-drinker, so Brody hoped he went to the kitchen before leaving for the courthouse.

When he'd cased out the place earlier, he'd noticed a police car out front. There was some kind of surveillance on Jefferson, but the man in the past had refused police protection. This time he had agreed to a cop outside the house. For his purposes Brody was glad that was all. He didn't want to call Jefferson or meet him at the office, and he wasn't familiar enough with the man's daily routine to plan a chance encounter somewhere else. Besides, time was very limited.

A light came on in the kitchen. Two sets of blinds opened. Brody caught a glimpse of Jefferson staring out one of the windows. When the man turned away, Brody surveyed the backyard then hurried to the deck and knocked on the back door. This was the tricky part. Would Jefferson answer or notify the police out front?

A minute passed. Standing exposed on the deck, Brody felt vulnerable, every nerve alert, every muscle tense. He wanted to be able to get Arianna to the court-house and immediately into the courtroom to testify. Jefferson could quietly tighten security on the floor and pave the way for Arianna. He could also ruin every-thing if he was on Rainwater's side.

The door flew open. Jefferson held a gun pointed at Brody's chest.

Arianna stood in front of the mirror in the master bedroom at Dan's house, staring at herself. The dark circles under her eyes attested to the lack of sleep she'd endured over the past few days. The cuts and bruises she could hide with clothing confirmed the trauma she'd gone through to get to this point. Now she was only hours away from walking into the courtroom to end this ordeal. At the moment waiting for Brody's return from the prosecutor's house, she looked and felt like a wreck.

But that couldn't be the case when she sat before the jury. Not only what she said was important but how she said it mattered, too. She had to make it clear that there was no doubt in her mind that Joseph Rainwater killed Thomas Perkins. And there wasn't. Now she just needed to convey that to the twelve men and women when her body and mind were on the verge of exhaustion.

Lord, You've brought me this far. I know You'll be with me the rest of the way. Please guard the persons protecting me. Don't let anyone else die to keep me safe. I'm trying very hard not to let my fears interfere with what I must do. Rainwater can't win. But I've been in the middle of so much death that leaving here for a new life will be a relief.

Except for Brody. Tears smarted her eyes, and she pivoted away from the mirror. That was all she needed to fall apart right now.

I won't think about what could have been. He's my bodyguard. That's all.

Then why was she fretting that he wasn't back from the prosecutor's?

Jefferson scowled. "What are you doing here?"

"To fill you in on Ms. Jackson and what will happen today." Brody didn't take his gaze off the gun still aimed at him.

The prosecutor lowered his weapon and stepped out of Brody's way. "Come in." After he shut the door, he faced Brody, still grasping the .38 but held down at his side. "Where is she?"

"Safe."

The man's frown deepened even more. "We weren't sure you were alive. All we knew was she was missing. In fact, I'd come to the conclusion that Rainwater's men had taken her and killed her somewhere else. Then yesterday some information came to me that made me think I might be wrong."

"I figured by now you've heard about the wreck on Richardson Highway and all the activity on the roads into Anchorage."

"Yes. I knew something was going on. I don't want Rainwater walking on this. Law enforcement officers have been injured and killed because of him. There were two firefighters hurt, too, trying to put out that forest fire. It's still smoldering in places. This has got to stop."

"I'm bringing Ms. Jackson to the courthouse this morning. First thing, I hope. I have protection for her, but I want her to go right into the courtroom and testify. The longer she has to wait the more chances Rainwater will do something desperate."

"Why aren't you relying on the U.S. Marshals Service?"

"There's a mole. I don't see how else the location of the safe house could have been leaked. To be on the safe side, I have to go on that until proven otherwise. We nearly died several times getting here."

"Your boss isn't going to like that you came straight to me rather than through him. Not protocol."

"My primary—actually only—concern is Ms. Jackson's safety." Nothing can happen to her. The thought it could curdled Brody's gut like corrosive acid.

"Fine. We'll deal with the fallout after this is over."

The doorbell rang. Brody stiffened. "Are you expecting anyone?"

"My escorts to the courthouse. I have been persuaded under the circumstances to accept a police officer outside my house and an escort. There really isn't any reason to go after me. Another prosecutor in my office can step in and wrap the case up. But the police chief, your boss and the mayor insisted."

"I should probably wait until you leave before I do."

"Stay in here." Jefferson grabbed his coffee mug for traveling and started for the front of his house to answer the door.

Brody moved closer to see and hear who was taking Jefferson downtown. While he glimpsed Carla in the entry hall, Ted Banks' booming voice filled the air. "Are you ready, sir?"

"Yes," Jefferson murmured, "let me get my briefcase. We'll go directly to the courthouse."

"I thought you wanted to go to your office first," Carla said.

"Changed my mind."

Footsteps sounded on the hardwood floor, and Brody popped back into the kitchen in case it wasn't Jefferson. Brody wasn't happy that Ted and Carla were escorting the prosecutor. He didn't know if he could trust them, but Jefferson was right. Killing him wouldn't accomplish anything, and he didn't think Ted and Carla were both on the take. Actually he didn't think either one was, but he'd learned to reserve judgment of guilt or innocence until all the evidence was in.

When he heard the front door close and silence permeated the house, Brody left the kitchen and planted himself in the dining room to watch Jefferson leave. Brody peeked through the blinds to see Jefferson climb in the back with Ted next to him while Carla started the engine and pulled away from the curb. The police car followed behind the marshal's car.

Not seconds later across the street in a neighbor's driveway, a dark van backed out and turned in the same direction as the small convoy going to the courthouse. If that was someone tailing them, Ted and Carla were good marshals and would spy the vehicle behind them and take measures to evade. He couldn't worry about Jefferson. He had to get back to Arianna and implement their plan to get her to the courthouse in a couple hours.

Brody hurried to the back door. When he came earlier, he'd gone through a hedge at the back of the property that separated Jefferson's place from his neighbor's. His car was parked two streets over.

As he neared the seven-foot wall, someone behind him said, "What are you doing here?"

TWELVE

Arianna prowled the kitchen. "Why isn't he back by now? He said the prosecutor didn't live that far away. He should have been in and out."

Charlie shut down the laptop. "He's fine. Brody knows how to take care of himself." He rose. "I think I've gotten this computer back to the way it was. All traces of me erased. How about the rest of the house?"

"Done. Ten minutes ago. Where is Gus?"

"Getting the truck we're going to use. It's nice knowing someone who has a lot of relatives."

"And Pete?"

"Gone to work. He'll be ready for us when we show up."

Arianna kneaded her thumb into her palm. "I just want this over with. I want Brody back safe." *I want my old life back.*

Not for the first time she asked God why she had witnessed the murder. If they had been half an hour later, her life would be so different.

Charlie's throwaway cell phone rang. "Yeah. Okay."

"Was that Brody?"

"No, Gus. He'll be here in five minutes."

Arianna collapsed back against the counter, gripping its edges. "When he gets here, we're going to get Brody, and if you say no, I'll go without you. Once we get Brody, we can leave for the courthouse from there."

Brody slowly rotated toward the man behind him. It was a man he'd seen before in the forest—Boris Mankiller. And behind him was Stefan Krasnov. Each held a gun in their hand. Brody calculated his chances of getting away without being killed and came up with nil. There was nowhere to run at the moment.

Brody glanced at the van he'd seen following the marshal's vehicle. "You're going to lose the prosecutor's car if you don't hurry."

"We know where he's going. Even if we're wrong, it's being tracked. No, you're the reason we doubled back. Your car is being towed as we speak. There'll be no trace of you."

"How did you know I was inside?"

"We bugged Jefferson's house and have been listening in on his conversations. We've gotten some good info, but today was the best because you're going to tell me where you stashed Ms. Jackson."

"You think?" Brody's gun was holstered at his side. Grabbing it and firing it before both men shot him was impossible. He wasn't a quick draw, just a precise shooter.

"Yes. It's over for her. I'll promise you one thing. If you tell me now rather than after I torture you, I'll make sure she dies fast. She won't even know what hit her. But if you make me draw this whole ordeal out, I'll make sure she dies slowly and painfully. The same goes for you."

"And once I tell you, what guarantee do I have you'll keep your word? I've heard you enjoy killing."

Mankiller grinned, a sinister expression that wordlessly confirmed the rumors circulating about him. "My word."

Brody laughed, relieving the tension that had a chokehold on him. But only for a second.

Mankiller's face firmed into a deadly look, and the assassin closed the short space between them bringing the back of his hand across Brody's face. "That's for your disrespectful attitude."

Pain tumbled around inside Brody's head. His ears rang, and the taste of blood coated his lips.

"Let's go. We're gonna leave a little message for Jefferson. He may not be as safe as he thinks. Your dead body in his bed will get that message across."

Arianna sat in the telephone company's truck with Gus driving. Going up and down the streets around Jefferson's house had produced nothing. No Brody. No car he'd driven. Arianna's concern mushroomed. Every nerve shouted that something was wrong.

"I don't see how we missed him. There's really only one direct route from here to Dan's place. We didn't see him on the road." Arianna sat behind Gus with Charlie in the front passenger seat. The only way for her to look out was the windshield and part of Charlie's side window that his body didn't block, but they had all been looking for the white Chevy.

"What do we do now?" Gus asked, the truck idling a few houses down from the prosecutor's.

"Maybe the man is there and can tell us when Brody

left," Arianna said and finished piling her hair up then putting on the hard hat.

"No way," Charlie said between clenched teeth.

"The street is deserted. It's early. We're in disguise and we all have vests on as well as hard hats."

Charlie shoved his door open. "I'll go to the house and check around. You two stay here. If I have to I'll ring the doorbell and pose as a telephone repairman."

"No, we need to park in front and really appear as repairmen. We're dressed for the part. Besides, I'm not sitting here and waiting. I don't have a good feeling about this." As the truck crept forward, Arianna pointed toward the prosecutor's place. "There's a van in the driveway. I've seen it somewhere. What if some of Rainwater's thugs have Brody and Mr. Jefferson? If we sit here having a little discussion about it, they could be murdered by the time we make a move. I won't lose him. It's not up for any more debate." She withdrew her gun. "If I have to, I'll go alone."

Charlie glared at her. "Girl, you're stubborn."

"She's got a point." Gus increased his speed until he was at the house and parked the truck along the curb.

Arianna crawled over a few boxes of equipment and put her hands on the back doors to open them.

"Hold on. The least you can do is wait and walk between us. We'll come around like we're checking on something in the back and you can get out then." Charlie threw a frown over his shoulder before he climbed from the truck.

A few seconds later, Arianna hopped down to the street, her gun back in her pocket with her hand on it. "Let's go. From the street about the only house that has a vantage point to see Mr. Jefferson's place is right across the road from him. Thick vegetation blocks the other neighbors. That'll shield us some while we snoop around."

"When we find Brody, he is going to chew us up and spit us out for putting you in jeopardy," Charlie said.

"You haven't. I would have gone by myself. You're protecting me."

Sandwiched between Gus and Charlie, with her gaze trained on the house, especially the windows which were mostly shuttered, Arianna went down the drive toward the back of the two-story house. At the van Charlie signaled Gus to go around one way while he and Arianna circled it in the other direction. She tried the van's door. It was locked. She pressed her face against the dark window and saw some rope and a couple of guns down on the floor.

"Something is wrong. Even if Brody isn't here, the prosecutor might be in trouble."

"Let's go inside." Charlie removed his set of picks and made his way to the back door, which protected him from prying neighbors.

Arianna withdrew her gun from her pocket with Gus doing likewise. They stood guard while Charlie worked on the lock then opened the door into the kitchen.

Mankiller's fist connected with Brody's jaw. Again and again, knocking him farther into a desk chair in what must be Jefferson's office. The other thug worked to tie Brody's hands behind his back.

For a second Mankiller paused as he switched fists. Stars swam before Brody's eyes. Krasnov yanked the ropes around Brody's wrists so tight his blood flow was cut off, and the ends of Brody's fingers began to tingle.

"That was just me letting off some steam because you sent me on a merry chase up north." Mankiller stepped away and pulled a switchblade from his pocket. "What I'd really like to use is this."

"Who's the mole in the Marshals' office?" Brody asked, through swollen lips.

"Wouldn't you like to know?" Mankiller flicked his attention to his partner working on tying Brody's legs. "Make sure his feet are bound tight, too." When his gaze reconnected with Brody's face, he grinned that sinister smile that turned a person's blood to ice. "I'll tell you right before you die. That is if you don't test my patience. Now you tell me. Where is Ms. Jackson?"

Arianna heard the noise—flesh hitting flesh—followed by a man saying something. She only caught a couple of the words, but the sound of her name confirmed her sense of danger. Whether it was Brody, the prosecutor or both being tortured, she didn't know. She caught Charlie's attention then Gus's and gestured toward the hallway where another male voice responded to the first one. Brody. For a second, relief washed through her until the sound of flesh hitting flesh began echoing again, filling Arianna with anger and concern.

Gus indicated he would check the other part of the house while she and Charlie found Brody and the man with the coarse voice. Memories of when she had interrupted Rainwater interrogating Thomas Perkins flashed into her mind. Perkins ended up dead.

Please, Father, keep Brody safe.

Arianna sneaked down the hallway toward a room at the end. The feel of her Glock in her hand gave her comfort. This would end better than with Perkins. Surprise was on their side. When she came to the door into the room, her position afforded her a clear sight to what was going on, and her blood boiled. Brody's face was worse than after he encountered the man outside the cabin. Two men towered over Brody who was tied to a chair. The smaller one, Stefan Krasnov, held a gun but his arm was straight at his side, the barrel pointed at the floor.

Thank You, God.

Then Arianna swung her attention to the large, bulky man with short, dark hair. He clasped a switchblade in his hand, which accounted for a thin line sliced across Brody's neck. The wound bled down his front.

"Tell me where she is and this will end quick." The big man pointed at Brody's face with the knife. "Do you need more motivation?"

Brody's response was a glare.

Arianna shoved down the anger rising in her. It could hinder her efficiency. She looked at Charlie and indicated two, then pointed in the direction she wanted him to go when they entered the room.

Charlie nodded, his gun up.

Using her fingers, she counted to three, then swung into the office. "Drop your weapons," she said in the deadliest voice she could muster.

She cocked her gun, ready for the men to resist. The large man, the one she had her Glock trained on, whirled, rage mottling his face. Mankiller glanced from her to Charlie, who pointed his weapon at Krasnov's chest.

Mankiller started to bring his arm up and back, as though to throw the knife.

"I'll shoot you before it leaves your hand. Drop the knife."

The thud from Krasnov tossing his gun on the floor resonated through the air—a sweet sound. Now if only Mankiller would do the same.

"Now," she clipped out.

Indecision warred in Mankiller's face for a moment, then a noise from the hallway pulled his attention away from her.

"Good thing I brought a couple of pairs of handcuffs along. Looks like we'll need them," Gus said as he came into the office.

Mankiller released the knife, which fell to the floor.

"Kick it away." Arianna didn't drop her vigil and wouldn't until these two were behind bars.

"You, too. Kick the gun away," Charlie said, next to Arianna.

"Gus, this would be a great time to use those handcuffs. Brody?" It took all her willpower not to go to him. Not until the two thugs were secured.

"I've been through worse." His words sounded garbled from his swollen, cut lips.

After both men were handcuffed, Arianna made sure Charlie and Gus had their weapons on the pair before she put hers back in her pocket, then rushed to untie Brody. As soon as she freed his hands, she turned to his legs and undid the rope about them while he used his shirt to help stop the bleeding at his neck.

"Be right back. I'm going to get you something better to use." Arianna hurried to the kitchen and grabbed a towel then looked around for a first aid kit. Nothing.

After she returned with the dishtowel, she went from bathroom to bathroom until she found some items to take care of his injuries. She knew he would refuse to go to the hospital until after she had testified.

When she came back into the office, Charlie had used the rope to tie the two men together on the floor. "Where's Gus?"

"Getting the rest of the rope in their van. They won't get away until we can call the police to come pick them up." Charlie tightened the loops around both Mankiller and Krasnov's legs, making it difficult for them to roll or stand up.

"They look like mummies made out of rope," she said and bridged the distance between her and Brody.

"I think that's appropriate." Brody tried to stand and swayed.

Arianna steadied him. "Is there any chance I can talk you into going to the hosp—"

"Not a snowball's chance in the Mojave Desert."

"That's what I thought. I've got gauze to wrap around your neck."

"You're not going to make *me* look like a mummy, are you?"

She laughed. "I'll pass. We don't have the time. I'll patch you up the best I can and the second I have testified, you're going to the hospital. No arguments."

"I'm fine—"

"If you could see your face right now, you wouldn't be saying that." She helped him to a loveseat and sat down next to him. "Now this may sting some."

"Not as bad as before, when you used patching me up to take out your frustration because we didn't give ourselves up to Mankiller in the forest."

"True. This'll be a piece of cake." Arianna opened an antiseptic swab and as gently as she could, started taking care of the worst first—the cut on his neck. The sight of Brody, battered and cut, knotted her stomach. All because he was protecting her.

The two assassins lay trussed on the floor while Charlie and Gus anchored them to the massive mahogany desk nearby so they couldn't scoot to the door.

"You aren't going to make it. You've got a large bounty on your head," Mankiller said with a cackle.

Charlie took the towel Brody had used and stuffed it into Mankiller's mouth. "There's no reason we have to put up with his ravings."

Ten minutes later Arianna held on to Brody, and they all headed for the truck.

"As soon as we get to the courthouse and inside, Charlie, call the police on those two guys in Jefferson's house. I'll tell the prosecutor what happened so he'll know." Brody hoisted himself into the back of the phone truck.

Arianna climbed into the back with him while Gus drove and Charlie sat where he had before.

The former FBI agent tossed a phone repairman's uniform for Brody to Arianna. "He needs to put it on."

She started to help Brody when he grasped her hands and said, "I can do it myself. I'm not an invalid."

She frowned. He'd allowed her to hold him as they'd walked to the truck, which surprised her. The closer they had come to the vehicle the stronger Brody appeared as though he'd used the trek to regain what he needed to finish his job.

"Fine." She turned her back on him and gave him privacy while Gus pulled away from the curb.

Every muscle tightened into a hard ball as Arianna stared out the windshield and into the right side mirror as they traveled toward the courthouse. The traffic picked up as the truck neared downtown. The hammering of her heartbeat increased, too.

Dressed in his uniform, Brody sat behind Charlie and kept an eye on the left side mirror out front. "When we pull up to the service entrance, we need to act as if we're telephone repairmen. I'm sure there's someone watching. We'll take out equipment to carry inside, but make sure you can get to your weapon fast. Without making it too obvious we're guarding you, Arianna, you'll be in the middle. Gus, you'll be on one side. You two are almost the same height. I want them to think she's a man. The moustache should help."

Arianna removed it from her pocket and used facial glue to put it on. "Is it on straight?"

Brody nodded, a smile lighting his eyes. "You don't look half-bad in a moustache."

"That's just what a gal wants to hear," she said with a chuckle. The act of laughing eased some of the tension in her body.

He winked at her. "I aim to please."

The heat of a blush moved up her neck and onto her face. She rarely flushed. She'd learned with three older brothers not to. It only made their teasing worse. That Brody could get her to blush only reinforced the effect this man had on her. But before her doubts and regrets about her life to come took over, she pushed them away. If she had thought of not going into WitSec after testifying, what Mankiller had said earlier about a bounty on her head clinched it. She couldn't risk hurting the people she loved—including Brody.

Gus pulled up to the service entrance. Both men in the front climbed from the truck and opened the back doors. Arianna and Brody hopped down, along with the equipment that would make their disguise believable. Together they strode to Pete's entrance. He passed them through, giving them badges to wear. Not a word was exchanged except what was necessary. Gus cased the right side of the hall while Brody the left. Because Charlie was taller, he peered over Arianna and kept an eye out in front as well as behind them.

Arianna stuck her hand into her pocket with her gun and clasped its handle. Brody slowed his step as they neared the elevator and paused, waiting until they could ride it alone. But at the last moment a man stopped the doors from closing. When they reopened, two men entered the elevator. Brody fixed his gaze on the one closest to him while Gus checked out the other rider.

Sweat coated Arianna's forehead and upper lip. Her pulse rate accelerated. When the doors slid open on their floor, for a few seconds her feet were rooted to the ground. Brody touched her arm, and she moved forward. The courtroom where the trial was taking place was only yards away. Two guards stood at the double doors. What if one or both of them were killers?

Another couple of steps and a commotion at the end of the hallway riveted the attention of the few people in the hallway. In their planning for this, Brody had stipulated that Charlie be the one in their group to check out anything that might be considered a diversion while Gus and he kept to the plan—moving forward with Arianna, scanning their designated area.

"A man and woman fighting. The woman slapped the man. Two men pulled them apart," Charlie said matter-of-factly.

Staged? Arianna's heartbeat continued to thump rapidly against her chest.

As they neared the door, Brody and Gus withdrew their badges and IDs. "We're delivering a witness. Arianna Jackson. Mr. Jefferson is expecting her."

Each guard scrutinized the identification then looked them all up and down. Arianna removed the moustache and hardhat, shaking out her long silver-blond hair.

"Just a moment." One guard went into the courtroom.

A rivulet of sweat trickled down into her eye. Her three protectors squeezed in close, forming a semicircle around her while panning the long hallway. The hairs on the back of her neck rose.

The guard came back with Mr. Jefferson who smiled at her. When he looked at Brody, the prosecutor's forehead creased. "What happened?"

"I'll tell you after she testifies."

"She is to come in with her escort," the prosecutor said to the two men on guard at the door.

The guard to her right ran the wand down Gus's length and his gun set it off.

"We're all carrying our weapons," Brody said to the man. "She's under protection of the U.S. Marshals Service. Myself and state trooper Gus Calloway must be by her side."

Both guards looked at Mr. Jefferson. He nodded his agreement.

Back at the house, Charlie had said he would like to stay in the hallway and keep an eye on the courtroom from out there.

As the guard started to wave the wand down Arianna, she reached in and removed her gun. "I'd like it back when I leave."

The guard began to argue with her.

"I'll take her weapon when we leave." Brody stepped forward with Arianna.

The guard frowned. "Fine," he said and moved out of their way into the courtroom.

Everyone turned to look at her, dressed as a telephone repairman with two men at her side, one with a face of a fighter after a tough bout.

Brody leaned close and whispered, "Go get him. I'll be here when you're finished."

Brody listened to her testimony and his respect for her grew even more. Arianna's integrity and straightforwardness were so refreshing. The sacrifices she'd made and would make increased his admiration many times over. He cared about her more than he ever thought possible.

He love—

No, he couldn't go there. She would be gone tomorrow. He couldn't walk away from his job. He made a difference. He—

"Thank you for testifying, Ms. Jackson. You are free to go," the judge said, signaling Brody and Gus next to him to stand.

The next stop was to deliver her to the U.S. Marshals office. Charlie was to notify them and tell Brody's boss what they suspected about a mole—they had ruled him out. At least they could work with him and hand Arianna over to the two marshals who were to escort her to her new home, wherever that was to be. Although he didn't think it was Ted or Carla, he didn't want them involved in case he was wrong. He suspected it had been Mark, with all his debts.

As Arianna stepped down from testifying and walked toward the gate that separated the public gallery from the trial participants, she looked right at Rainwater. She didn't back down when the man's eyes narrowed. A tic twitched in his jaw.

When Arianna saw Brody, she beamed, her eyes dancing as though she felt free for the first time in days. And yet, she would never totally be. His throat closed when he thought of her flying away to some unknown location. He swallowed several times.

"Let's go. I need some fresh air," she said when she approached Brody.

He took up her left side while Gus fell into step on her right. A guard opened the double doors, and they went into the corridor. The guard passed Arianna's gun to Brody. As he suspected, his supervisor stood with Charlie and two other men wearing their Deputy U.S. Marshal badges. The rest of the hallway was empty.

Arianna slanted a look toward Brody. "Who are the two with your boss?"

"The marshals who will take over for me. They'll process you and settle you in your new home."

"So all this is over." Emotions flitted across her face—from relief to sadness to resignation.

"Almost." Brody continued toward the group.

Nearby, a door opened. A police officer stepped into the hall. The ding of the elevator sounded at the other end. Brody glanced toward it to see who was getting off. Empty.

In that second he swiveled toward the police officer as the man drew his gun and aimed it at Arianna. The blast of the weapon shook the air at the same time

Brody threw himself in front of Arianna. The bullet ripped into his arm then another struck him. Blackness engulfed him.

With a third shot, Brody collapsed to the floor. Arianna went for her Glock in her pocket. It wasn't there! Brody still had it.

A barrage of gunfire went off around Arianna, all directed at the police officer by a door a few yards from her. He staggered back, collapsed against the wall and slid down to the floor. The gun he'd used to shoot at her dropped from his hand.

While pandemonium broke out around her, Arianna fell to her knees next to Brody. *He can't be dead. He can't be.*

Everything around her faded from her consciousness. All she cared about was Brody. With a trembling hand, she checked his pulse at his neck. Beneath her fingertips she felt one beat.

She looked up and shouted, "Call 911." His vest had stopped the second bullet.

The two marshals along with Brody's supervisor came to her side. "You've got to leave. Now," the blond one said, grasping her arm to help her to her feet.

She fought him. "I'm not leaving him. Get him some help."

The second marshal took Arianna's other arm. "They'll take care of him. You can't stay. Too dangerous."

"I don't care." She tried to wrench herself from their hold.

Their grip tightened about her. One thrust his face into hers, demanding her full attention. "But we do. It's our job to get you out of here in one piece."

Tears burned her eyes. "I can't leave him. He's shot."
Because of me.

The marshal in her personal space moved away enough for her to see Gus and Charlie with Brody. "He'll get the help he needs. Now let's go."

Charlie glanced up at her and tipped his head toward her.

Her chest hurt so much it was as though she'd been shot, not Brody. She couldn't take in enough oxygen. Her lungs were on fire. "Please, I need to stay. Make sure he'll be all right." His arm had been a bloody mess and that was all that occupied her mind.

"Go now and I'll see what we can do later," the blond marshal said, a look in his eyes that told her he understood.

She nodded. As she strode toward the elevator, she looked back again and saw Brody move. Her heart cracked. The farther away from him she went the more it ripped until it seemed to be in two pieces—one moved forward with her, and the other stayed behind with him.

"I won't leave Anchorage until I see Brody. You all owe me that. He put himself in front of a bullet for me. I can't walk away without thanking him, and making sure with my own eyes that he's all right." Arianna paced the conference room at the U.S. Marshals office.

"I'll get a message to him. You can write one, and I'll make sure he gets it." Supervisory Deputy U.S. Marshal Walter Quinn sat at the table with the other two marshals now responsible for her.

She stopped, balling her hands at her sides. "No. I won't go until I see him. I'm losing everything. The least you all can do is give me this."

"Fine, I'll arrange it tomorrow morning," Marshal Quinn said in a tight voice.

The stress knotting her insides unraveled some. She'd be able to thank him. To see him one last time. Say goodbye. She took the seat nearest her. "What's being done about the leak in this office?"

"We're wading through the information you all gave us and we're interrogating Boris Mankiller and Stefan Krasnov. We'll give the first one a deal that'll be hard to refuse if he gives up the person responsible for the leak."

"Have you identified all the people found at the cabin and the surrounding area?"

"Yes, and one was Kevin Laird. The person not far from him worked for Rainwater. We're not sure the fire was deliberate. There's evidence it was started by a cigarette. Kevin smoked. We have theorized that he was smoking when he was killed by Rainwater's man. It looks like his throat was cut. From the way the bodies were laid out, it seems that Rainwater's guy was trying to put out the fire, but somehow the flames engulfed him."

"Probably not long after, Kevin notified Mark Baylor he was coming back to the cabin." Arianna rose again, too restless to sit long.

Marshal Quinn's eyes grew round. "We thought it was Baylor, with the kind of debt he had."

"The more I think about this the more I think it was Kevin, not Mark. When we were looking into each marshal's background, I noticed Kevin's brother was in the military here. He works in supplies at the base. I also read there have been some supplies missing over the past year—weapons. One of the things Rainwater deals in is arms. Kevin wanted this assignment. When he first came to the office in Anchorage, he told everyone he was there to be near his brother, but I think it was more than that. Because your agency staff is small, you work with all the law enforcement groups in the area. Not a bad person to have on your payroll if you're a criminal like Rainwater."

"Then why would Rainwater have him killed?"

Arianna gripped the back of the chair. "I don't think Rainwater wanted Kevin found out. It would give him a chance to turn on him. Maybe Kevin's usefulness had come to an end. I imagine it won't take too long for the military police to find the person responsible for the missing weapons. Kevin's brother may even be dead by now. Things are falling apart for Rainwater. He's getting desperate, especially because he's probably facing life in prison."

A frown slashed across Marshal Quinn's mouth. "We need evidence. Even with the man dead, I can't function if there's any chance a mole is in my department."

"You can get it. Dig into his financial records. Kevin, in all his youthfulness, was smart. His major in college was finance. He hid his money well, but with time you have the resources to find where he buried the money Rainwater paid him. Also, if his brother isn't dead, he'll be an asset." She began pacing again. "But the most telling thing was that Mark let the assailants into the cabin. He wouldn't have if Kevin had given him the signal indicating he was being forced. Kevin never did. When I looked at the suspected marshals from all angles, that was what made me think it could be Kevin. It would have been hard to jump Kevin outside unless he was expecting someone. Shooting him yes, but not up close and personal with a knife."

Ted came into the conference room. "Brody is out of surgery and the jury is out on Rainwater."

A pounding behind her eyes intensified. "I should have been at the hospital," she said more to herself. Then louder, she asked, "The defense didn't have too many witnesses?"

"No. Three, then each attorney gave their closing remarks." Ted studied her. "Brody will be all right. The doc said the bullet that hit his vest cracked a rib, the one that grazed his head didn't really hurt him except to leave a scar. And the doctors were able to repair his arm. They feel he'll regain full use of it in time."

Arianna massaged her temples. "Thanks, Ted." She swept her gaze from one marshal to the next. "I'm tired and would like to rest."

They all scrambled to their feet as if they were remiss for keeping her so long.

"We have a place here for you. We don't want to move you but once. That'll be tomorrow morning." Marshal Quinn waved for her to go ahead of him out of the conference room.

All she wanted was peace and time by herself. She knew she wouldn't sleep until she saw Brody alive. There would be plenty of time in her lonely future to sleep.

In an office where they had set up a cot for her, she sat and stared at the floor. *God, I'm Yours. Whatever You have in store for me in this new life, I'll do it the best I can. Thank You for saving Brody. I don't know what I would have done if he'd died because of me.*

The next morning, the two marshals who were taking her to her new home escorted her to a car. The blond one opened the back door for her, and she started to climb inside when she saw Brody sitting in the backseat. She'd thought they would take her to the hospital.

"What are you doing here? You're supposed to be laid up in bed." She smiled and slid in beside him, wanting so badly to take him into her embrace, hold him and never let go. She stayed where she was, clasping her hands tightly together in her lap.

"I broke out. At least temporarily, with Walter's help." Brody gestured toward the driver in the front seat.

She drank in the wonderful sight of him, battered but alive. His left arm was in a sling, a white bandage on the side of his head. "You should be in the hospital." The bruises from Mankiller the day before had swollen one eye and his lips, with a cut across the bottom one.

"I heard you demanded to see me before you left." His mouth curved into a smile for a few seconds, a gleam sparkling in his eyes. "It was too dangerous to take you to the hospital. I know how stubborn you can be, and even if they tried to take you away, I was afraid you would evade your protective team and come anyway to the hospital. So I told them I would come to you. Did you write a letter to your parents?"

She fumbled for her purse, her hands shaking. "Yes, and one to each of my brothers. I appreciate you delivering them to my family. That means so much to me, but…" Her throat swelled, making it difficult to say what was in her heart.

"I'm glad to do it. I'll have some time to. It'll be a while before I'm fully recuperated to work again. I'll probably pester the doctor weekly until I can go back to my job."

"You enjoy your work like I did."

"It's all I know really, and despite how I look, this last assignment turned out a success. On the way over here my boss got a call. The jury came back half an hour ago with a guilty verdict for Rainwater. Also, Walter told me they arrested Kevin's brother in the late hours of the night. He was hiding from Rainwater's men. He'll testify to what he knows about the man's weapons trafficking. He'd been working for him for several years, even recruited Kevin for Rainwater, but when he heard Kevin died at the cabin, he knew he was next. You were right. I was still thinking it was Mark."

"Praise God everything is wrapping up—except for Esther," Arianna said. "Marshal Quinn told me they still haven't found her or her body." She didn't want to talk about the case, but there was something about Brody, a restrained, aloof posture, that told her anything else would be met with silence.

"No, and they may never. But Rainwater's organization is beginning to unravel. Even Stefan Krasnov is making a deal with the prosecutor."

"Not Mankiller?"

"I guess he'll be loyal to the end." Brody began telling her about the fake police officer that tried to kill her yesterday.

She heard his words, but they barely registered in her mind. She wanted to tell him she loved him and beg him to come with her. But she wouldn't. She couldn't ask him to give up his life as she had to. It was too hard for a person. He deserved better.

She glanced around and noticed they were pulling up to a private hangar. "I guess it's time for me to go— wherever. I—I—" she cleared her throat "—want to thank you for saving me several times. You took a bullet for me. That—"

He put his fingers over her mouth. "It's my job. You know it. You're a bodyguard."

His touch melted the defenses she was desperately trying to shore up. She wanted so much more. "No, you went beyond your job. You and I both know that. You'll always have a special place in my heart." That was the closest she would come to telling him how she felt in person. When her door opened, she peered over her shoulder at the blond marshal. "Just a minute."

"I'll walk you to the plane," Brody said in a thick voice. He swallowed hard.

"No. It's bad enough you escaped the hospital. This is goodbye. I've never worked with someone so professional and dedicated as you." Arianna leaned forward and gently took his face in her hands, aware of his injuries. She whispered her mouth over his, again aware of his wounds. She found a place on his cheek that looked relatively safe to kiss and she did, then pulled away, clambered from the car and hurried toward the airplane. She wouldn't cry until she was inside. She didn't want him to see her tears.

Brody watched her go and wanted to go after her. He wouldn't. What they had experienced was surreal. She'd begin a new life; he'd go back to his old one. Life would continue.

He settled his hand on the seat next to him. His fingers encountered the envelopes she'd given him. The top one had his name on it. He tore it open, not wanting to read it. But he knew he had to. It was her last communication with him.

A short note greeted him. All it said was, "I love you, Brody. Have a great life. You'll always be in my heart. Arianna."

He looked up to see the small plane with her on it rise into the air. She'd taken his heart with her.

The sound of a car coming toward her small ranch drew Arianna to the door of her barn in Wyoming. A green Jeep barreled down the gravel road toward her house. She didn't recognize the car—none of her neighbors or friends in town had that color Jeep.

She grabbed her rifle and waited in the barn entrance to see who got out of the vehicle. It could be a buyer for one of her horses, but she wouldn't take any chances. She'd been in Wyoming for nine months, and she had started to do well with her stock of horses. Although the winter had been particularly tough and very lonely, she might be able to make a go at this after all. Getting involved with the playhouse this spring as a makeup artist for its productions had helped, but nothing would heal the deep loneliness she experienced when she allowed herself to think about Brody or her family she'd left behind.

The Jeep came to a stop near the front of her one-story farmhouse. Its door opened. She lifted her rifle in case it was a stranger. She didn't know if she would ever feel totally safe—not after all that had happened in Alaska.

When the person stood, she saw him. Brody. Shock held her immobile for a few seconds before she lowered her rifle and ran toward him.

Closer to him, she slowed. Why was he here after

all this time? Maybe something was wrong. With her parents? Rainwater?

"What brings you to these parts? And more important, how did you find me?" She stopped a few feet from him, the feeling of vulnerability swamping her.

"You've brought me here and I pulled a few strings with Walter's help. It's a good thing you put me on your list to join you if I chose to or no matter how much I pleaded I would never have gotten this far."

She'd remembered doing it before leaving the office in Alaska, thinking she might say something to him at the hospital. Give him a choice of coming with her. But she'd changed her mind so she hadn't thought anything about it—until now. "Is something wrong?"

"No, everything is great now that I'm here." He slammed the door and strode to her. "I thought once I got better and was back at my job that I would be fine. I'd convinced myself that what we had between us wasn't reality. That I didn't need you. That my job was all I needed."

Arianna's heartbeat kicked up a notch. "And it isn't?"

"No. It took me five months of physical therapy and desk duty before I was allowed back in the field. But it was never the same. No matter how hard I tried I couldn't get you out of my head or heart. I began to hate going to work. That never has happened to me. I'd thought when I gave your parents the letters I would feel better. That made it worse."

Her thundering heartbeat clamored in her head. "Why?"

"Your dad cried when he read your letter. I felt very uncomfortable witnessing that. I tried to leave, but they insisted I stay with them for a few days and tell them all about my time with you. I did. When I left, they gave me some letters for you. I took them, not wanting to tell them I didn't have a way to get them to you." He halted for a few seconds and sucked in a deep breath. "Leaving them was hard, but not as hard as watching you fly out of my life. I love you. I've left the U.S. Marshals Service. I'm not leaving here until I convince you to marry me." His intense gaze seized hers.

"So you're physically all right now?"

He nodded. "I wouldn't have been able to go back to work if not."

"Good." Arianna threw herself at him, winding her arms around him. "I didn't want to hurt you. The last time I saw you I was nearly too afraid to even kiss you goodbye."

"And if I remember, it wasn't even what I would call a proper goodbye kiss."

"How about a proper welcome one?"

His embrace caged her against him as he slanted his mouth over hers. She poured nine months of bottled up emotions into the kiss, taking and giving at the same time.

When he pulled a few inches away, he captured her face in his palms. "I love you, Arianna."

"My new name is Kim Wells."

He chuckled, laugh lines at the corners of his brown eyes. "I love you—Kim."

"I love you," she murmured right before she planted another kiss on his mouth.

* * * * *

Trust in the Lord with all thine heart; and lean not unto thine own understanding. In all thy ways acknowledge him, and he shall direct thy paths.
—*Proverbs 3:5–6*

BODYGUARD REUNION

To my husband, Mike. I love you.

ONE

Her first day on the job as a bodyguard for the Zimmermans and Chloe Howard already wanted to quit. In a limousine heading for the Dallas Community Christian Church, Chloe sat next to her client, Mary Zimmerman. Across from her, T. J. Davenport guarded Mary's husband, Paul. If Kyra Hunt, her employer at Guardians, Inc., had told her she would be working with T. J. Davenport, she would have declined the assignment. Instead, she would be around the man for the entire month of the Zimmermans' book tour.

Chloe kept her gaze trained out the side window, but occasionally felt the brush of T.J.'s dark gaze. He was probably trying to figure out how to back out of this assignment, too.

She'd worked with him nine years ago when he was a Secret Service agent and she was a police officer for the Dallas Police Department. From the beginning she'd been attracted to him, and when they had started dating, the attraction had grown into love—or so she'd thought. But his job had taken him away, and now she'd discovered he was back in Dallas, no longer a Secret Service agent.

The limo driver turned onto the road that curved up to the covered vestibule of a megachurch, where they would exit the vehicle. People crammed the entrance, waiting for the couple to arrive. Even on this windy, cold day, a large crowd was here, hoping to get a glimpse of the couple whose book, *Taking Back America*, had rocketed to number one on the *New York Times* bestseller list. This was the third such appearance by the Zimmermans, who wrote about putting God back into daily life. Off-duty police had roped off a path for the Zimmermans to the double glass doors, and each officer had taken up a post every few feet to hold the throng back.

Was it enough? Whoever had targeted Mary and Paul at their second stop in the book tour could be in the multitude waiting for them to climb from the car. So far, no description had been obtained of the person or persons in Paris, Texas, who had thrown stink bombs into the gathering, scattering everyone. Mary had nearly been trampled before her husband had gotten to her. Knowing what Mary and Paul stood for and the effect it must have had on them tightened Chloe's gut. That incident had led to the Zimmermans' publisher hiring two bodyguards for the third stop and the rest of their book tour.

Chloe straightened, scanning the area through the windows while T.J. did the same, his large body poised and alert. The Zimmermans had only reluctantly agreed to protection, not totally convinced there was a threat against them. They'd always had dissenters and had even received hate mail. A particular nasty letter had arrived at their first stop in Longview, Texas, and might be tied to the incident in Paris.

Chloe had wanted to sneak the couple into the church through a back way, but the Zimmermans didn't want to go that far. They wanted to be accessible to the people who had come to hear them speak. She'd tried to convince the pair of the potential danger, and to her surprise, T.J. had agreed with her.

Their parting in the past had been intense, filled with anger and hurt. He'd wanted to continue with a long-distance relationship. She'd seen too many of those fail—like her parents' marriage with her dad in the navy and gone a good part of the year.

As she did a final check of the huge crowd before exiting the limousine, her gaze collided briefly with T.J.'s. Not one emotion showed on his face, creating what she had come to think of as his professional facade. Cold. Determined. At one time she'd known a side to him apart from work. His laughter and smiles had always fulfilled a need in her for more of that in her life. There had been little of that growing up with a mother who hadn't been happy her husband was gone so much.

Chloe had even begun to picture what it would be like married to him—the children they would have. She'd wanted a family since she'd worked as a teenager in the church nursery each Sunday. She'd fallen in love with caring for children. No, she wasn't going to think about what could have been with T.J. if circumstances had been different.

She quickly focused on Mary Zimmerman, who had insisted on being addressed by her first name. "We need to escort you inside as fast as we can. Keep moving. I'll be right behind you."

Dressed in a powder-blue suit with a pencil skirt,

Mary uncrossed her legs, her forehead crinkling. "But these people are out here because they want to hear us speak. The seating inside has been sold out for weeks. I can't ignore them when they took the time to come here."

"Someone in that crowd might want to harm you and your husband." T.J. slid closer to the door and gripped the handle. "Stink bombs may seem like a prank, but two people were hurt seriously enough to go to the hospital. Thankfully you all took care of those hurt, but if your husband hadn't gotten to you when he did, you might have needed to be hospitalized, too."

"But what if that was kids in Paris and our publisher overreacted? I know that sort of thing happened at my high school several times when I was a teenager." Paul Zimmerman took his wife's hand.

T.J. looked from Mary to Paul. "How about the threatening letter delivered to your hotel in Longview? Another teenage prank?"

Chloe swiveled her attention to T.J. He plowed his fingers through his thick, wavy black hair—one of the few habits she'd noticed before that indicated he was worried about something.

T.J. continued, "It described in detail what he wanted to do with you two, beginning with torture. That doesn't sound like a teenager. I've read some of your hate mail, and that one had a different feel to it."

He'd read some of the Zimmermans' hate mail? When? How had he gotten it? She'd been assigned this case only hours ago. Other than being apprised of what had happened in Longview and Paris, she had nothing else to go on. Not even the hate letter they'd received in Longview. Time had been limited when she had met with Kyra this morning.

The thought that T.J. knew more than she did irritated her, but mostly she felt she didn't have all the information to do the best job possible because this job had come up so suddenly. When this event was over, she would have a few choice words with the man. Just because he'd been the team leader on the one case they had worked on together didn't mean that was the situation now. The only way she could do this job was to be totally professional and an equal partner.

Paul frowned. "This is curtailing our mission to reach the masses as personally as we can, and that certainly isn't from behind bodyguards and police lines. They need to see we aren't afraid to fight for what is right."

"Honey, maybe that's the point of the threats. To keep us from connecting with the people." Even in the midst of a tense situation, a smile graced Mary's lips. "The Lord is our protection, but our publisher will cancel this tour if we don't agree to—" she waved her hand toward Chloe and T.J. "—them being our bodyguards. I think spreading our message is too important to cancel the tour."

A long sigh escaped Paul's lips. "Fine, but I'm having a talk with the publishing house after this is over with. Let's go."

Chloe studied T.J.'s reaction to the declaration, and not one emotion crossed his face. She'd worked with him and knew that expression, but she'd also seen its opposite. When he'd been waiting for a chance to protect someone on the level of the vice president and finally got his promotion, she wouldn't move to Washington to be with him. Anger, hurt and disappointment had swirled between them that day.

She'd had her reasons. He'd had his. They'd parted. After a few calls from T.J. trying to persuade her to come to Washington, she'd never heard from him again until this morning when Kyra had introduced her to her partner in this assignment.

Before he could catch her staring at him, Chloe busied herself with opening the door and exiting the limo. The wind whipped through her, its cold sting biting. She surveyed the crowd, looking for any potential threats. Too many people pressed together. Too many possibilities.

Cheers rose from the spectators, the din assailing Chloe's ears as the crowd closed in around the Zimmermans, who started toward the entrance. This beloved couple's message touched many people. Chloe herself was a fan of their grassroots movement to take back the family and this country. They were full of integrity, compassionate and straightforward in what was important. Who wouldn't believe in their ideas?

But someone out there wasn't a fan. And she knew firsthand how hate could fester, exploding outward to include everyone. She'd seen more than her share, to the point that she wondered how much longer she could do what she was doing. But this was what she was good at.

Chloe moved forward on Mary's right toward the massive double glass doors. T.J. took the left side of Paul, steering him through the people wanting to shake hands with the couple before they headed into the church.

Every sense on alert, Chloe kept her hand near her

holstered gun. Something didn't feel right. Or was she confusing this with an assignment she'd had a year ago under similar circumstances? Her shoulder still ached where she'd taken a bullet defending her client.

Mary had stopped and leaned close to an older woman, taking her hand. "I'll be praying for you and your family."

Tears glistened in the fiftysomething spectator's eyes. "That means so much to me. I don't know what else to do anymore."

"Praying is important. I'll be addressing some of the issues you're dealing with today. I know our talk will be piped out here for the people who couldn't get seats." Mary lifted the rope standing between her and the woman. "But I'm sure we can find one extra place for you."

Chloe inched closer to Mary, especially as the crowd surged forward with the vacant spot left by the lady. Several people nearby shouted various problems they were dealing with, but the words jumbled into incoherent sentences.

"We need to keep moving," Chloe whispered to Mary while her full attention remained fixed on the throng. "Your husband is at the door waiting."

Mary nodded and replied to a few close to her as she shuffled forward, shaking hands with as many as she could.

They were only yards away from the entrance now. The feeling of being watched tickled up Chloe's spine, leaving goose bumps in its wake. She'd learned not to ignore that sensation. She glanced back, but couldn't tell anything because everyone's eyes were on them.

Then a middle-aged man, going bald, pushed past

the off-duty officer and grabbed Mary, making her stop. "I want to sit inside, too. Take me."

Chloe stepped forward, putting herself between Mary and the man, forcing him to let go of her client and back away. Anger flashed across his face. Tension whipped down Chloe as others began to shout they wanted inside.

Mary smiled, although Chloe could see the corners of her mouth twitching from holding it in place. "I'm sorry. The fire codes are specific about how many people can be in the auditorium."

Finally, Mary and the older lady entered a large church foyer with lots of windows and skylights. Mary paused to talk to one of the coordinators to make sure someone took care of the lady and to see about letting the crowd outside stand in the foyer, where it was warmer.

Having no time to do a walkthrough beforehand, Chloe swept her gaze around her surroundings as she crossed the threshold, noting where everyone stood, where the doors and exit signs were, as the floor plan she'd seen indicated. "I don't think that's wise under the circumstances," she whispered to Mary, imagining the chaos that could cause.

The young coordinator called over an older gentleman, who must be the person in charge, and they talked together.

The man turned to Mary. "We'll try to accommodate as many as we can."

"Will they be able to hear our talk?"

"We can pipe your speech out into the foyer. But we can't fit everyone in here."

"I understand. I'd appreciate anything you can do

to make it better for the people outside. Bless you for trying." Mary made her way toward her husband, taking his offered hand.

The love that flowed between them made Chloe wonder when she had given up on her dream of having a family—a husband who loved her like that and at least two children. But everyone she'd dated since T.J. hadn't been right, especially her last boyfriend, Adam. He'd cheated on her. At least T.J. hadn't done that.

The noise of the crowd in the massive auditorium at the end of the lobby grew to a deafening roar the nearer they came. With every seat taken, there were over fifteen hundred cheering people here to listen to the Zimmermans. Chloe wouldn't relax until they were all back at the house where the couple was staying.

The young coordinator escorted the guest speakers toward the stage area. As the Zimmermans stepped out to greet the crowd, the people all rose, clapping and yelling. A wall of sound assaulted Chloe. As the audience finally quieted, Chloe stationed herself behind the Zimmermans, positioning herself so the lights didn't obscure her view of the spectators. Her quick glance took in where T.J. was. He tipped his head toward her, his signal he would take the left side of the auditorium while she cased the right. Even with her and T.J. each taking half the auditorium, it was hard to keep an eye on everyone since people crammed the place.

After the presentation by the Zimmermans, T.J. paced the room above the church auditorium like a bear he'd seen at the zoo. He should be used to waiting. It was a big part of his job, but this assignment was different—and all because Chloe Howard prowled the other side of the room. From the surprised look that had flashed across her face this morning before she masked it, he was sure she hadn't known he was the other bodyguard on this case.

In fact, he was positive she hadn't or she wouldn't have taken the case. Not after how they had parted nine years ago. He'd been falling in love with her when he'd been given a choice assignment to be part of the detail covering the vice president. He had been a Secret Service agent at the time, assigned to Dallas working counterfeiting cases and financial crimes, sometimes in coordination with the Dallas Police Department. He couldn't turn down a chance to move into the protection part of the United States Secret Service, a move that would make his career in the agency. He'd wanted Chloe to move to Washington and see if their relationship would grow into a lasting one. He'd known from his fellow agents how hard being a law enforcement officer could be on a marriage, and that a marriage would only survive if it was based on a deep friendship. He'd decided he would only marry once.

She wouldn't leave Dallas. Her widowed mother had been fighting cancer, going through chemo, and she'd needed Chloe. He'd understood that, but she also hadn't wanted to have a long-distance relationship. He'd realized it would be difficult, but he'd been willing to try it, even though he had trouble trusting others—collateral damage of his law enforcement days. He'd never found someone like Chloe. Was that the reason he'd decided to settle in Dallas when he'd left the Secret Service?

Now, having seen Chloe, he wondered at the wisdom of asking to team up with her, even though she was an excellent bodyguard. From working with her nine years ago on a counterfeiting case in conjunction with the Dallas police, he'd seen her dedication, and that had impressed him enough to persuade her to go out with him after their assignment was over.

He turned from watching her out of the corner of his eye and peered out the only window in the room that overlooked the church entrance hall. Finally the crowd was thinning and soon they could leave. He'd feel better when they were back at the couple's temporary residence, the house of one of their good friends who was on vacation, although T.J. could never totally let down his guard. The chances of something happening increased during transport from one place to another.

He was still amazed the Zimmermans had had to be convinced to have two bodyguards. Today, at their talk, he'd sensed a person in the audience calculating how to get to the pair, but he hadn't noticed anyone who stood out. He'd learned, though, not to ignore that gut feeling. It had saved his life several times.

The couple might think the past threats had been pranks. They hadn't been. He glanced at them, talking with the organizers of the event. When he'd insisted on bringing Mary and Paul into the church the back way, they had told him they were in the Lord's hands and were safe.

He'd believed in God fervently at one time. Now he was at a crossroads in his life, especially concerning the important aspects of life. He was good at guarding people, but he'd become jaded in his job. He needed something more. That was the reason he'd resigned from the Secret Service after fourteen years and approached Kyra Hunt about going into partnership with her and expanding Guardians, Inc. While he took this assignment with Chloe, Kyra would consider his proposition of taking the business to the next level.

He sensed Chloe advancing toward him, although her footsteps were quiet. He glanced over his shoulder, locking gazes with her. In the past those sea-green eyes had been warm with emotions developing between them. Now they were cold. Her demeanor was totally professional and reserved—at least where he was concerned. He had known going in that might be the situation, but he'd wanted the best female bodyguard as his partner. In that moment, though, he acknowledged he had wanted more. Were there lingering feelings?

A memory of their first kiss years ago taunted him, stirring emotions he'd tried to forget and thought he had. They hadn't been right for each other nine years ago. Why should now be any different?

"We should be able to leave in ten or fifteen minutes. I'd prefer to wait until most of the people have left before we do." T.J. assessed her long auburn hair pulled back in a ponytail and remembered a time when her hair had been chin length and straight. What else was different?

Chloe stiffened, but her expression remained blank. "Is there a problem?"

She released a long breath. "No, I agree with your plan, but before you whisk *my* client anywhere, please inform me of your intentions. If this is going to work, we'll need to be equal partners. A *team*." Emphasizing the last word, she looked him directly in the eye and held his gaze as though waiting for him to challenge that claim.

"I totally agree, and I'm sorry I acted without consulting you after their presentation. However, there may be times when it'll be necessary for one of us to act and then explain. The lobby is still full of people from the crowd outside." He refused to break visual contact.

Her chin tilted up a fraction, and she squared her shoulders even more. But the look in her eyes, a stormy green like the sky right before a tornado struck, mellowed. "I know the only time we worked together you were the team leader and used to giving orders. My first priority will be Mary Zimmerman. I was hired to protect her. You were hired to guard her husband. I've been working for Guardians, Inc., for four years. I'm not a novice anymore." The tense set to her body relaxed. "I've changed since we knew each other."

He had changed, too. He realized if they were together very long on this assignment they would have to discuss their parting nine years ago, but with one glance around the room, he knew this wasn't the time or the place. "I know you aren't. I've read over the assignments you've done this past year. I'm impressed. That's why I asked for you. I felt a woman would be better suited for guarding Mary, so I contacted Kyra." He wouldn't go into the details about the possibility of buying into a partnership with Kyra for Guardians, Inc. He wouldn't be part of Guardians, Inc., if he and Chloe couldn't at least call a truce between them.

"You know my boss?" Her body visibly relaxed.

"Yes, I've known her since the first time I lived here. We've kept in touch through the years." And he'd asked from time to time about Chloe. Another tidbit he wouldn't tell her.

Chloe peered out the window, confusion clouding her eyes for a few seconds. "She didn't tell me. I didn't even know you would be guarding Paul."

"I told her not to say so because there was little time to get someone and I didn't want you to refuse before meeting the Zimmermans. There's so much that's changed in nine years. I didn't want our past together to affect you taking the assignment."

She blinked several times.

"Their publisher didn't contact me about the job until late last night. So I went to Kyra early this morning and was glad to learn you were available."

"But—" she looked away again "—after what happened between us, I'm surprised."

A silence fell between them peppered with murmurs from Paul and Mary's conversation with the organizers. T.J. inched closer and lowered his voice. He touched her arm, not sure if she would yank away or not. She didn't. "We need to talk later. I don't want anything standing in the way of this partnership. I'm not the same man I was. Life has a way of redirecting your dreams."

Chloe opened her mouth, but instead pressed her lips closed before saying anything and fastened her attention out the window. An uncomfortable moment later, she said, "It looks like the crowd is gone. I'll feel better when we get them back to the house. Everything went well, but I couldn't shake…" Her eyebrows slashed downward.

"I got the feeling someone was out there watching the Zimmermans, waiting for the right moment."

She faced him. "I did, too, but then nothing happened, even with the last-minute change Mary insisted on with the crowd coming inside. I was beginning to wonder if my instinct was off. Generally, it isn't."

In that brief moment a connection sprang up between them as if their breakup had never occurred. "I don't think it is. Someone in the audience could have been casing the Zimmermans. Just because he did something at the first and second stops in the tour doesn't mean he will at this one. The security was tightened, and he might not have expected that."

Finally, as though she'd realized his hand was touching her, she stepped back. "You keep saying *he*. Is there a reason you think it's one man?"

He shook his head. "I need a way to refer to the person or persons since we don't have any names."

"I just want to make sure I know everything connected to this assignment. No clues to who is after them?"

"From what happened in Paris with the multiple stink bombs, I figure it's more than one person. But frankly, I know so little at this time." T.J. glanced at the pair they were guarding. "I'm concerned mostly about their lack of concern."

"It could lead to problems. Mary puts everyone else first."

"You know her?" T.J. kneaded his shoulder, aching from holding himself taut and ready to move at a second's notice. There was still tension with Chloe. He'd thought the past was just that—the past—that they could forge a working relationship because Chloe was good at her job.

"Not personally, but I know of her. I've read her books, and they have a great message. We need to put God's principles into action."

"In theory, the concepts they promote might work, but in practice we need more law enforcement officers and tougher laws." When he saw her forehead crease, he continued, "We should leave, but we'll talk later, and I'll make sure you know everything I do. There won't be any confusion with this assignment."

One of her perfectly arched eyebrows lifted, a smile flirting with her mouth. "Promise?"

He chuckled. "Yes, we made a good team once before. There's no reason why we can't now." Her smile gave him hope that they could at least work together.

"I suppose anything is possible."

"Let's get the Zimmermans to a more secure location. Okay?"

She nodded.

Turning toward the couple, T.J. said, "It's time for us to leave."

While the Zimmermans said goodbye to the organizers, T.J. withdrew his phone from his pocket and called the limo driver to pull the car around to the back exit. Now that the crowd was gone, the couple shouldn't mind going out that way. He let it ring five times, then it went to voice mail.

"The Zimmermans are ready to leave. We'll stay put until you call back." His grip on the cell tightened. That gut feeling he'd had earlier clamored against his skull, demanding to be heard.

Chloe watched him as he slipped his phone back into his pocket and evened out his expression. Although she wasn't as easy to read as in the past, it was clear when concern invaded her eyes.

He moved closer to her and whispered, "The driver didn't answer. I'm going out to the parking lot to see what has happened. You stay here and guard the Zimmermans. I'll call you and let you know what's going on. Lock the door after I leave."

He started to turn away, but she grasped his arm. "I won't open that door unless you tell me it looks like it's going to rain. Okay?"

"Yes."

She didn't release her grip. "Be careful. I don't have a good feeling about this."

Just like I don't. Which only reinforced the suspicion something was wrong.

Nodding, he strode toward the exit, ushering the two organizers out of the room in front of him. The sound of the lock clicking into place didn't quiet the alarms going off in his mind. He could think of a hundred reasons the driver hadn't answered the call—most of them bad.

He left the church through the back door, his gaze sweeping the area around him before he stepped out into the cold February day. A brisk wind blew from the west, slamming against his torso as he headed around the side of the church where the driver was supposed to have parked the limousine. Fifteen yards away, he spied the car where it should be.

The windows were darkened, so when T.J. stared into the vehicle, he couldn't see the driver. Anywhere, inside or out.

Then T.J. noticed the tire nearest him had been slashed. From where he stood he could see the back one, too. Flat. His stomach clenched. Adrenaline pumped through his body as he pulled his gun from his holster. While he scanned the parking lot, he made his way to the limo. His heartbeat picked up speed as adrenaline flooded his system.

He circled the limo quickly. Two more flat tires. No one hiding behind the car. When he returned to the driver's side, he yanked open the passenger door. No one hiding there, either. Then he turned his attention to the front. When T.J. opened the door, there was no sign of the driver or where he might be.

T.J. pushed a button on the side panel, then hurried to the back of the limo. When he lifted the trunk, his breath bottled in his lungs. He'd found the driver.

TWO

Chloe paced in the room above the auditorium. She should have heard from T.J. by now. This didn't bode well. Tension held her tighter with each minute that ticked away until she felt like a walking statue. When her cell rang, she came to a halt. It was T.J.'s phone calling.

"Yes?" she said with wariness. *Please let him be okay.*

"The driver was knocked out and locked in the trunk of the limousine. All the tires have been slashed. I'm coming into the church now with the driver. I wanted you to know what happened before I call the police." A slight breathlessness to his words indicated he was hurrying to get back to the room.

"I'll call. I know some people on the police force." She disconnected and immediately placed a call to a detective who was a friend and filled him in on where they were and what had happened, then she called for an ambulance.

A knock cut through the sudden silence in the room as Mary and Paul listened to Chloe's conversation with Detective Rob Matthews. Paul started for the door.

"Don't! Let me." Sliding her phone into her pocket, then drawing her gun, Chloe hurried to cut him off. He stopped, his eyes huge as he looked from her to Mary.

"There was a problem at the limo. Someone knocked out the driver and slashed the tires." Chloe clasped the handle and motioned for Paul and Mary to stand in the corner, out of the line of fire. When they had moved, she asked, "Who is it?"

"T.J. here. It looks like it's going to rain." His deep, husky voice penetrated the barrier of wood between them.

The smooth sound of his words sent relief through her—and something else, a flutter deep in her stomach. She dismissed the reaction, chalking it up to being glad he was all right. She couldn't afford to fall for T.J. again. She unlocked the door and swung it open while keeping her gun ready at her side.

T.J. helped the stunned driver into the room as Chloe shut the door and threw the lock—not that it would stop someone really determined to get inside. In fact, she could probably pick the lock in under a minute.

Mary rushed from the corner with Paul right behind her. When she reached the driver, she waved her hand toward the nearest chair. "I've had some first-aid training. Let me check him."

The Zimmermans tended to the man, who responded to Mary's questions about how he felt as she looked into his eyes, then examined the back of his head. When she probed with her fingertips, the young man winced.

"How long until the police and paramedics arrive?" T.J. asked Chloe, drawing her attention to him.

"I called a friend, Rob Matthews, who is on duty

and will send some patrol officers. He's on his way, too, but they'll get here first. Maybe ten minutes out. Does the driver know what happened?"

"He was groggy. I wanted to get in here before questioning him. I kept thinking it might have been a diversion."

"It's been quiet."

Mary crossed the room to the counter where there was a sink and wetted some paper towels. As she made her way back to the driver, Paul walked over to them, his color pale.

"What's going on?" His voice wavered.

"Not sure. At best, another harassment." T.J. started for the driver and Mary.

"And the worst?" Paul followed.

"The attacker is out there waiting to do something else, most likely to you and your wife."

T.J.'s declaration caused Paul to falter.

Chloe grasped his arm and steadied him. "That's why we're here. To protect you and Mary." She looked toward T.J. and was comforted he was her partner. He exuded a self-assurance that would keep the Zimmermans as composed as possible under the circumstances. She'd discovered that was important when events turned bad.

"What should we do?" Paul asked Chloe.

"Pray. The police are on the way. They'll check the surrounding area and the church. Right now it's best if we stay in here until we're given the all-clear sign from them." She schooled her voice into a calm, even tone.

"How are we getting back to the house?"

"I'll ask my detective friend to take us. The driver needs to be checked out by a doctor. The paramedics coming will take care of him. From the looks of it, he might have a concussion."

As T.J. paused next to the driver, Mary finished tending to the man with her limited resources. Chloe moved with Paul toward the trio. She needed to know what had happened to the driver.

"I think he'll be fine. He's coherent." Mary backed away while Paul wrapped his arms around her.

"Did you see who did this to you, Ben?" T.J. sat in a chair in front of the young man, whose dazed look had cleared.

Ben Johnson leaned against the table, cradling his head in one hand. "Not really. That parking space was one of the few left after I dropped y'all in front." Closing his eyes for a few seconds, he rubbed his fingers across his forehead. "I parked and sat in the car for a while before I decided to use the restroom. I came into the church, found the men's room then went back to the limo."

"Did you see anyone in the parking lot?"

"A large man came out of the restroom as I was going in, but otherwise no one else. I heard the general rumble from the auditorium and saw people down the hall toward the front of the church—I guess in the foyer."

"Can you describe the man coming out of the bathroom?" T.J. gripped the back of his chair.

"Big. Maybe six and a half feet. Dark hair. That's all I can remember. I wasn't really paying attention. The boss doesn't like us away from the limo for long. I was only gone five minutes." Ben swept his gaze across the group.

Chloe stepped next to T.J. "What happened when you went back to the car?"

"I saw the slashed tires on the left side and hurried to see how bad the damage was. All I could think was how mad my boss would be. The next thing I know someone hit me over the head. Everything is fuzzy after that. I vaguely remember being dumped in the trunk. I must have passed out."

"So you don't know where your attacker came from?" T.J. asked the driver, but he looked at Chloe.

She tore her gaze away and focused on Ben.

He squinted and stared off into space for a moment. "He must have come from behind the car next to the limo on the right side. I think."

"But you aren't sure?" Chloe asked as though she and T.J. had silently agreed to take turns with the questions.

"No. It happened fast."

"Can you describe the car on your right?" T.J. rose suddenly, invading her space.

Ben's eyes lit up. "Yes. I may not remember people, but I do remember what they drive. It was a red Mustang, last year's model. A beauty. The car gleamed."

"Anything else?" Chloe moved back several steps, her heartbeat increasing from T.J.'s nearness.

"There was a pine-tree air refresher hanging from the rearview mirror. I love the smell of pine."

Chloe's cell phone rang. She walked toward the window that overlooked the front of the church and answered a call from Rob. "What's going on?" Outside, three patrol cars pulled up to the entrance.

"The officers are there and will check out the church. I'll meet them there in ten with my partner.

They'll let me know when it's safe for you all to come out."

"Thanks. We're in the room above the auditorium in front. I'll be able to see you pull up."

T.J. joined her as she put her cell back into her pocket. He looked at the police fanning out and heading into the building. "We don't have much to go on."

"Do you think the driver could be involved?"

"I don't think he's lying. There are no big tells. But some people are quite good at lying."

His shoulder brushed against hers when he shifted. The casual touch zipped through her, making her acutely aware of the man beside her at the window—almost as if only days had passed since they had been together instead of years. It disconcerted her, and she had to fight to think what she needed to say. "So I'll have Kyra check the company and driver out. But I don't see how the description of the car next to the limo will produce anything."

"While you were on the phone, Ben remembered the last three numbers of the license plate. It's probably nothing, but we should tell your detective friend about the Mustang."

"In other words, we're no closer to who or why someone is after the Zimmermans. Ben referred to the assailant as 'he.' Does he think it was a man who attacked him?"

"I didn't ask. I will, but Ben is over six feet tall and a hefty guy. To knock him out and stick him into the trunk would take someone large and capable of managing that physically."

"The man from the restroom?"

T.J. shrugged. "As you said, we have little to go on."

A movement out of the corner of her eye caught her attention. A black Crown Vic drove into the parking lot and stopped next to one of the patrol cars. Not far behind the police was the ambulance that pulled up to the door to the church. "Rob and his partner are here as well as the EMTs. I told Rob where we were. He'll let us know when it's safe for us to come out of the room."

T.J. massaged his nape, a frown marring the hard planes of his face. Although he wasn't classically handsome, his strong features gave off an air of capability and confidence. On closer examination, she realized he must have broken his nose between the time they had been together and now. How had it happened? Had there been other injuries? She didn't want to care, but she did.

Before she became fixated on that, she swung toward the window and observed her friend entering the building. But every part of her was strongly aware of the man standing next to her, their arms only inches apart as they watched the same thing.

"When we get back to the house, I'll need to contact the Zimmermans' publisher," he finally said as all the police disappeared inside.

"Are you going to recommend that the couple cancel the rest of the tour?"

"Yes. Their message might be important, but not if they are hurt or killed."

"They feel this country is at a crossroads. One road holds destruction. The other is a chance for salvation. They're out there fighting for us to take the right path. I'm not sure they'll quit."

"Then we'll have to do what we can to protect them." He'd said *we'll*. She used to think of them in terms of we. She knew the danger of doing it now, but they had to form a solid partnership in order to protect the Zimmermans, who were clearly in danger. The more she and T.J. were a united front, the better Mary and Paul would be.

But at what cost to her feelings? When he'd left her to go to Washington, she'd been alone dealing with her mother and her chemo treatments. She'd missed her father, who had died two years before, and T.J. She'd never felt so alone. She couldn't go there again.

T.J. made his rounds of the two-story house, checking all the doors and window to make sure the place was locked up tight. It had been a long day, and the Zimmermans had retired early. Now all he and Chloe had to do was keep them alive. He'd worked with others in his duties as a Secret Service agent, and usually he was the lead. Chloe had made it clear, though, that they needed to be partners, and she was right.

When he entered the kitchen, the scent of perking coffee saturated the air. After the day he'd had, he would need the whole pot to keep going.

Chloe turned from the counter, a grin gracing her lips. "It's almost done."

For a few seconds that smile whisked away his worries. She'd made the day bearable; he'd known his back was covered. "I hope it's not decaf."

"What's the point in drinking coffee without the caffeine?"

He chuckled. "True. I remember you like your coffee like I do—strong and caffeinated." He recalled many things now that he was around her again. Her laugh—filled with so much joy. Her favorite dessert—

anything with caramel. Her caring nature, especially for the underdog.

"It's strong. We'll have to take turns standing guard tonight, so when the coffee runs out, make some more."

"I'll take the first watch. Coffee won't keep me up when I do get a chance to sleep. I don't think anything will." He covered the distance to the pot and poured a mugful. "This house isn't as secure as it should be. I wish they weren't staying here, but they insisted. Their friend invited them to use it while he was away on a skiing vacation."

"We'll only be here a few more days, then on to San Antonio. Let's hope the next place they're staying is better."

"The alarm system is old and could be circumvented easily, not to mention the locks and door frames aren't as sturdy as I'd like."

Her large eyes trapped him. "Maybe we should try to find a more secure place tomorrow. Then both of us can stay up tonight. Just in case there's a follow-through with what happened today?"

He didn't remember her eyes being so green—like a peridot crystal—when they had been together before. "I'm a light sleeper. I'll leave the door open. We both need some sleep in order to do our jobs. Even no sleep for one night could impair our abilities."

Chloe took a sip. "I was thinking of stretching out in front of the entrance to the Zimmermans' bedroom. The easiest way to get to them is coming in the front door and up the stairs."

"I'll be planting myself on the stairs when not making my rounds. That way you can sleep in the room across the hall from the Zimmermans'. I can't imagine the hard floor being comfortable."

"I'm a light sleeper, too, so if you need help, just give me a holler."

The more he was around her, the more he realized they used to have a lot of things in common—but not enough for a commitment. "Wish we had a big dog right about now, but we'll have to rely on the alarm system."

"The one that's easily disarmed." Her eyes twinkled, a dimple appearing in her cheek.

Her look warmed him, although the old house they were staying in had a draft as if the cold wind blew right through it. "Afraid so." He cupped the mug between his hands and took a slow sip. "This might be a good time to talk. As crazy as this first day was, we may not have time later."

Putting her cup down, she leaned back with her hands grasping the counter on either side of her. "I would prefer we leave the past in the past. What happened nine years ago can't be changed."

She made it sound so easy. Just forget the past—the moments he'd shared with her, his decision to go into law enforcement rather than become a preacher and what his job had meant to him at the time. In the end it hadn't made any difference. They had gone their separate ways, and he needed to remember that.

"I made a choice to go to Washington—to take the promotion. I wanted you to come, but I understand why you didn't. You had other obligations. Looking back on that time, I don't think we were meant to be together. Sometimes people meet and begin to fall in love, but it doesn't work out. I don't want our past to interfere with the present." As he spoke to her, he wondered if he really believed it couldn't have worked out if circumstances had been different.

"I don't, either. I can put it behind me. Can you?" Her knuckles whitened as her grip tightened on the granite edge.

"Yes, because I may be working with Guardians, Inc., and I can't think of anyone I'd want more than you as a partner, if the need arises."

"Kyra is expanding?"

"Maybe. I've given her a proposal to consider."

She pushed off the counter. "What kind?" Wariness entered her voice.

"I have a lot of contacts for potential personnel and clients from my years working in the Secret Service. I'd buy into the business, and we would expand, hiring male bodyguards to complement the female ones already working for Guardians, Inc. I'll take over some duties from her. I think she wants to have more time with her family." T.J. swallowed some more of his drink, relishing it. She made a good cup of coffee.

"So you'd become my boss?" Her forehead crinkled; her mouth pinched into a frown.

"Yes. Can you work for me?"

Chloe tilted her head to the side, her gaze fastened on him as if studying him. "I don't know if I can. Working on a case with you is one thing. We've got a past—one serious enough that you wanted me to follow you to Washington and I asked you to stay in Dallas. You didn't. You made your choice."

"I'd been working for that promotion for five years. I thought when your mother was better, you'd come. I asked you to. Why didn't you?"

"I wanted to be more important to a man than a job. It's the past. I don't want to go through this again. No good will come of it."

"So we'll put the past in the past as you said and proceed forward?"

She nodded, stepping away from him.

"That's all I need to know." He finished the last few sips of his coffee.

"What made you quit the Secret Service? Nine years ago it was obvious your life revolved around your job." Tension threaded through each word.

"Probably the same reason you quit the police department. I needed a change." He busied himself pouring another cup of coffee. He couldn't tell her about the government figure he'd protected while the man had had an affair. After a while, he hadn't been able to look away as if nothing was wrong. He believed in marriage and wanted to get married only once in his life. When his respect for the man had plummeted, he'd realized that it was time for him to seek employment elsewhere.

"When you feel up to telling me the whole story, I'm willing to listen." Her expression neutral, she passed him and headed toward the dining room. "I'll do a walk-through, then go up to the bedroom across from the Zimmermans. Wake me in four hours."

He watched her leave, then turned off the light and positioned himself at the bay window in the breakfast nook. Stepping close, he cracked the blinds open to survey the area outside. With all the security lights on, there were still pockets of shadows that could conceal a person from the patio to the wooden fence that surrounded the half-acre backyard. He had a bad feeling about this house. Good thing they were moving to San Antonio soon. He had a better place in mind for the Zimmermans to stay there, and the fewer people who knew the couple's plans, the better to keep them safe during their off hours.

Now all he and Chloe needed to do was get the Zimmermans to San Antonio safely.

Before falling into bed, Chloe walked toward the window at one end of the upstairs hallway. She tried to dismiss the conversation she'd had with T.J. She couldn't. When her mother had gone into remission, she'd actually considered resigning from the police force and going to Washington, D.C., to be with T.J.

But as she'd taken care of her mom, she'd seen the sadness and hurt she had held inside for years. While her mother had struggled with her battle with cancer, she had shared her disappointment in her marriage to a captain in the navy, who had been at sea for half their marriage, and how alone she'd felt for years. She hadn't wanted to end up like her mother—married to a man married to his job. She'd never contacted T.J. and refused his calls. She wouldn't settle for anything but what she deserved—a man who totally loved her and put her first rather than a career. She wasn't sure about T.J.'s true feelings. He'd left because of his career—like her father.

Chloe approached the window, keeping the overhead light off so she could see better when she looked out. The security lamp on this side of the house illuminated every crevice. She made her way to the other end and studied the terrain more carefully because the soft glow didn't cover every patch of ground. She started to turn away and go to bed when a movement out of the corner of her eye seized her full attention.

Someone was out there.

THREE

Chloe whirled away from the hallway window and ran to the stairs. As she descended, she drew her gun. "T.J., we've got a visitor." She shouted the words and raced for the alarm system to turn it off so she could go outside.

"Where?" T.J. rushed into the foyer, his weapon in his hand.

"Right side of house." Heart pounding, she punched in the off code, then hurried toward the front door at the same time he did. "I'll check outside. You stay in here and guard the Zimmermans." She reached for the handle first.

Her comment stopped him. He let his arm drop back to his side, a frown slashing his face. "I'm bigger. More capable of stopping an assailant."

"We're not going to get into an arm-wrestling match right now. I won't jump the person." She pulled open the door, narrowing her gaze on him. "I'm using my gun."

He charged out the entrance. "So am I. Lock the door, turn on the alarm and call the police."

Short of tackling him and knocking him out, Chloe had no other choice but to do as he said. But when this was over with, he would hear from her. She didn't need protecting, too.

She flipped the lock in place, then stabbed in the code to turn the alarm back on. Anger and frustration surged through her veins. Pushing those emotions down, she called her detective friend.

"You wanted to know if anything unusual happens. T.J. is outside trying to apprehend an intruder." She gave him the address.

"On my way."

As she hung up, she hurried up the stairs to check on the Zimmermans and let them know what was happening. When she knocked on their bedroom door, no one called out or let her in. She heard something hit the floor and reached for the knob.

Gun drawn and up, T.J. crept around the right side of the house, his full concentration on protecting his client. A picture of Chloe's furious face taunted his attention for a couple of seconds until he shoved it away. He'd deal with her anger later. His first priority was keeping everyone safe, including Chloe, whether she liked it or not.

A dog barked in the still of night—probably two or three houses away. His nerves taut, T.J. rounded the corner, ready to duck if shot at. He searched the shadows. Something moved beside a holly bush against the eight-foot fence. A man darted out from behind the foliage and ran toward the backyard.

T.J. gave chase, his strides lengthening. The intruder headed for the rear of the property, glancing over his shoulder at T.J., then sprinting faster.

T.J. increased his speed, cutting the distance between

them. He catalogued the man's build—over six-and-a-half feet tall, slim, gangly, his limbs disproportionate to the rest of him, reminding T.J. of an octopus.

The intruder lunged for the top of the fence, trying to hoist himself over it. T.J. leaped toward him and grabbed his legs as the man dangled half on this side of the property. T.J. yanked hard and the trespasser fell into him, sending them both crashing backward. T.J. hit the ground first with the intruder landing on top of him.

The air swooshed from T.J.'s lungs. His head bounced against the ground, causing the world to spin before his eyes. The hard impact wrenched the gun from his hand, and his Glock flew across the grass.

The man rolled off T.J. Scrambling for his weapon, T.J. drew in a breath. But the prowler barreled into T.J. before he could grab his gun.

Chloe twisted the Zimmermans' bedroom door handle. Locked. "Mary. Paul. Open up." She threw her shoulder against the barrier between her and her client. Pain radiated through her body as she hit the door again. Solid. Not budging. She stepped away to shoot the lock.

"Coming. Coming," came Paul's deep husky voice through the wood.

Chloe poised, ready at a second's notice to react if he was being forced to let her in.

When he opened the door finally and stuck his head out of the gap in the entrance, worried lines mixed with the exhaustion on his face, his eyes blinking at the dazzling light in the hallway. "What's wrong?"

"What was that crashing sound?"

"When I got out of bed, I bumped into an end table. Why are you waking us up?" He shook his head as though to wake himself totally.

"There's a prowler outside. T.J. has gone to check on the situation while I secure you two. I need to come in and check your bedroom."

"No one's in here. I'd know."

"Humor me."

He flipped on the overhead light and stepped to the side to allow her to pass. Lying in bed, Mary groaned and hid her face as illumination flooded the room.

"She took a sleeping pill. After what happened today, she didn't think she would get to sleep any other way." Dressed in a long robe, Paul moved toward the bed. "What do you need us to do?"

"You two need to get up in case I have to move you quickly." Chloe made a tour of the room, inspecting the closet and the connected bathroom. She stopped at the window and peered out the front of the house before checking to make sure it was locked. Satisfied no intruder was in the room, she crossed to the door. "Get dressed. I'll be out in the hall."

The muscles in her neck and shoulder taut, Chloe paced the corridor, examining the stairs and foyer below each time she passed them. Finally, when Mary and Paul left their bedroom, Chloe glanced at her watch. It had been ten minutes since T.J. had gone outside. She didn't like not knowing what was going on.

What if something happened to him? No, I won't think about that. T.J. can take care of himself. He's been protecting people longer than me. He's in Your hands, Lord.

The couple approached Chloe. Mary leaned against her husband, trying to wake up.

"What do we do now?" Paul asked, his arm around his wife.

"Sit down there—" Chloe gestured toward an area where their backs would be against the wall "—and if I tell you to move, do so immediately. Don't be alarmed. I'm turning off the hallway light so I can check outside and see what's happening."

She inspected the ground where she'd seen the intruder on the side of the house. Nothing. Where was T.J.? The prowler? If he ran from T.J., he would go for the backyard most likely. She flipped the hallway light on again, then entered a bedroom overlooking the rear.

The sight of a tall, thin man pouncing on a figure on the ground stiffened her. She leaned closer to see what was going on by the fence, the security lights not quite reaching the place where two men wrestled, rolling away from her view. The urge to go out and help was overpowering, but her job was to stay with the Zimmermans.

One last time, she searched the darkness at the back of the yard. The night shadowed the pair enough she couldn't tell what was going on. T.J. had had some of the best training in the world, but she hated the helplessness she felt. She shook it off and hurried toward the hallway. She needed to get Mary and Paul into the closet under the staircase—no windows and only one way in. That way she would be able to know if someone breached the lower level right away and defend them better until the police arrived.

T.J. threw a punch that connected with the intruder's jaw. The man returned it with a right uppercut, sending

T.J. staggering back against the fence. The guy rushed in, pinning T.J. then pounding his fists into his stomach and torso. One. Two. Three jabs. The breath left his lungs. Lightheaded, he blocked the next assault and brought his knee up into his assailant. The man dropped to the ground, groaning. T.J. hammered him until the prowler went still.

T.J. wanted this to end. Still feeling dazed, he stumbled toward the place where his gun lay. An iron grip on his left leg, then a sharp jerk, sent him down. He shook off the assailant's hand and scrambled away, then struggled to his feet and faced his opponent. The man's features were obscured by the dark. The man drew himself up tall, his arms held out from his body as he sidled to the right. T.J. mimicked his moves, taking a reprieve in order to inhale deep, fortifying breaths.

"The police are on the way. I'm not letting you leave." T.J. made a full circle. The sound of the intruder's raspy breathing wafted to him. "You aren't getting away. You might as well make it easy for yourself and give up."

The prowler cackled. "I haven't done anything wrong. You attacked me. I welcome the police."

"You're trespassing on private property."

"You aren't going to stop me from getting my story."

Maybe the guy had hit T.J. one time too many. "Story?"

"Yes, I work for the *Texas Inquirer News*."

"That's great. You can tell the police." In the distance a siren blared, a welcome sound. T.J. angled closer to his Glock, slicing a glance toward it.

In that split second, the man rushed T.J., taking him

to the ground and rolling toward the gun. He'd never lost his gun, and he wouldn't let this be the first time.

The prowler kept reaching toward T.J.'s Glock. Inches from it, T.J. knocked the lanky guy's arm away, lurched across the short space and latched on to his weapon. With all his strength, he shoved the man away from him and swung the gun around, aiming it at the intruder's chest.

"Don't move." T.J. scooted back, then rose, keeping his Glock trained on the prone man.

The siren stopped, not far from the house. In spite of the cold air, sweat drenched T.J. The sound of the gate opening reverberated through the air, quickly followed by someone shouting, "Police!"

The prowler pushed to his feet, the security light illuminating the fury on his thin face. "Help. This man is going to kill me."

T.J. suppressed the urge to laugh, because until the police could straighten this out, he would be suspected, too.

"Drop the gun," the first of the two officers said, his own weapon on T.J.

T.J. followed his order and then raised his hands. "I'm T. J. Davenport. This man is trespassing."

With the patrol cars' lights flashing in the driveway, Chloe stood on the porch with Detective Matthews as two officers led T.J. and the intruder from the backyard. Both of them had their hands cuffed behind them. She might be mad at T.J. for cutting her off and rushing outside after the prowler, but the sight of his cuts, his rumpled clothing and the bits of dead grass in his hair and on his sweatshirt emphasized she'd fared better than he had. She could take care of herself in most situations, but after one look at the size of the intruder, she had to admit in this case she might not have been able to. She gave a wry smile. Maybe she did have limitations.

But with the Lord all things are possible. You kept us safe. Thank You.

Rob stepped forward, waving his hand toward T.J. "He's the good guy. You can release him."

"Oh, please keep them on him for a few more minutes," Chloe whispered behind Rob.

Her friend chuckled. "Behave, Chloe."

The police officer took the handcuffs off T.J. "What do you want us to do with the other one?"

"I want to talk to him, then you can take him to the station," Rob said as he descended the steps.

Rubbing his wrists, T.J. plodded up the stairs to the top of the porch, where Chloe stood. "Where are Mary and Paul?"

"In the living room with an officer. They're safe."

"Good, because I want to be in on this interrogation." T.J. backed down several steps but glanced over his shoulder. "And I heard the crack about keeping the handcuffs on me."

Serves him right for playing the macho male. She presented an innocent expression. "You okay? You should be checked out by a doctor."

He turned toward Rob and the intruder. "I'm fine. It's happened before. Don't worry."

"I'm not. You know how to take care of yourself," Chloe fired back, not wanting him to think she had been worried about him. *But I was. Yeah, and that's the problem. My focus needs to be on Mary and Paul, not T.J.*

Though she tried not to, Chloe slanted a look toward T.J., his strong jaw set in a hard line, his usually neat and professional medium-length black hair messy from wrestling with an assailant. A vision of her running her hand through that hair was quickly replaced with another memory of the touch of his day-old beard beneath her fingers as she framed his face and leaned in to kiss…

Chloe shook the thoughts from her mind. That was the past. T.J. had made it clear that he had no room for a wife in his life, and then he'd flown to Washington to guard the vice president. She made a mistake only once—never twice.

"What were you doing here?" Rob asked the tall, lanky man, dragging Chloe's attention to their current situation.

"I don't deserve this kind of treatment. I'm not a criminal. I demand these handcuffs be taken off me, too." The trespasser tossed his head toward T.J. "He chased me. Tackled me. I'm the victim here."

"What were you doing here?" A steel thread ran through her friend's voice. "Or if you can't answer that question, maybe you can manage telling me who you are?"

The guy drew himself up even taller. "I'm a reporter for the *Texas Inquirer News* and was here to interview the Zimmermans."

"At ten o'clock at night?" Chloe asked, all three men turning their attention to her.

The prowler shrugged. "The lights were on, so I thought they were up."

Chloe folded her arms over her chest, trying to ignore T.J.'s gaze on her, which she was finding was next to impossible. "So you decided to go around to the back of the house and knock on the kitchen door? Is that your normal way to interview people? Perhaps you wanted to peep into windows to make sure people were up at this hour."

T.J. laughed and looked back at the intruder. "Who told you the Zimmermans were even here?"

The trespasser's forehead creased. "They aren't? My source sounded like they knew."

"They? More than one?" T.J. moved to the bottom of the stairs.

"Only one, but you aren't getting anything else from me, not even if male or female." With blood streaked across his face, the reporter lifted his chin and glared at T.J.

"Who are you? Who is your source?" Rob asked, throwing a look to be quiet at Chloe and T.J.

"I'm Artie Franklin. I won't tell you my source. I don't have to. You'll find my credentials in my wallet in my back pocket."

Rob approached the man, removed his billfold and flipped it open. "Being a reporter doesn't give you free rein." He indicated to the officer nearby to take the man to the station, handing his patrol partner the wallet. "I'll be there soon." After the pair left with Artie Franklin, Rob climbed the stairs. "Let's finish this inside. It's freezing out here."

Chloe hadn't felt the cold because energy had been

charging through her, the adrenaline only now beginning to subside. "I want to know who told him the Zimmermans were here."

"So do I." T.J. held the door open for Rob and Chloe, and then followed them into the house.

"I'll do my best to put pressure on him, but I've dealt with a few like this Artie Franklin. They will protect their sources at all costs."

Chloe swung around in the spacious foyer. "Give me a chance to talk to him. He might tell me. I didn't pound him into the ground and threaten him with a gun."

T.J. quirked a grin, then winced. "Hey, you wanted me to stop him. I did."

"The bottom line is that he found us when only a few knew the Zimmermans were staying here. We need to find out who leaked the info."

"It only takes one person saying something for it to get out. That's why in WitSec there are such strict protocols in place." T.J. looked her in the eye. "We're going to have to do the same thing."

She nodded. "We'll be moving from here, but I'll check in with you, Rob, to find out what you get from this Franklin character."

Rob frowned. "I don't like y'all being out of contact with me. I understand the Zimmermans have two more stops in the Dallas area. Will they be attending those?"

"I think they should cancel the tour, but it—"

"Yes, we'll be going to them." Paul interrupted Chloe. "We have people who are expecting to see us. We'll be attending both of those events. Mary and I have prayed about this and feel it's what we have to do."

Chloe spun around and faced the man. "Someone

is after both of you. The wise thing to do is to put a stop to this tour."

Mary came up beside her husband. "That's why our publisher hired you and T.J. You'll protect us, but more important, the Lord will."

"Oh, great. Logic won't sway them," T.J. mumbled close to Chloe.

"Hush," she whispered, then faced the couple. "We're moving. That's the least we can do, since someone knows you two are here. Go pack. I want to be gone in half an hour."

As the Zimmermans mounted the stairs, Chloe shifted toward Rob. "I'll keep you informed, but we're going to have to be careful." She began walking her friend toward the door.

"Aren't you going to pack?"

"I never unpacked."

"I'm leaving him here." Rob waved toward the third officer standing in the entrance into the living room. "I'd feel better."

She opened the front door. "Fine. But he isn't to follow us. Okay?"

"I figured you'd say that. But you've got to promise me you'll call if there's more trouble."

"I will. You and I go back years." She watched him leave before turning toward T.J. "I may not have to pack, but it looks like you need to clean up. When we get to the new safe house, we need to decide which one of us is in charge. Both of us can't be. It isn't working." The best way to resist T.J.'s appeal was to concentrate on the job and keep everything professional. Or she would find herself falling in love again.

"Agreed." T.J. headed toward the rear part of the house.

Just before he disappeared down the hallway, a scream pierced the air.

FOUR

Chloe hit the stairs before T.J. and the police officer, but the pounding of their footsteps indicated they were right behind her as she rushed toward the Zimmermans' bedroom. Paul came out into the hallway, as pale as if he hadn't seen the light of day in months. He held in his hand a soft blue dress shredded to ribbons.

Chloe skidded to a halt in front of the man, dropping her hand with the gun to her side. "What happened?" She looked beyond and saw Mary sitting on the bed, trembling and hugging her arms to her chest.

"Someone..." Paul gulped, glancing at T.J. and Officer Bryant right behind her. "Someone did this. It wasn't like this—" he raised his hand, shaking the destroyed garment in Chloe's face "—this morning. She wore it last night. She..." He opened and closed his mouth several times, then snapped it shut, clamping his lips together in a thin line.

"Officer, we'll take care of our clients. You should call Detective Matthews about this development. It's obvious someone was in the house sometime today."

T.J.'s calm voice floated to Chloe as she took Paul's arm and guided him back into the bedroom. She hadn't seen Mary this distraught even with all that had happened today. But cutting up one of her dresses was more personal.

Chloe sat next to Mary. "Where was your dress?"

"I brought two suitcases, and use one for putting my dirty clothes in. I—I thought I would do a load of laundry tomorrow since it was going to be one of our down days without an appearance." Mary dropped her head, scrubbing her hands down her face. "Sorry, I'm babbling," she finally said, lifting her gaze to Chloe.

"Was this dress in with the other dirty clothes? Was anything else cut up?" Chloe noticed T.J. standing at the entrance, scanning the room.

"Yes, it was with the other clothes. This was the only thing ruined. The dress is—was—my favorite one. Paul gave it to me on our last anniversary. Twenty blessed years. He picked it out himself. I even wore it to the event in Paris." Eyes glistening, Mary took a deep breath, then another, raising her quavering hand to comb her fingers through her hair. "I must look a mess. I...I..."

Chloe placed her arm around Mary. "You look fine. Why don't you let me pack the rest of your clothes? You can sit downstairs with Officer Bryant. When we wrap up everything here, we'll move to a new house. I don't want you to tell anyone—" she looked up at Paul, then back to Mary "—where you're staying."

"But my family needs to know." Mary blinked the tears from her eyes.

"I'll get you a number they can call. It's my employer's. She'll relay all messages to me. Remember, do not tell anyone, even family, where you're staying," she repeated, not sure the couple fully understood the importance of keeping their location a secret.

"But this isn't my family's doing." Mary's voice quavered with each word.

"They might accidentally let something slip. It's very important. No one should know." Chloe stood.

Paul moved to the bed and sat on the other side of Mary, wrapping his arm around his wife. "How about the publicist for the publisher?"

"She can use the same number. We'll set up a network so your whereabouts can't be traced, but you'll still be able to stay in touch if you are needed." Chloe walked to T.J. "We'll give you a few minutes, but please don't touch anything in the closet until Detective Matthews gives his go-ahead."

T.J. stepped into the hallway. "Matthews should be here soon. I want him to dust for fingerprints and take Mary and Paul's to rule them out. Maybe we'll get something from that. But the question I want answered is how did the person get inside to destroy the dress? I know the alarm system isn't the best, but unless they knew the code, the alarm should have gone off."

"But as we talked about earlier, some systems can be circumvented if a person knows what he's doing. Were the windows wired?" Chloe asked. "I found two unlocked on the second floor when I did a walk-through earlier."

"No. Why didn't you say something?"

"Both weren't easily accessible and nothing seemed out of place. I thought maybe the owner left them unlocked. On the second floor, some people aren't as vigilant about locking them. Every closet and hiding place was checked, so no one was in the house after we came home."

"Which means they were here while we were away."

"Since the Zimmermans' schedule was public knowledge, that wouldn't be difficult to coordinate."

Footsteps coming up the stairs interrupted their conversation. Chloe glanced down the corridor as Rob and the police officer made their way toward them. Rob scowled, his long strides eating up the distance between them.

He stopped a few feet away from her. "What happened?"

"Someone cut up Mary's dress. It was in her suitcase with some other dirty clothes." Chloe observed the officer who moved around them and positioned himself at the bedroom door. Rob was taking this very seriously, which pleased her. Someone was toying with the Zimmermans. No one had been harmed—yet. But it was only a matter of time. She couldn't shake the feeling a lot more was to come. Ripping Mary's dress was personal. Had they known it was her favorite? "Just a sec." Chloe parted from the group and stepped back into the bedroom. "Paul, have you checked all of your clothes and belongings?"

"Not everything. Mary brought the suitcase out first and opened it on the bed—" Paul gestured toward the bag on the other side of the couple "—so I haven't had time to check. Should I now?"

"Wait until Detective Matthews talks with you two and gives the go-ahead. I want you both to make sure you have everything and your items and clothing are intact."

Rob entered, surveying the bedroom before bridging

the distance to the Zimmermans. Chloe had intended to stay and listen, but T.J. clasped her hand and pulled her out into the hallway.

"I'd like to check the two windows that were unlocked. Also the ground below them."

"The first one is at the end of this hall." She pointed to the window on the side of the house that was well lit. "It's a straight drop with no trees or way to climb up to it unless a person uses a ladder."

"Maybe they did. A lot of people don't think anyone can get into their house through their second-story windows. They leave them unlocked and not wired to an alarm. That may be the case here. The Zimmermans arrived early this morning and didn't have a lot of time before they had to leave for the church. Where's the other window?"

"In the corner bedroom at the front of the house, which, if someone was using a ladder, wouldn't be their first choice."

T.J. walked to the first window at the end of the hall and examined it, without touching it, then checked out the second one nearby in the bedroom. "I'm assuming you didn't see anything unusual or you would have said something to me, but let's check outside. It rained yesterday, so the soil would be soft. If the intruder used a ladder, it would leave an indentation in the ground."

"I'll tell the officer where we're going and grab a flashlight."

When she went outside with T.J., they first checked the window facing the front of the house. An intruder would have to put the ladder on the driveway. "If he entered here, there's no way for us to tell."

"This wouldn't be the one. This entry is too obvious. They would check each window in the back of the place first." T.J. opened the gate and let Chloe go through ahead of him.

She stood under the window and inspected the ground around a bush directly under it. "This looks like someone put a ladder here."

"I'll have Matthews check for fingerprints here especially on the outside and the upstairs windowsill. You didn't touch that or the screen, which would have been removed to allow someone to climb inside, did you?"

"No, not other than the lock which I clicked shut."

T.J. made a full circle, taking in the surroundings. "That elm near the property blocks much of this side of the house from the next-door neighbor, but it wouldn't hurt for Matthews to talk to them in case they saw something like an unfamiliar car parked near here."

"Rob is thorough. Maybe he'll find evidence to help ID the person stalking the Zimmermans after he talks with them."

"Until then, let's get them moved to a safer house and let him do his job."

"Sounds like a good plan. None of us are going to get much sleep tonight, but tomorrow is a rest day and I figure we'll all need it." She headed for the front of the house. "Of course, that's only if no one discovers where we're going."

"This is a fortress," T.J. said and took a long sip of his coffee, relishing the jolt of caffeine. He turned from the window overlooking the large front yard of the new safe house, bathed in the morning sunlight.

Chloe closed the few feet between them. "And what's even better, no one knows about this place ex-

cept the Zimmermans, you, me and Kyra. Paul and
Mary are taking a nap. Paul was quite upset about his
computer being wiped clean by the intruder. Apparently he and Mary have been working on another book
in the series. It seems someone doesn't want them to
write it. Fortunately, they have a backup."

"Going after a writer's computer is as personal as
Mary's dress. Have we found out how anyone could
know the significance of that piece of clothing?"

"Good question. I asked Mary about that. She
opened the anniversary present at a party attended by
a group of close friends. She made a big deal out of
it because Paul actually went out and bought it. She
called it her power dress. He usually has Mary's cousin
who lives with them buy her gifts." She faced the window, side by side with T.J.

Her presence charged the air around him. Distracted
a few seconds, he stared at her as she swallowed some
of her drink. He pulled his attention away and continued his perusal of the yard, enclosed all the way around
by an electrified six-foot fence. "I like that this is a
much smaller house. Easier to defend."

"No one in our agency has used this yet. Kyra
amazes me with her connections."

"Well, I'm in love with the security system. Everything is wired and will go off if someone tries to circumvent it."

Chloe chuckled. "Only someone in security would
get excited about that."

"Or someone running for his life."

"The only thing we're missing is dogs patrolling
the grounds."

"I guess we can't have everything." T.J. shifted toward her. "You wanted to talk about who should be the lead in this detail."

"Not anymore. The publisher contacted you about this job. You should be it."

He stuck his forefinger into his ear and wiggled it. "Did I hear correctly or has no sleep finally sent you over the edge?"

"Cute. I'm being practical. There needs to be one person in charge, and I wouldn't be here if you hadn't suggested it to Kyra. We can't debate tactics in the middle of a crisis. I trust you."

I trust you. Those words reverberated in his mind, leaving a warm feeling in their wake. He didn't trust. What had happened to him? His job certainly had taught him to be cautious, but he was even questioning the Lord. Was this innate distrust the reason he hadn't tried to stay in Chloe's life even after she didn't come to Washington? Had he been afraid in the end she would disappoint him, as so many people had in his line of work?

She grinned, two dimples showing. "Besides, if the publisher needs to talk to anyone about the security, that'll be your job."

"I've got big shoulders. I think I can handle it," T.J. said, forcing a laugh. He pushed his thoughts into the background. This wasn't the time to contemplate his trust issues.

"You'd better. That's the part of the job I don't like. Thankfully Kyra does that task."

"The publicist will be at the event tomorrow. I'll make sure she doesn't corner you."

"See, we're already working better together by talking about this."

A strand of her hair had come loose from her pony-tail. T.J. clenched his hands tightly to keep from hooking it behind her ear. He moved toward the kitchen. "Do you want some more coffee?"

"No. I'm going to lie down while the Zimmermans are asleep, if that's okay with you. Then you can rest after me."

"I was going to suggest that very thing. We both need some sleep, and although this place is a fortress, I think we should take turns guarding tonight, especially since there are only two bedrooms." As he entered the kitchen, he glanced back at her following him. "Okay?"

"Great. I feel so much better that we don't have a limousine service involved. Thanks for using your car to come here. It's been a *long* twenty-four hours since we started on this assignment." Chloe finished her coffee and put the cup in the sink. "I'd better snatch some sleep or I won't be able to keep my eyes open tonight."

"I know better. Kyra told me about one of your cases where you had to stay awake for over forty-eight hours and be alert until help got to you."

"I was younger then."

"Yeah, by a whole six months. That would make a big difference. See you in a couple of hours. Do you want me to wake you up?"

"No," she said quickly, her eyes widening slightly. "I always bring an alarm clock with me. I'll use that." She backed away. "See you in a few."

When she left, she seemed to take some of the energy with her. There was something vibrant about Chloe. He took his mug of strong coffee and walked through the small house, rechecking all points of entry before he stood at the large window in the living room and stared outside.

When the police officer had finally taken them to T.J.'s house to pick up his car early this morning before the sun was up, he'd grabbed an untraceable cell phone for communication with Kyra, Detective Matthews and the publisher. Then as he'd driven to this safe house, he and Chloe had kept an eye out for any car that might be following them. With less traffic at that time of day, it would have been easier to spy a familiar vehicle behind them.

And yet, beyond the six-foot chain-link fence, he sensed someone watching the place. Nothing concrete. Just a gut feeling.

Maybe that was his problem and the reason he distrusted so easily. He was always looking over his shoulder, always scanning the crowd searching for someone who had evil intentions. He'd been taught to suspect everyone. He'd left the Secret Service and gone right into private protection. What was it like to have a normal life? To go to a nine-to-five job and come home—to a family. Would he ever do that with someone like Chloe?

Whoa. Where had that thought come from? Seeing Chloe again? He'd given up on having a family years ago when he was so often on the road with his job after his relationship with Chloe ended. He was still doing the same type of job—still gone from home a lot—which made him realize he needed to press Kyra about taking on a partner. Maybe then he could consider a life outside his job if he didn't travel much.

The next morning after showering and getting dressed, Chloe came into the kitchen for her first cup of coffee. The scent of it brewing drew her to the room. "Good morning. Did you two sleep all right?"

she asked Mary and Paul. She'd slept soundly for four hours. She'd known T.J. stood guard and trusted him. That was a good feeling.

Scrambling eggs at the stove, Mary glanced over her shoulder. "Like a baby. I knew there was a reason we planned a couple of rest days in our month-long speaking tour. After all that has happened, I feel re-energized. How about you?"

"I slept as well as I usually do on the job." She was thankful she could operate on little sleep for short periods of time and still perform as she should.

"I hope you're hungry. I love to cook, but I don't get to as much as I used to. I thought we would have a big breakfast before we left. We have a long day ahead of us." Mary turned back to stir the eggs.

"Where's T.J.?" Chloe crossed the kitchen and filled a mug with coffee.

"He's in our bedroom, looking for bugs," Mary said.

"Bugs?"

"Listening devices." Paul buttered the toast after it popped up from the toaster.

"Be back in a sec." As Chloe moved through the six-room house, she scanned her surroundings, checking outside as she passed a window. When she arrived at the entrance to the bedroom the Zimmermans were using, she leaned against the doorjamb, took a sip of her coffee and asked, "Do you suspect there is a bug in their belongings?"

T.J. shrugged while running his bug sweeper over the couple's room. "Just a gut feeling we're being watched. I can't shake it. But if that's the case, how did they find us?"

"How did you get that?" Chloe gestured toward a black rectangular box on the end of a long, black pole.

"Kyra brought it to me first thing this morning. I think I woke her up."

"Why didn't you get me up?"

"Because it was your turn to sleep and you needed to. I'll wake you when we have a problem. Kyra talked to Matthews about the case late last night. It seems she knows him, too."

"Yeah, years ago they worked together on the police force. He's one of the reasons I went to work for her. What did she tell you?"

He walked toward her. "What prints they gathered were either Mary's, Paul's or an unknown person's."

"Were there any on the outside windowsill or the pane?"

"Surprisingly, those areas were clean of any prints."

"Like they had been wiped off?"

"Exactly. At least that's what Matthews thinks, or else gloves were used."

"Or they didn't use the window. There generally won't be prints on an upstairs outside windowsill that has a screen."

"That still is the most likely way they got in and out. The alarm wasn't set off or tampered with, so the intruder didn't come through the door unless he knew the code."

As he moved through the doorway, his arm brushed against hers. She caught a whiff of his lime aftershave. Her heartbeat revved for a few seconds. She stepped away while T.J. crossed the hall to the bedroom she'd slept in.

"I've already checked my bag. Yours is the last one.

Oh, by the way, I'm having Kyra call the limo company and check for a GPS tracker on the one we used. It would be nice to find out if that was the way they discovered where the Zimmermans were staying."

"The limo company the Zimmermans were using wasn't public knowledge."

"But certain people knew—like the publicist who set it up."

"Why would the publicist do this?" Chloe tensed as he approached her suitcase on the floor on the other side of the bed.

T.J. ran the bug sweeper over her belongings, but it didn't sound. "That's it. Nothing on any of the items we brought from the other house. But I still feel something isn't right."

"Maybe you're being overzealous. Of course, I'd rather you be that than the opposite."

He strode into the hallway, inhaling a deep breath. "I'm sure glad Mary likes to cook."

"So am I, since I don't do much but the basics. Cooking for one doesn't inspire me to learn more."

"I feel the same way. Living in hotels will do that to you." T.J. waited for Chloe to go into the kitchen first.

Paul sat at the table while Mary carried the platter of scrambled eggs and bacon and put it in the center next to the stacked pieces of toast and the coffeepot.

"Good timing. Did you find anything?"

T.J. eased into the chair across from Paul while Mary and Chloe took a seat. "Nothing. That means most likely the person who came into the house two days ago was only there to wipe your computer and damage Mary's dress."

"But at least he doesn't know where we are now. That's a good thing." Mary spread her napkin in her lap.

"Yes," Chloe said, although a person could look at it from a different angle. If breaking and entering to plant a bug was the object, then the motive didn't seem as personal. It became much more personal if an intruder risked capture to taunt the couple with how easy it was for him to get to them. That meant the person was playing with them.

"Let's pray. I've worked up an appetite." Paul bowed his head and blessed the food, then began passing the platters around the table.

As Chloe handed T.J. the eggs and bacon, their gazes connected. In his dark eyes, full of concern, she could see he'd been thinking the same thing. Instead of being relieved he'd found no tracking devices, his expression reflected apprehension, his mouth tightening in a frown. No tracking device meant someone close had leaked the whereabouts of the Zimmermans. This could be another long day.

In the large auditorium, Paul wrapped up their appearance to a standing ovation. T.J. kept scanning the crowd, larger than the one at the church two days before. The place was packed. A detail of police was stationed around the room. Paul, dressed in his usual gray suit, had removed his coat early in their presentation and laid it over a chair behind him. He turned and shrugged into it, then straightened the red rosebud pinned to his lapel.

"Ready?" T.J. asked his client.

"Just a moment." Paul moved forward to meet some of the audience who had approached the stage.

He and Mary shook people's hands as they had before the presentation.

Chloe paused next to T.J. right behind the couple. "If only we could get them to come, speak and immediately leave," she whispered close to his ear, with her attention focused on the throng in the auditorium. She left him to watch the smaller group near the Zimmermans.

From the moment they had driven to the large school auditorium, he and Chloe had fallen into a rhythm where she often knew what needed to be done without him saying anything. She was making it easy to work with her. She was experienced, controlled and totally professional. He appreciated and admired her for that.

When Nancy Carson, the publicist for the publisher, walked out onto the stage and signaled for the Zimmermans to accompany her, Paul and Mary disengaged from the crowd after saying a prayer for the group.

"That's what I love about them. They're always thinking of others even with all the trouble they've been having." Chloe fell into step behind the couple while T.J. took the lead and went through the double doors first. The corridor was clear except for a half a dozen individuals, rendering the situation manageable.

As Paul and Mary walked side by side toward a room where a book signing was set up, T.J. took Paul's left and Chloe Mary's right. The publicists hurried before them, and when the Zimmermans stepped through the entrance, T.J. understood why. A television reporter with her camera was there, along with hundreds of people waiting for the couple. Why weren't they told about this? This made a difference in how they controlled a room.

T.J. hadn't fully realized the scope of their popularity until today. Before Nancy could draw Paul and Mary to be interviewed by the young woman from a TV station in Dallas, the crowd pressed toward the Zimmermans. Someone knocked into T.J. He swiveled around to face an older gentleman, maybe seventy years old.

"Sorry. Someone pushed me from behind," the man said, but still jostled for a chance to speak to Paul.

T.J. glanced at Chloe being squashed against Mary. Why in the world had he thought this was manageable? Nothing about it was.

"Step back, please," T.J. shouted to the throng. When no one responded and kept pushing forward, he stuck his fingers into mouth and whistled, loud enough that the people around him backed away.

"Please move back and give the Zimmermans a chance to get to their table so they can sign your books." Chloe's clear, authoritative voice sounded above the murmurs.

The crowd parted and allowed them to escort Paul and Mary toward the area set up for the book signing. T.J. noticed Nancy beaming and the cameraman capturing the frenzy on tape.

After the couple had settled behind the table with a barrier between them and the crowd, T.J. still didn't let down his guard. The way the publicist was looking victorious, he wondered if she had set up that little scene when they had come into the room. Standing behind and to the side of Paul, T.J. looked toward Chloe, his tension reflected in her features.

"I hope we don't repeat that little scene at any other stops. Nothing happened today, but the person after them could cause some havoc. Perfect time to," she murmured, while her gaze swept the winding line that filled the large room.

"We'll make sure more police are in attendance next time they sign books and make sure with Nancy Carson there are no surprises like today with the television reporter." T.J. threw her a quick, assessing look. "You okay? I saw you getting pushed around."

"Besides my foot being stepped on, I'll survive. We might as well settle in here. This is going to take a few hours."

T.J. looked from one side of the room to the other. "Yep. At least."

By the end of the book signing, T.J. and Chloe hadn't left their positions for a couple of hours.

Tension vibrated the air, his every muscle taut and his nerves on edge as he waited for something to go wrong. He slanted a look at Chloe, her posture ramrod straight. At least their job was getting easier as the crowd finally thinned and the reporter got her story and left.

T.J. returned his focus on the large man pausing in front of Paul. The guy smiled at Paul and requested the book signed to him and his wife. Most of the people remaining were those who had sponsored the speaking engagement. Paul slid the book toward Mary to add her signature, then she passed it to the large gentleman. The couple had a good system down, but they had been autographing hundreds of books for almost two hours nonstop. T.J. didn't know how they did it.

The publicist bent over and checked the last box, then rose and said, "Sorry, everyone. These half a dozen are the last books." Nancy Carson waved at the short stack between Paul and Mary on the table. "I have a sheet where you can write down your address, and we'll send you a signed copy."

A few in line grumbled, but most hurried to Nancy Carson to sign up.

After autographing the last book, Mary rose. "If you'll excuse me, I'll be right back."

While Chloe went with her, Nancy stepped over to Paul. "This event was a huge success. At each stop more and more are attending and, even better, buying your books. I'm glad we've arranged a book signing at most of the rest of the stops on the tour. We've gotten good coverage."

A scowl descended over Paul's features. "Not the kind of coverage I want. I've been following what has been written. It seems the reporters are only focusing on the bad things happening."

"But that hasn't discouraged anyone from coming. Any publicity is better than none. This has gone national. I won't be surprised if you two sell tons of books over the next couple of weeks. *Take Back America* has risen to number one at all of the major online bookstores and is still on the *New York Times* bestsellers list. You two are spreading your message. That's what you wanted, as well as your publisher."

Paul shifted toward T.J. "I'm ready to go. It's been a long day."

Nancy started toward a bookstore employee as she addressed Paul. "A television station wants you to appear on their morning show the day after tomorrow before you head to your next town. I told them you two will be ecstatic."

Paul's frown deepened. "I would have appreciated

you running it by my wife and me before agreeing. Squeezing in any more doesn't give us much time to regroup and rest."

"You can do that at the end of the tour." Nancy smiled and continued toward the employee.

"That woman only looks at Mary and me with dollar signs in her eyes," Paul said when Nancy was out of earshot.

"A television station is a safer place to protect you than a large crowd. Why don't you do more of that?" T.J. asked.

Paul's mouth twisted, then settled into a neutral expression. "Mary and I want to touch people personally. These speaking tours give us a better chance than being in front of a camera. I'm not a big fan of television anyway. Too many people are wrapped up in watching it rather than living the life they were meant to. They use it as a form of escape."

"The room is clearing out. Let's get Mary and Chloe and leave. We need to meet Kyra Hunt to trade cars again."

"You really think someone would put a tracking device on the car in the parking lot?"

"Yes."

Paul shook his head. "How do you live distrusting everyone?"

"It's my job. If I wasn't so cautious, someone could be killed."

"Still, it has to affect you. I find it so much easier to trust the Lord. He'll prevail."

"In the meantime, I'm here to protect people who need it." But he couldn't argue it hadn't affected his personal life. When had he stopped trusting in God?

T.J. met Chloe and Mary returning from the restroom. "Ready?"

Chloe nodded. "I'll call Kyra to meet us."

"Stay inside by this door. I'll bring the car around." T.J. pushed out of the double doors leading to the side parking lot and jogged toward the rental car he'd exchanged with Kyra en route to the event. The still air cooled him, and he relished being outside after being stuffed in a room with so many people, all wanting the Zimmermans' attention. He should be used to that scene after the Secret Service.

T.J. slipped behind the steering wheel and drove toward the side of the building. When he pulled up near the double doors, Chloe rushed the couple to the rental. She sat in the back with Mary while Paul clambered into the front passenger seat.

Although T.J. would switch back to his gray Jeep Grand Cherokee before continuing to the safe house, he would have Kyra check the rental for a tracking device. Ten minutes later, he parked behind his car, which Kyra sat in. "I'll only be a sec. Stay in here until I give you the go ahead." He made his way to the Jeep's driver's side.

Kyra climbed out. "Everything go okay?"

"So far so good, but I won't breathe easy until we're at the safe house. Before you turn in this rental, see if anyone attached a tracking device. We'll follow the same procedure with a new rental car tomorrow. At least that way I'll know we aren't being tracked."

"I will, and I checked your Jeep. It was clean. Not that I was expecting to find anything. But I like to take every precaution possible." Kyra exchanged keys with T.J. "Drives my husband crazy at times."

"Tell Michael hi, and congratulations on another baby."

The owner of Guardians, Inc., smiled. "I will, and when this is over, I hope you'll come to dinner. I want to discuss your proposal to become my partner. With another baby arriving in five months, I need to stay home more."

T.J. walked toward the rental with Kyra. "Great." At the car he opened the front passenger door. "Let's go."

As Mary and Paul exited the rental, T.J. introduced them to Kyra.

"I wish we weren't meeting under these circumstances. I'm a fan of yours." Kyra shook hands and then hugged Chloe. "You'll be just fine with T.J. and Chloe."

T.J. escorted Paul to his Jeep. Although on a residential street Kyra had picked at random, he was still alert for anything unusual. When a blue van turned the corner and headed toward them, he hurried his pace and quickly ushered Paul into the front seat while Chloe helped Mary into the back. The van picked up speed, the driver rolling down his window.

FIVE

As the blue van grew nearer to the Jeep, Chloe said, "Get down." With her hand on her gun, she stood in front of the back window to block Mary.

T.J. followed suit. Tension poured off him as the van came to a stop and the driver leaned out his window. "Do you know where 1245 South Fourth Street is? My GPS sent me here, but this isn't Fourth."

"Sorry. I can't help you."

"Oh, okay." The driver moved his van slowly forward ten yards and asked Kyra, who had positioned herself by the rental.

"There isn't a Fourth Street around here, but there is a Forest. That sort of sounds like the one you're looking for. Could there be a mix-up?" Kyra asked while waving T.J. on.

Chloe climbed in T.J.'s Jeep and kept her eye on Kyra and the van driver as T.J. pulled away. When T.J. rounded the corner, she said, "You all can get up now."

Paul glanced back. "What's going on? The guy was only looking for an address."

"We don't know what his real intentions were, so we prepare for the worst. If we don't, we could be caught off guard." T.J. made another turn, then quickly a third one.

"How sad you have to suspect everyone. I couldn't do your job."

Mary's words stayed with Chloe the whole way to the safe house. For a good part of her life as a law enforcement officer and then a bodyguard, she'd had to be tough and strong for others around her. Even as a teen with her father gone a lot, she'd had to be there for her mother, but she had dreamed of having her own family and doing things differently from her mom. Somewhere along the line, that dream had gotten pushed to the background. Was it because she couldn't quite forget those times her mother had cried, lamenting how much she and her husband had been in love?

But seeing Kyra's pregnancy starting to show had revived Chloe's yearning to be a wife and mother. At first, when dating Adam, she'd thought he would be the one, but she must have instinctively known he wasn't suited for her because she hadn't been totally able to commit to him. He'd ended up dating another woman behind her back.

After T.J. and Adam, she wasn't sure having a family was in God's plan for her. If she couldn't make a total commitment, a marriage wouldn't work. She'd seen that firsthand with her parents.

Later that night, Chloe entered the living room and found T.J. staring out the front window. He threw a look over his shoulder at her, then went back to studying the landscape outside. "Do you see anything suspicious?" She planted herself next to him and gazed into the darkness.

"No, but Kyra called. She found a tracking device on the rental by the rear left tire. She's working with a sketch artist to draw a picture of what the man in the blue van looked like. The police will have it with them tomorrow at the last speaking engagement in Dallas."

"Good. I know you took down the license number. Have they tracked the owner?" She found herself narrowing her eyes, trying to see into the blackness.

"Yes, and as you guessed, it was stolen and found abandoned about ten blocks away."

"Any fingerprints?"

"Tons, but none on the steering wheel or the driver's door."

"With a picture of the guy, they can run a facial recognition program for a match."

"True—maybe we'll get a break and he'll be in the system."

T.J. shifted toward her, his eyes shielded by the shadows.

But Chloe felt them pierce through her as though he were assessing her and trying to figure something out. "I guess we scared him away since there were three of us, ready to draw our guns."

"Plus we were blocking Paul and Mary from his view. Before he got a second shot off, he'd have been dead." He narrowed the space between them and grasped her hand. "But we came close today. One of us could have been shot."

The feel of his hand around hers sent her heartbeat racing. Memories of their past deluged her. If her mother hadn't been sick with cancer, would she have gone with T.J. to Washington? She'd asked herself that many times over the years. But when her mother had recovered, she still hadn't been able to shake her doubts about T.J.'s true feelings, or she would have moved to Washington. Even though she'd ended up comparing all men she dated to T.J.

"And we know he doesn't care if others get hurt while he's hunting the Zimmermans." She barely strung the words together to form a coherent sentence, but T.J. was waiting for her to say something.

"Right. He gave the Zimmermans' driver in Dallas a concussion, and that little stunt in Paris injured a few spectators. Thankfully not bad, but still, the potential was there." He shrank the space between them even more. "I do know one thing. I didn't want anything to happen to you today."

Her mouth went dry, and she swallowed several times. "You don't need to worry about me. I can take care of myself. I've been doing it for years."

"I know. But that doesn't mean I don't want you to be careful."

"What are you doing, T.J.?"

"Telling you I care about you." He ran his free hand through her loose curls.

Her pulse throbbed. "We didn't work in the past."

For a long moment, he searched her face as though probing for some insight into what she was thinking. He released his hold on her and stepped back. "You're right. I don't want anyone to get hurt, whether it is the client, a spectator or my partner," he said in a professional voice, erasing the past few minutes as if they hadn't occurred.

Disappointment flitted down her length. What was going on between T.J. and her? Had what she'd felt the past few moments been her imagination? "I agree."

Tall, his posture straight, almost rigid, he stared outside again, his hands stuffed into his pockets. She studied his hard profile, part of it in the dark, and wished she could read his thoughts. He could still affect her, even when she steeled herself against his charms.

"Have you ever wondered what would have happened to us if you had gone to Washington?" he said, finally breaking the silence.

"Have you wondered what would have happened to us if you had turned down the job to guard the vice president and stayed in Dallas?"

He dipped his head. "Touché. And to answer your question, yes, I have thought about it."

Her eyes grew round. "What?"

"It wouldn't have worked out. You needed to stay and take care of your mother. If you hadn't, you would have been resentful that I took you away. And if I had turned down the position, I would have become resentful, wondering what opportunities I had passed over because I didn't take the job. We were both young and trying to find a place in our field. We weren't ready for that kind of commitment."

Are we now? Will you ever be ready to let go of our distrust and fear? She wanted to ask that question, but bit the inside of her cheek to keep the words inside her. "You left the Secret Service early. Do you regret being an agent?"

He swung around with several feet still between them. "Yes and no."

She waited for him to elaborate, but when he didn't, she examined the planes of his jaw line. "That's a complete answer?"

"Let me ask you if you regretted being a Dallas police officer. I thought you would make a career out of being one, but you only remained one five years after I left."

"I stayed because of my mother. After Dad died, she moved from Houston to Dallas because she needed her family and I was it. I think she knew something was wrong with her. Not long after she came, she got sick."

"Yeah, I remembered when we started dating she'd just moved to Dallas and was staying with you."

"I'm glad I had that time with her. If I hadn't, I would have regretted it. I was the only family Mom could turn to."

"Why did you quit the force? You were good at what you did. I could see you moving up the ranks quickly."

"I made detective and was excited that I could work on homicides. My mother had passed away from a reoccurrence of her cancer about six months before that and I thought a change was what I needed. Day in and day out was too much for me." For a moment, surprise gripped her. She'd never given an indication that too much death was taking the life out of her. "I left because I needed more in a job than it could provide. How about you?"

"Yes." He paused, as though trying to compose what he said next. "It was pretty much that for me, too."

His evasive tone indicated he was holding something back. Her curiosity piqued, she wanted to ask him what, but instead said, "Not being a human shield? Isn't that what we're doing?"

"Yes, but we have a say in who we protect and more control over the situation. With that said, I have something I need to tell you."

She tensed. "This doesn't sound good. What's wrong?"

"I've proposed to Kyra to buy into Guardians, Inc. Today she expressed interest. I believe she'll take me up on my proposition. She wants more time at home, especially since the new baby is coming soon."

"Why are you telling me this?"

"Because you work there. I don't want you to feel uncomfortable about the situation."

"And if I was?" She held her breath waiting for his answer because this was her job—a good one with an added bonus she felt she was helping people in need.

"Then I would look for something else. I'm not tied to Dallas. I have connections in other cities."

The thought that he would move away again if she said she was uncomfortable bothered her. Why wouldn't he fight for her? Change her mind? She'd known Kyra was pulling back from the agency, that her family was demanding more of her time. Her taking on a partner wasn't a surprise but a logical step for her employer. But that would mean T.J. would be her boss. How did she feel about that? Maybe it was time to make a change, possibly even in her job. She'd been thinking more about that lately.

"Chloe?"

There was a wealth of inquiry in that one word. Seeing him again, being around him, she had begun to realize what kind of relationship they could have after the assignment was over. Could they return to the way it had been in the past? She needed to say something to him, but… "I don't have an answer for you. We have history. Although I know you wouldn't intend for it to stand between us, it might."

"Fair enough. This may be a moot point. I don't have a definite answer from Kyra. We'll talk about it when we finish protecting Paul and Mary. I told you now because I didn't want any secrets between us. Not that my interest in Guardians, Inc., is a secret, just not public knowledge." His mouth curved into a smile.

"Good partners are honest with each other."

"Agreed, and that's why I appreciate your honest opinion about the situation."

In that moment, something shifted in this new relationship between her and T.J. In the past, she'd never felt totally on equal footing with him. He'd been her team leader on a big counterfeit case she'd worked on as an undercover operative. Even when they'd started dating, always in the back of her mind had been the fact he was older and a more experienced law enforcement officer. She hadn't been a rookie, but close enough.

For the first time she felt on equal footing—what would happen if he became her boss?

"Over the years I've learned to stand up for myself and give my opinion. I've changed." Nine years ago she hadn't been fully honest until the end of their relationship when she'd refused to go to Washington and stayed to help her mother.

"I've noticed. I've changed, too. More mellow."

"Mellow? Not from where I am," she said with a chuckle. "You rushed right out the door to catch the intruder a couple of nights ago."

His laugh filled the air. "You aren't going to let me forget that. You got the better end of that deal."

"Yes, and *now* I'm grateful for that. But at the time I wanted to clobber you." She tried to force the tight muscles in her neck and shoulders to relax, but it wasn't working.

"That's okay. I got clobbered by Artie Franklin. And speaking of that reporter, Kyra said he's still remaining quiet about his informant. She's going to dig into his life and see what she finds."

"If anyone can get him to talk, it will be Kyra. Anything else?" *What really made you quit the Secret Service?*

"Nothing really. Matthews can't find the car that was parked next to the limo at the church. The driver is fully recovered, but can't give us any more information. Kyra is checking into his past, too, to make sure he wasn't in on it."

"Could he be the leak to the reporter?" Weariness blanketed Chloe, and she turned to lean against the windowsill.

"Kyra mentioned that. It's possible, but for some reason it doesn't feel right to me. You should get some rest. I'll take the first watch tonight."

"Are you sure?"

He moved closer and put his hands on her shoulders. "Definitely. You're wound tight. I can feel the knots."

"I get like this during an assignment. All my stress ends up on my shoulders."

"Turn around. Let me see what I can do."

When she did as he said, his fingers kneaded the base of her neck and along her shoulders, working to ease the tension. Bit by bit it fell away. "You're hired. No matter what I do, I always feel this tense after a few days on a job. I've tried putting heat there, but your massage is much better."

"It's because those knots have to be broken up."

A sigh slipped from her lips. "When did you get so good?"

"This can be pretty common in our line of work. Our stress has to go somewhere."

"Where does yours go?"

"Into sleepless nights."

Finally, she swung around, needing to put some space between them. "I think I got the better deal. I need my sleep, which is my cue to leave and get some before it's my turn to stand guard. Thanks."

"Good night, Chloe. See you in four hours."

She left T.J. standing at the window, staring out front again. At the doorway, she looked back at him, rubbing her hand over her neck and shoulder. The deep ache had vanished, but not the questions their conversation had raised. They both had changed in nine years. He wasn't the same man she had fallen in love with once, and she wasn't the same woman. That should be reason enough to guard against his appeal.

Standing backstage at a downtown hotel with a theater-style auditorium, Chloe watched the throng filling up the large area—a sea of red chairs with almost two thousand people in them. Rob Matthews was in the dressing room waiting with Mary and Paul for the crowd to be seated. At least the couple had agreed to come early and not to use the main entrance into the building after hearing that the driver in the blue van hadn't been legit and the rental had had a GPS tracker attached to it.

All the uniformed police watching the auditorium, double the number after yesterday, had a drawing of the driver, which Chloe thought looked remarkably like the man she'd seen.

She studied the audience as they filed into the massive room through the main sets of doors in the back while T.J. positioned himself on the other side and observed the individuals coming through the right entrance. Rob thought it would be better if they scanned the crowd while he stayed with the couple because they had seen the driver yesterday.

As much as she wished she saw the perpetrator in the auditorium, not one person looked similar. That didn't mean he wasn't here somewhere, disguised. The sheer numbers entering made it impossible to be sure he wasn't among them. And no amount of trying to persuade the Zimmermans to cancel had worked.

The lights dimmed two minutes before Mary and Paul were expected on stage. The people, most still standing, moved to their seats. Mary and Paul would speak for an hour, then sign books at the table set up for them in the lobby. A copy of their most recent book had been included as part of the ticket sale. Probably not everyone would want an autograph, but enough would that it would be hours before they left for the security of the safe house. Then they would repeat it all in San Antonio, their next stop.

Paul joined T.J. while Rob escorted Mary to Chloe's side of the stage. The lights came back up and the couple strolled onto the stage with Chloe and T.J. closely behind them. A story had run on the news the day before about the fact the Zimmermans had two bodyguards because of threats made against them, and still the whole auditorium was crammed with people eager to hear their message, to fight for their families, their communities, to stand up to gangs and criminals who wanted to defy them.

As before, Chloe took the right side while T.J. canvassed the left side. The bright lights shining in their faces made the task difficult. Paul began speaking, then Mary. Throughout their talk the audience erupted into applause at different points.

"This is our country. We'd better determine what is acceptable and not let just the vocal people determine it. The silent majority has a responsibility not to be silent any longer," Paul said about halfway through the talk.

The people rose, cheering, the sound deafening. Chloe tensed. This would be a good time to make a move. But within minutes the crowd took their seats and silence ruled as Mary spoke.

A woman in the back of the front section screamed. Red smoke billowed into the air from the center section while from behind the curtains smoke flooded the stage as the audience surged to their feet, yelling. Chloe grabbed Mary's arm while T.J. took Paul's. The people from behind the stage poured out of there, running away with the fleeing crowd as red smoke rolled and swelled from the back, too.

Chloe started for the steps when she caught sight of Rob carrying a woman from behind the curtain. Her long curly dark hair flowed over the detective's arm, her face turned toward his chest.

"There's another one down near the dressing rooms. I think these are smoke bombs, but we need to get out of here in case there's something else coming," Rob shouted.

T.J. looked at Chloe.

"Go. Rob's here," Chloe said, moving between Paul and Mary on the far right by the stairs leading to the theater floor.

Paul wrenched away from Chloe's grasp. "I'm going with T.J. There may be more hurt backstage. Please make sure that Mary gets out all right."

"No, Paul. I'll stay and help, too."

He swung around and took hold of Mary. "Get out of here." Then he hurried after T.J.

Chloe started after him, but Rob blocked her passage. "You and Mary need to leave with me. I'll get some help back here."

"I can't leave. What if..." Mary's eyes glistened.

Reddish-gray smoke continued to roll across the stage like dense fog, its stench spreading. Chloe tightened her hold on her client. "T.J. will take care of Paul. Let's go."

Mary didn't resist, but kept looking back while Chloe focused on a way out of the theater—the nearest exit was a third of the way to the back of the theater. She kept Mary close to her. All around Chloe, the mob tried cramming through the few exits—two sets on the sides and another two in the back, six double doors with two thousand individuals hurrying to leave.

Mary gasped and all color drained from her face. Chloe glanced back. Flames licked up the curtains on the left side of the stage—where T.J. and Paul had disappeared.

SIX

T.J. turned and saw the burning curtain fall onto the stage and the blaze engulf the material. Flames ran across the stage, completely cutting them off from getting out of the theater from that direction. That left only one other—the backstage door, which felt like riding into an ambush.

"We'll check the dressing room area. Start praying that the back door isn't blocked." Coughing, T.J. used the crook of his elbow to cover his nose and mouth, his eyes stinging.

Paul did likewise, staying right at his side as T.J. plunged into the smoky air. Up ahead through the haze, he saw a figure lying on the floor. T.J. increased his pace, and when he reached the prone body, he knelt and felt for a pulse. With coughs racking his body, Paul squatted next to T.J.

"He's alive. Help me get him up and we'll drag him between us." T.J. hoisted the obese man up by the left side while Paul took the right.

"Why isn't the sprinkler system working?" Paul shouted over the crackling noise of the fire.

"Good question." Sweat rolling down his face, T.J.

started again for the back of the theater. With a look over his shoulder, he spied the fire moving away from him but toward the audience—and Chloe and Mary.

At the door, T.J. slammed his hand down on the bar to open it. Nothing happened. The lever didn't budge. Locked?

Someone in front of Chloe went down, tripping over another person who'd fallen. With Rob carrying the unconscious woman, Chloe and Mary were left to grab the two on the floor and pull them up before the stragglers behind them ran them over. One man leaped over Chloe, barely missing her and the young lady she was helping. An older gentleman plowed into Mary and sent her flying into the teenage girl trying to get up with her assistance. They both went down again. Chloe managed to haul the woman to her feet before she turned her attention to her client and the teen.

All the while heat, smoke and flames headed their way faster than the people could move through the exits. She would be a fool not to be afraid, but she didn't have time to give in to her fear. She could when she got Mary outside.

The sound of something crashing onto the stage spurred the mob to hurry even more. The pounding of her heartbeat thundered against Chloe's skull. Smoke from the fire reached outward, engulfing the whole theater.

"Let's put him down and both of us try to open the door. It's not locked. It seems like something is blocking it," T.J. said right before a ceiling beam ten yards away from them collapsed onto the stage. "No wonder everyone fled out of the stage area."

Coughing, Paul dropped the man, who slid down, almost taking T.J. with him. He released his hold before they were a tangled mess on the floor.

Facing Paul, T.J. said, "One, two, three."

Both slammed their shoulders into the metal door. It inched open.

Again T.J. and Paul struck it. Fresh air blew in from the small gap and fueled T.J.'s determination to budge whatever was on the other side—but also fed the fire with oxygen.

The third attempt moved the obstruction enough that T.J. squeezed his shoulder through the space and poked his head outside. The big Dumpster had been dragged in front of the door. The stench of garbage mixed with the smell of smoke. The wail of sirens echoed down the alley. Police and a couple of firefighters charged toward them.

Relieved, T.J. ducked back in, staying next to Paul low to the ground. "Help is coming." When he heard the Dumpster being moved, he said, "Let's get this guy up, so when the door can open all the way, we can get him out into the fresh air."

As Paul helped him hoist the huge man up, he looked at T.J. over the top of the victim's head. "We'll be all right, but what about Mary and Chloe?"

T.J. stared at the wall of fire edging its way toward them, seeking the fresh air. "They're fine," he said and prayed to the Lord he was right. *Chloe and Mary are in Your hands.* He didn't know what he would do if something happened to Chloe—or Mary.

* * *

Screams erupted around Chloe as the fire danced along the front of the stage and up the walls toward the back. Panic mushroomed as the fire exploded nearby.

"Get behind me," Rob said to Chloe and Mary.

"Lord, put a shield of protection around these people," Mary said as she looked around.

"Amen." Chloe had seen this kind of crowd chaos before. From what she'd read about the stink bombs in Paris, that was mild compared to this.

A man near Chloe pulled another guy back and surged into his place. The first man returned and jumped on him. In the midst of the mob, a fight broke out. The sight shot adrenaline through Chloe, and her heartbeat accelerated even more. People circled past the two wrestling on the floor and kept heading for the exit. Sweeping her gaze through the theater, Chloe glimpsed the same thing happened at all the doors—panic taking over.

Chloe grasped Mary and pulled her even closer. With Rob in front, Chloe covered the area behind them and to the sides.

Finally the double doors loomed a few yards ahead.

"We're almost out of here," Chloe said close to Mary's ear as the noise around them kept rising.

Tears running down her face, Mary nodded, then started coughing.

Gray smoke like a menacing veil mingled with what red was left in the air above them, becoming thicker—darker.

Rob, carrying the passed-out woman, burst through the exit, followed by Mary and Chloe. The mob dispersed out into the lobby, charging for the bank of glass doors that led outside. Fire trucks lined the front of the building while firefighters and police swarmed the area inside, helping the crowd to move in a safe manner. Some of the firefighters were pushing into the auditorium against the tide of people.

Out in the fresh air Chloe propelled Mary farther from the theater. Police waved the throng past the barricades set up. Rob sought paramedics for the woman. As Chloe scanned the crowd for the perpetrator, she searched for T.J. and Paul, too.

Were they still in the theater behind the stage where the fire had started? She *needed* to see T.J. and Paul— that they were alive and safe.

The paramedic took the oxygen mask from T.J. "I'm okay," T.J. said. "How is the man we brought out?"

"He's being transported to the hospital, but he did recover consciousness."

"Praise God." Paul also gave his mask back. "Can we go now?"

"I'm fine with that, but the police officer wants to talk with you." The paramedic waved his hand toward a young woman waiting a few feet away.

She approached them when the EMT left. "What is your name and contact information?"

After T.J. told her, he asked, "Please see if you can contact Detective Rob Matthews. I'm a bodyguard hired to guard Paul Zimmerman here." T.J. indicated his client next to him. "I need to know if the detective and the women with him made it out okay." T.J. went on to explain why Matthews was involved.

The woman officer stepped away and spoke into the receiver at her shoulder.

Paul shifted from one foot to the other. "We should go around front and see if we can find Mary and Chloe. I need to know they're okay."

So do I, especially Chloe. She's here because of me. A vision of Chloe, concern deep in her eyes, as she'd left with Mary, taunted him.

"You think this area is a madhouse? The front will be twenty times worse as all the audience exits. I'm hoping she can track down Detective Matthews and he'll have Mary and Chloe with him." Safe. *Please, Lord. I haven't asked much lately. Please let them be unharmed.*

As T.J. waited for the officer to return, Chloe haunted his thoughts. Her smile could melt him, although he did his best not to let her know the effect it had on him. Her long, wavy hair down around her shoulders—the memory of letting it slip through his fingers. Her scent that teased him every time she came near him.

The policewoman retraced her steps to T.J. and Paul. "Detective Matthews is on his way and he told me to tell you he would bring Mrs. Zimmerman and Chloe. You're not to go anywhere until he arrives. You two can sit in my patrol car. He asked me to stay with you."

Paul collapsed on the backseat behind the driver while T.J. slipped in next to him, his gaze intent on the direction Chloe and Mary would come from. Until he saw Chloe with his own eyes, he wouldn't be satisfied she was okay. He knew all the things that could happen in a crowd during a disaster. Pandemonium ruled, and that made it possible for the person hunting Mary to take her out. Chloe would protect her client, putting herself in harm's way. The realization iced his blood.

* * *

Coming around the side of the theater about a hundred yards from the building, Chloe glimpsed a woman officer standing next to a squad car. Through the windshield she noticed two figures in the back of it. "Is that them?" she asked Rob, who flanked Mary's other side as they weaved their way through the throng milling behind the barricades.

"I think so. I'm not personally familiar with Officer Parks."

As she swept her glance over the crowd, Chloe caught sight of the smoke churning from the roof of the theater. "What happened in there? We saw red smoke bombs first, then a real fire."

"The woman I carried outside came from the back area of the stage, where some of the red smoke was. Once she is tended to at the hospital, I plan to talk with her. Maybe she saw something, or maybe she's the one who set off the smoke bomb."

"Why would she do that? I don't know her. What have I done to her?" Mary stared straight ahead, a dazed expression on her face as though in overload.

Chloe couldn't blame her after all that had happened to Mary and Paul this week. She knew one thing. This tour could not continue. If need be, she would decline the assignment and hope T.J. would, too. Mary and Paul had no business being out in public until whoever was after them was caught. She'd never walked away from a job in the middle before, but she cared about Mary and Paul and wanted to keep them alive, so she would leave if that would keep Mary and Paul from continuing the book tour.

"What sets someone off can be one of a thousand

reasons, big or small. Some you can't even comprehend. When dealing with situations like this you need to look at everyone as a suspect," Chloe finally answered.

"I agree, Mrs. Zimmerman. What Chloe says is true. If you want to stay alive, there's no question the person doing this wants you and your husband harmed. This isn't a prank like Paris." Rob stepped up to the officer and introduced himself. "Can you drive these folks to their house and stay there until I arrive?" Then he turned to Chloe. "I'm staying here and working this scene. We'll talk later."

"No. I don't want Officer Parks driving us. We can take care of it. The fewer people who know where we are the better."

Rob pulled her away from Mary and lowered his voice. "I can't force you, Chloe, but the Zimmermans are in danger."

"Why do you think T.J. and I were hired? But yesterday the guy after them put a tracker on the rental so he would know where they were staying. I need this evening to convince Mary and Paul to cancel their tour and retreat to a safe place. Maybe even stay where we are until you find whoever is doing this." The sound of the car door behind her opening and closing alerted her a few seconds before T.J. joined them.

"I suggest you quit the chitchatting and let's get out of here. The person responsible for this is probably somewhere in this crowd." T.J. gestured toward the theater where the firefighters were beginning to bring the blaze under control. "I called Kyra and told her what happened. She'll meet us to exchange cars again."

Chloe swung her attention to Rob. "Will it appease

you if Officer Parks follows us to the exchange in our rental to make sure everything goes all right?"

Rob nodded. "But we're still talking tonight. I need your address, and I promise no one will track me. Where's your rental?"

T.J. pointed to a green Chevy not far away.

"I'll talk with Officer Parks, then walk with you to your car."

As Rob approached the police officer, T.J. escorted Paul to Chloe and Mary. Paul embraced his wife for a long moment. Chloe heard the words *I love you*, and turned away to give them some privacy while watching the people around them.

"Let's go," Rob said when he came back. As they walked toward the Chevy about a hundred yards across the parking lot, he continued. "Mr. and Mrs. Zimmerman, are you sure you can't think of anyone who would do something like this? There was a lot of anger behind what happened today. Four red smoke bombs were set off to cause panic much worse than the stink bombs at the Paris event. Then there was a fire, too."

Paul scowled. "Can a smoke bomb start a fire?"

"Not likely." Rob opened the back door for Mary. "A flash bomb would be more likely to do that."

Mary climbed into the rental. "Then why the smoke bombs if the person was setting a fire?"

"Don't know the answer, but I may know more when I talk with the fire investigator about how it started. That may be a while, though."

"Thank you, Detective." Mary leaned back against the seat and closed her eyes.

After shutting the door, Chloe faced Rob. "I echo her thanks. I hope you can give us some answers this evening." She gave her friend the address of the safe house. "Call when you arrive at the gate and I'll open it."

"Take care, Chloe. We're coming up empty with the clues we've found so far. I have my partner tracking down one lead from the photo of the man yesterday."

"Why didn't you tell me this right away?"

"I found out right before everything started and since then we've been kind of busy."

"Thanks for being here today." Chloe gave Rob a small smile.

T.J. shook Rob's hand. "See you later."

Her friend started back toward the theater, homing in on the fire captain in charge. Chloe expelled her breath slowly. "We have our work cut out for us. We need to convince the Zimmermans to cancel."

"They will. If not, I'll get the publisher to cancel it."

As T.J. slipped into the driver's seat, Chloe rounded the rental and slid into her position next to Mary.

Paul angled around and peered at his wife. "Before we go, I want to make it clear that Mary and I agree that the tour has to be canceled. We can't put people in danger, and today this person made it clear he didn't care who was in his way."

Thank You, Lord. Now we have a chance to protect Mary and Paul.

"We caught a break, or so we thought," Rob said when he entered the safe house later that evening.

T.J. closed the door behind the detective and turned toward him. "I like the first part of your sentence. You need to improve on the last bit, though."

"I wish I could." Rob surveyed the entry hall.

"Where's everyone? I want to say this only one time. I need to return to the station as soon as possible."

"Chloe, Paul and Mary are in the kitchen cleaning up the dinner dishes. I volunteered to be on door duty."

"I wish I could do that at home. My wife won't take any excuse. All the duties are split fifty-fifty, and I can't really say anything since she works as much as I do."

T.J. started for the back of the house. "More than a detective in a big city?"

"Yep. She's a doctor in the E.R. Since we don't have children, she fills in when needed, if possible."

"It sounds like you have an understanding wife."

"Yes. It was a great day when I met her."

T.J. listened to the love in Matthews's voice, and he was bothered by the fact he didn't have what the detective had. For a long time, he hadn't even considered having a wife and family. Then he'd met Chloe and that had changed. He'd started thinking about the possibility of getting married. But on one occasion when they had dated, she'd expressed how she hoped to have children one day, and he hadn't seen that in his future as a Secret Service agent. Was that one of the reasons he'd jumped at the chance to go to Washington, D.C., and be on the vice president's detail? He'd never thought he had a commitment phobia. Did he? Or had the timing been all wrong? And even if it had been, that didn't mean it was right now.

When they entered the kitchen, Chloe looked at Rob. "Do you know how the fire started?"

"Not yet, but by morning the rubble should have cooled enough for the arson investigator to go through it. I have a few things to ask and tell you."

Mary crossed the room. "Then let's sit down in the living room. I'm exhausted. I'm sure you'll want me to be fully awake, but I can't stand much longer."

Paul took her hand and accompanied his wife out of the kitchen.

T.J. liked the way Paul and Mary supported each other. There were times he'd needed that but hadn't experienced it. He settled on the couch across from Paul, Mary and Chloe.

Matthews stood at the end of the coffee table, his mouth set in a grim line. "There were sixteen people who went to the E.R. Five of them were hospitalized."

Stiff, Mary blinked several times. "Anyone critical?"

"No."

Her shoulders sagged, and Mary wilted against the couch. "Thank You, Lord."

Matthews scanned his notes. "It has been confirmed the sprinkler system was tampered with. From what we can piece together, four red smoke bombs went off pretty close together. I suspect someone used a detonator to set them off. The back part of the theater has been searched, since the fire didn't reach that far and the devices were attached to the seats. Several hours earlier the theater owner had had a dog sniff for bombs before setting up for the event. Only people who had been vetted were allowed inside after the stage was set up. The doors were locked and guards posted until the event opened. People were checked as they came in."

"So how were the smoke bombs planted?" T.J. asked, not liking where this was going.

"There are security cameras, but not all over the theater. Interestingly, the smoke bombs were placed where the cameras didn't reach."

"Inside job?" Had this job been hired out to a pro? T.J. began to wonder if there was more going on here.

"I think so, and we're looking at staff employees, but that will take time. I'll keep you informed if we get any kind of lead. Mary, Paul, can you think of anyone who is holding a grudge against you?"

"You don't think it's our message?" Paul asked.

"It's possible, but I think this is tied up in a more personal angle." Chloe rose and prowled the room, stopping to stare out the window.

"I have to agree with Chloe." T.J. leaned forward and placed his elbows on his thighs, clasping his hands together.

"No, when we aren't writing or speaking, we have a quiet life at our ranch. We treat our employees like friends."

T.J. stood across from the detective. "We're leaving early tomorrow morning for the Zimmermans' ranch between Houston and San Antonio. We're making a slight detour to pick up their sixteen-year-old son at Bethany Academy in Houston. You have my number. Call if you find out anything."

"Will do." Matthews nodded toward the couple then Chloe. "I've got more I have to do tonight so I need to get back, but let me know if you can think of anyone who would want to hurt you."

T.J. saw the detective out of the house and waited until he went through the gate before returning to the living room. "I'll take first watch again tonight since I'll be driving tomorrow. Mary, are you going to call your son and let him know what you're doing?"

"Yes, now that we know we can leave. I was afraid Detective Matthews would need us to stay, but I really have no idea why this is happening, especially today. What was done was bolder than in Paris or at the church the other day." She delved into her pocket. "Can I use my phone? He'll know that number. In fact, he's probably expecting a call after what happened and wondering why I'm not answering my cell. At least I was able to call the school and let them know we were okay since he was on a field trip."

T.J. handed her his untraceable one. "Use this one. If he wonders why you're calling on a different phone, chalk it up to me being cautious."

Paul came to sit beside Mary while she made the call to their son. T.J. left the room with Chloe to give the couple some privacy. In the entry hall, he turned toward her. "Ready to go?"

"As I said at the other house, I haven't unpacked. Maybe at the ranch I actually will."

"On the ride to the ranch, we need to have a conversation about how the ranch operates. Who does what? Who works there? How long? I know Mary called her cousin, who takes care of the home, and Paul talked with his foreman to let him know he would be returning earlier than expected to the ranch."

"Mary has mentioned a Vickie Campbell. Is she the cousin?"

"Yes. The foreman is Zach Bradley. I overheard Paul arguing with him about selling some cattle. He told him to hold off until he got home."

Chloe's forehead scrunched. "Paul's the owner."

"Who is gone a lot of the time. Maybe Zach is used to running the ranch without someone looking over his shoulder."

"I'm just glad that Mary and Paul called off the

tour, but they are doing a TV interview after they get back home. The TV crew has agreed to film it at the ranch, so at least the Zimmermans won't have to go to the studio." Chloe kneaded her hand into her neck. That had been to appease Nancy, who was throwing a fit about canceling the interview tomorrow morning. "But if it's not safe at the ranch, that TV interview will be canceled, too, no matter what Nancy says."

"You're still tense."

"Your powers of observation are amazing." A twinkle sparkled in her eyes. "I'm trying to loosen those knots the best way I can."

"I can help." He winked.

"If I can't work them out, I might take you up on that."

"Good. Whatever makes my partner—"

Mary appeared at the living room entrance, tears gleaming in her eyes. "Aaron insists no one is after him, just us. He refuses to leave school and come to the ranch. He hung up on me."

SEVEN

Passing through the iron gates of the Sizzling Z Ranch, Chloe noted their sturdy structure, a plus as far as security was concerned, but the black fence along the property where the highway ran could easily be vaulted. From a distance she spied a large two-story redbrick antebellum home. The white trim stood out between the trees—mostly pine. Not far from the house, maybe two hundred yards, sat a black barn.

As they neared the home, a thin woman, who was five foot seven or eight inches and about forty years old, came out onto the verandah. Her blond hair pulled back in a tight bun, she held her hand up to shield the sun slanting across the porch.

T.J. parked his car in front. "Is that your cousin Vickie?"

"Yes. I don't know what we would do without her. She keeps the house running smoothly, especially when we're gone," Mary said, sandwiched between Chloe and her pouting son in the backseat.

The second the vehicle stopped, Aaron Zimmerman shoved open the door and scrambled from the Jeep.

Mary climbed out of the car. "Aaron."

He threw a glare over his shoulder and kept going while Chloe quickly exited the vehicle and came around to Mary.

She leaned close to Chloe. "Sorry about the attitude. He has always felt like he's living in the limelight because of who we are, and now he feels even more restricted." She trailed after her son with Chloe right behind her.

The sixteen-year-old pushed past Vickie and charged through the entrance to his home. The sound of him stomping up the steps echoed through the large foyer, which was the size of Chloe's living and dining room at her apartment. Mary went after her son, waving Chloe back.

She respected Mary's desire to talk to Aaron alone, so she would give mother and son a minute, then follow. She hadn't had a chance to even canvass the house and see what kind of security was in place. The description the Zimmermans had given them on the way hadn't told her much. They had a several-year-old alarm system. That could mean anything. The front gate was controlled by a remote or a keyed-in number and remained locked. That was good, but then as she'd observed that wouldn't stop a person on foot.

A minute later, Chloe started up the steps, glancing back while Paul and T.J. brought in the luggage. Vickie closed the front door behind them, then peered at Chloe. Vickie welcomed Chloe with a warm smile before turning her attention to Paul and T.J.

On the second floor, there was a long hallway to the right and left with four rooms on either side. She strolled down the corridor to the right but couldn't hear any voices. She traversed the left hall to the end and checked out the barn about two hundred yards away as well as the lock on the window. This house's configuration was similar to the first house they'd stayed in Dallas, which didn't leave her with a comfortable feeling.

The sound of a shrill, angry voice pierced the air, coming from the nearest room to her right. The door slammed open and Aaron rushed into the hallway, sending her a narrow-eyed look before stalking off toward the staircase.

Chloe moved toward the room to see if Mary was inside and all right. She came face-to-face with Mary, an ashen tinge to her features. Her client tried to shrug and smile. Both attempts collapsed.

"I'm a psychologist and should be prepared for my son's rebellious behavior. I certainly counseled enough parents concerning that." Tears returned to Mary's eyes, and she averted her head, swiping her hand across her cheeks.

"I didn't eavesdrop—my job is just to be with you and keep you safe."

"I've got to have some freedom in my own home. Paul said he would do what needed to be done so that the family could move about without always having someone with us, especially for Aaron's sake. I'm not sure what he would do otherwise. He was furious with us this morning for staying on tour as long as we did. I assured him we were all right, but that didn't appease him."

"You and Paul are celebrities in a sense, and I've seen this before. That can be hard on the children. I imagine T.J. has stories about the children of the vice president rebelling over their confinement. We'll tour the house and grounds and make this work for you and your son."

Mary enveloped her in a hug. "Bless you. This has been difficult on all of us. I have a hard time thinking about someone out there hating me so much he would set fire to the theater and risk harming so many innocent people."

"The fire still could be an accident. I'm calling Detective Matthews later to see what the arson investigator said."

"I guess we need to have hope. That's what helps people keep going forward. Please tell Paul I've decided to lie down."

"Where's your room?"

Mary pointed to the door across from her son's. "I thought I would have you stay in the room next to ours and T.J. in the one beside my son's. Is that okay?"

"Perfect. Where does Vickie stay?"

"She has the room at the far end of the hall."

"How long has she been living here?"

"Ever since she had to file for bankruptcy three years ago when her business failed. She had no place to go, and we were happy to open our home to her. Since she didn't want a free ride, she asked to be the housekeeper when our other one left unexpectedly. She's a jewel. She also keeps the ranch books and works with Zach to make sure it runs smoothly. Now do you see why we are so appreciative for both of their help?" Mary took a few steps and opened her door. "I'll be down later."

"Let me come inside and at least check out your room."

Mary chuckled. "I don't think anyone can get under my bed."

Chloe looked around, checking to make sure the windows were locked, before crossing to the bathroom, drawing the shower curtain back then inspecting the huge walk-in closet. She'd seen bedrooms that were smaller.

"Anyone behind the dresses?" Mary's mouth tipped up for a second, then quavered. "What have we done so wrong that we deserve this kind of harassment?"

Chloe closed the space between them and took her client's hands. "Some people don't need a good reason. In their mind they have twisted everything around to suit their need."

"Thank you, Chloe. I'm usually the one holding someone else up."

Chloe gave her hands a squeeze, then walked into the hallway. "Rest. You'll stay safe if I have anything to do with it."

When she descended the staircase, T.J. and Paul stood in the middle of the foyer next to the round glass table with a huge floral arrangement. The scent of roses, lilies and some kind of flower she didn't know the name of drifted to her as she paused in front of the two men deep in conversation.

T.J. smiled at her. "Is Mary okay?"

"Yes." Chloe glanced around the foyer and the sur-rounding rooms. "Where did Aaron go?"

Paul's thick eyebrows slashed almost together. "Knowing my son, he's left the house out the back. He'll probably go to the stable, which is not far from the barn."

T.J. straightened. "Is he going riding?"

"If he's going there, it's to ride."

"He can't. At least not without one of us with him. We don't know what we're dealing with. The person might have been trying just to stop your tour. If so, then nothing else will happen, but most likely there's more to it." T.J. looked at Chloe. "Do you want to go after him or should I?"

"I will."

"If you think my family is in danger, not just me and Mary, do we need to bring in bodyguards for him and Vickie?" Paul asked, his frown deepening. "Because I don't think Aaron will stay inside the whole time. When he comes to the ranch, he spends a lot of his time outside. He even helps Zach and the other hands with the cattle."

Chloe gritted her teeth. "He needs to be made to realize the seriousness of the situation."

Paul exhaled audibly. "At the school when we talked with him in his room while he was packing, he was so angry. He seems to be that way all the time lately. I've tried everything with him, but nothing seems to work. If I ground him to the house, he'll find a way to escape his prison, because that's what he'll think it is."

"Since you've agreed to get a couple of security dogs, I can bring in some men to handle them and walk the perimeter outside. We need to be prepared for the long haul."

"While you two discuss the issue, I'd better get Aaron before he rides off." Chloe headed for the front door.

"Do you ride?" Paul called out.

She swiveled around at the exit. "Yes, so I'll go

after him if I have to. This will be a good time to meet some of your men."

Beyond the barn, Chloe spied the stable, a long black building. Aaron led a horse out of the open double doors. He patted the animal, then hiked his foot into the stirrup. Five yards away. Instead of calling out, she hurried her pace.

As he mounted, Chloe reached his side and snatched hold of the reins and then the bridle. "You aren't going anywhere. In case you didn't understand your parents earlier, there is a madman out there bent on hurting them."

"But not me."

"How do you know that? One of the worst ways to hurt a parent is to do something to their child."

"Just great! The one thing I enjoy at the ranch, riding, and now I can't even do it because of them."

He sent her a look that screamed he intended to defy his parents anyway.

She shot him a hard stare. "Don't even think it."

"Think what? Are you a mind reader now?" the boy sneered.

"One of my many talents. You're thinking by the time I could get a horse saddled you'd be long gone." She narrowed her eyes. "I'm prepared to hold on if you try. Are you ready to face the consequences?"

"What?" His glare challenged her.

Inching more toward the middle of the horse while holding on, Chloe watched for the slightest indication he would try to ride away. A tic in his jaw line twitched as he sat forward and kicked the sides of his horse. Letting go of the reins, she vaulted into the saddle right behind him and locked her arms around him. The mare set out in a canter.

"Where are we going?"

Aaron pulled back on the reins, his shoulder hunching over. "Nowhere."

"Good choice."

"I don't have a choice. I can hardly breathe. Can you loosen your hold?"

"Are you going to get off?"

He huffed. "Yes. It's not like I could get very far with you hounding me."

After Chloe slid off, keeping her grip on the saddle, Aaron dismounted, anger raging in his eyes.

"Take care of your horse, then we'll go back to the house."

As he removed the saddle, he said, "You must ride a lot to be able to do what you did."

"I grew up around horses, so yes, you might say I have."

He looked her up and down. "You're quick."

"I'm a bodyguard. I need to be."

He finished tending his mare in silence, and then turned it loose in the paddock next to the stable before storming toward the house. On the trek back, Chloe assessed the outside security issues. Most would be taken care of with dogs and a guard patrolling. But nearer the antebellum home, she noticed the lack of lights for the grounds. A brightly lit place was less likely to be hit.

Aaron disappeared inside, the back door slamming closed. Now all she and T.J. needed was for everyone to follow the security procedures. That might be the hardest part of this assignment.

* * *

That night, Chloe took her seat next to Mary at the dining room table while T.J. sat between Aaron and Paul. Vickie rushed through the swinging doors and put the last dish in the middle of the table for eight, then eased onto her chair on the other side of Chloe.

Mary reached for her son's and Chloe's hands, bowing her head. "I'd like to say the blessing tonight." After everyone joined hands, she continued. "Dear Heavenly Father, thank You for delivering my son, husband and me safely home. Please heal Joy, Samuel, Bill and Kitty so they can be home with their families, too. Thank You for sending Chloe and T.J. to protect us. Paul and I forgive the person who is after us. Heal his hurt and anger. And last, bless this food that Vickie prepared for us. Amen."

Quickly releasing his mother's hand, Aaron kept his head down as though he'd found an interesting spot on his plate. Since coming back from the stable four hours ago, he'd been in his room, refusing to come out when his mother had tried to coax him to join them.

"Who are Joy, Samuel, Bill and Kitty?" Vickie asked as she passed the platter of roast beef.

"We found out those are the people still in the hospital from yesterday's fire." Paul took the meat from Vickie, speared a thick, juicy slice, then gave the platter to T.J.

Aaron lifted his chin and looked at his dad. "There were people hurt?"

"Yes, I'm surprised you didn't hear about it. It's been splashed all over the news. Some were injured and taken to the hospital."

"I don't look at the news. All it talks about is what's

bad in this world. I didn't know anything had happened to you until the school told me and then said you two were all right." Aaron spooned the broccoli rice casserole onto his plate and then gave the vegetable dish to his mother without even looking her way.

Chloe watched the terse exchange between Aaron and Paul, most of the tension—not just tension, but anger—coming from the son. Even though he was upset at his mom and dad, it was strange Aaron didn't turn on a TV to see what was going on or go on the internet. But then, when did she? She didn't purposefully check the news every day, especially when she was on a job, unless it directly affected the assignment.

"Have you heard from Detective Matthews about how the fire got started?" Mary asked Chloe while cutting her roast.

"Not yet. With all that happened at the theater, he's been busy tracking down leads."

"Any good ones?" Vickie sipped some water.

"A couple, from what he told me this afternoon. I promised I wouldn't bother him until later this evening. He was interviewing the people behind the stage. The woman he carried out shouldn't have been there. She's disappeared. We think she was filling in for a sick employee of the event-planning company." Chloe had just gotten off the phone with Rob right before dinner and hadn't gotten a chance to tell T.J. or the Zimmermans. He was going to talk to the arson investigator and would elaborate when he called her after that meeting.

Mary sat forward. "Then they might actually find the person?"

"Maybe. It could be nothing, or it could lead to the

person behind this. The Dallas police will continue to investigate every piece of evidence." Chloe scooped up some broccoli and rice. "Vickie, this meal is delicious."

Vickie grinned and started to say something, but Aaron cut in, "Do we have to sit here and talk about this all the time? It's bad enough I'm a prisoner here in my own home."

"Actually, son, that's a good suggestion. When we're eating, we won't from now on." Paul swept his gaze around the table.

Silence fell over the table as everyone dug into their food. Except Aaron. He toyed with his meat and vegetables, moving them around on his plate, not even pleased at what his father had said.

The doorbell rang.

Chloe's hand tightened on her fork as she finished her last bite. Sitting nearest the foyer, she rose and glanced at Paul. "Are you expecting anyone?"

"That'll be Zach. I told him to come up to the house when he was through for the day. We have some business to discuss. He just returned from being gone for a week and some issues need to be tied up."

Chloe started for the entry hall. "What does he look like?"

"Tall, thin with salt-and-pepper hair." Paul stood. "I'll let him in."

Chloe whirled around. "No. Either T.J. or I will do that, even with a person you know."

Paul covered the distance between them. "Surely you don't think it's Zach. He's worked here for years."

"Where was he last week?"

Paul's mouth dropped open. "I've known him for eight years."

In the foyer, Chloe stopped. "Was he on vacation?"

"No, his father was ill and not doing well. He asked for the time off to go see him in Dallas."

"He was there at the same time you were?"

Paul frowned, folding his arms over his chest. "It's not Zach."

"Still, I need the information to make sure he was where he said he would be." Chloe put her hand on the knob, then pulled it open to keep Paul from responding. It was always hard for a person to realize someone close might be the one after them. She and T.J. had to look at all possibilities, especially the ones in direct contact with Mary and Paul.

As she let the ranch foreman into the house, T.J. came to the dining room entrance. After Paul introduced her and she shook Zach's hand, T.J. crossed to the foreman and greeted him.

"I missed you at the barn a couple of hours ago." T.J. studied Zach.

The foreman removed his cowboy hat and held it by the brim. "I went into town to see about some feed problems."

"Come in, Zach. Let's go to my office. I'll have Vickie bring in coffee and a piece of the chocolate cake she baked today."

T.J. strolled behind the two men, but Paul paused at the end of the hallway that led to the back part of the place. "You don't need to come. I don't want Zach to think I suspect him, because I don't. Stay here. Please."

T.J. nodded, but when he turned toward Chloe, his jaw was set in a hard line. He walked to her. "They don't really understand the danger they're in. They think now that they're home everything will return to normal."

"I know. That's the most dangerous time—when they let down their guard. I'll try to get that point across to Mary again."

"And I'll talk with Paul. But he's a lot like his son. I caught him earlier going out the back to go see Zach. He'd forgotten to tell me he was going to the barn. Freedom is hard to give up."

"We do every day. We're as much a prisoner as they are."

T.J. chuckled. "But we're in control, dictating the rules."

"I'm not hungry anymore." Aaron's loud voice wafted to Chloe. "At least I can go upstairs by myself." He appeared in the doorway to the dining room. "I would appreciate no one bothering me." As he swung around, his glare drilled into T.J., then Chloe. "That includes you two." Then he tramped up the stairs.

"Good thing there's only one child or my patience would have been exhausted by now."

T.J. leaned close to her ear. "Mine was gone about an hour after I met Aaron. And there was a time I wanted to be a father. Being around that boy has definitely made me reconsider."

The idea T.J. had considered having children flushed her cheeks, heat spreading down her face. She'd wanted a family, too—still did. "I agree. Having children is a serious decision. Once my mother told me I should take care of young children before I decide, so I babysat a lot when I was Aaron's age. Young children are a piece of cake next to a teen like Aaron. I think taking care of teenagers should be the criteria."

"I wonder where all his anger comes from—how long he's been this way."

"I had a cousin who hated the world his freshman, sophomore and junior years in high school. She actually became bearable during her senior year. I'll see what else Mary has to say about her son. It might help us protect him better if we know where he's coming from." She turned to head into the dining room.

T.J. fell into step beside her, his hand casually at the small of her back. "I'll see what Paul has to say, too."

The brief connection between her and T.J. spurred her pulse to a faster rate. How had they gotten on the subject of having children? Dangerous territory when she was trying to keep her emotional distance. But it was hard when they fell into such an easy partnership—a true team.

T.J. moved through the living room, checking each window to make sure it was locked, a habit he'd formed because once one of them had been unlocked. In that situation, it had turned out a maid was working for the person targeting the man he was protecting as a Secret Service agent. It never hurt to be extracautious.

For a moment he lingered in front of the window overlooking the verandah and yard. He would be relieved with the addition of the dogs and outside guards. The number of people he and Chloe were guarding had doubled, not to mention one was rebellious and hostile about his situation. He'd protected enough family members as a Secret Service agent to know a young person didn't always see the danger until it was too late.

He'd chosen the right partner with Chloe. They had fallen into a pattern that complemented each other.

But as he'd waited to hear that she was out of the

building and safe, the fear he'd felt had made it clear that his feelings for her weren't dead. At the moment, his life was at a crossroads. He'd always known what he wanted and had been focused on that goal. Now he wasn't sure. Should he walk away from what he'd been doing all his life—guarding people in danger—or continue in some other capacity? In the middle of all this, he certainly didn't need to fall in love with Chloe again. He trusted her as a partner, but to trust her with his heart was totally different. Or was it? He didn't like this confusion, this lack of control.

"I'm going to bed," Chloe said as she entered the living room.

The soft sound of her voice penetrated his thoughts and only heightened his dilemma. They had been good together once, but it hadn't worked out. Did he want to be hurt again? He could still remember the pain he'd felt when she hadn't come to Washington.

He rotated toward her slowly. "It'll be nice when we have a guard outside, patrolling the grounds. It'll give us a chance to get a good night's sleep. At least I hope. I can go without sleep for a while, but it does catch up with me eventually."

Chloe came further into the room. "All this emotion can be draining. Earlier when I talked to Mary about Aaron, I could see she was barely holding it together."

"It's been a rough week and her son isn't helping things." T.J. walked to the last window and examined the lock. "Did she tell you anything about Aaron that might help us?"

She joined him, inches away. "I don't know about helping us, but she did share something concerning Aaron. He had a younger brother who died about seven years ago. Aaron took it as hard as Mary and Paul did. As a result of Mary and Paul's grief, they turned all their energy to helping others."

Her vanilla scent, the same one she'd had when they had dated, surrounded him with memories. The first time they had met. The first time he'd kissed her. The last day, when they had parted. A constriction in his chest reminded him of the hurt that had stayed with him for years.

"How long has he been at the Bethany Academy?"

"Since he was a freshman. The school he went to wasn't academically challenging, so they sent him to Bethany Academy. It's close enough that he can come for the weekends when he wants."

"Does he like the school?" He started for the foyer, needing some space before he decided to see if she still kissed as well as she had nine years ago.

"She thinks so, but she confessed her son doesn't confide in her like he used to when he was a young boy. But that's often normal with any teenager." She trailed behind him, that soft, husky voice tempting him to take her into his arms.

T.J. held them tight against his side. The brighter lights in the entry hall sobered him. They were working, not on a date. He turned toward her. "Have you guarded many teenagers?" He needed to keep focused on business.

"I don't know if you consider it a lot, but in four years, maybe ten or so, mostly girls, and a couple of boys. One was thirteen. The other sixteen. The thirteen-year-old was a challenge." She grinned, two dimples appearing in her cheeks. "But Aaron could prove to top him." Her eyes widened. "You aren't leaving me to deal with him all the time. Surely we can take turns."

"I have a feeling he'll respond to you better than me. A beautiful woman usually does that to a sixteen-year-old," T.J. said with a chuckle.

Occasionally he'd seen Chloe blush, and this was one of those times. As though it had a will of its own his hand lifted, and he brushed a finger across her cheek. "You *are* beautiful. Inside and out. Because of you, I became serious about my relationship with the Lord. Maybe this is the reason we met again. That faith has wavered."

"Why?"

"Life and the things I've seen. People aren't who they say they are. I knew that before I became a Secret Service agent, but some of my assignments made that very clear."

"Do you want to talk about it?"

Though he wanted to inch closer, T.J. stepped back. "I can't, and sometimes that's the problem. What I saw as an agent remains a secret. That's part of the job."

"I've often used Kyra as a sounding board when I needed one having to do with my job. Sometimes we just need to talk it out. If you can't with another person and I can certainly understand that with the job you had, then talk to the Lord about it. He's always there to listen."

"Praying."

"Not exactly. Sharing your thoughts with Him isn't always praying."

"I've missed you" slipped out of his mouth before he could stop it. Then, as though he needed to qualify it, he added, "I've always been able to tell you things I never could others."

One corner of her mouth tilted upward. "We did have that once."

"Yes, maybe—"

"Chloe. T.J." Mary's frantic voice came from the second-floor landing. "I went to say good night to Aaron. He's not in his room, and his window is wide-open."

EIGHT

Chloe whirled around and raced up the stairs.

Fear held Mary rigid, her hand clutching the railing. "He's been here. He took my son."

"None of your bedrooms can be accessed without a tall ladder, and Zach took care of that for us. They're locked up in the barn."

T.J. came up behind Chloe. "Where's Paul?"

"I'm here. What's going on?" Paul left his room and stood across from Aaron's, confusion clouding his expression.

"Aaron isn't in his room," Mary said in a clogged voice. "Remember how that person came into the house in Dallas. He's done it again. He's…"

"Aaron's downstairs." Paul bridged the short distance to Mary and took her in his embrace. "I doubt someone brought his own ladder, and ours are at the barn locked in the shed."

Chloe hurried toward the boy's room. "He isn't downstairs."

The color washed from Paul's face. "Then he's hiding to make us worry."

Chloe and T.J. entered to find the window wide-open, the curtains blowing in the cold wind. Careful not to touch anything, Chloe made a full circle while T.J. pushed back the sheers and examined the window and outside it. She noticed the bed was minus its sheets.

"There's a rope made out of sheets that goes most of the way to the ground. I suspect Aaron snuck out." T.J. faced the couple as they stood in the entrance. "Would he go to a friend's house? Anywhere you can think of?"

Paul shook his head. "Most of his friends are at school. He's lost contact with the ones he had around here."

"Except for Brett. He might be with him. We can call him and see," Mary said, her chest rising and falling rapidly.

Chloe was concerned for her client. "Mary, you need to sit down. We'll take care of this. He's most likely being a teenager and doing what he wants."

"But you don't know for sure."

"Paul, call the sheriff and let him know Aaron is gone," T.J. said. "Let him know what's going on. I have a feeling he's aware of what happened in Dallas. I'm going outside to inspect the ground below the window. Chloe, go through the house in case Aaron slipped by us." T.J. headed for the stairs.

Paul settled his arm over Mary's trembling shoulder and pressed her close. "I'll see to Mary and call the sheriff. We're friends. I'm sure he'll want to come."

Chloe glanced around. "Where's Vickie?"

"Probably in her room. Sometimes Aaron will talk to her, especially when he's mad at us. We'll get dressed and come downstairs." Paul escorted his wife into their bedroom.

"I'll check there first." Chloe strode to the other

end of the long hall and knocked on the woman's door. When it opened and Vickie peered out, Chloe asked, "Is Aaron with you?"

"No." She stepped out into the corridor, dressed for bed with a robe on. "What's happened?"

"We believe he went out his window. Hopefully on his own."

"How?"

As Chloe explained, the deep lines in Vickie's forehead faded.

"Aaron has done that before."

"Mary and Paul didn't say anything about that."

"That's because they don't know. It happened last summer. He was grounded, but they were away for a weekend retreat. I discovered him sneaking back into the house and he told me everything. He thought his parents were too strict and he had plans to meet Brett, so he did anyway."

"Please go tell Paul and Mary while I check the rest of the house."

As Chloe descended the stairs, she thought of finding T.J. outside and letting him know, then decided instead to wait until he came back in. No point in having two people wandering around in the dark.

T.J. shone his flashlight over the ground directly under Aaron's bedroom window. Signs of the same tennis-shoe size indicated only one person was involved. Aaron. It didn't surprise him when he thought of the teen's behavior today.

He looked up and made a full circle trying to see beyond the few security lights into the night beyond. A noise like an engine starting to the left caught T.J.'s attention. He jogged toward it, sweeping his flashlight in front of him the farther away from the house he went.

Is that a pickup parked off the drive? The hairs on the back of his neck prickled. He spun around as something hard connected with his head. His legs gave out, and the black swallowed him.

Chloe paced the foyer at the bottom of the staircase and for the sixth time glanced at her watch. More than ever, she wanted to go out and see where T.J. was, but if he was in trouble, she needed to be here to protect the Zimmermans and Vickie. She checked the gun she'd strapped to her side. He'd been gone ten minutes. He shouldn't have been gone that long.

She mounted the steps and made her way toward Mary and Paul's bedroom. The door was open and Vickie stood just inside.

"I need Zach and a few of the men to search for T.J. He hasn't come back and all he was going to do was look around under Aaron's window."

Paul picked up the phone. "I'll call him."

"I'm returning to the hall and positioning myself on the stairs. Keep this door open unless you hear me tell you to shut it."

Mary's face whitened. "It's happening again."

As she moved into the hallway, Chloe looked back. "I don't know what's going on, but we need to be prepared for anything."

In the distance, T.J. heard the sound of a vehicle driving away. His eyes fluttered open. The scent of earth filled his nostrils. The feel of grass cushioned his left cheek. Bright lights—a beacon that called to him—shone through the darkness that encased him. But the one sensation he couldn't ignore was the pain hammering against his skull.

For a moment he tried to remember what had happened. Where he was? Why he was here with a gong thundering in his head?

Aaron. Gone. Slowly the words filtered through the pain, and he struggled to sit up. He remembered the vehicle—a pickup, he thought—and the noise of it leaving. He couldn't have passed out for more than a few seconds.

The black spun around.

Closing his eyes, he sat still, trying to right his twirling world.

"T.J.," someone shouted through the fog surrounding his brain.

"Over here," he said while he eased his eyelids up halfway, the sound of his voice thundering through his head.

Circles of light illustrated his whereabouts. He averted his head, panning the area as he pieced together what had occurred.

A vehicle had started. He'd gone to investigate. Then someone must have hit him from behind. He felt the back of his head and winced when he encountered a sticky wetness.

As flashlights came toward T.J., he lowered his chin while his eyes adjusted to the brightness.

When the ranch foreman knelt in front of him, he asked, "What happened?"

T.J. looked at Zach and a ranch hand named Shane behind the foreman. "Someone knocked me out." As he said those words, alarm rippled through him. Chloe and the others could be in danger. "I need to get to the house." He tried to rise—too quickly—and collapsed back to the ground.

"I'd suggest slow and easy." Zach moved around to examine the back of his head. "You're gonna have a doozy of a headache."

He didn't have time for an injury. He pushed himself to his feet with Zach next to him, poised to help if needed. "Have you seen Aaron?"

"Not since he came to the stable earlier."

T.J. started for the Zimmermans' home, his gait slow but steady. The nearer they came, the faster the haze over his brain faded. Zach made a call to Paul and let him know T.J. was all right and coming back to the house.

The door flew open, and Chloe positioned herself in the entrance, one hand on her gun. She took one look at him, and her severe expression melted into relief, but a slight frown still tugged at her mouth.

"What kind of trouble did you manage to get into? It was a simple task. Check the footprints under the window." She settled her fist on her waist.

"Someone else had a different plan." T.J. cocked a grin. "But I'm fine, as you can see."

Chloe motioned with her hand. "Turn around and let me see for myself." She sucked in a deep breath. "Your idea of fine is different from mine. So tell me what happened." She stepped to the side to allow him inside. "Thanks, Zach. Can you and your men check the grounds out from the house and let me know if you find anything unusual? The sheriff is on his way."

Once she'd closed and locked the front door, T.J. made his way to the stairs and sat. "I heard a vehicle start and went to investigate. Then, a minute later, I saw a pickup stopped on the side of the drive."

"Did you see Aaron?"

"No. I didn't see anyone. The person who hit me came up from behind."

Chloe took out her cell phone and made a call. "Zach, this is Chloe. Check to see if any vehicles are gone. Maybe a pickup." She paused, her eyebrows scrunching. "Just a minute. I'll ask him."

"Can you describe the pickup?" She held her cell between them so Zach could hear.

"No, I didn't get close enough. I heard it coming from the left side of the house. I went around the corner and started into the yard. The lighting over there isn't good. I saw a tire and was lifting my flashlight to get a better look at the vehicle when I was struck."

"Did you get that? Okay. Thanks." Chloe slipped her phone back in her pocket. "Zach said that's where the old Ford F-150 is kept. Aaron drives it when he's home."

"So Aaron hit me?"

"Maybe. What did you find with the footprints?"

"Only one set under the window, which leads me to think it was Aaron. Probably alone, but maybe with a friend."

"I'll go up and get Mary and Paul. We'll need a description and license number if the Ford F-150 is gone. Then you're going to the hospital."

"No. I'm okay. I promise I'll tell you if the signs of a concussion worsen. I'm not dizzy anymore, and I can take something for my headache. See if they have something for one. Aaron may have decided to leave, but he's still in danger. He's a kid. He doesn't realize the danger he's in. The kidnapping of a child is a parent's worst nightmare."

"Don't say anything to Mary or Paul. They are already beside themselves." Chloe ascended the stairs and disappeared down the hall.

T.J. clutched the railing and pulled himself to his feet. There was a guest bathroom off the foyer. He went in and did the best he could to wash the blood off the side of his head behind his left ear. Grimacing, he patted the area with a wet cloth.

When he reappeared in the foyer, Paul, Mary and Vickie stood at the bottom of the steps.

Vickie saw his injury and scurried toward the kitchen, muttering about a bandage and some pain relief in the first-aid kit.

"The sheriff is almost here. Aaron has a 2006 Ford F-150. This is the license number." Paul handed T.J. a slip of paper. "The pickup can't go over fifty miles an hour without problems. It's really only good for around here or in town."

"Where do you think he went?" T.J. dug into his pocket for his set of keys.

"Not Brett's. I talked with the kid's parents. I would guess back to school, but then I really don't know my son as well as I should. I didn't think he would be stupid enough to leave." Frustration and concern weaved through Paul's words.

Chloe snatched the keys from T.J. "He hasn't been gone that long. I'm leaving and heading back toward Houston. I can make up some time in your car and possibly catch up with him." She held out her hand. "The license number, please."

"I'm going with you."

"You can't. Someone has to stay back here with our clients, and if you have a problem, you need to be near medical help." Chloe took the paper from T.J. and then turned to Paul. "If you need to, ask the sheriff for assistance keeping you all safe."

"He'll give it to me. Bring my son home, then we'll have a heart-to-heart about his leaving." Paul set his mouth in a deep frown, but his eyes were full of concern—two intense emotions fighting for dominance.

Chloe walked toward the front door.

"Wait," T.J. called out and made his way to her.

"Call me every twenty minutes and let me know what's going on."

She grinned. "I'm not going to take offense to that, but I'm a big girl and have been a bodyguard for years."

"That won't stop me from worrying."

Her smile grew. "I know. I'd worry about you, too." Then she was out the door.

"There you are," Vickie said behind him. "C'mon and sit down so I can tend to your injury. I've patched up the ranch hands and have become quite good at doing it."

T.J. released his frustration in a long, drawn-out exhalation.

With her cell phone hooked up to T.J.'s car, Chloe could call safely and still go sixty-five. The sheriff had arrived as she left the ranch and was having his two deputies work with the cowhands to search the area.

Checking in with T.J. for the first time, Chloe scanned the cars as she approached and passed them. "What if Aaron is somewhere at the ranch having a good laugh right about now?"

"He won't be laughing when I get through with him."

"You okay?"

"I've had better days. Paul has a friend who's a doctor. He's paying us a call and will take a look. If I didn't agree, Paul was going to have the sheriff drive me to the hospital."

"A doctor making a house call? I guess it pays to know people. Did the sheriff put a BOLO out on Aaron and the Ford F-150?"

"Yes, and he and his deputies are canvassing the area, especially around the main house."

"Good. Take it easy. Bye."

As she started to hang up, she heard T.J. say, "Don't forget to call in twenty minutes."

Chloe punched the off button and increased her speed by five miles per hour. She didn't like being away from her client, but then she guessed Aaron was their client, too—whether he liked it or not.

Ten minutes later, she saw the black Ford F-150 with the correct license plate number. She came right up behind him and flashed her lights. The truck picked up speed. She easily kept up with it, and after five miles, she passed Aaron to force him to stop. Slamming on her brakes, she turned the wheel and blocked the two-lane highway. Aaron came to a halt a couple of feet from T.J.'s Jeep.

She got out of the car, and when the teen opened his door, she shouted, "Park on the side of the road. You're coming back with me."

"I can drive back." Frustration and something she couldn't quite put her finger on filled his voice. Fear? If he had been afraid, then why did he run away?

"No. Move it now." She poured all her anger into her words, determined the kid understood she wouldn't put up with his antics. Part of her prepared to chase after him in the opposite direction, if need be.

But to her surprise, the teenager did as he was told and stormed to T.J.'s Jeep, glaring over the roof at her. "I can make my own decisions. I'll be seventeen in a few months. I *need* to go back to Houston."

"Then start acting like the mature adult that you claim you are and get in my car. Your life is more important than attending school at the moment. Your parents have it worked out with Bethany Academy. Your friends will understand. If not, they aren't your friends."

He wrenched open the door and climbed in. Chloe peered up at the nearly full moon. *Lord, I need Your help to get through to this child the danger he could be in.*

As she restarted the car, she slanted a look at Aaron. "What did you think your parents would do when they discovered you were gone? Let you stay at school in danger? They love you."

"They have a great way of showing it," Aaron mumbled and averted his head to stare out the side window.

"Before you go into your pouting routine, use the phone and call your parents to let them know you're coming back to the ranch with me."

"You do it. I don't feel like talking to them. I want to be in Houston."

One. Two. Three. Giving up counting to ten, Chloe chewed on her bottom lip to keep her retort inside. At the moment, Aaron wasn't listening to anything she said.

Chloe called the ranch. "Mary, I've got your son with me. We're heading back to the ranch. We left the truck at the side of the road. Someone should go and pick it up tomorrow."

"Thank You, Lord. I'm so glad you found him. Tell him I love him and don't want anything to happen to him."

"I will. How's T.J. doing?" She wished she were there in person to make sure he was okay.

"The doc says he should be all right, but if anything changes, he'll need to go to the hospital for tests."

"See you all in about half an hour." When she hung up, she looked toward Aaron.

With his shoulders hunched, he'd almost turned his whole body away.

"Did you hit T.J. over the head so you could get away?"

"No," he mumbled, hunkering over even more, his arms folded over his chest.

Chloe suspected if he could crawl under the seat, he would have. "You're the only one who had a reason to."

He swiveled toward her. "I'm not lying! I didn't!" His shouts bombarded her. The fury flowed off him.

She gritted her teeth and concentrated on getting them back to the ranch. Aaron wasn't out of danger. There was thirty miles between here and the ranch.

After a search of the area around the house, T.J. and Paul went to talk to Sheriff Landon and Zach in the living room. When they entered, T.J. found the sheriff, a deputy and Shane Clapton, who had been with Zach earlier.

"Where's Zach?" T.J. asked, not sure of Shane's position at the ranch other than ranch hand.

"I fill in for the foreman when Zach's busy somewhere else. One of the horses is giving birth and there's a problem." The man, who was about thirty-five years old with a receding hairline, glanced at Paul. "Zach can handle it, Mr. Zimmerman. He told me to tell you not to worry."

"I'm sure he can. Did you find anything to explain who attacked T.J.?"

Shane glanced at the sheriff, who answered, "No signs. There are a lot of footprints around in the dirt near where you were found, but a lot of them were Zach's and Shane's. The tennis-shoe print under the window matched the one where the car was, which I'm gonna assume is your son's."

"Were the tennis-shoe prints found around where T.J. went down?"

"No, but there's a lot of grass in the area and the footprints wouldn't show up well there." The sheriff put his cowboy hat back on. "I understand you're hiring some guards for outside and bringing in dogs? I'll be back tomorrow to have a word with your son, Paul. In the meantime, I'm leaving a deputy out on the verandah."

"Yes, Sheriff Landon. Thanks for coming." T.J. escorted the trio to the door, then locked it behind them and pivoted toward his client, who was hanging back by the living room.

"If my son did this to you, I'll…" Paul's face fell, his coloring pale, his eyes haunted.

"Let's not speculate. Let's hear what he has to say."

"But he was trying to get away. Who else would have done it?"

"I don't know. But we need to assume the person in Dallas did it. I'd rather think the worst-case scenario."

Paul laughed, no humor in the sound. "I think my son doing it is the worst-case scenario."

T.J. didn't say anything else. He'd rather deal with the teenager than an assailant moving freely around the ranch. If there was someone out there, T.J.'s appearance outside might have prevented Aaron from being kidnapped, which only reinforced the fact the dogs and guards were vital.

Ten minutes from the ranch, Aaron finally broke the silence in the car. "I didn't hit Mr. Davenport."

"You'll get a chance to tell him and your dad. But if you're right, then that probably means the stalker after your parents has been at the ranch and could be hiding somewhere there now."

"Why? They aren't doing their book tour anymore."

"The person's purpose may be more than stopping the tour. Maybe he hates what your parents stand for or has some grudge against them."

"Then wouldn't they know that?"

"Not necessarily. Some people simmer until rage finally explodes in them."

Chloe crested a hill and saw the four-way stop sign at the bottom. She began to slow down, putting her foot on the brake. It went all the way to the floor and nothing happened. T.J.'s car picked up speed, careening down the incline.

NINE

"What are you doing? Slow down," Aaron shouted at Chloe.

Chloe gripped the steering wheel, pumping the pedal. "I can't. The brakes have gone out."

"What? Do something!"

She didn't see any headlights approaching the four-way stop, but she lay on her horn as she flew through the intersection. A stretch of level road with a shoulder gave her an idea. She drove off the highway and along the graveled edge as she pulled the emergency brake up.

The car came to a stop half off the pavement. Chloe leaned against the steering wheel, her hands still clasping it so hard, pain streaked up her arm.

Aaron collapsed forward, sucking in short, shallow breaths. "We could have died. What if a car had been coming?"

"There wasn't one, and we're all right. That's what is important." Her hands shaking, she placed another call to the ranch.

When T.J. answered, he asked immediately without saying hello, "Where are you? I'll feel better when you get back here."

"I'm about six miles away on the highway going east about five hundred yards from the four-way stop sign. I didn't have a wreck, but I need someone to come pick up Aaron and me. The brakes gave out on your car."

"You had no warning?"

"No. It was sudden."

"Both sets of brakes failed?"

"Yep, back and front."

"I'll get someone to pick you up. I think I can catch the sheriff. I want a mechanic to check what caused them to fail at the same time."

With T.J.'s injury and the brakes going out in his car, it was obvious the assailant would go through the bodyguards to get to the couple.

T.J. came into the house through the front door and walked into the living room, where Mary, Paul and Chloe sat, discussing the addition of two dogs and several extra guards the day before. "The mechanic just delivered my car. Someone tampered with the physical linkage from the pedal to the brake master cylinder. I'm moving my Jeep into your three-car garage where we can protect it with your two vehicles. I don't want them sitting outside unattended. We don't need a repeat of last night." T.J. glanced around. "I thought Aaron was going to join you all."

"No, he's been holed up in his room on the phone a lot." Chloe shoved to her feet and began prowling the room. "Once we started talking about suspects, he was out of here. And I just came back from checking on him. It won't be as easy for him to try running away with the guards and dogs in the yard. That's why he took off two nights ago."

Mary stared out the window. "What a gray morning. The weather isn't helping my mood." She angled toward Paul next to her on the couch. "I'm not looking forward to going to Harrison's memorial service. What if something happens there?"

"It's outside in the park that he helped fund for the town. He was a good friend and he specifically asked for me to speak at his memorial service. I can't say no. His family is expecting me."

"After what happened in Dallas, I would think they would want us as far from the memorial service as possible."

Paul swallowed hard. "He was my best friend, and he passed away on his trip to Europe, his last hurrah before the cancer took him. I need to say goodbye to him."

"The sheriff and deputies will be there, as well as me and T.J. It's hard to hide something in an open field." Chloe leaned into the back of the lounge chair, grasping the top of the cushion.

"I'm just not myself lately. I'm tired, mentally and physically." Mary twisted her hands together in her lap.

Paul cupped them. "You should stay here with Chloe and the guards we hired. I'll feel better if you rest. We both don't need to be a target."

Mary blanched. "Don't say that."

"I've got an even better idea. You haven't had a chance to work in your greenhouse since we went on the speaking tour. I know there are things you need to do in there. Show Chloe some of the orchids you're growing."

"I can't do that. What will people——"

"We've never done things because of what people will think," Paul interrupted his wife. "Harrison wasn't your friend, but mine, and under the circumstances they'll understand."

Mary collapsed back against the couch. "I've been fretting about that since you reminded me of the memorial service yesterday. So much around here has changed. It's hard to take it all in."

Paul kissed her cheek. "Now you don't have to worry. You were supposed to work in the greenhouse yesterday, but then the day slipped by before you knew it."

Watching the married couple only reinforced T.J.'s desire to experience a relationship like what Paul and Mary had. That respect and understanding of each other was what he wanted, the same as what he'd seen when his parents were together.

His gaze skipped to Chloe observing the couple, too. Why hadn't it worked for them? Too young? They hadn't wanted to make that kind of commitment? Or was it fear? He'd known about Chloe's father being in the navy and always gone and the effect it had had on her mother. The type of job he and Chloe had chosen often caused them to be away from their home for weeks, possibly months, at a time. She wasn't exposed to two parents openly sharing their respect and love for each other like he had been, and yet he had hesitated, too, nine years ago. He should have come back to Dallas when Chloe's mother was better and persuaded Chloe to follow him to Washington. But then, that had been the first time he'd encountered a man he respected a lot and guarded dallying with a woman who wasn't his wife. Although not unusual for a person to have an affair, he hadn't thought the man he was assigned to was like that. His trust had been shaken and he'd never totally gotten it back.

"T.J."

He finally heard his name being called and dragged his focus away from what could have been. "Yes," he said to Chloe.

"When are you and Paul leaving?"

"In two hours. We'll probably be gone until four."

"You taking your car?"

"Yes, since the mechanic just finished working on it, I figure it's the safest car here at the ranch."

Paul snorted. "I never thought I would be sitting in on a conversation about a person being after me and one who would go to those lengths."

After talking with Aaron when he'd come back to the ranch, T.J. had been even more convinced whoever had targeted the Zimmermans on their tour had been here the other night and assaulted him. "You aren't the first person I've protected who has said that. Most people don't set out to make enemies."

"That doesn't comfort me." Paul shot to his feet. "I'll check on Aaron and let him know what I'm doing this afternoon, then I'll work on what I'm going to say at the memorial service. With all that's happened, I haven't had much chance."

T.J. watched Paul head up the stairs. Now that the windows were all hooked up to the alarm system, he could breathe a little easier concerning Aaron trying to leave again or someone getting into the house through a second-story window.

"For an active family, this all must seem like a

prison. That's how Aaron feels." Chloe came up behind him.

Her presence—the sound of her voice—melted some of his tension. There were times he felt he had a whole household to protect, including Chloe. He didn't want anything to happen to her. He was responsible for her being here. What had happened when she'd driven his car had only strengthened that feeling. Yes, she was a good driver and a quick thinker. She didn't panic easily, but she and Aaron could have been seriously hurt that night—or killed. He shuddered at the thought.

She laid her hand on his shoulder, still slightly behind him. "You okay? All day yesterday you were quiet."

"I was supervising the changes in the alarm system and overseeing the new guards. You're a natural with the two German shepherds."

"Thanks. I've worked with dogs before. But I'm not letting you change the subject. You're upset about your car, aren't you?"

He pivoted. "What do you think? You could have been hurt."

"Or you, if you had been driving. The good news—I wasn't hurt and took care of the problem just fine. That night you were hurt, not me. You knew this could be a dangerous assignment. We're in a dangerous business. I was when I was a police officer. Every day I went to work, there was the potential of getting hurt."

"When I was younger, I thought of myself as invincible. I was trained well. I could deal with anything. Now I've seen how foolish those thoughts were. Nobody is invincible."

"But we have both been well trained. We're using

our skills and abilities to help others." She slid her hand from his shoulder.

He missed her touch—more than he should. "Have you ever thought of giving it all up and doing something totally different?"

"Sure, I thought about doing something else. I seriously considered it a year ago when I was shot in the shoulder. I helped Kyra at the office for a while and liked that. But when I went back into the field, I fell right back into the groove, because I bring a sense of safety to people who need it. That's a good feeling. How about you? You quit the Secret Service, but you're still doing what you were doing for them—guarding people."

"It's crossed my mind, too. As I told you, I'm also looking at other options. Right now I feel unsettled."

"Our jobs don't help that. We're always going from one job to the next in different places." She smiled, her green eyes sparkling. "We are who we are. We have to do what we think is best, what our purpose in God's plans is."

He stared into those glittering eyes and wanted to lose himself in them, to forget where they were for a few minutes at least. He wished they were anyplace but here in the middle of a case. He grazed his forefinger across her cheek. "It should have been me in my car," he whispered, trailing his touch to her chin as he leaned toward her and tilted up her head.

Her allure was too much to ignore anymore. His mouth caressed hers with feathery brushes before he drew her to him, his hands framing her face, his lips possessing hers with a deep kiss. For a moment, he allowed himself to focus totally on her. The house faded from his consciousness, and it was only Chloe and him together in their own private world.

Then a noise intruded on their interlude, forcing T.J. to step away and swing his attention to Vickie coming down the hall from the kitchen.

"Where is everyone?" Mary's cousin asked as she crossed the foyer.

"Upstairs." T.J. wondered if Vickie had seen anything. From her expression, he didn't think so, but the incident confirmed in his mind he couldn't do that again. For a moment, he'd lost his awareness of his surroundings. Chloe consumed his focus, which in a dangerous situation wasn't wise.

"I came to tell y'all lunch is ready."

Chloe strode toward the staircase. "I'll let the family know."

She glanced at T.J. before proceeding to the second floor. Every part of her was aware of the man across the entry hall. His kiss had rocked her from the top of her head to the tip of her toes. It should never have happened. Yet she touched her lips and imagined it all over again. Warmth spread through her. She hated to think how flushed her cheeks were.

When Chloe started down the upstairs hallway, Paul came out of his bedroom, spied her and stopped. "Is something wrong?"

"No. I told Vickie I would let you all know lunch is ready."

He gestured toward a room down the corridor. "Mary is in our office. I'll get her."

"And I'll let Aaron know."

The teen had stayed in his room most of the time

since he'd run away. When they had returned to the ranch, his face had been as white as the trim on the outside of the house. His eyes had still been dilated in fear. When he'd entered, he'd ignored everyone and raced up the stairs, his door slamming so loudly she wondered if the painting on the wall near his bedroom was still hanging up.

"No, find him," came from Aaron's room.

She paused and bent close to the wooden door. Was someone in there with him? Or was he on the phone? Either way he wasn't happy.

"Call me back. Soon." Sharpness hardened each word.

She knocked and waited. A minute passed, and she rapped again. If he didn't answer in five seconds—

Aaron swung his door open, a scowl etched into his features. But behind the expression she glimpsed something else. Fear? Worry? She hoped so, because both of those emotions would help keep him alive.

She peered around the teen and couldn't glimpse anyone else in his room. "Is there someone here?"

"Why do you ask?"

"Who is in this house is my business."

"No one is. I was on the phone. What do you want?"

"To talk," Chloe said, surprised at her words.

"What are you? Some kind of bodyguard/therapist?"

She chuckled, trying to ease the tension vibrating from the teen. "Hardly. But I do know something about stress from a harrowing experience."

"I'm not…"

She looked him in the eye. "Scared?"

"Yeah. Brakes fail all the time. It was just an accident."

Since the teen hadn't joined the family much since the *accident*, he didn't know the brakes had been tampered with. T.J. had only just found out. Aaron needed to know the truth. "It wasn't an accident. Someone wanted the brakes to fail."

Aaron paled. His knuckles on the hand gripping the door whitened. He blinked, shook his head and said, "Then someone is after you and Mr. Davenport, not my parents."

"I wish that was the case, but that has been the car we've used to go places. It's okay to be worried about your parents, but they're in good hands. I know my job and will do my best to protect them and you." She stepped to the side to let him go first. "You coming downstairs for lunch?"

"No, I'm not hungry. I'll get something later."

While descending the stairs, Chloe couldn't get the picture of Aaron out of her mind. He was angry and yet scared at the same time. She was so glad she wasn't a teenager. She could remember being angry with her dad for always being away. Most of the time she hadn't really felt she knew him. Did Aaron feel the same way about his parents?

Chloe sat back in her chair at the kitchen table. Paul and T.J. had left twenty minutes ago for the memorial service, and Vickie and Mary had cleaned up after lunch, then decided to have some hot tea. Chloe was a coffee drinker and declined the tea. Her thoughts kept straying to Aaron still in his room and Paul having to deliver a eulogy for a good friend while someone was after him.

"How have my orchids been doing in the greenhouse?" Mary sipped her tea in a china cup with tiny red roses.

"I'm not you, but I followed your watering instructions and none died," Vickie said with a laugh. "I'm surprised you didn't run out there the first chance you got when you came home."

"That speaks to how upset I've been. Until Paul mentioned them to me today, I'd forgotten about my orchids." She put her hands to her face and rubbed it, then turned to Chloe. "I've been raising orchids and showing them for years. My cousin has been gracious enough to fill in for me when I'm gone, but she's right. I always check on them when I get home. I didn't this time, and I can't believe it."

"That's what I said to Paul earlier this morning. I've been worried about you." Vickie rose and brought the pot of hot tea to the table and topped hers off. "Are you sure you wouldn't want any, Chloe?"

"Yes. I'm fine with water."

"Do you remember how we used to have tea parties all the time while we were growing up?" Vickie eased into her chair and sighed. "It's good to get off my feet."

Mary's forehead wrinkled with worry. "Is your gout bothering you again?"

"No. Thank goodness for that. It's just been a lot keeping up with all the people coming and going the past few days. Didn't the sheriff call right before Paul and T.J. went to town? Has Sheriff Landon discovered anything about who was here the other night and tampered with T.J.'s car?"

"Yes. He called. No evidence was found in T.J.'s car to point to who could have tampered with the brakes and hit T.J. over the head. All we know is someone knew what he was doing. But there was no guarantee the brakes would have failed at a certain time." Chloe sipped some water.

Vickie cocked her head. "So why do it?"

"There was a good chance it would have been driven with either Paul or Mary or both of them in the coming days. For instance, Paul's attending the memorial service. He was even going to come home in the middle of his speaking tour to do that. And where Paul goes, T.J. does, and he likes to drive his own car."

"Who in the world would do something like that? I've known you all my life. You wouldn't hurt a fly." Vickie patted Mary's hand. "You're like a big sister to me. If your parents hadn't taken me in…" She blinked, and a tear rolled down her cheek. "I might have gone into foster care."

"No, you wouldn't. The family wouldn't have allowed that. You're part of the Benson family."

"I'm a third cousin."

"But still family. So that's that." This time, Mary patted Vickie's hand. "And just for the record, I'm only six weeks older than you."

Vickie laughed. "I always used to kid her that she was my elder. When she turned thirty and I gave her some antiaging cream, it became a running joke between us. She got me back when my birthday came up that year, although I think the walker was a bit much."

"Did you have any sisters or brothers?" Mary asked Chloe.

"No, just me. I always wanted a big sis."

"Not a younger one?" Mary finished the last swallow of her tea and pushed back her chair.

"Nope. I had a friend who had a younger sister who was a pest."

"I have a feeling I have a lot of work to do in the greenhouse so I think I'll head outside. It will be a good time for me to pray and think." Mary put her cup in the sink, grabbed her sweater and started for the back door.

"Wait a sec. Let me grab my jacket." Chloe rushed from the kitchen and took the steps two at a time. After retrieving her coat, she paused at Aaron's door and knocked again.

This time he answered right away. "I knew it was you. It's different from my mom or dad's knock."

"Just wanted to let you know your dad has left and your mom will be out in the greenhouse. It's all clear if you want to get something to eat."

He pulled himself up straight. "I'm not avoiding my parents."

"You aren't? You could have fooled me."

Chloe hurried down the stairs and to the kitchen. When she entered and Mary was gone, she asked, "Did she go to the greenhouse alone?"

"Yes, I tried to stop her, but it's only ten feet from the back door."

It was hard to get clients to realize the normal freedom they had at their house had to be suspended completely while they were being protected. Even going out on their front porch could be problematic or dangerous.

Chloe stepped out onto the deck and headed for the greenhouse off to the side. Halfway there a scream coming from inside the glass building shuddered down her length. Her first instinct was to rush in. But caution stayed her actions. Through the window she couldn't see where Mary was. Chloe withdrew her gun and clasped the handle, then inched the door open, peering into the building.

Frozen, Mary stood against a post, her eyes wide with fright as she stared at an area under a table halfway down the middle row.

"Mary, what's wrong?"

She slowly rotated her head toward Chloe. "A snake. Under the table." Then she returned her attention to where the reptile must be.

"What kind?"

"A rattler." Mary flinched when the snake began rattling its tail.

TEN

"It's going to get me again," Mary said in a high-pitched voice, frantically looking around the greenhouse as though searching for a place to hide.

"You've been bitten?"

"Yes, on my leg."

Chloe dropped her gaze and found where some blood seeped through Mary's cotton tan pants. "Can you move this way slowly?"

"No. It's looking at me. It's huge." Mary's voice rose with each word as hysteria took hold of the woman.

"Stay still. I'm going to try to kill it."

The rattling sound bombarded off the walls. Chloe gave the snake a wide berth to come up behind it and get a shot at it. She didn't have anything to kill the serpent with but her gun, and if Mary was bitten, she needed help immediately.

When Chloe eased closer, she locked on to a coiled greenish gray snake with diamonds down its back and its rattle shaking. A diamondback? She inched toward a place where she had a good view of the reptile, which had arched its back and brought up its head as though it would strike again.

Making sure she was clear of hitting Mary, Chloe aimed her Glock at the head and squeezed off a shot. She hit her target, and it collapsed to the floor, but the body twitched.

Chloe saw a shovel leaning against a wall and snatched it, then crept cautiously toward the rattler to make sure it was dead. Some animals moved after they were killed. She prayed that was the case with this snake.

When she approached the serpent, she brought the shovel down on the reptile right behind its head and cut it off. The body still jerked, but at least the rattler couldn't bite anymore. She shoved it as far away as she could, then turned her attention to Mary, who had slid down the post.

Her face etched in pain, Mary clasped the bite area on the calf of her leg.

"Take deep breaths. Calm down. Think of God holding you in His arms right now. I'm going to get some help."

The first call she placed was 911 to have a helicopter airlift Mary. She would need to be flown to the nearest hospital with a supply of antivenin. Then she called Vickie and asked her to bring soap and water with a cloth. Next, she called Zach and asked him to come to the greenhouse because Mary needed to be carried into the house. Last, she got hold of T.J.

"What kind of rattler?" he asked.

"I think a diamondback. There are diamonds down its back."

"Send me a picture. I'll show it around. When giving antivenin, the hospital will probably need to know exactly what kind of snake."

"Just a sec." Chloe took several pictures from different angles and sent them to T.J.'s cell phone.

"Thanks. I'll give you a call when I find out anything."

"Where's Paul?"

"Speaking with the family. The memorial service is about to start. I'll grab him and we'll be there as soon as possible."

"The AirLIFE is coming from San Antonio, but you should be back before it arrives."

As Chloe hung up, Vickie came into the greenhouse, followed by an out-of-breath Zach.

"Where's Mary? Did she fall?"

Chloe hadn't gone into details with Zach or Vickie because that would delay Chloe from finishing all the calls she needed to make. And time was working against Mary. "A rattler bit her. Do you know much about that kind of thing?"

"Sure. I've been bitten by a diamondback here on the ranch, but it's cold right now. They aren't out at this time of year." His jaw clenched with that statement.

"Maybe he found his way in and made his home here."

"I guess it's possible." Zach knelt next to Mary. "Let me take a look. Vickie, wash the area, then put the cold cloth over it. We need to make sure you keep the wound lower than your heart." He glanced around and saw the snake. "I'll carry you to the house once Vickie cleans your injury."

"Thanks, y'all. I never expected to see a rattler in here in February. I know we've had some warm days, but it's cold most of the time."

Zach inspected the still-twitching snake. "Its reflexes will react long after it's dead. We'll need to carefully dispose of the head where the venom is. It's still as lethal even after death." Zach took out his phone and took several pictures. "I have a friend who is an expert on rattlers. I'm sending this to him and I'll call him once I get Mary inside and make sure he looks at it."

"It's not a diamondback?" Chloe stared at the dark diamonds on its back.

"I'm not sure, and you need to tell the doctor exactly what type of rattler." He lowered his voice and moved away from Mary. "She doesn't need to get excited. We need to keep her blood pressure down, if possible. There is a kind called the Mojave rattlesnake that looks like a diamondback, but its venom is different. It's a neurotoxin, very deadly if not treated correctly. The venom is much worse than other rattlesnakes. I think it's a Mojave one because the diamonds don't go all the way down its back. This rattler is a different color, too, but I may not be familiar with all the colors of a diamondback."

"I'm all done," Vickie said, and rose, her hands trembling.

As Zach lifted Mary, she winced. He trudged out of the greenhouse while Vickie ran ahead to open the back door. "I'm putting you in the living room on the couch." He looked at Chloe. "Are Paul and T.J. on their way back to the ranch?"

She nodded.

"I'll go and let Aaron know." Vickie began to mount the staircase.

"No." Chloe hurried toward Vickie and continued in a whisper. "I don't want him upset about his mother.

It's important that she remains calm. After we leave, you can tell him and blame it on me."

"But—but..."

Chloe released Vickie but didn't go into the living room until Vickie descended to the foyer. "Tea. Get her some calming tea. The helicopter is probably twenty minutes out. And when it does land, please keep Aaron back if he hears it."

"I'll sit here on the bottom stairs after I get some tea for Mary."

Chloe went into the living room as Zach checked the bite, then stood back.

"Mary, I know it hurts like the dickens, but you'll be able to get the help you need. I'm calling my friend. Once we've accurately ID'd the type of rattler, the rest is a piece of cake."

"Really?" The creases in Mary's forehead emphasized her worry.

Chloe walked with Zach toward the entry hall. "Will you watch for Paul and T.J. and the helicopter?"

"Yes, and I'll find out what kind of snake it is. If my friend isn't sure, he'll know someone who will be. Rattlesnakes are common around here. But not the Mojave variety. They're only in the southwest corner by El Paso." He tipped his hat toward her. "Leave it to me."

As Zach left the house, Chloe sent a silent prayer to the Lord. Mary was in His hands now.

Back in the living room, Chloe pulled up a stool and sat beside Mary. "Okay?"

"I'm trying to be. Will you pray with me?"

Chloe held Mary's hands, cold and clammy, and bowed her head. "Father, I know Mary is in the best hands there are. Please give her the calmness she needs, knowing You are here for her. Pave the way for her to arrive at the hospital quickly and help there to be a fast response to her snakebite. Blanket her in Your love and assurances. Amen."

Carrying a mug, Vickie entered the room. "Here you go, Mary. A nice cup of tea. I know how much you like this flavor."

"Thank you. It's sweet you thought of that." Mary took the tea, her hands shaking.

Chloe wrapped her hands around Mary's and steadied the mug while her client brought it up to her mouth.

By the time Mary had drunk half her tea, the noise from a helicopter flying over the house flooded the room.

Mary pressed the mug into Chloe's hand. "Where's Paul?"

"They're coming as fast as they can."

A few minutes later, the front door banged open, and Paul rushed into the living room a few steps ahead of T.J. Chloe rose quickly to allow Paul to sit with Mary.

"Okay, hon?" Paul smiled, but Chloe could see the effort it took as his gaze latched on to the swelling leg.

"I'll be fine. Chloe has arranged everything. From that sound, the AirLIFE helicopter is here to take me to the hospital."

"I'm coming with you." Paul brushed Mary's hair back from her forehead, then wiped away the sweat that had popped out on her face.

Chloe exchanged glances with T.J. If there was only one spot, she needed to go. If the snake had been put into the greenhouse, what did the perpetrator have in store for Mary? He would know she would be flown to the nearest hospital that could treat her.

While T.J. held the front door open, Zach showed the AirLIFE medical team into the house with their gurney as he said, "The snake was a Mojave rattlesnake. I had it ID'd by a zookeeper I know."

"We'll notify the hospital so they have everything ready when we get there," the medic said as Paul moved back to let the team prepare Mary for transport.

"I'm coming with you. I have several photos of the snake I killed on my cell," Chloe said to the man in charge, noticing T.J. had stepped outside.

"Who are you? A relative?"

"No, I'm Mary's bodyguard, and she needs protection. There have been some attempts on her life. This being the most recent one."

The team leader swept his attention to Paul. "Are you the husband?"

"Yes, and she is right. Will you have room for me, too?"

T.J. came back into the house with Sheriff Landon as the man replied, "This is highly unusual."

"I'm the sheriff of this county, and Mary Zimmerman will need protection. Please do what you need to make it happen."

The team leader glanced from one person's face to the next, then said, "I'll take care of it. You both can come. Anyone else will have to drive." Then he gave the name of the hospital where Mary would be transported for emergency service.

Paul took Mary's hand as they wheeled her out of the house, sitting up on the gurney to keep her heart higher than her leg. All color was bleached from her face. She bowed her head and began murmuring a prayer.

As Chloe followed, T.J. walked beside her. "Where's Aaron?"

"About forty minutes ago when I checked last, he was in his room. He doesn't know. He was listening to his music using earphones, so he must not have heard the helicopter land."

"I'll bring him with me." T.J. squeezed her hand. "Take care."

Chloe stared down at the ranch as the helicopter took off. How had the snake gotten into the greenhouse in the dead of winter hundreds of miles from its territory?

From the highway, the lights of San Antonio glittered in the dark up ahead. T.J. glanced at Aaron sitting still next to him in the front seat, staring out the windshield as he had most of the trip from the ranch. When T.J.'s cell phone rang, Aaron flinched but didn't look his way.

"T.J. here."

"We made it safely to the hospital. Mary is in the E.R. being treated. They gave her the antivenin for the Mojave rattlesnake. They had to wait for it to be flown in from El Paso. Now it's wait and see. I'm seated outside Mary's room with Paul."

"How was she when she went into the room?"

"Feeling nauseated and having some problems breathing."

"Make sure Paul stays with you until I get there. I'm probably half an hour or so away." T.J. kept his attention shifting from the road to Aaron to the cars around them.

"How's Aaron holding up?"

"Okay. Vickie is staying at the ranch since we have those guards."

"See you in a while."

T.J. hung up. "Your mom has gotten the antivenin."

"Will she be all right?" The teen's voice quivered, as did his hands. He fisted them.

"Most people recover."

"Most?"

"Some arrive too late for the treatment to work."

"Did she?"

"I believe she arrived in time. We got her there as fast as we could."

Aaron sank back against the seat as though he'd released all the air from his lungs. "What's a rattlesnake doing in the greenhouse?"

"Good question. Chloe and I believe it was put there on purpose. That species of rattlesnake's range in the U.S. is southern California, Arizona, New Mexico and a small area in Texas's southwest corner. Not between Houston and San Antonio. Its habitat is desertlike land. Not to mention it's winter and has been too cold for snakes."

"Maybe it found its way in because the greenhouse is heated."

"I don't think so."

"The person after Mom and Dad came on the property and put the snake in there?" Fear shook Aaron's voice.

"A definite possibility. He could have put it in the greenhouse the evening you ran away, or the snake could have been there for a while. Your mother usually goes into the greenhouse several times a week, if not more. If he did it earlier, it was only a matter of time."

Aaron crossed his arms over his chest and lowered his head.

"We have to consider everything and prepare for the worst."

"Someone has been at our ranch," Aaron mumbled, keeping his chin down.

"Don't worry about it. Chloe and I will protect you and your parents. That's why it's important to follow our instructions. Your mom went out to the greenhouse without waiting for Chloe. We always like to check a place out before you go inside. That's also why it's important you don't go outside without one of us."

"I never meant this to happen. I…"

T.J. shot a look at Aaron. "What do you mean?"

The teen remained silent.

"Aaron?"

"I've wished my parents were regular people, not always in demand to speak and attending events. Everyone wants something from them. I've missed the time we were a normal family living on the ranch."

"They have an important message. They're trying to help others."

"Sometimes *I* need their help myself, but they're always unavailable. It didn't use to be that way." Aaron lifted his head and peered at T.J. "I've given up on getting any of their time."

"Since you've been back at the ranch, all you've wanted to do is return to school. You've got their undivided attention, and you stay in your room. Why?"

"They're there but not really. If they aren't on the phone, they're working in their office or…" Aaron shrugged. "What's the use? I *need* to get back to school. I belong there."

"We need to catch who is after your family first. I suggest making an effort with your parents when they return to the ranch. They're trying to fill their time so they don't think about what's happening around them."

Aaron harrumphed and turned to look out the side window.

Something wasn't right. Aaron wasn't telling him everything. Was it because of his emphasis on needing to get back to school? He'd said the same thing to Chloe when she'd picked him up on the highway to Houston. From what he'd gathered from Paul, Aaron's grades at Bethany Academy were passing, but that was all. Aaron used to love the ranch, according to Paul, had even talked about running it one day.

Fifteen minutes later, T.J. parked in the hospital's visitor lot. As they strolled toward the main entrance, T.J. placed a call to Chloe to see where they were now.

"Mary is still in the E.R. For sure she will be staying overnight. Beyond that will depend on how fast she starts to recover."

"We'll be there in a few minutes."

When T.J. and Aaron came into the emergency room, Paul spotted them and headed straight for his son. He enveloped Aaron in a hug. "You're safe."

The teen squirmed from Paul's arms. "But Mom isn't. You aren't. This is all happening because of you, Dad." Aaron stomped toward Chloe.

His son's words hurt Paul. T.J. could see it in the Paul's eyes as he fought to recover from what Aaron had said.

"This isn't your fault, Paul. The person doing everything is at fault. Don't let Aaron's frustration and anger convince you otherwise," T.J. said.

"Aaron and Mary have always been closer than he and I have been. I've tried. We don't seem to speak the same language. I thought the ranch would help us grow closer, but lately he's lost interest even in that."

"He's scared. I could tell by his tone in the car coming here. He's worried and struck out at the safest person—you."

The doctor came out of Mary's room in the E.R. Paul hurried back to him. T.J. followed, giving his client some space to talk privately with the man. When the doctor finished and left, Paul's shoulders lifted, then fell.

"Is Mary going to be all right?" T.J. said in a whisper, in case the news wasn't good.

Paul nodded, then turned toward Aaron and Chloe sitting across the hall. "They're moving her to a room for a couple of days if all goes well. She didn't have an allergic reaction to the antivenin and it seems to be working."

"Can I see Mom, then?"

"Yes, the doctor suggested we grab something to eat while they get her settled in her room."

Aaron pinched his lips together for a moment then said, "I'm not hungry. I'll stay and follow them up to the room."

"I think getting something to eat for dinner is a great suggestion, Aaron. I know your mom would want that. I'll stay with her and make sure nothing happens to her and see you all in a while." Chloe smiled at Aaron. "Do me a favor. Bring me a large cup of coffee. Okay?"

"I guess I can." The reluctance in Aaron voice carried over into his slow moves as he rose, his gaze straying to the room where his mother was. "We'll get to stay with her, won't we?"

"Yes. Let's go." Paul started to put his hand on his son's shoulder, but Aaron dodged the attempt.

T.J. stepped between the two. "I'm starved. I hope the food is half as good as Vickie's." He glanced back at Chloe. "Call and let me know which room."

"I will. You all let me know what is good or not."

As T.J. walked away from Chloe, he noticed what adrenaline had gotten her through the crisis was fading and weariness was beginning to set in. But he knew and trusted Chloe. No matter what, she would do the best she could to keep Mary safe.

Chloe sat on the small sofa in Mary's hospital room with Aaron pacing. Twenty-four hours had passed, and she was improving. The doctors were pleased with her progress.

"She sure has been sleeping a lot. I don't think the doctors are telling us everything." Aaron kneaded his thumb into the palm of his hand.

"Her body is resting, which is the best thing she can do at this time," said Chloe.

Aaron walked to the door and peeped out into the hall, not for the first time since Paul and T.J. had left. "How long does it take for them to meet with the hospital? What if something happened? What if—"

"Aaron, it's only been twenty minutes. Working everything out concerning payment and insurance can take time. And besides, T.J. knows what he's doing. He worked for the Secret Service for years."

Aaron swept around, still working his thumb into his hand. "Who did he guard?"

"I know for quite some time he was on the vice president's detail, but there were other government officials he protected, too."

"Really?" For a moment Aaron's tense features relaxed, then a movement out of the corner of his eye caused him to pivot toward the bed.

Mary blinked several times. When she finally fixed her gaze on her son, she attempted a smile. The corners of her mouth twitched, then the grin collapsed.

"Mom, you're awake. I've been worried about you."

Mary licked her lips and reached toward the plastic glass on the table near her.

Aaron rushed to her and picked it up, then helped her take a few sips.

"Thanks. I missed seeing you this morning."

"If I'd known you would wake up, I'd have waited to eat. Are you all right? Any pain?"

Is this the same angry teen from a few days ago?

"I'll be fine, Aaron. You don't need to worry about that. Worrying is a wasted emotion."

Chloe rose. "I'm going to give you two some time alone. I'll be outside the door if you need anything."

As the door swung closed, she heard Aaron say, "I didn't mean for this to happen to you. I wanted us to have more time together, but not this way."

Could Aaron be responsible?

ELEVEN

For a few seconds in the hospital hallway, the thought rolled around in Chloe's mind, and yet while the attacks had been organized and planned out, Aaron had been at school. She and T.J. had been keeping an eye on the teen to make sure he didn't pull another stunt like he had the first night. So how could he have put a snake in the greenhouse? Although she couldn't totally dismiss the possibility Aaron was responsible, she wouldn't say anything to Mary or Paul unless she had proof. She would do some digging around and talk with Kyra and T.J.

The elevator at the end of the hall swished open, and T.J. and Paul exited it. T.J. smiled when he caught her gaze.

As they neared, Paul asked, "Is the doctor or nurse in there with Mary? Where's Aaron?"

"He's talking with his mom. He's been upset, and I gave them some time alone."

"Mary's up?"

"Yes. You should go in and spend some time with the two of them. Aaron has been struggling with this whole situation." T.J. grasped the handle. "I'll stay out here with Chloe."

"That's a great suggestion. We need to bond as a family again." Paul walked into the room as T.J. held the door open.

Chloe turned to T.J. "When I was leaving a few minutes ago, Aaron said something strange. The first thing he said to Mary was, *I didn't mean for this to happen to you.* Could he be involved in what is happening to his parents?"

"I don't know. We can never rule anything out. He's been very upset since the incident with the rattlesnake. I don't think he's acting. That doesn't sound like a guy who planned all of this."

"That's what I was thinking, but I'm going to have Kyra look into his friends and Bethany Academy."

"We shouldn't tell Paul and Mary. They have enough to deal with. Besides, I talked with your friend Rob. They discovered who leaked the information where the Zimmermans were staying in Dallas, which led to the reporter paying us an unorthodox visit that night—Nancy Carson."

Chloe blew a soft whistle. "The publicist. What was she thinking?"

"According to Matthews, Nancy was trying to stir up publicity for the Zimmermans. She was capitalizing on the pranks being pulled at their events. Her words, not mine. She was quite proud of her handiwork until the last stop and the fire. She told the police she knew nothing about the actual pranks and certainly not anything about the fire. She took a lie-detector test. I informed the publisher about what Nancy Carson had done and she is no longer the Zimmermans' publicist."

"You and I both know people can pass a lie-detector test. That's why they aren't permissible in court as testimony."

"But she probably isn't behind what's happened at the ranch. She even canceled the interview the Zimmermans were going to have the morning after the fire. She didn't even complain."

"Mary has received a lot of publicity over this snake-bite, so anything is possible. I won't rule her out until we discover who is doing this to the Zimmermans. Did Rob say anything about the cause of the fire?"

"Yes, the arson investigator ruled it arson. In fact, the police are looking for the woman Matthews carried out. After interviewing the man Paul and I helped out of the backstage area, it seems he had discovered the woman fleeing from the room where the fire was started. He stopped her and they ended up in a fight. She hit him over the head with something. As he went down, he grabbed on to her and took her down, too. That's the last he remembered before passing out."

Chloe thought back to the time Rob had carried the woman out from behind the curtains. She'd never gotten a good look at her face. "All I can recall about her is curly long dark hair draping over Rob's arm with thick black framed glasses. Her head was turned away, but there was a big mole on her left cheek. I was too busy trying to get Mary out of the theater alive. You might ask Mary if she remembers anything about the woman, but she was so worried about you and Paul, her focus was on the stage."

"Matthews said when she arrived at the E.R., she left before the doctor could see her. She also gave a false name to the paramedics. He's going to work with the sketch artist for a picture. He'll send it to us."

"So the person after Mary and Paul could be a woman?"

"Or more than one person."

"I need to get some coffee. Maybe two or three cups."

"I'll come with you." T.J. kept his eye on Mary's room as they walked a few yards down the hall to the vending machine. "I also talked with Sheriff Landon about the snake investigation."

"Tell me he found the culprit." Chloe inserted her money and punched a button. Her cup plopped down and her coffee squirted into it.

"I wish I could. In one sense, a culprit was caught, chopped in half, even."

As she slid her cup out, she glanced at T.J. "Quit teasing me. I'm sleep deprived."

His eyes softened. "I'm sorry. I shouldn't dangle the carrot in your face."

She gave him a mocking frown. "I'm not a rabbit you're trying to lure into a trap."

He chuckled. "I'd never think that of you." His gaze bound to hers. "Ever." He started back toward Mary's room.

She couldn't shake the feeling of being cherished. Boy, she must really be sleep deprived if she was thinking that. "'Fess up. What are you holding back?"

He lounged against the wall next to the door into Mary's room. "After we left, Shane, Zach and the sheriff searched the greenhouse. They couldn't find how the snake got inside if it supposedly crawled in, but Shane did find another one in the back by the orchid supplies. It wasn't happy to be disturbed, but the cow-hand got him out without being bit."

At the thought there was another deadly rattler in the greenhouse, her knees went weak, and she leaned back next to T.J. "So there were two snakes. I guess whoever put the rattlesnakes in there wanted to make sure Mary got bitten. Did I ever tell you I hate snakes?" She sipped her coffee, her hand quivering.

T.J. grasped it, steadying the cup. "It's surprising what we can do because of our training when it's necessary."

"Yeah, but it doesn't stop the reaction afterward. The whole time I was in the helicopter I kept replaying those fifteen minutes in my mind. I knew if I'd missed hitting the rattler, it might strike Mary again, or me." Taking another drink of her coffee, she angled toward T.J. "God was looking out for us."

"Through this whole assignment I've felt that. I find I've been turning to the Lord more and more. I think that's your influence. You have reminded me how important putting my trust in the Lord is. For so long, my distrust was there under the surface, ready to rise at a second's notice."

She nodded once. "I'm glad to be of help. I know I've been trained well to do what I do, but there are just times all I can do is rely on Him."

"And yet you fear snakes." A grin tugged at the corners of his mouth, and a sparkle danced in his eyes.

"I suppose you have no fears."

"I wish that were the case. Sadly I do. Spiders."

"Spiders!" She pressed her lips together to keep from laughing. "Most of them are small, no more than your thumbnail."

"Not all of them. I know it's irrational to feel that way, but I have ever since I was a kid and I found a tarantula in my cabin at camp. It was huge." His eyes widened. "And I was small. My first time to go to camp. It bit me."

"A tarantula isn't poisonous."

"But I had an allergic reaction to its bite. I ended up in the E.R. the next day and went home from camp early. Needless to say, I didn't go again."

"Okay. I'm not going to laugh." But Chloe couldn't contain the smile that demanded its release.

"Let's just agree you'll take care of any spiders we encounter and I'll deal with the snakes."

She stuck her hand out. "A deal."

He closed his around hers but didn't shake it. He inched closer. "You know, I used to think I knew you well, but I didn't know that tidbit. What else about you are you keeping a secret?"

She chuckled, a bit shakily as the warmth from his touch spread through her. "It wasn't a secret. It never came up. Believe me, if I had seen a snake when we were dating, you would have known how I felt."

"I'm even more impressed by how you handled the situation yesterday."

Her pulse rate increased. Her breaths shortened. She wished they weren't in a hospital guarding three clients. She wanted him to kiss her again. Could they work out the second time around? What kind of relationship could they have when they both were on the road so much? Seeing Mary and Paul, who worked so well as a couple, she wanted that. They had problems, but they dealt with them together—that was one of their themes in their books. Working together to solve what was wrong. This was the first time she'd had a partner as a bodyguard, and although it was different and she'd needed to get used to the idea, it had worked well so far. Was that because it was T.J.?

"Do you think we've given them enough alone time?" Chloe finally asked, needing to remind herself that she and T.J. were still working.

"Probably not, but it's getting close to dinner." T.J. waved at the dinner cart coming down the hall for the patients. "We need to make some decisions about what we'll do this evening for food and rest. I think you need to go back to the hotel and catch some sleep before you stay tonight."

"Good suggestion."

T.J. pushed open the door, and Chloe went into the room first. Mary, Paul and Aaron had their heads bowed and their hands intertwined as Paul finished up a prayer. The scene gave Chloe hope everything would work out for the couple and their son.

Mary, who was sitting beside Chloe in the backseat of T.J.'s car late the next day, sighed loudly. "I'm so glad to be back at the ranch."

Paul, on the other side of Mary, clasped her hand. "I never want to see you in a helicopter again."

Mary smiled at him. "Me, either, and I hardly remember the journey."

Chloe's throat tightened at the love gushing from the two. The evening before had been a shift in the couple's relationship with Aaron. Their son had even participated in the conversation. She'd seen some of it before she'd gone to the hotel to shower and take a nap. Another thing she liked about T.J. He seemed to know what she needed before she did. The rest had rejuvenated her.

When the car came to a stop in front of the house, T.J. climbed out first, slowly scanned the landscape and approached the guard with one of the dogs. They talked for a few minutes before T.J. made his way to the car and opened the back door for Chloe, then went around to the other side to let the Zimmermans out.

Chloe stood, doing her own survey of the ranch. In the distance she spotted Zach working on a pickup while two cowhands repaired the fence a couple of hundred yards away. The late-winter day was unseasonably warm, which made for a great one to spend outside. She wouldn't be surprised if Aaron wanted to go riding. She'd like to.

Aaron was first through the entrance and headed up the stairs, announcing he had some friends he needed to call.

When Mary walked into her home, Vickie engulfed her in a hug. "I was so worried about you."

Mary leaned back. "What is that smell?"

"Your favorite dish, beef stew. I thought we would celebrate your safe return." Vickie rotated toward the living room. "Shane's been helping me decorate a little."

Mary strolled to the entrance and gasped. "Y'all did this for me?"

The room was filled with balloons and vases of flowers. Above the mantle hung a big sign with Welcome Back, Mary written across it. Mary glanced at her husband, tears shining in her eyes.

Paul shook his head. "I didn't have anything to do with this. It was all Vickie's idea. She wanted to surprise you."

"You shouldn't have."

"I had to do something," Vickie said. "You didn't want flowers or anything in your hospital room."

"I was only there a short time."

Chloe almost laughed out loud, because by the time they had left a few hours ago, the hospital room had been overflowing with flowers and potted plants from different people who had read about what happened to Mary. Finally, after the first twelve hours, Chloe had had the nurse's aide take what was delivered and pass them out to other patients.

Vickie waved toward the living room. "The balloons and sign are from me, but the flowers are from people in town."

Shane tipped his head. "Ranch hands and I have done a thorough search of the house, greenhouse, garage and any other place you might go to make sure there aren't any more surprises for you, ma'am."

Mary blushed. "Thank you, but really, all this fuss isn't necessary."

Paul came to Mary and clasped her upper arms from behind. "I know Chloe and T.J. didn't want a lot of people coming to the ranch, but tomorrow at church be prepared to be smothered with love. They have planned a celebration for you."

Chloe tensed. On the drive from San Antonio, Paul had insisted they would all go to church and give the Lord thanks for Mary's quick recovery. No matter what protest T.J. had thrown at the man, he had insisted they would be all right there. No one was going to keep him from being in God's house. They had a lot to celebrate. Mary was alive. Chloe had to agree with Paul, although it made T.J.'s and her job more difficult.

Shane started for the foyer. Vickie walked with him to lock the door after he left. The cowhand leaned down and gave the housekeeper a quick kiss on the cheek. Vickie's cheeks flushed a deeper shade of red than her cousin's had earlier.

When Vickie rejoined the group, Mary grinned. "Are you dating Shane?"

Vickie lowered her head and fiddled with her apron, smoothing it over and over. "He's sweet on the sweets I bake for the ranch hands a couple of times a week."

"That's wonderful. You should invite him to have dinner with us some time when everything isn't so up in the air."

"Oh, that does remind me. Sheriff Landon is coming by later. I took it upon myself to invite him to dinner. He and his deputies combed the ranch, but couldn't find anything to indicate who had tampered with T.J.'s car or put the snakes in the greenhouse."

"Before all the festivities begin, I'm going to rest or I'll fall asleep at the dining room table." Mary crossed to the staircase with Paul close behind her, carrying the bag T.J. and Aaron had brought to San Antonio for the family.

Vickie scurried toward the back of the house, leaving T.J. and Chloe alone in the entrance to the living room. Chloe felt T.J.'s gaze on her and shifted to look at him. "We need to check the interior and exterior of the house."

"Definitely. A lot could be changed in two days. I'll talk with the guard outside and walk around the house, then I'll go down and talk with Zach and make sure the shed is still locked. It's not as big a deal now that the upstairs windows are wired into the security system, but the harder we can make it for someone to get inside, the better."

"I'll go through the house and talk with Vickie. See if anyone came by the house. She does the ranch accounts for Mary and Paul. Could this have to do with the ranch, not their books and stand on certain issues?"

"Not a bad idea. I'll talk with Zach. I saw him earlier at the barn."

"I just want to make sure we're looking at this from all the different angles. At first it looked like someone wanted to stop the speaking tour. Now I don't know."

T.J. invaded her personal space, and usually when someone did that, it set off alarm bells clanging in her mind. But not this time. When they had worked together years ago, they hadn't been on equal footing. He'd been in charge of the task force trying to bring down a counterfeiting ring. Technically he was the lead on this assignment, too, but in reality they were partners. He'd gone out of his way to always consult her and get her input. How would she feel if he became her boss? Their dynamics might change yet again.

His gaze dropped to her mouth for a long moment, then lifted to her eyes, his look heart-melting. "I'll be glad when this is over. We have a lot we need to talk about when we don't have all these distractions."

Her heart rate kicked up a notch. Thinking about a possible future with T.J. made her realize she was falling in love with him again. And yet she'd loved him nine years ago, and it hadn't worked out.

T.J. passed the ranch pickup Zach had been repairing. The open hood stood up, and a toolbox was still sitting next to it on the ground. T.J. strode into the barn and headed for Zach's office to the left.

"The check is in the mail. If you don't receive it in a few days, call me back," Zach said, the sound of the phone slamming down echoed through the cavernous interior.

A cowhand at the other end glanced toward the office, then went back to moving some hay bales.

T.J. stuck his head through the doorway. "Having trouble?"

"The feed company. They're insisting they haven't received the check for last month's bill. I saw Vickie write it and put it into an envelope to be mailed. I guess I'll have her stop payment on it and reissue the check if they don't get it in a few days. I don't like this new company, but Paul wanted to help them." Anger infused the foreman's voice.

"Are there problems at the ranch?"

"Don't get me wrong. Paul is great to work for, but when he tries to run the ranch, things happen. He's good at what he does, and I'm good at what I do. He usually gets territorial about this time every year. With spring approaching, we get very busy."

"And you don't have time to babysit?" T.J. cushioned his shoulder against the door frame, his arms folded over his chest.

"Exactly. Although I guess it isn't exactly the same. You must know what it feels like. Your job is kinda like babysitting someone."

"Except the stakes are a lot higher." T.J. jerked his thumb to the left. "What's wrong with the pickup outside?"

"Sluggish and knocking."

"Do you work on all the vehicles for the ranch? I wouldn't think that would be part of your job description."

"I do sometimes. Also Willie or Shane. It's kinda nice as a change of pace." Zach stretched his arms above his head. "Office work is not my favorite part of the job. I appreciate it when Vickie comes down and sometimes helps out. Is Mary really all right? I've missed Vickie not being able to help the past week or so."

"Yes. It will take a while to be back to her old self, but she should be soon."

Zach rose. "Is there a reason you came to see me?"

"Not particularly. I was just trying to understand the ranch operations, and if there would be any reason for someone to be after the Zimmermans because of the ranch. I'm not so sure what's been happening is connected to Paul and Mary's books and campaign to make a change."

Zach blew a long, low whistle. "Paul and Mary pay good money for their help. They're fair, and I can't see one of my men upset with him. I'm usually the one who fires a ranch hand, after checking with Paul. So if someone had a beef, it would be with me."

"Have you fired anyone recently?"

"One, a month ago for continually smoking on the job."

"Smoking?"

"It's not allowed at the ranch, especially around the stable and barn. This area has been going through a drought off and on for a while."

"Who was the man?"

"Bo Moore." Zach came around his desk.

"Do you know where he went?"

"He lives in town. I wouldn't have given him a second chance when I caught him the first time, but Paul believes in second chances. I'm not as tolerant as Paul. And sure enough, I found him smoking again right outside the back door of the barn." Zach gestured in that direction.

T.J. pushed away from the doorjamb and moved out into the barn. "If you can think of anyone else, I'd appreciate if you'd tell me, no matter how small the reason. I've been surprised at some people's motivations. But usually it revolves around love/hate or greed."

When he exited the barn, a horse in the pasture across from the barn neighed. A light breeze blew from the south, the air warmer than it had been the past week.

T.J. took a couple of steps, stopped and turned back to Zach. "Have you replaced Bo Moore yet?"

"Actually, about a week before y'all came to the ranch."

"Where is the ranch hand?"

Zach frowned. "You're thinking the person could be my new guy?"

T.J. shrugged, not wanting to commit either way. "I suspect everyone."

Zach pointed to his chest. "Even me?"

"Yes."

The foreman's expression darkened. "Well, I'm not. Dave Cutter is repairing the fences in the far pastures. That's been his main job since he started. He couldn't have done the prank with the stink bombs because that was when he arrived at the ranch. He interviewed a few days before. He had excellent references. I don't hire just anyone."

"I'd appreciate talking with Dave Cutter when he comes in from working today."

"I'll send him up to the house."

"No. Call me and I'll come down here."

Without saying another word, Zach went back to work on the pickup. T.J. strolled toward the house. When he'd first come to the ranch, he hadn't thought it might be someone who worked at the place, although he'd had Kyra start a background check on everyone, especially the ones who were in contact with Paul and Mary. Even though Kyra hadn't alerted him to an anomaly in an employee's background, he knew that would take time to uncover. Now he didn't know if the attacks were connected to Paul and Mary's speaking tour and their message. But he would check in with her and add Bo Moore to the list.

When Sheriff Landon arrived at the front gate, Chloe accompanied T.J. out onto the verandah to wait for him to pull up to the house.

Chloe waved at the guard who passed with the dog. "How's Kyra coming with the background checks on the employees?"

"So far Zach, Vickie, Shane and Willie have checked out—at least their references. Nothing in their background was a red flag. She's going to look into Dave Cutter and Bo Moore for me next before completing the list of the rest of the ranch hands."

"Have you noticed the interaction between Shane and Vickie? I think she's sweet on him, and he returns the feelings. When you were down at the barn, he came up to the back door with some lame excuse he was making sure Vickie didn't need any more help setting up for the party for Mary tonight. Vickie blushes every time I've seen them together."

The corners of T.J.'s eyes crinkled. "Love must be in the air."

"No comment," Chloe said with a laugh and pretended a great interest in the sheriff's SUV approaching.

T.J. shook hands with the man first, then Chloe did. "I didn't want to talk about this in the house. Did you talk with Bo Moore?"

"Yep, and he has an alibi at least for the tampering with your car. He was gone to his brother's in Phoenix at that time. In fact, he found a job there and was boxing up his stuff to move soon. He didn't appear to have any hard feelings toward the Zimmermans or Zach. He was excited about the job he found in Arizona working on a dude ranch in the northern part of the state." Sheriff Landon rubbed the stubble of his beard. "In my opinion, he didn't do it."

"I respect your opinion. When's he moving?"

"In a few days."

"That sounds like good news to celebrate along with Mary's recovery," Chloe said. "We'd better head inside or they'll be wondering what is keeping us." She started for the front door when T.J.'s cell phone rang.

While he answered it, she escorted the sheriff inside and to the living room. Then, staying back by the entrance, she waited for T.J. to come inside. When he did, a scowl grooved his face.

She met him halfway across the foyer. "What's wrong?"

"That was Zach. Remember I said he was going to let me know when the new employee came back to the barn? He never did, and Zach went out to the area where he was supposed to be repairing the fence. The wood, barbed wire and tools were there, but not a sign of Dave Cutter. When Zach returned to the barn and checked where the ranch hand parked, the guy's car was gone."

TWELVE

"**K**yra is tracking down the references that Zach checked for Dave Cutter, and so far she hasn't been able to get in touch with the first one. She'll call me when she gets something. What did Sheriff Landon say?" Chloe asked later that night when the celebration for Mary's homecoming was winding down.

T.J. sidled closer to Chloe, standing in the entrance to the living room, and lowered his head to whisper, "He's checking for a driver's license photo so we have a picture of him, but the deputy that went by the man's address said he wasn't there. The owner of the property isn't there, either. He's renting a garage apartment. Hopefully one of them will come home soon."

"For the first time, I feel we might be getting closer to what is going on. Look at Mary. She's trying to be the gracious hostess, but this has taken its toll on her." Chloe noted the dark circles and puffy eyes that Mary had tried to disguise with makeup.

Sitting on the couch, Paul cupped his wife's hand and put one arm around her shoulder as though he was trying to shelter her. "As much as you've enjoyed this little celebration, Mary, I think it's time you consider going to bed."

Mary looked at Aaron, then Vickie, before her attention skipped to Sheriff Landon and finally settled on Zach. "Thanks, y'all. This has touched my heart, and I wish I could stay up, but Paul's right."

Her husband grinned, his eyes lighting up. "You heard it. Mary has said I'm right. I want you all to remember that."

The sound of laughter sprinkled the air, but beneath it was the unspoken threat that still existed for the Zimmermans. Everyone quickly sobered. Zach and Sheriff Landon rose almost simultaneously.

Zach reached for his cowboy hat. "Ma'am, glad to see you're all right."

As the party broke up, T.J. walked with the sheriff and Zach toward the front door to let them out, then lock up and arm the alarm system.

Paul paused next to Chloe. "I'm seeing Mary to bed, then I need to talk to you and T.J. about tomorrow."

Aaron followed his parents upstairs while Vickie made her way to the kitchen.

"I'll take the right side of the house. You the left," Chloe said to T.J., and rotated toward the right to begin her perimeter check of the first floor.

With all windows and outside doors locked, she returned to the foyer to find T.J. talking with Paul.

He crossed his arms. "Mary and I don't want Aaron or Vickie to go to the event at our church."

"Too bad," Vickie said to Paul as she came into the entry hall. "I'm going. I agreed to not go to the store and sent Zach for the items I needed, but I'm determined to be part of the church celebration. I'm getting claustrophobic. I need to get out of here. Besides, you don't know if the person is after me. I'm not part of the immediate family." Lifting her chin, she fixed her hard stare on Paul. "I agree Aaron should stay away."

For a long moment, Paul and Vickie exchanged looks before his mouth set in a frown. "Fine."

"Good night." Vickie ascended the stairs to the second floor.

"I personally wish you all would stay here," T.J. said in a steely voice, as if that would make a difference.

"Not an option. Mary and I are determined to make a statement that we are not afraid. We aren't stupid and will take precautions, but we won't be prisoners, either. Right now our lives are revolving around this madman."

"Does Aaron know?" Chloe asked, imagining the teenager's reaction. He'd shared the same thoughts as Paul on a number of occasions.

"No, but I'll tell him tomorrow morning. I do want an extra guard on duty in the house while we're gone."

His frown carving deeper lines into his face, T.J. nodded. "I'll see to it. The sheriff told me earlier he'd have deputies at the church."

Paul attempted a smile that failed. "I know how you feel about this, and if this wasn't for Mary, I would insist she stay home. Actually, I tried, but she wouldn't listen to me. It's become very important to her to show whoever is doing this that she's not afraid. I don't want to lose her, but she's right. If our message is to take back America, which means everyone fighting for what they believe in, I can't tell her not to go." He heaved a deep breath, then released it slowly. "I'd better go to bed, too. It's going to be a long day."

When Paul disappeared down the upstairs hallway, T.J. plowed his fingers through his hair and massaged his neck. "I want to shake some sense into Paul and Mary."

"We've guarded other clients who still went about their jobs. We can do this."

"I know we'll do the best we can, but ultimately if someone wants to get to them, he could, especially if he didn't care if he was caught."

"I don't think that's the case here. The guy is bold, but he's gone to a great deal of trouble to keep himself hidden."

"Don't forget the woman in Dallas at the last stop. She's still missing and could be involved."

"If the woman is involved, then there is more than one person. Whoever it is seems to enjoy messing with Mary and Paul."

"Maybe it's Dave Cutter and the police will find him."

"So you've decided—"

T.J. laid two fingers on her lips. "Shh. No more speculation tonight. It's not really our job. Our job is to be alert and keep our clients alive, although it would be nice if we could solve it so the Zimmermans have their life back." He took her hand and tugged her toward the stairs. "Let's sit and enjoy each other's company until everyone has gone to sleep. Tonight's my turn to sleep on the couch in the living room."

"But you did it the last time we were here."

"And you spent two nights with Mary in the hospital. I owe you a bed to sleep in."

"I imagine we're both light sleepers no matter where we lay our heads."

"True. That seems to come with the job." A smile slid across his mouth and spread to encompass his whole face, forming deep crinkles at the corners of his sparkling eyes. He was totally focused on her.

Tension slipped from her shoulders, easing the tightness there. "Have you ever wondered what would have happened to us if I had moved to Washington all those years ago?"

"Yes. Have you?"

"Of course. For months after you left. And again recently."

"And?"

She stared at the front door, knowing in her heart she needed more than what her mom had had with her dad. "We wouldn't have worked out."

He touched her chin and turned her head toward him. "I agree. We needed different things from a relationship. Although I'm not a navy guy like your dad, I needed a port in a storm and you needed an anchor."

Surprised flittered through Chloe. "Exactly, but I haven't changed. How about you?"

"I don't know. My life has been in a bit of turmoil lately with me quitting the Secret Service and coming to live in Dallas. Working in the field gives me satisfaction that I'm doing something to make a person's life better or at least safer."

"Why did you pick Dallas?"

"It was familiar. I like the area. I wanted to be based in a large town with good airline connections to make it easy to travel."

"Did I figure into the decision?" She held her breath, the seconds ticking by slowly.

Finally he hooked an errant strand of her hair behind her ear. "It crossed my mind."

"I've been wondering about that." She smiled, more stress melting away. So much had happened since they'd become partners and, yes, they hadn't seen each other for years, but T.J. was still the same person deep down. Although she'd stated she had changed, she was also the same. She wanted the same things: something more than she had, something she'd been looking for. She'd decided T.J. wasn't that something nine years ago, but now she wondered if she'd been wrong.

He angled toward her, taking her hands in his. His look wiped away the time they had been apart, and she felt whisked back to when they had been dating. He cupped her face, the feel of his roughened fingers caressing her cheek sent shivers down her spine. "I wish we were somewhere else."

He bent close to her, his breath whispering against her lips. Goose bumps rose on her arms. Then his mouth connected with hers in a kiss that removed the last vestige of tension. All her senses homed in on T.J. as he deepened the kiss.

Someone coughed at the top of the stairs. T.J. pulled back at the same time she did.

Aaron descended, a smug expression on his face. "Sorry I interrupted you. Going to the kitchen to get a snack." He continued his path toward the back of the house.

"I'm sure we'll hear about that tomorrow." Chloe tamped down the sensations rampaging through her. She'd wanted that kiss more than she had realized.

T.J. straightened, putting more distance between them on the step. "Probably. Which brings me to another decision I have made. Working with you isn't a good idea. You're a distraction, as a moment ago illustrated. No matter what I do or say, I've found myself thinking on occasion of you when the Zimmermans should be paramount in my thoughts."

Even though they worked well as a team, she had to admit the same thing. This was neither the time nor the place. "Should Kyra send someone else to replace me?" Although she knew where he was coming from, the idea she would be replaced with another bodyguard bothered her.

Leaning forward, he settled his elbows on his thighs and clasped his hands, his head averted. "We'll talk about it after tomorrow. But if I had to make a decision tonight, I would say no, because we do work so well together. I know the Zimmermans wouldn't like it. We're professionals. We know how to suppress our emotions when we need to." He rose and put some space between them. "We have so little downtime when we're on a job. It's hard not to touch you, relax, enjoy getting to know you all over again when we do have a moment for ourselves."

As he said those words, she could see a neutral expression descend over his features, as though the kiss had never happened. His hands, which were at his sides, opened and closed.

Chloe pushed to her feet, weariness blanketing her. She couldn't shut down her emotions as easily, but she had to. Being in this profession wasn't conducive to a relationship. Adam had taught her that. And right now this was her livelihood, and she intended to do the best job she could.

"I'll check the second floor before going to bed. See you in the morning."

As she climbed the stairs, his gaze bored into her. She felt it deep in her heart. She refused to look back. She was better off by herself rather than with a man married to his work. *Nine years ago he was, and now he still is.*

The next day, after the event at the Zimmermans' church, T.J. pulled up to the entrance of the ranch, releasing his tight grip on the steering wheel to push the button for the gate to open. Slowly—too slowly for him—they swung wide, and he drove through, heading toward the house. Although the event at the church had gone without a problem, he wouldn't breathe easy until Paul, Mary and Vickie were inside their home.

"Does everyone still have their bulletproof vest on?" Using the rearview mirror, T.J. looked at Vickie and Mary to make sure, because the two women had complained about the awkwardness of wearing it.

"Yes, we do," Mary said, twisting her mouth into a thoughtful expression. "How in the world do the police wear these all the time? It's uncomfortable. The sheriff can have this back gladly."

"It depends on the officer and the situation." A chuckle accompanied Chloe's words.

T.J. wished they had agreed to wear them into the church, but when the sheriff had offered them to the Zimmermans, they'd drawn the line at walking into the celebration in bulletproof vests. So T.J. had pulled up to the back door within several feet so his clients hadn't had far to go. Then Chloe had rushed them inside.

When T.J. stopped in front of the antebellum home,

he started counting down the minutes until the Zimmermans were safe.

"See, nothing happened," Mary said with a long sigh. "It was good to see everyone. A lot of people are praying for us."

"Stay in the car until Chloe and I come around and open the door. Hurry inside. Chitchatting can take place in the house."

"At least we're home safely," Vicky said with a shaky laugh.

T.J. climbed from the vehicle at the same time as Chloe did. Surveying the area, he skirted the front of the car while Chloe went around the rear. As he reached toward the handle, his gaze snagged Chloe's. He tipped his head, and then opened the door.

Paul rose quickly and started to help Vickie and Mary out, but T.J. ushered him toward the house. "Chloe will take care of them."

A cracking sound split the air, and the column splintered inches from Paul's head. The second T.J. heard the noise he tackled Paul to the ground, the car partially shielding them.

Another bullet hit the concrete step not covered by the Jeep. T.J. pushed Paul until the car blocked him.

"Get down." As T.J. drew his gun, he swung his attention to the women. Mary was still inside the car hunkered down while Vickie and Chloe used the Jeep as protection.

The two guards let their dogs go while one man ducked behind the verandah and the other used a tree as a shield.

The front door banged open, and Aaron ran outside

waving his arms and shouting, "Stop! Stop! You aren't supposed to do this."

T.J. ran low toward the teen and barreled into him, sending them both flying into the house. T.J. hit the tile floor and rolled the kid out of view. "Stay down. Don't move." Then he crept toward the door and peeked out. "Okay, everyone?"

"We're all right," Chloe answered.

T.J. called 911, then shouted out the door, "Help is on the way." He hoped whoever was firing on them would hear and try to make his getaway.

The guard behind the tree zigzagged toward the pecan grove across the drive.

When there weren't any more shots, T.J. rotated toward Aaron. "Stay." Then he headed outside at the same time the guard by the verandah moved forward and the second one near the paved drive ran across the road and took cover behind a tree.

"Get them in the house one at a time when I give you the go-ahead," T.J. said to Chloe as he passed her.

Scanning the trees, T.J. quickened his pace and plunged into the thick woods directly across from the house. Pecans, not gathered last fall, crunched beneath his feet, making moving harder.

The sound of the dogs' barking grew louder, and then a shot went off, followed by a yelp.

Shielding Vickie, Chloe hurried her toward the front door, then came back for Mary, all the while keeping vigilance on the pecan grove across the drive. She spied T.J. vanishing in the thick of the vegetation.

Paul helped Mary out of the back, his wife's face the

pasty white that Chloe had seen when the snake had bit her. She took Mary's arm. "Run as fast as you can."

As Mary straightened, she froze when she heard the noise: the gunning of an engine coupled with a dog yelping echoed through the stand of trees.

"Go. Now." Chloe pushed her forward to get her to move. Again she used her body to protect Mary.

When she was safe inside, Chloe came back for Paul, who was already part of the way to the house. Frowning, she fell into step behind him.

More gunfire blasted the air as Chloe slammed the front door closed and locked it. "Sit on the stairs." Then she took up watch, using the window in the living room. Every ten seconds or so, she glanced at the family huddled together on the bottom couple of steps.

She saw no movement in the pecan grove.

Please be all right, T.J.

When T.J. saw one German shepherd down by an oak, he waved to the nearest guard a few steps behind him. "See to him."

Near the highway about four hundred yards from the front lawn of the house, T.J. spied the back of a red pickup pulling away and squeezed off a couple of shots, knowing the low probability of him hitting one of the tires. As T.J. jogged to the road, the other dog gave chase after the old Chevy truck without a license plate. When the vehicle had disappeared around a curve, T.J. whistled for the dog to return. The black-and-tan German shepherd loped toward him, his tongue hanging out the side of his mouth.

T.J. patted him on the head and rubbed his back.

"Good boy. Let's return to the house after we check on your buddy."

When he arrived where the other dog had gone down, the guard already had the animal in his arms and was starting back toward the house. Over his shoulder he said, "There's some material with some blood on it by where Rover was. I think he bit the shooter."

"How's Rover?" T.J. squatted by the trunk.

"He should be okay once the vet patches him up."

A piece of tan cotton, possibly from pants, with red drops on it lay on the ground. Was the blood from the assailant or the dog? That would be easy enough to discover, and this could be good evidence to help convict the shooter.

Paul had been inches away from being shot in the head. The assailant had gone for the head when the chest area was an easier and bigger target—he must have somehow known Paul was wearing a bulletproof vest under his coat. Something to mull over.

T.J. left the cloth to be processed by the sheriff's office. Straightening, he weaved his way through the pecan trees and dense brush beneath them. When he reached the paved drive, the front gate opened to let in the sheriff and two deputies in a car behind Landon's.

Out of the corner of his eyes he saw a couple of ranch hands with grim expressions on their faces coming toward him.

"Where's Zach?" T.J. asked Willie.

"He's out repairing the fence Cutter was supposed to do. I'm sure he heard the shots and will be back shortly."

Two more cowhands jogged toward them while Sheriff Landon climbed from his four-wheel drive.

The law officer pushed the front of his cowboy hat up on his forehead. "We need to quit meeting like this."

"I'm in one-hundred-percent agreement, but someone else isn't." T.J. shifted toward the arriving ranch hands. "We've got everything under control, but be extra-alert. The guy who shot at Paul was driving an old red Chevy pickup, probably a late-nineties model." Then to the sheriff he added, "No license plate. But one of the dogs got hold of the man. He tore off a piece of his pants with blood on it. I'll show you."

After the sheriff had the deputies cover the back and front of the house, he went with T.J. A taut constriction around his chest still had hold of T.J. Slowly his adrenaline began to subside.

"The sheriff and a couple of deputies are here," Chloe said from her position at the side of the living room window.

"What about the dog?" Mary asked, her voice barely carrying across the space.

"The guard took him to a truck and is leaving."

"I pray he's all right," Vickie said at the entrance into the room.

So do I. "Please stay back on the stairs." Chloe gritted her teeth. "What if there's a second shooter waiting for our vigilance to drop?"

Vickie's eyes widened. "Really?"

"You have to think of as many possibilities as you can and plan for them."

Vickie backed away and retook her seat next to Aaron, who hadn't said a word since he'd run out of the house shouting for the shooter to stop. But she hadn't forgotten his words. Why would he do that unless...

She let the thought fester in the back of her mind as she walked to the front door to unlock and open it for T.J. and the sheriff.

With grim determination stamped on his face, T.J. entered the house. "He got away in an old red Chevy pickup. Do you all know anyone who owns one like that?"

Paul rose from the step. "No, but check with Zach. He's more aware of that kind of thing."

Sheriff Landon removed his hat. "We'll keep an eye out for a vehicle like that. Without a license plate number, that's about all we can do. I'll let the police in the surrounding towns and counties know. Maybe something will turn up. In the meantime, we'll scour the area to see if we can find anything besides the torn piece of fabric."

T.J. directed his look at Aaron. "Before you leave, Sheriff, I think we need to talk with Aaron."

The teen dropped his head, his hands curling then uncurling.

In the midst of a long silence hanging over the group, Vickie hopped up. "I'm gonna see what I can fix for dinner. If you need me, I'll be in the kitchen."

"Let's go into the living room, where it's more comfortable." Chloe moved toward the entrance, then waited for the family.

Paul put his arm over Mary's shoulder, and she gave him a hug. His soft gaze glided over her face. "Next time we leave we'll need to wear soldier's helmets, too." He tipped one corner of his mouth up in a lop-sided grin.

"How can you joke about what happened? You were

this close to being killed." Mary indicated a couple of inches with her thumb and forefinger.

"But I'm not dead, so obviously the Lord still has things He wants me to do."

"Remember how you felt when I was bit by a rattlesnake? That's how I feel right now."

Paul sobered. "I'm sorry. I can't let this person win. He's already affected our lives. He will not affect my hope this will be taken care of soon."

When Paul, Mary and Aaron settled on the couch, T.J. stood behind the wingback chair. "Aaron, why did you run out of the house when someone was firing at us? Why did you think you could stop him?"

Aaron lifted his chin, his mouth slashed in a frown. "He was there because of me. I paid him to play pranks to get my parents to cancel their speaking tour."

Mary gasped.

Paul grew rigid. "Why, son?"

"You canceled the skiing trip we'd planned for spring break next week because of this speaking tour. You two were gone most of the Christmas holiday. Yeah, I joined you the last part of that tour, but it isn't fun being stuck at a hotel with nothing much to do. These past two years we have seen less and less of each other and it's not because I'm at boarding school. Is that why you sent me to Bethany Academy, so you could travel more?"

"Of course not. We sent you because the school has an excellent academic program." Paul's mouth pinched together.

"We've been together this week and you've stayed in your room," Mary cried out.

"The guy didn't do what I asked. He caused a fire

in Dallas. I couldn't face you all knowing that. I tried and tried to get hold of him and tell him to stop after the first two places. I left a message on his voice mail. Then at the last event you all almost got killed. Again I tried to get hold of him. I wanted to go back to Houston and find him, but she—" Aaron pointed at Chloe "—came after me."

"You should have said something. Told us." Paul's stiff posture deflated.

Aaron surged to his feet. "It got so out of hand. I don't understand. All I wanted was for the tour to be canceled. Then I thought maybe we'd go skiing together. We used to do stuff as a family all the time. I miss the ranch. I don't want to be at Bethany Academy."

"You never said anything." Tears ran down Mary's face.

"Yes, I did. You weren't listening. I mentioned finishing my last two years at the local high school. You said I would get a much better education where I was and I should finish at Bethany Academy."

T.J. came around the chair and took a seat, waving his hand at the couch. "Sit and tell us who this guy is. How did you find him? You saw firsthand his intention isn't to play pranks anymore." Out of the corner of his eye, he glimpsed the sheriff moving farther into the room, but he remained quiet.

Aaron glanced from Sheriff Landon to T.J. "One of the guys at school from Houston knew of a person who did this kind of thing. Fixed problems. I met him in a parking lot downtown. I paid him a couple hundred dollars and was to give him another couple after he finished the job. I had a phone number I was to call with any details from my parents. The letters were perfect. He delivered them to the hotel. No one saw him. The stink bombs would have been fine, but a few people were hurt. Not too bad thankfully—" the teen gulped "—but I changed my mind when I saw what could happen."

"So you told him not to do anything after Paris?" the sheriff asked from behind T.J.

"I didn't leave a message until after the first event in Dallas when the driver of the limo was hit over the head. I thought everything was all right when nothing happened at the second speaking stop in Dallas."

"It wasn't publicized, but someone put a tracking device on the car." Chloe rose and headed for the foyer. "I have a picture I want to show you of that person we think tagged the rental. It could be your guy."

"What's his name and who is the person who told you about him?" The sheriff pulled out his pad and pen.

Fear washed over Aaron's face. He bit into his lower lip and slanted a glance toward his mother. "I'm afraid of him. Look… What he's been doing. I never told him to do that."

T.J. leaned forward, resting his elbows on his thighs. "Tell us his name. The police will catch him, and you'll be safe."

"He might be in a gang. I never asked." Aaron twisted his hands together, and his mouth clamped shut for a long moment.

His father settled his hand on the teen's shoulder. "We're here for you."

Swallowing hard, Aaron looked straight at the sheriff. "Lenny Woods—at least, that's the name I know him by."

When Chloe returned to the living room, she

crossed to Aaron and showed him the picture the Dallas police had come up with from Kyra's description of the man driving the blue van.

Aaron's eyes grew wide. "That's him." He shrugged away from his dad's clasp and shoved to his feet. "This shouldn't have happened. I asked him several times to quit, and if he didn't, I wouldn't pay him any more money." His voice rose several decibels. "Are you taking me in?"

Sheriff Landon shook his head. "Not at this time. I'll be talking with the Dallas police. You'll have to answer for putting this guy into motion, but at this time, I think you're safer here under T.J. and Chloe's protection. I'll be leaving a deputy posted here until we can track down this Lenny Woods." He approached Chloe, who held the picture. "May I take that? I'll be spreading this man's sketch around and contacting Houston. Who was the student that told you about Woods?"

"Do I hafta tell you? I don't wanna get him into trouble."

"I'm afraid so, son. Your cooperation will go a long way in determining what the police in Dallas and Paris will do concerning your part in all of this."

Aaron paled, his body quaking. "Anderson Stokes."

"I'll be in touch with what we find," the sheriff said to T.J., then made his way to the front door.

Chloe followed him to let him out.

"Why didn't you say anything after your mother was bitten by the snake?" Paul asked, squeezing Mary's hand.

"I tried. I couldn't. I was—am—scared of this guy. I didn't know this would happen. Never thought it would.

You're always helping every…" Aaron snapped his mouth closed.

The doorbell rang. T.J. heard Chloe answering it. Ten seconds later, Zach came into the living room with Chloe.

"Tell them what you told me." Chloe gestured to the family and T.J.

Zach took the toothpick in his mouth out and said, "Bo Moore has an old red Chevy truck. I heard from some of the cowhands about the pickup driving away from ranch. I'm sorry, Paul and Mary. Me firing him last month must have set him off."

Chloe unfolded another copy of the assailant tracking them in Dallas and showed Zach. "Is this Bo Moore?"

"Nope. There is some similarity, but Bo has a cleft in his chin. This guy doesn't and his eyes are blue, not brown. Hair is lighter, almost blond. I told the sheriff before he left and he's going to get a warrant for Moore's house and see if he can find his truck."

"There are two people?" Paul's eyebrows scrunched together.

"I didn't hire two people." Aaron collapsed on the couch and laid his head on the back cushion, closing his eyes. "This is a nightmare. How did it get so out of control?"

"Okay." T.J. held up his hand. "It won't do us any good to start speculating about what has happened. Thanks for the information, Zach. Hopefully the sheriff and police here or in Houston will find the truck and Bo Moore as well as this Lenny Woods. At least now we have some names to follow up on."

While Chloe walked with Zach to the door, Mary

looked up at T.J. "We would like some private time with our son. Is it okay in here?"

"Yes. I'll make sure no one bothers you." T.J. strode to all the windows in the living room and closed the blinds. "I'll be doing that in the whole house."

T.J. met Chloe in the foyer. "Let's shut the blinds. We might as well not give a sniper a target."

"I just got off the phone with Kyra. She said one of the references for Dave Cutter checked out. The other two didn't."

"Which means?" T.J. stood at the bottom of the staircase.

"He's worked at one ranch for about six months. No other experience. Zach told me he called the first one and the man had good things to say about Dave. Zach had been short a cowhand for a while and with spring approaching he decided to hire him on a trial basis. At that time, nothing had happened in Dallas and Zach thought the Paris incident was just a disgruntled person."

"I'll take care of the windows downstairs while you do the upstairs."

T.J. met Chloe back in the foyer five minutes later.

"Aaron's bedroom is a mess. That's unusual. Mary told me he's neater than she is."

He shook his head. "I knew on the trip to the San Antonio hospital that something was wrong with Aaron. I should have pressured him to talk."

"He wasn't ready. He's in trouble now and will have to face the consequences. It could be jail time, depending on what the police and DA discover." Chloe snapped her fingers. "I almost forgot. The other guard got a call. The German shepherd will be okay. The second guard will get another dog and return soon. I suggest we keep two patrolling outside and also that wooded area across the ranch road."

"Agreed. I'll make the arrangement with the agency to double up. I'm hoping Lenny will be found soon and this will all end."

"Maybe for us, but not for Mary, Aaron and Paul."

T.J. started to step toward her but stopped himself. It shouldn't be long before this assignment was over. Until then he needed to rein in his feelings for Chloe. Afterward, he had decisions to make. He was falling for her again, but then, he had nine years ago and neither of them had been able to make the commitment to the other. He didn't want to go through that again.

"I thought you were taking a nap," Chloe said when she entered the kitchen and found Mary staring into her mug in front of her on the table.

"I can't. I don't think I got two hours' sleep last night. I keep waiting—praying for the phone to ring and the sheriff to tell us the person who's been doing this has been caught."

Chloe eased into the chair across from Mary. "It's only been twenty-four hours. No one knows where Bo Moore or his truck is. The sheriff talked with Bo's brother in Phoenix, and he wasn't due to show up for the new job for another week, so Bo told his brother he would hang around here a few more days with some of his friends."

"Did the sheriff talk with his friends?"

"Yes and they haven't seen him in over a day. He'd mentioned to one of them he had an opportunity to make a little cash before he left for Arizona."

Mary's eyes widened.

"Don't worry. The sheriff has everyone looking for him and his pickup. It's been on the news in this county and the surrounding ones."

"I hope something gives soon. Look at me." Mary held her trembling hand out flat. "I've prayed and prayed. Paul has and even Aaron joined us last night." She made a fist that shook, too. "Then we have to deal with what our son has done."

"Did you call your lawyer this morning?"

"Yes, and he'll be here this evening to talk to Aaron and us." She laughed, but there was no humor in the sound. "We go around the country talking about taking back our communities and not tolerating violence. How can we do that with what Aaron set in motion? What kind of authority are we now?"

"I never got the feeling from your message you were speaking from a place of authority. More from a place of concern for the type of future we'll leave our children. You're a parent. You have a right to talk about that. I hope more will start being concerned about where our future is going and take a stand."

Tears in her eyes, Mary swallowed over and over. "I've cried so much in the past week. In the middle of this, about all I can really do is turn it over to the Lord. I can't function on two hours of sleep a night. I've got to find a way to push this worry away and keep my eye on God. This has been my biggest test. I tell people to do that, and now I'm struggling to keep my focus on the Lord myself."

"Because it isn't easy. It can be one of the most difficult things a person does in the midst of a crisis. Let the worry go. I've done my fair share of worrying over the years, and I'm sure I will in the future. We want to control everything, and we worry when we can't."

"Thanks." Mary tried to smile while a wet tear coursed down her face. "I need to listen to the advice I've given others." She swiped her hand across her cheeks. "I'm not the type of person to have a pity party. Let's talk about something other than my situation." This time one corner of her mouth lifted. "What's going on between you and T.J.?"

Had Aaron said something to his mother about the kiss she and T.J. shared last night? "What do you mean?" she finally said while trying to decide how to handle this conversation.

"I've seen how you look at T.J. Not often, but every once in a while. I may have missed the signals my son was sending me, but I think you care about T.J.—more than just as a partner. Am I right?"

Chloe stared into Mary's understanding eyes and knew she could trust the woman with her emotions, which seesawed between committing herself to T.J. and seeing if they could work out as a couple and cutting her losses and making a change in her life that she'd been thinking about for months.

"Yes, but it's complicated."

"Love often is."

Love? She wanted to deny that, but the words wouldn't come out. "I grew up in a family with a father who was rarely around. I saw what it did to my mother. He broke her heart. I vowed that I would come first in a man's life—first before a job—but then I fell in love with T.J. nine years ago. I knew I shouldn't and I was right. He got a promotion and moved to Washington, D.C."

"He just picked up and left without talking to you about it?"

"Well, no. He wanted me to follow him after my mother was better. For me to leave my job and my mother, who had just recovered from cancer, I couldn't. What if it hadn't worked out? What if..."

Mary covered Chloe's hand on the table. "We can't predict the future. All we can do is believe in the Lord and trust Him to lead us in the right direction. If you aren't ready to commit to T.J. one hundred percent, then you shouldn't. But don't try second-guessing what might happen in the future. I never in my wildest dream thought what my family is going through would happen. And I'm glad I didn't know ahead of time. I would have spent all that time worrying. Worrying doesn't change the situation and often compounds it. When you became an adult, what did you see your future as?"

"I wanted to be a wife and mother."

"In spite of what happened to your parents?"

"I love children. It was a dream I had since I was a young teenager. It wasn't until I was seventeen that I really saw what was going on with my mother and father. She'd tried to shield me from her problems, but when my father took back-to-back assignments so he would be gone much longer from home, she fell apart. From then on, I was who she confided in."

"That's quite a burden for a teenager."

"She needed me. I had to be there for her."

"Yes, but you are not your mother and your situation isn't the same."

Uncertain about what to think anymore, Chloe rose. "I'm not so sure."

"Pray, Chloe. Talk to the Lord."

Chloe started to say something, but the sound of someone approaching the room filtered through her confusion. She swallowed back the words.

T.J. walked into the kitchen, holding his cell phone to his ear. "Thanks for letting us know. I'll pass the information on to Paul and Mary."

When he hung up and looked at them, Chloe knew the news wasn't good. Although his expression showed little emotion, the taut lines of his body conveyed a different impression.

"That was Sheriff Landon. They found Bo Moore in his pickup in a lake. A rifle was in the cab with him."

THIRTEEN

"Is it over?" Mary massaged her temples.

"No. Moore may be responsible for the shooting earlier, but we have no reason behind the attack. Lenny Woods is still out there." T.J. slipped his cell phone into his pocket. "I'm going to let Paul know. At least we probably won't have someone out there shooting at us, and the sheriff said the Houston police have a lead on where Lenny is—the hospital. Apparently he got into a fight two days ago and ended up shot."

"Will he recover?" Chloe rolled her knotted shoulders, then kneaded her fingers into her nape. At least some answers were falling into place.

"The sheriff didn't have all the details, but he's coming by later to talk with Aaron. I told him your lawyer would arrive at six, so he'll be here then. Maybe he'll have more information for us at that time."

"How did he end up in a lake?" Something bothered Chloe about that, but she didn't know what.

"From what little the sheriff could figure out, Moore lost control of his truck."

"Were there any witnesses?" Chloe crossed to the pot of coffee on the stove and poured a mugful.

"No. A passerby from the road saw the rear end barely sticking out of the water early this morning."

Mary took her teacup to the sink. "All this discussion has tired me out. I'm going to see if I can sleep some before the lawyer and sheriff come. Vickie thought she would prepare some sandwiches and buffet-type food, so if Sheriff Landon and Henry Calvin want to have something to eat, they can. No telling how long all of this will take tonight." Hugging her arms to her, she shivered. "But this meeting will have far-reaching consequences for Aaron and for all of us."

When Mary had disappeared down the hall, T.J. grabbed a cup of coffee, too. "She looks exhausted."

"She's not sleeping."

"Paul isn't, either."

"Where is he?"

"With Aaron, in his office. Aaron is writing down everything he remembers surrounding hiring Lenny to cause trouble on the speaking tour."

"Where did Aaron get that kind of cash?"

"He worked last summer and had it in his saving account. He's finally telling his dad how unhappy he's been at Bethany Academy. I decided to leave them alone. I think Aaron will talk more freely without me in the office."

"A breakdown in communication can destroy a relationship. I'm glad to see them finally talking."

"Like you and me?"

Chloe tilted her head and studied him a moment. "Yes. We should have talked more in the past. I think, though, we were in two different places in our lives." And she was beginning to feel they were in two different places now. Talking to Mary over the course of this assignment, as well as just a few minutes ago, Chloe realized she wanted more from life than what she had. She wanted roots and a family. She didn't want a husband wrapped up in his job. Look at what was happening to the Zimmermans because their work took over their lives. "Some people are meant only to be friends."

His look sliced through her. "Us?"

"You're looking at going into business with Kyra and expanding it. That's going to require a lot of time and work. I'm looking at simplifying my life. I've realized I haven't read a good book in years because I'm always working. I have an apartment in Dallas, but no pets because I'm always gone. In fact, my place doesn't feel like a home. It means no more to me than a hotel room. I've been thinking about what Mary and Paul say about considering what's really important in life. Is it money? Is it possessions? What rules your life? At the moment, my job rules mine and I'm finding out that's not what I want. I want more." Chloe started for the back door. "I'm going to walk around the house. I need some fresh air, and I want to make sure everyone is doing what they need to."

T.J. called out to her as she left, but she kept going. She needed a change. She wasn't sure what she would do, but she needed something different.

Chloe opened the front door to let the Zimmermans' attorney, Mr. Calvin, into the house that evening. She noticed that the sheriff was pulling up. "The family is in the living room. Go on in. Sheriff Landon has arrived. I'll wait for him."

Passing the lawyer in the entrance into the room, T.J. approached her with a determined expression on his face. She'd been avoiding him the whole afternoon. For the past half a year, she'd been dissatisfied with what she was doing. She'd always love helping people feel safe, but not this way. She'd dodged one too many bullets.

Instead of staying inside, she moved out onto the verandah as the sheriff headed toward the house. The smile on the man's face prompted her to ask, "Do you have good news?"

"Yep." The sheriff's gaze shifted to a place behind her. "The Houston police found Lenny Woods getting ready to leave the hospital. They took him down to the station and are questioning him now. The detective will call me with any additional information after the interrogation. They searched his place and found a few hundred dollars, which fits what Aaron said. Also they found a burner phone with half a dozen messages on it from the teen. The last one was a plea to stop what he was doing before he killed someone."

Chloe stepped to the side, spying T.J. behind her. "Come in. They're in the living room. Your news isn't going to get Aaron off the hook, but it will help his case."

Her gaze latched on to T.J.'s as he entered the house. She started across the foyer.

T.J. blocked her. "We need to talk."

"About what? Leaving the ranch?"

"No. About us. You're doing exactly what you did nine years ago. I think we have a chance as a couple, but I sense you're backing away from me. What do you want from me? I've moved to Dallas. I'm going to be doing what you're doing."

"Is this why you came to Dallas? To see if you and I could make a second go of it?"

Fury hardened his features. "Yes. I didn't realize it, but it was the reason I came here. I could have moved anywhere and made a fresh start. I chose here because we did have something special once—enough that you spoiled me for any other woman."

Her eyes blinked wide. "I did? Don't blame that on me." She pushed past him and marched across the foyer to plant herself in the entrance into the living room. She clenched her hands so hard pain spread up her arms. This wasn't the time to make that important decision she'd talked with Mary about earlier.

T.J. joined her, leaning close to her ear. "You're scared. You think I'll be like your father—an absentee husband. I'm not your father. If I make a commitment, I put my whole self into it."

She turned her head slightly. "As you did your job all these years?" Before he could reply, she put her finger to her lips and said, "Shh." She couldn't deal with this now.

T.J. lounged against the opposite doorjamb with a look of thunder on his face.

With T.J. feet from her, Chloe had a hard time focusing on the interview between the sheriff and Aaron. Sheriff Landon finished walking the teen through what he'd done to procure Lenny Woods's services and why. Paul sat on one side of his son while Mary was on the other. She could imagine what was going through their minds as they listened again to their son explain he'd needed more from his parents and had gone about getting it the wrong way. So much of what Aaron said reminded Chloe of how she'd felt as a teenager, especially toward her father.

At the end of the interview Sheriff Landon said, "After I was notified about Lenny Woods being taken into custody in Houston, I called Detective Matthews. Tomorrow he's driving to Houston to interrogate Woods and arrange for the man to be transported to Dallas. He wanted to know if I felt y'all were out of danger. I told him yes. We had a few loose ends to tie up, but it appeared the two perpetrators involved have been accounted for."

"Did you ever find Dave Cutter?" Chloe asked, wondering where the man had gone.

"He left because his divorced wife was closing in on him for child support. He's disappeared again." The sheriff shook his head. "That's a pity for his children."

The lawyer sat forward. "What about Aaron?"

"Detective Matthews wants Aaron to turn himself in the day after tomorrow before noon in Dallas. That'll give you time to drive there from the ranch. Okay?"

Mr. Calvin glanced at Paul before answering, "Yes. I'll be accompanying the Zimmermans to the police station in Dallas. Aaron wants to cooperate with the police any way he can."

The sheriff stood and shook the lawyer's hand and then Paul's. "I'm sorry all this happened, but at least now you can go about your life without worrying about someone being after you."

"But we don't know why Bo Moore did it," Paul said.

"My guess, since he can't tell us, is that he was madder than Zach had thought about being fired from the ranch, and since you're the owner, he saw you as the one behind the smoking ban. The rifle he had in the cab of his pickup was like the one used by the sniper in the pecan grove. The ballistics checked out. They matched." Sheriff Landon plopped his hat on his head and made his way toward the foyer.

T.J. walked with the man to the front door. Chloe stayed, not wanting to be alone with T.J. at the moment.

"What's going to happen to me?" Aaron began pacing in front of the fireplace.

"I'm going to try to have this taken care of in juvenile court since you're still sixteen." The lawyer stood, buttoning his suit coat.

"Will me being seventeen in a couple of months make a difference?"

"Maybe, but we should be able to show your intent and what you did to change what was happening. That might help your case. But I'm not going to kid you. You could serve time and your parents may be open to lawsuits. We need to expect the worst and hope for something better, which is probation and community service."

"You will have to face the consequences, but you won't be alone. We'll be by your side." Paul bridged the distance between him and his son and embraced him. "You should have come forward sooner, but at least you did."

"I've ruined everything for you and Mom."

"The Lord wants us to go down this path for a reason. He's never wrong. Maybe He has other plans for your mom and me. We'll just have to wait and see."

Mr. Calvin gathered up his papers and stuffed them in his briefcase, then rose. "I'll be talking with the prosecutor in Dallas tomorrow. I'll let you know what he says."

"Thank you, Henry. I'll walk you out. It will be nice to be able to go outside without worrying about someone being after us." Paul accompanied the lawyer to the door.

"This meeting didn't take as long as we thought. I forgot to invite the sheriff and Henry to dinner." Mary stood, closing her eyes for a few seconds, weariness in every line of her body. "I hate for Vickie's buffet to go to waste, but I'm too tired to eat. I'm going to bed early."

"Mom?"

She smiled at Aaron. "I'm fine, honey. Y'all have to remember I was in the hospital recently and don't have the energy I usually have." Mary strolled toward her. "Chloe, maybe you can see if any of the ranch hands are still here. If so, they're invited to dinner. Since Zach lives on the ranch, at least he should come."

"I'll walk down to the barn and check with Zach. We'll take care of the food. Won't we, Aaron?"

"Don't worry. I'm starved. I'll eat your share."

"Thanks. At least tonight I should be able to sleep. And, Aaron, I'm not worrying. Not when I remember who is really in charge."

Chloe watched Mary climb the stairs slowly. Sleep was the best thing for her right now. "Aaron, your mom is a strong woman. She'll be fine."

"I know." The teen paused next to Chloe. "I'd like to come with you to the barn. Okay?"

Chloe glimpsed T.J. and Paul entering the house. "Sure. Let's go out the back." She didn't want to talk to

T.J. She had some serious praying and thinking to do. She didn't want to mess up her future and act recklessly. *Besides a change, what do I want?*

Chloe descended the stairs to the foyer and set her piece of luggage by the door. After breakfast, she and T.J. would leave the ranch. Although they had offered to stay an extra day and follow them back to Dallas, Mary and Paul had insisted they were fine and needed some alone time with their son before he turned himself into the police. They needed to feel their life was normal at least for a day.

T.J. called Sheriff Landon and he said the Houston authorities were interrogating Lenny Woods. "He hadn't said much except he wanted a lawyer. But Lenny couldn't give an alibi for the event at the theater in Dallas. He said he had been sleeping off a hangover in a Dallas motel at the time. I called the place he said he was staying, and the manager couldn't say one way or another if he had been there the afternoon in question."

When she entered the kitchen, Mary, Paul and Aaron were already seated as Vickie set a platter of blueberry pancakes in the middle of the table, and then took a chair.

T.J. finished pouring a cup of coffee and held up the pot. "Want some?"

"Yes." Chloe sat at one of the two places left, realizing T.J. would be next to her. Last night she should have gotten a good night's sleep, but for hours she'd kept replaying scenes from when she and T.J. had dated years ago. She'd gotten out of bed and paced her bedroom, thinking about their time together, especially at the ranch. The kisses they had shared had flashed in and out of her thoughts until she'd given up trying to get any rest. She'd lain down and stared at the ceiling in the darkness, and some time in the night she'd finally fallen asleep in exhaustion, a prayer for help running through her mind. She'd barely dragged herself out of bed half an hour ago.

T.J. took the seat next to her and slid her mug toward her. She reached for it, needing the caffeine.

"What are all of you planning to do today?" Chloe asked after several sips of her coffee.

"I need to go shopping later." Vickie poured hot maple syrup over her pancakes. "I'm thankful one of the ranch hands did it for us, but it's hard to think of everything we need and put it down on a list. I've never been a person who could only shop by what I had on a list."

"I appreciate you taking over the household account while I've been gone so much, but Paul and I have decided we aren't leaving for the next year. All this has made us reconsider what we need and want to do." Mary patted Aaron's hand. "I want my son to feel he's the most important one in our lives."

"We're thinking of riding over the ranch after lunch. Getting out and enjoying this beautiful day God created and reconnect with Him. We haven't done that in nine months. Then we'll prepare ourselves for what's to come concerning Aaron." Paul snatched another piece of bacon off a plate in the center of the table. "How about you and T.J.?"

"I don't know about T.J., but I'm crashing for a few days. I forgot to water my one plant, a cactus, and I'm afraid it might have bit the dust by now. I used to have more houseplants, but traveling makes it hard to keep any."

"I have Vickie. She takes care of us." Mary smiled at her cousin across from her.

"So what are you going to do next, T.J.?" Paul stabbed his fork into pieces of pancake.

T.J. glanced sideways at Chloe. "I'll be finalizing my partnership with Kyra Hunt. She called this morning to tell me she has accepted my offer."

"Congratulations. That's great. You and Chloe are good at your job. We appreciate you two." Paul took a bite of his pancake. "But we're ecstatic we don't need you all anymore."

Chloe had been pretty sure Kyra would take T.J. on as a partner, but with her second pregnancy, how much would she be involved in the business? Would he be out in the field any or working at the main office? How much did he want to expand? T.J. knew the business and could go far, especially with his background and connections. He wanted to go forward. She wanted to go in a different direction. Again they were at divergent places in their lives.

When breakfast was over, Mary hugged Chloe, whispering, "I recently discovered what's more important in my life than my work. My family. I hope you get your heart's desire and find those answers you're searching for." Mary looked at T.J., then pointedly back to Chloe. "You saved my life. I imagine you have done that for others, too. That's a gift the Lord gave you. I wish you the best, and don't be a stranger. I want to stay in touch."

After saying their goodbyes, Chloe and T.J. climbed into his Jeep for the three-hour drive to Dallas. Chloe had a lot to think about, especially Mary's parting words. For the first few minutes as they left the ranch behind, a strained silence dominated the atmosphere in the car.

Then T.J. said, "What I didn't say back in the kitchen was that Kyra won't be coming back to the agency. I'll slowly buy her out and have full ownership, probably in the next two years. How do you feel about that?" Tension wove through his words, his hands clenching the steering wheel.

She told him what Mary had said to her at the end, and then added, "I don't know."

"Why not? When I first saw you and talked with you, I never felt you were unhappy with your job. Did this assignment, working with me, make you unhappy?"

She chewed her lower lip, trying to figure out what to say. "I'm not unhappy about my work, just not satisfied like I used to be. The more I was around you, the more I began to think about what I used to dream about and what I have put on the back burner for all these years. A family. I need more than my job. I need to feel grounded and I'm not right now."

"Are you telling me you're leaving Guardians, Inc.?"

"I don't want to continue as I have, on the road three-fourths of the time. What husband would want his wife traveling all the time?" She immediately thought of Adam and her father. "I know what that does to a relationship."

T.J. pulled off the road and parked the Jeep, then twisted toward her. "I love you, Chloe. I think we can make it work. I want a family, too. I don't want to pass this second chance up for us. I told you when I make a commitment I make a total one. If I stand before God and pledge myself to you, you will have me one hundred percent."

"I don't see how you can do that with the plans you have for Guardians, Inc. I don't want a husband that is married to his job, too. I need more. I see that now. You're right. That was why in the end I didn't come to Washington after my mother's chemo treatments were finished. I used that as an excuse. It was hard enough for us to find time together with me being a cop and you a Secret Service agent working in the counterfeiting unit."

He reached for her hand and held it. "Let me make myself clear. I'll run the agency, not be a bodyguard. I've gotten a lot out of my work, but it's time for me to move on to something a little different. I want you to be my partner in marriage and in the business. I'm looking to expand, which means more work running the agency. I can't think of a better person to work with because I wouldn't want you traveling for your job. I want to go home to you every night. I want to be there for you and you for me. I want to stay in one place and make a home filled with love and the Lord."

She tugged her hand from his grasp. His touch made her forget her rational side, and this was too important to let feelings swamp her, with no regard to the consequences of her decision. This was for the rest of her life. "I want children. At least two. I used to babysit as a teenager and loved being with kids. I even considered becoming a teacher, but police work called to me more."

"I'd love to be the father of your children. You can work as much as you want at the agency. As I said, we will be equal partners in all things. This assignment showed me how well we work together. I think the Lord brought us back together again because we're perfect for each other."

The emotions she tried to hold at bay overwhelmed her. There had never been another man for her, but would this really work? Could they make the change they needed? *Is this Your answer to my prayers, Lord?* "Are you sure once you get back and take over the agency you won't get sucked into your job? Look at what the Zimmermans' career did to their family."

"If we have good employees in place, we don't have to work all the time. Kyra has made it work. It can be a regular job. So what do you say about going into partnership with me? And to make myself clear, I mean in marriage *and* the agency."

"I love you, T.J. I always have, but I need some time to think. I'm exhausted from this job, and I don't want to rush into a lifelong commitment without making sure it's what is best for the both of us. You need to do the same thing. It'll be a big change for us. We've been on our own for years."

He cocked a grin. "Always the practical one. Okay." He took her hand and pulled her toward him. Framing her face, he touched his forehead to hers. "If we get married, I'm more afraid I'm not going to want to even go to work. You'll have to kick me out of the house or we might starve."

He kissed her, laying claim to her with heart-shattering possession. When he straightened and switched on the engine, he threw her a look that melted any reservation she had. In that moment she knew it was the Lord's answer to her prayers last night. She loved him.

He loved her. She needed to put her faith in that and cherish the time they had together rather than be governed by her past.

"T.J.—"

His cell phone rang, spoiling the moment.

"That's Sheriff Landon." He answered it. His smile quickly evolved into a frown. "Thanks for the information. We're going to turn around and head back to the ranch. We're about ten minutes away. I'll call you later."

"What's wrong?"

T.J. made a U-turn. "Sheriff Landon got the autopsy report back on Bo Moore. He was full of sleeping pills and tranquilizers. He drowned, but he was unconscious when it happened. They're going to scour where the truck went off the road. He doesn't think it's a suicide, especially when he talked with Bo's girlfriend. Yes, he was angry about losing his job, but he was mad at Zach. Bo and his girlfriend were planning to elope next weekend and settle in Arizona. Doesn't sound like a suicidal man."

"No. So that means we don't know who shot at the Zimmermans when they returned from the celebration at the church."

"It's possible they still aren't safe. He called the Houston police, and Lenny Woods keeps saying the last thing he did before he received Aaron's message was put a tracking device on the rental car and follow us from the second event in Dallas."

"Which leaves the fire at the theater, the snakes and the sniper. Do you think someone took advantage of the fact someone was after the Zimmermans?"

"Yes." T.J. increased his speed. "I can't see Nancy doing it, because she's no longer the publicist for the

Zimmermans. She has nothing to gain going after them. I'm the one who got her fired, so if she is angry, it should be at me." He tossed her glance. "But we can't rule out anyone."

"Someone at the ranch or in town? Or we could be back to someone upset at the Zimmermans' message. They're particularly vocal about gangs in communities."

"When we get back to the ranch, we'll sit down with them and go through the people they know again."

At the gate he phoned the main house, but no one answered. Then T.J. placed a call to Zach, who had the ability to let someone into the ranch from his office. T.J. knew yesterday's gate code, but he'd trained Paul to change it every morning.

As they approached the main house, Chloe pushed her exhaustion away and focused on the job to be done if someone was still after the Zimmermans. The second the Jeep stopped, she was out of it and striding toward the front door. She rang the bell while T.J. joined her on the verandah. When no one came to answer, she pressed the button again and rested her hand on her gun.

The door swung open, and Vickie appeared in the entrance. "Sorry. I was in the kitchen making a list of items I needed at the store. Did you forget something?"

"No, but I don't think this is over yet. Where are Paul and Mary?" T.J. looked beyond Vickie into the foyer.

Vickie glanced over her shoulder. "They went to meet the lawyer in town. Some new development concerning the charges against Aaron. He went with them. I was finishing up and gathering my purse, so I can go meet them there for lunch before I go shopping." Hugging her handbag under her arm, she rambled.

T.J. barged past her. "We'll follow you, but first I want to search the house to make sure everything is okay since security hasn't been tight the past eighteen hours. Someone could have snuck something in here. You all stay there. I won't be too long."

While he went into the living room, Chloe skirted Vickie to stand inside the entrance. T.J. came back out and headed across the foyer to the dining room.

"Vickie, where are you? I'm here to finish the job," a deep masculine voice said from the kitchen.

Mary's cousin's eyes grew round. She took a step back, then whirled and raced out the front door.

Near the dining room door into the kitchen, T.J. smelled gas. Coming from the kitchen? They had a gas stove. Something wasn't right.

Then he heard Shane call out to Vickie. He slapped his palm against the swinging door and pushed his way into the kitchen. He caught sight of Mary and Paul lying on the floor.

His attention was riveted on Shane, who was standing near them, surprise registering on his craggy face. He turned and ran for the back door. T.J. flew across the room and threw himself at the ranch hand. They fell to the floor, T.J.'s arms locked around the man's chest. Shane flung T.J.'s body back against a set of cabinets nearby. Then he did again. T.J.'s head struck the wooden door. His ears ringing, he hung on and tightened his hold.

Shane grunted and tried to shake T.J. off him. Bringing his hands up, Shane clutched T.J.'s arms and pulled down. He broke T.J.'s grip on him. The ranch hand rotated at the same time, scrambling back from T.J. Shane brought his fist back and drilled it into T.J. Through the haze in his head, T.J. returned a punch. Then another. The stench of gas filled his nostrils, and he knew he needed to get the family out of there. Soon.

Vickie was halfway down the sidewalk, not far from her car, which was parked in front of T.J.'s.

Chloe drew her Glock and aimed it at the woman. "Halt or I'll shoot."

Vickie glanced back and veered onto the grass but tripped over a stone. She went down on her knees, and Chloe fired her weapon off to the side of the woman to scare her.

Vickie froze, lifting her shaking arms. "Okay. Okay."

"Lie face down on the grass and don't move. All I can think about is that I hate snakes, and you're probably the one who put two in your cousin's greenhouse." Chloe approached her, keeping her attention focused on Vickie.

The sound of pounding footsteps forced Chloe to look briefly toward the barn. Zach. Still not sure who to trust at the ranch, she shouted, "Go get some rope to tie her up." Then she watched to see if he would.

Chloe let out a bottled breath when the foreman headed back to the barn. She knew that T.J. could take care of himself, but who was the man who had shouted from the kitchen?

A shot rang through the air, fueling T.J.'s determination to finish this, to get the family outside and check on Chloe. He willed all his strength behind his next blow to Shane's jaw. Pain streaked up his arm as his fist connected with the man's face. But the hit flattened Shane back on the floor, his head cracking against the tiles. Shane passed out, his body going limp.

T.J. didn't waste any time. He scrambled to his feet, clutching the side of the counter to get his bearings then he hurried and switched off the stove and closed the oven. Mary lay nearby, and he picked her up. After carrying her outside, he checked to make sure Shane was still out and dragged Paul out the back door. In the corner, he spied Aaron slumped against the wall. T.J. had little strength left but managed to haul the teen to the doorway. Stepping outside, he sucked in a deep breath of fresh air, then continued with Aaron out the back and down the steps to the backyard—away from the house.

When he returned to the kitchen, he used the cords on the blinds to tie Shane up, then pulled the man free of the house. As he headed to the front, he called the sheriff, explained briefly what had happened and requested some ambulances.

With gun in hand, he rounded the corner to the front yard to find Zach tying up Vickie while Chloe held her Glock on the woman. When Vickie was secured, Chloe's shoulders sagged slightly, but she still kept her gun at her side as though prepared for anything else.

As he approached, she peered at him and grinned.

"I'm glad you caught Vickie. I took Shane down in the kitchen. The gas was on. I turned it off and got everyone outside. The family was passed out on the floor."

Zach straightened, glaring at Vickie as he dragged

her to her feet. "Why did you do this? Mary and Paul gave you everything."

"And they never let me forget that they took me in and saved me from bankruptcy. All my life Mary got everything. Paul. An important job. A big house and ranch. People who loved her. I always got her leftovers. When I was a child living with her family. When I was adult and had financial problems. I was tired of always coming in second and having to be nice or fear I'd be kicked out of the house."

Zach shook his head. "Mary and Paul aren't like that, but you're too full of hate to see the goodness in them."

"Look what they did to their own son. Shuffled him off to boarding school. They couldn't be bothered to raise him and when he was home, I had to play mother because Mary was too busy." Venom dripped from each word.

"Keep an eye on her, Zach. I'm going to the backyard to check on Paul, Mary and Aaron." T.J. grabbed Chloe's hand and tugged her to his side.

As they walked around the house, he slung his arm around Chloe. "When I heard a gun go off, I was so afraid you'd been hurt. It gave me the extra incentive to finish off Shane."

"Shane was helping Vickie?"

"I knocked him out, but when he wakes up, we'll see what his story is. Vickie had to have outside help. She may have put the snakes in the greenhouse, but Shane had to be the one who fired at us after the celebration. You know it was Shane that pointed us toward Bo Moore and his red pickup."

"I thought Vickie was interested in Shane. Obviously more than I thought."

T.J. rounded the corner and immediately found the couple and their son where he'd left them. Paul was leaning over Mary while Aaron stirred on the ground nearby.

T.J. hurried to their side with Chloe next to him. "Are you okay?"

Confusion clouding his eyes, Paul glanced up. "She's alive, but still out. What happened to us?"

"An ambulance and the sheriff are coming. Vickie had the gas on. I found you three passed out on the floor. Do you remember anything?"

"Mary and Vickie were in the kitchen talking at the table. I came in to talk with Vickie about some discrepancies I found in the account books." He looked to Aaron, who sat up, touching the back of his head and wincing. "What's wrong, son?"

Aaron brought his hand around and showed them his bloodied fingers. "She...hit me."

"Vickie?" Chloe asked.

"Yes." Aaron closed his eyes for a few seconds. "I came into the kitchen—saw my parents on the floor." He peered at his mom. "Mom." He started to get up, but collapsed back onto the ground.

Chloe went to Aaron and knelt next to him. "She'll be all right." She glimpsed Mary moving her hand. "See. You need to stay put until the paramedics get here."

The blare of the siren echoed through the air.

Before the couple and Aaron were taken away, T.J. squatted next to Paul. "Why were you looking at the books this morning?"

"Zach told me there was something wrong. I thought I would see before we had to leave for Dallas. When I said that to Vickie, she smiled and agreed we should do it now. With what was happening, I thought she had probably added a few things wrong. She went to the coffeepot and poured a cup for me and refilled Mary's, then sat to talk about the accounts."

Mary moaned. "The last thing I remember—" her voice sputtered to a halt and she blinked "—is you opening the books on the table."

"Yeah, you fell over as I was talking with Vickie."

"Did you drink some coffee?" T.J. noticed the paramedics coming around the side of the house, relieved help had arrived.

"Yes. You think she drugged us?"

"Probably. Was she drinking the coffee?" T.J. caught sight of Sheriff Landon right behind the EMTs.

Paul frowned. "No, and she loves coffee." He snorted. "I didn't get very far going through the books with her before I must have blacked out."

"I guess she was going to use the gas leak to cover everything up. When it builds up, it doesn't take much for an explosion." T.J. stood and backed away as paramedics started working on the family and readying them for transportation.

After making sure the Zimmermans would be all right, Sheriff Landon crossed to where Shane lay, trying to get free. The sheriff slapped his handcuffs on the cowhand. "You aren't going anywhere. I'm taking you to the station along with Vickie. We have all day to straighten this out." He hauled Shane to his feet, then looked toward T.J. and Chloe a few feet away. "I guess you two will have to stay around another day.

When Mary, Paul and Aaron are taken care of, I'd like to see you two at the station, too. I intend to close this case once and for all."

"That you'll be able to do. We'll be there shortly. Tell your men to be careful in the house. Vickie had the gas on in the kitchen." T.J. slipped his arm around Chloe.

The sheriff tipped his hat, then strode with Shane toward the front.

"If you hadn't pulled over to talk to me about our future, we might not have made it back in time to save them." Chloe nestled closer to T.J, turning her head up toward his and reaching up to kiss him on the lips. "Yes."

T.J.'s gaze gleamed with love. "Yes? To what?"

"Yes, I'll marry you. In the car before the sheriff called you, I was going to tell you I didn't need time to think it over. But then the timing wasn't right and possibly the timing isn't right now, but I don't want to risk any more time passing without telling you."

He bent his head toward her and returned her kiss. "I love you."

"Good because I love you, too. I don't want to take a chance and lose you. Life's too short, and if we love each other, we can work anything out. And I do love you. I've never stopped loving you. No man lived up to you in my eyes."

T.J. embraced her and swung her around. "It might have taken us a while to figure out we're perfect for each other, but I'm not going to let you forget one day of our marriage how important you are to me." He'd finally found a place to call home—anywhere with Chloe.

EPILOGUE

Ten months later

"Is my husband busy?" Chloe asked T.J.'s secretary when she came into the office.

"No, he just got off the phone."

Chloe crossed to his door and went into the room to find T.J. working at his desk. He looked up, and his dark eyes gleamed. A slow smile spread across his face as he rose.

"What did the doctor say?" T.J. covered the distance to her and drew her into his arms.

"It's official. I'm pregnant. In seven months you will be a daddy."

He beamed. "That's the best news you could tell me."

She stretched up on her tiptoes and gave him a quick kiss on his mouth. "We need to celebrate tonight."

"A few minutes ago Paul called to tell me the verdict in Vickie's trial came in. Guilty of murder and attempted murder as well as the arson at the theater. Paul saw Rob at the trial. He was still upset that he carried the woman out of the fire who was responsible for setting it."

"Vickie was wearing a good disguise. She was a bitter, sad woman. For years, her envy of Mary festered, and when the pranks started, she hatched this plot to finally get rid of Mary. She didn't care if she took Paul and Aaron with her. She was set from embezzling money out of the Zimmermans' accounts."

"I felt sorry for Shane. He loved her, and she used him. She'd planned to leave the country with the money she'd stolen, leaving him behind. She didn't think he would say anything because he was involved, too. Actually, Vickie and Shane killed Bo Moore to set him up to be their patsy."

"With Lenny's, then Shane's trial a couple of months ago, that's the last person involved in Paul and Mary's harassment and attempted murder. It's over." Chloe inhaled a deep breath, the scent of lime aftershave filling her nostrils. She would always associate that smell with T.J.

"Paul wanted to take us to dinner before he and Mary drive back to the ranch. I said yes. Okay?"

The warmth of his look made her feel cherished. "Sure. We can celebrate when we get home. I want to share the news with them. If it hadn't been for Mary and Paul, we might not be married today."

He cuddled closer. "Oh, I don't know about that. After all, I came back to Dallas because of you."

"And it took you six months to figure that out. Is Aaron with them?" She would never tire of being in T.J.'s embrace.

"No. He's finishing up his community service at home. He can't miss any school unless he's sick. He's staying with his pastor's family until Paul and Mary return home tomorrow."

"Then all he has is four more years on probation until he turns twenty-one."

"According to Paul, Aaron has changed. He's involved with learning how to run the ranch. Paul is, too."

"It took a tragedy to make them a family again."

T.J. bent his head and settled his lips over hers. "A lesson we need to remember. Not to let our work consume us."

"Nothing is more important than you and this baby."

* * * * *

*When Amos Burkholder steps in to help the
Miller family, he soon discovers that middle daughter
Deborah disappears for hours at a time.
Where does she go?*

*Read on for a sneak preview of
Courting Her Secret Heart by Mary Davis,
available September 2018 from Love Inspired!*

Amos Burkholder looked out over the Millers' fields to be plowed
in the spring. He couldn't help but think of them as partly his. Of
course, they weren't his fields, and he might not even be here to do
the plowing and the planting. But if he was, he would take pride in
that work.

Bartholomew Miller appreciated everything he did around the
farm, so Amos worked harder than he ever had at home.

Bartholomew had never had a son to help him with all the work
around the farm. How had he run this place without sons?

But on the flip side, Amos's *mutter* had been alone doing the house
chores, cooking, cleaning and laundry for six men. How did she do it
without help?

On the far side of one of the fields, a woman emerged from a bare
stand of sycamore trees nestled next to a pond. She walked across the
field.

The woman came closer and closer.

Deborah.

Where did she go all the time? She had disappeared every day this
week and would be gone for hours. He was about to find out.

With her head down, she didn't see him approaching. He stepped
directly into her path a few yards in front of her. When it looked as
though she might literally run into him, he cleared his throat.

She halted a foot away. She was so startled to see him there, she
appeared to lose her balance. Her arms swung out to keep herself
upright.

He reached out and took hold of her upper arms to stop her from tumbling to the ground. "Whoa there."

She gasped. "I'm sorry. I didn't see you."

"Where have you been all day?"

"What? Nowhere." She tried to pull free of his grip, but he held fast.

He shook his head. "You've been somewhere. You've left every day this week and been gone for most of the day."

"I—I went for a walk."

"Where? Ohio?"

"We have a pond just over there. I like to sit and watch the ducks. It's a nice place to think and be alone. You should go sometime."

"I did. Today. You weren't there."

Her self-satisfied expression fell. "I was for a while, then I walked farther."

He sensed there was more to her absence than a walk. "Where?"

"Why do you care?"

"With your *vater* laid up, I'm responsible for everyone on this farm."

"I'm fine. I can take care of myself. May I go now?"

He didn't want to let her go but did. "I don't want you to leave the farm without telling me where you're going."

"Are you serious?"

He gave her his serious look.

She huffed and strode away.

Where did she go every day? He had wanted to follow her, but he realized it was none of his business. But curiosity pushed hard on him. He still might follow her if she didn't obey. Just to see. Just to watch her from a distance. Just to know her secret.

Something inside him feared for her. Feared she would walk out across this field and never return. Feared her secret would consume them both. She was a mystery.

A mystery he was drawn to solve.

Don't miss
Courting Her Secret Heart *by Mary Davis,*
available September 2018 wherever
Love Inspired® books and ebooks are sold.

www.LoveInspired.com

LIEXP0818

Save $1.00

on the purchase of ANY
Love Inspired® book.

Available wherever books are sold,
including most bookstores, supermarkets,
drugstores and discount stores.

Save $1.00

on the purchase of ANY Love Inspired® book.

Coupon valid until October 31, 2018.
Redeemable at participating retail outlets in the U.S. and Canada only.
Limit one coupon per customer.

52615896

5 65373 00076 2   (8100)0 12379

Looking for inspiration in tales
of hope, faith and heartfelt romance?

Check out **Love Inspired**® and
Love Inspired® **Suspense** books!

New books available every month!

CONNECT WITH US AT:

Harlequin.com/Community

Facebook.com/HarlequinBooks

Twitter.com/HarlequinBooks

Instagram.com/HarlequinBooks

Pinterest.com/HarlequinBooks

ReaderService.com

Love Inspired®

LIGENRE2018